FEEL NO EVIL

FEEL NO EVIL

Rosemarie Aquilina

Porch Swing Press

ANN ARBOR, MICHIGAN

1 Dec 17

Janie —
To an outstanding, caring woman — May you always be happy! My pleasure to know you —
I hope you enjoy the adventure —
All best
Rosemarie Aquilina
30th Circuit Court Judge

sabieha@aol.com

For more information please write:
Porch Swing Press
2258 Courtney Circle Court
Ann Arbor, MI 48103
Telephone: (734) 213-1370
Facsimile: (517) 769-1865

Or, contact the Author:
Rosemarie Aquilina
Aquilina Law Firm. P.L.C.
229 N. Pine Street, Lansing, Michigan 48933
Telephone: (517) 371-4144
Facsimile: (517) 371-4148.

Library of Congress Catalogin in Publication Data

Aquilina, Rosemarie
Feel No Evil

1. Mystery/Thriller. 2. Fiction.
I. Title

ISBN: 0-9724166-1-7

Ordering information is located on the back page of the book.

Feel No Evil, First Edition 10 9 8 7 6 5 4 3 2 1

**This book is lovingly
Dedicated to
The best people I know,
David, Jennifer and Johanna:
My children,
My inspiration,
My reasons for reaching my goals, and
Without whom I would be lost.**

ACKNOWLEDGMENTS

There were times when I thought I would never finish this book. The encouragement that I received from my children, family and friends must be acknowledged with a special thanks to *everyone* for helping me. I only wish I could acknowledge everyone!

Nick and Mary Rose Aquilina, my grandparents, who always believed in me no matter what.

Joseph and Johanna Aquilina, my parents, who always supported my crazy schemes especially when they failed.

Joseph and Susan Aquilina, my brother and sister-in-law who sent me many articles of encouragement and inspiration.

Thomas and Carey Aquilina, my brother and sister-in-law for their constant interest and guidance and for Carey reading and praising every word of every draft.

Helen Hartford, my sister, for her reading and editing skills, her friendship and honest criticism made the story better.

Denise Thompson-Slaughter, my extraordinary editor.

Susan Pitts, my secretary and friend who faithfully made revisions and keeps my life on schedule.

Michael Gleissner, my uncle, and Sr. Teresa Aquilina, my aunt, each of whom helped me pull the final draft of this book together.

Katarzyna Sudak, a brilliant artist whose talent instantly brought the book cover to life.

And finally, Christine Cook, my friend and publisher, who finally pushed me into organization and completion, despite my hectic life.

Chapter 1

Samantha sat limply, remembering and reliving those moments of terror as she listened to his voice on the recorder. Her stillness did not betray the loud pace of her pounding heart. To courtroom viewers, her beauty and fine features did not match the circumstances they were hearing. She shut the courtroom out. She shut out everything, for the moment, except the turmoil inside. She remembered it. She remembered it all. But she no longer remembered who she used to be. Samantha could not identify with any of her childhood memories or dreams. He took it all from her after what she already thought was the worst thing that could have happened to her.

She was wrong. He was the worst thing that had happened to her.

Closing her eyes, she tried to shield herself from the voice and visualize better times. None came. Samantha drew in her limbs tightly and she tried to mask the flood of memories and pain. She tried to keep the voice from harming her and controlling her again.

Brought back to the present by the silence of the courtroom, Samantha felt uncomfortable. The only sound, other than the tape recorder, was the scratching graphite on the news reporter's pad as his sketch gave life to the once-friendly familiar face she had grown to despise. She stared at the emerging picture. The artist had given Skyler more gray hair than she remembered and darker circles and lines around his eyes. How is it she never saw those things? Could fear have blinded her, making her see only his savage strengths, not his weaknesses?

She didn't want to remember or to feel. But she did. Emotions flooded in as the terror rose inside and the painful past rushed in. She had to remember; she had no choice.

Panic. She felt panic. Her body was on the alert. She feared she was not alone as she watched her shadow move with her through the alleyway. She turned, listening for footsteps. She turned the other way, suddenly, intuitively. The familiar face surprised her. She smiled, acknowledging him. And then she felt his grasp, hard and cold against her flesh. His aloof expression brought instant terror to her. Samantha tried to pull away from the strong grasp of the man's arm. She tried to calm herself, to take control, but her ragged breathing could not be quieted. She was not used to him touching her this way. Her brain couldn't connect his actions with her knowledge of him. Ever since she could remember, she had referred to him as Uncle Greg. For years she remembered teasing him and calling him "Geggy", even after she had mastered language and could pronounce the "r". He taught her to ride her two-wheeler and play basketball. He helped her with her math when her father was away on business. She knew Uncle Greg was not really related, but having been an employee and old college roommate of her father's, she'd grown up with him involved in her life.

She looked at his face—she'd never seen that expression. She felt his coarse beard tearing against her skin, the stench of his alcoholic breath, his immense body tearing at her clothes, clawing and ripping through, until her exposed flesh shone pale against the dark alleyway. He ripped the taut leather belt from his trousers and held it firm against her long neck, pinning her into breathless silence. She could not scream. She tried to wrench out his eyes, but could not. With all her might she tried to keep her body stiff and together, but it was no use. He pried open her legs.

She could do little as he pinned her. She looked for weapons. Her nails tore into his flesh as he pierced her body. She could feel his blood dripping against her, but his intensity did not lessen.

She tried not to feel, but it hurt. Piercing pain pulsed through her. Her most private flesh tore against his force and she felt the warm wetness. She couldn't tell if it was blood or him or both. She wasn't sure if she was breathing.

She vomited as he dropped her like a rag doll and fled. The dull thud of the pavement didn't hurt. She felt paralyzed. She knew she had to leave. To go home.

The next hours were a blur, but she remembered finding her way home. Her parents were in Washington. The governor wanted them there. Her father was handling some confidential legal matters and negotiations for the governor. Her mother, the perfect hostess, would keep the wives occupied.

The enormous empty house was comforting, safe. Her room. It looked the same as she had left it. She locked the door and entered her shower. Dazed, she turned the knobs, not feeling the scalding water against her skin or the stinging of the soap in her eyes and abrasions. She scrubbed every inch of her body until the water turned cold. She barely noticed the bloodied water as it drained. She focused only on erasing him from her flesh.

The shock of the temperature change sent her, still dazed, out of the shower. Samantha stood, momentarily confused about what to do next. She was shaking and couldn't stop as she pulled the familiar terry robe over her wet body. She couldn't look in the mirror. She didn't brush her long dark tangle of dripping hair. Instead she drifted around the room, as if she were a visiting spirit. Finally, she lay on her bed, the soft feather quilt pulled over her. Clenching her fists, she rocked her fetal-positioned body slowly until her mind succumbed to blackness.

When she awoke, she felt limp and heavy. She wasn't sure where she was and then, breaking into a cold sweat, she remembered. What should she do? Who should she tell? Who *could* she tell? Was she responsible? The loud clang of the doorbell interrupted the kaleidoscope of thoughts. Who would be calling on her at this hour? Everyone knew her parents were away. It had been highly publicized. Had he come back for more?

She found her way down the staircase and peered through the sheers to see the figure of a man. Skyler Marks. A man she knew she could trust. Fate brought him to her. Skyler Marks, the youngest attorney and partner in her father's law firm. He would know what to do.

Opening the door in a frenzy she hugged him for comfort. His broad shoulders felt comfortable and familiar. His cologne filled her nostrils and eased her spirit. Samantha watched Skyler's gaze as he took her in. He was obviously taken aback. She should not have let him see her so unkempt, so panicked, so needy.

"Calm down, Samantha. What's wrong? What happened?" Skyler grasped her shoulders and pushed her gently away from him.

"I'm in terrible trouble! I need to talk to you. I don't know what to do," Samantha whimpered, large warm tears splashing from behind her long black lashes.

"Let's sit in the living room. Can I make you some tea?"

"No. I don't want anything; you can help yourself, if you want something . . . I'm sorry to." Samantha found it difficult to continue.

"Let's just sit and, when you are ready, why don't you tell me what's wrong."

Samantha stared at Skyler, as if she could see right through him. Finally, finding her voice, she began speaking, despite her uneven breathing and her heart pounding loudly in her ears.

"I really shouldn't bother you, but . . . I'm sorry. . . Something happened to me last night. Something horrible."

"It can't be that bad! I'll help you. We'll fix whatever it is," Skyler said, with obvious concern.

"I was at the library late. I was studying for my finals. When I realized it had suddenly gotten dark I packed up my things and left in a hurry. I thought I'd take the shortcut . . . You know, through the alley. And, just as I entered it, I, I. . .," Samantha put her hands over her pale face. She turned ashen and felt suddenly both faint and nauseated as her flesh grew clammy. She tried to steady her hands but she couldn't.

"Take your time. It's okay. Can I get you something? A cool cloth perhaps?"

"No. I need to continue. Just let me collect my thoughts." She clenched her robe, taking a deep breath before continuing.

"I felt someone touching me. I turned around. I felt him hurting me. I couldn't stop him." She sobbed loudly, shaking.

"Couldn't stop him from what?" Skyler asked gently, moving closer to her, careful to only touch her hand.

"He, he raped me," Samantha whispered hoarsely, tears streaming faster and faster, her breathing unsteady.

"Raped . . . Raped you? Who raped you? Are you all right? Did you see a doctor? Did you report it?" Skyler asked.

Samantha felt his surprise as she watched him noticing

the scrapes and bruises on her neck, face and hands. Could he guess how many more there were under her tightly wrapped robe?

"No. I didn't report it. I didn't know what to do. I feel so badly. I should have stopped it."

"No. Then you might not be alive. Trust me, it's better to be alive. I can help you. You did the right thing in telling me. Can you tell me who did this to you?" Skyler asked in a soothing hypnotic voice.

Samantha's eyes grew wide. The tears stopped falling just long enough to fill her eyes before spilling into one large stream as she whispered his name, all the while rocking back and forth and back and forth, cradling her arms tightly around her stomach.

"Uncle Greg."

Skyler looked at Samantha. She saw the disbelief in his eyes.

"Greg Maston?"

Samantha closed her eyes and nodded her head as she continued rocking.

"Are you sure?"

Samantha couldn't speak. She could only shudder and nod her head as warm tears streamed down her delicate features. Skyler wrapped his arms around her to comfort her. She could feel her body stiffen into corpselike coldness. She pushed away from him. She took a deep cleansing breath, looking squarely at Skyler as he watched her. His actions unthreatening, she felt secure again. She could trust him.

"What can I do to help you?" Skyler asked. "I want to help you. I can help you, if you let me."

"I don't know what to do. I can't tell my parents, they won't understand. Maybe they won't even believe me."

"When are your parents due back from Washington?"

"They won't be home until Thursday."

"Good. You'll have almost four days to recover. Stay home from school tomorrow if you're not feeling well. Tell people you fell off your bike. You have some scratches and bruises that may be difficult to cover."

She hadn't looked in the mirror. Now she would have to. It didn't occur to her that her outsides might be hurt, just as her insides had been.

Samantha tried to hide the fear but Skyler saw her fear and shame.

Gently, Skyler said, "It'll heal in a few days . . .and makeup will cover the rest. Don't worry—although I think you should see a doctor . . ."

"No. I told you I can't do that! My doctor would talk to my parents. I know he would," Samantha said in a determined voice.

"Well, as an attorney, I can tell you that you should have gone to the police right after it happened and you should have been seen by a physician. You have showered all the evidence off, so for the most part it will be your word against his, unless there were witnesses. But, if you want to pursue it and get him behind bars, I'll help you. I believe you," Skyler said in a compassionate, but rhythmically hypnotic voice.

Samantha felt awkward as she watched Skyler staring at her. She was taller than other girls her age and felt self-conscious about her height. Even now. Even with Skyler. She listened as Skyler filled in her silence with his final argument.

"There are other factors that need to be considered—like sexually transmitted diseases and a pregnancy test. I can help you with all of those things, if you want me to."

"I don't think I can go through it . . . explain it to strangers, I mean. I can't face anyone. I want to forget it. I want to feel normal. I want to erase him from my life," Samantha said, her voice cutting through the burning tears.

"Well, if you pursue it, you will have to face him; and if you tell your parents and he denies it . . ." He didn't finish his sentence; he knew she was smart enough to complete the thought. He paused and then continued. "And then there's the media. If they find out, they will have a field day with all of you."

Samantha looked up, stunned. She hadn't even thought of that. She couldn't face that. She couldn't have her parents answer for her, have them dragged through the mud. They couldn't find out.

"No. Please I can't have that. Please forget I said anything. Forget it happened. Promise me you won't tell!" Samantha said.

Skyler nodded in agreement.

Samantha stared at him, then added, "Thanks . . . for talking . . . for everything. I, I have to go . . ." She fled up the stairs, matted curls bouncing fiercely behind her as she disappeared behind the safety of her locked bedroom door.

Skyler could do no more. It was time to leave. As he pulled the door shut behind him and stepped into the fresh air, he clicked off the microcassette hidden in his breast pocket, proudly, gently, patting it. A broad smile enveloping his tanned face, he began to whistle softly as he entered his emerald green Jaguar. He could hardly believe his good luck. It *was* good to be prepared; just like a Boy Scout, he laughed to himself. This tape would give him the things he most desired in the world: power—and Samantha Armstrong.

And what about that old lush, Greg? Had Greg guzzled one bottle too many and gone off his rocker? Had he, too, been lustfully watching beautiful Samantha grow up all these years? Or did he have a psychotic hobby of randomly assaulting women from alleyways in his free time? Maybe Samantha was wrong; maybe the rapist was someone who only resembled Greg Maston. But if not, Skyler grinned again, then he had a double dose of power in his pocket. Skyler smiled; he loved collecting secrets.

Samantha tried to put the rape behind her. But her dreams kept the rage and fear alive. Every night she prayed she would forget. But she didn't. She couldn't. She tried to think of happier times and to focus on good things, but they were all so minor and meaningless. She felt distanced from her family, her friends, herself. She knew she would survive. She had to. But *how*? And how long would it take?

Skyler called regularly to support her and see if there was anything he could do. He suggested counseling, but she resisted, not trusting her secret would be kept confidential. Besides, she knew she could always talk to Skyler. He seemed to understand. She appreciated his warmth and friendship. She had not known anyone in her life who was so caring and understanding. She took his interest in her problem at face value. He was a good friend to her and her family. He had everyone's interest in mind, and he knew how to keep her family protected. Eventually, he told her, she would forget and someone would come into her life who would help her forget. It would just be a bad dream, nothing more, nothing less. She tried hard to believe the possibility someday she would forget. But she worried constantly about being pregnant. She didn't believe in abortion. She was a good Southern Christian who believed in waiting until marriage to have sex. But all that had changed. She could no longer engage in schoolgirl laughter about alleged sexual prowess with her friends. She flipped through the sexual scenes in her novels, ignoring their content; made excuses about needing to go to the restroom during the love scenes in movies; and she moved away from any man who stood too close to her or tried to touch her even in friendship. Worst of all, she no longer liked her father kissing her good night and treating her as his "little girl".

And now she might be pregnant. As she lay in bed each night she could feel her body swell. Her hands rubbed a small hardening in her taut flat stomach. She wasn't sure if it was real or imagined. The fear. Was she just caving into her own fear or was she really pregnant? She couldn't wait too long. She had to do something. Skyler would help her.

Looking up at the overly adorned building, she felt the intimidation conveyed by the immense law building. Her father's law building. Through the foresight of her great grandfather and a winning poker hand, her father's family had acquired this antiquated historic building. Samantha walked in, trying to smile and act casually in case she was recognized by anyone. It seemed like hours before Skyler appeared in the elevator, briefcase in hand.

"Sorry I was late. Divorce clients, they never leave; they just talk your ear off. But at two hundred dollars an hour, I guess I can afford to listen," Skyler said nonchalantly, smiling confidently. "You look great. Feeling better? That's good."

"Well I . . ." Samantha cut off her response. He wasn't listening.

"I hope you're hungry. I've booked us a reservation at MacArthur Station. Best steaks in town." Skyler's white teeth flashed as he opened the Jaguar door and let her in.

Samantha looked at Skyler's deep tan. It made his shirt look whiter than anything she'd ever seen. She liked the diamond-cut cufflinks under the double-breasted pin-striped navy suit. His clothing made him seem older than his thirty-two years. She looked at him so hard she became entranced with his features. She focused on his thick salt and pepper hair and the way his face creased when he smiled. She focused on the soothing tone of his voice and wondered why he was a lawyer instead of a broadcaster in some exotic place. He was handsome enough to have been an actor.

Samantha was suddenly glad he was her friend and such a good friend of her father's. She knew she could trust him, but somehow it just didn't feel right to burden him or anyone else with her problems.

Samantha remained quiet as her mind kept wandering. She was losing her nerve. She had to tell someone, though. She needed to talk out her problems with someone she trusted. She needed help. That was the bottom line. Skyler was the only one she could tell. She would find a way.

The restaurant was only a few minutes away and, although she had always wanted to ride in a Jaguar, she barely noticed the drive or the small talk Skyler was making. Had she been herself, she would have been uncomfortable with the inspection his eyes cast upon her. She wished she'd worn something with a high neck instead of the scoop-neck dress. His probing emerald eyes were not those of a friend, but rather those of a man on the prowl. Samantha felt again how inexperienced she was with men.

The restaurant was nice. Her father had brought her here many times. She liked the food and the atmosphere, but she was not comfortable with its location, so close to her father's office. She hoped no one recognized her here with Skyler. She did not want to have to explain to her father what she was doing with him. He would not approve. She knew he would not like it; he would not understand. She began to worry. How would she explain it? Surely this would get back to her father.

Skyler had reserved a booth in the back of the restaurant. She hated the surrounding smoke, but the booth was more private than she had anticipated a table would be. Maybe she didn't have to worry about being seen, after all.

Once they ordered, she sat silent, staring at Skyler, waiting for the moment when she could express her thoughts.

"Samantha, you seem so preoccupied. Is this table okay? Would you prefer to move?"

"No. No, it's fine . . . I'm just wondering what I'll say to my father if we are seen together. He won't understand. I didn't tell him. He will be very upset with me; you know how he is."

"You leave that up to me. I'll tell your father I ran into you and I invited you to lunch. I'll tell him I was giving you the inside scoop about college. He'll be fine with that. Trust me," he said reassuringly, placing his hand over Samantha's, giving her his finest boyish grin. Samantha had no choice but to trust Skyler. She knew she was already in too deep with him to turn back. She needed his help.

"So how's school going? What are the seniors doing for graduation party? I remember my graduation night. We all went up to Lakewood and spent the night on the beach. Some of us were even brave enough to go skinny-dipping. It was great fun." He paused. "Ever been skinny dipping?" he asked lightly.

"Me? No. I couldn't. I wouldn't want to."

"Come now, a pretty thing like you? You must have all the boys asking you out!"

"No, not really. I have gone out some, but I've been focusing on my grades and college. Father says there's plenty of time for boys, and you know how strict he is," Samantha said uncomfortably. "Besides, being the youngest and the only girl, my parents are a bit overprotective. But really I don't mind. I'll miss them when I go to school."

"Aren't you going to stay close to home?"

"No." Samantha said, relieved the conversation had shifted. "I want to go to vet school and Michigan State has an excellent school. That's where I've applied. They have accepted me into the school but I haven't heard whether or not I've been accepted into the pre-vet program. From the photos in the brochures, their campus looks as beautiful as Arkansas in spring."

"Oh. I didn't know you wanted to be a veterinarian. That's quite an ambition," Skyler said. "Now, why don't you tell me what's on your mind? Did you ask me to lunch to ask for a letter for the pre-vet program? Because I'd be happy to support you, to send a letter, make a phone call or whatever."

"Well, no. I'm all set with my college plans, but thank you for your offer." Samantha began slowly, in deliberate contemplation of her words. "I wanted to thank you for all of your support and help over the past few weeks. Your phone calls and advice really meant a lot to me. But now . . . now I need more help." Samantha's voice began to quiver and her eyes were downcast.

Taking her hand in his, Skyler said, "It can't be that bad. You know I'll help you, whatever it is. Just tell it to me slowly."

"I haven't been feeling well. I thought it was the flu. I thought I was just upset from what happened . . . you know. But it's not. It's just awful." Samantha stared at Skyler. She tried to anticipate his response from his face but his law training had obviously left him with the ability to mask expression, to hide judgment.

"Continue, please. You know you can trust me. I will help you. I promise." Skyler said softly, his emerald eyes compassionate.

Samantha moved closer to him on the seat of the round leather booth. This excited Skyler. She did trust him. He liked that.

"I went to the clinic in Sherwood last week. I skipped out of my Friday classes. I was tested for AIDS . . ."

Skyler's eyes grew wide as he interrupted her. "You didn't use your real name, did you? I told you I would help you with all that. I could have protected you from anyone finding out." Skyler said plainly in spite of his promise of absolute support. "You don't have AIDS do you?"

"No. I 'm smart enough to not use my real name. I wore my hair differently; I wore it up and teased it a lot. I wore tons of makeup and I changed into old ragged clothes. I even borrowed Sally's car, telling her I felt like driving a convertible. We traded cars for the day. It was easy. I temporarily became someone else. The clinic was very impersonal. I paid cash for the exam and tests. I told them I didn't have insurance. Then I waited three days and called. I don't have AIDS or anything else. But . . ." Samantha paused taking a deep quivering breath as tears streamed uncontrollably down her face, "I *am* pregnant."

"Is that all?" Skyler said sympathetically, but relieved. "I know people that can help you. You're only about, what, seven or eight weeks, right?"

Samantha nodded silently, wiping the tears from her face. Shyly she looked at Skyler without meeting his eyes. She listened numbly to his solution, surprised at his cavalier response.

"No problem," Skyler said, with a boyish grin on his face, as if he'd heard this kind of news every day. "I'll set things up. I know a doctor who deals with these kinds of things. He'll give you an abortion without even asking your name. No one will ever know."

"Is it safe?"

"Perfectly. You just leave it all up to me," Skyler said, washing down his last bite of steak.

Samantha felt uneasy but couldn't think of any other options. She couldn't disgrace her family. She knew Skyler was right. She had disgraced her family already by being raped, and the need to have an abortion was another disgrace. Okay, she told herself, as she played in the mashed potatoes on her plate. She had no choice.

As Skyler outlined the plan, Samantha began to feel as if her body was slowly being paralyzed from the inside out. Her breathing was uneven and so shallow she wasn't sure she was even still alive. She felt as if she were suspended in limbo with no mind or thoughts of her own. She felt as if she could float away from her body.

The numbness encapsulated her like a sponge, but her mind absorbed the information needed to execute the deed; absorbed Skyler's voice, even though the words were like nails screeching along a chalkboard.

Samantha didn't want to listen but she knew she must. She heard the words but did not really listen to his tone. She couldn't. Her body was somewhere in between faint and nauseous. Her mind was racing. Her feelings remained numb, almost nonexistent. She felt as if she were in a theater watching someone else's life; like a puppet moving uncontrollably on carefully maneuvered strings.

Skyler told her to skip her Friday afternoon classes and tell her parents that she was spending the night with a friend to study for exams. She would be home Saturday afternoon as if nothing had happened. Skyler would take her. The clinic was almost two hundred miles away.

Was that far enough, she wondered, as Skyler recited over and over how safe it was and how no one would ever know, how it was the right thing to do, the *only* thing to do. It was almost a chant in her mind, and over the next few days it became a refrain, necessary to repeat to herself again and again until she believed it was absolutely true.

On the ride back to his office Skyler reminded her she needed to repeat the AIDS test in six weeks, then at three months, six months and twelve months. He reminded her to use another fake name. He reminded her to be careful and keep her actions as normal as possible so her parents wouldn't realize anything was bothering her. Samantha hated him reminding her of anything. She knew what she had to do. Most of all, she resented his reminder that he would, of course, be there for her for anything she needed; he would help her through everything. He made it clear she could count on him. Samantha knew she should be grateful, but she had an uncomfortable gnawing that made her apprehensive. For now she had to discard her feelings and follow Skyler's directions. They were all she had; she had to pay attention to them.

Chapter 2

The next few weeks passed slowly. The anticipation of implementing Skyler's plan caused Samantha to withdraw into a self-imposed cocoon. She couldn't help but feel everyone she was close to could see through her. Samantha tried to act as normal as possible, but she had a hard time forcing herself out of the house. She had turned down several invitations from her friends, using studying for finals as her excuse.

She wanted to be alone. She needed to be alone. She hadn't been eating breakfast with her parents, as she usually did each morning before school, and they had become concerned. Samantha did not want them to worry; she just couldn't be with them right now.

Samantha had tried to act casual the morning her mother walked into her room without knocking. She was dumbstruck when her mother practically ordered her to breakfast, after an unpleasant scene where she demanded to look at Samantha's naked body to make sure she wasn't "one of those girls who were anorexic or bulimic, or worse yet, on drugs." After several strained minutes, Samantha convinced her mother she was just preoccupied with exams and graduation and her friends going to different schools. When Samantha promised she would be there for breakfast from then on, her mother acted so relieved she could never tell her the truth.

Samantha's thoughts ran rampant as she carefully applied her makeup, trying to hide the dark circles under her eyes. She knew it was important for her to show her parents everything was all right. Samantha couldn't risk her parents asking any more questions or forcing her to see a doctor, as her mother had threatened.

Breakfast with her parents was the last thing she wanted. Samantha feared they could see right through her; her worst fears would materialize right in front of them. She hated the tenderness in her breasts and wondered how long it took before her stomach would show. Most of all, she feared the morning sickness that had become part of her before-school routine. How could she fool her parents when they sat inches from her at the breakfast table? Samantha, filled with anxiety, put on as cheerful a face as she could muster, all the while biting her inner lip so she wouldn't break down and cry.

"Samantha, that new Liz outfit we got you looks wonderful on you with that wonderful creamy complexion of yours!" Samantha's mother exclaimed as she studied her daughter. "At your age, you are very lucky to have such clear smooth skin. I was such a sight when I was young. My skin didn't clear up until after I had children."

Travis smiled behind his newspaper, understanding it was now his husbandly duty to tell her how beautiful she is, was, and always would be. "Anne, you have always been beautiful. I don't remember any unsightly mark on your face at any age."

"You are sweet, dear, and I'm glad you don't remember them. But they were there," Anne said in polite protest, trying to send her husband a cosmic message as their eyes met, she was trying to lift her daughter's spirits and her confidence.

Travis sensed, after years of acquiescence, he'd said enough, and he responded to her with a slightly raised eyebrow, utilizing his remaining moments by skimming the rest of the morning paper.

"Really, Samantha, those walking shorts and jacket are so practical, I bet you'll get lots of compliments from your friends. Those pastels give your face some color; you look like you're feeling much better," Anne said, noticing the silent shadows under her daughter's sapphire eyes.

"I am feeling a little better. But you know me, Mom, I always feel good in new clothes. The outfit is really comfortable. I'm glad you made me try it on." Samantha tried to smile as she shifted the eggs around on her plate with a whisper of movement, hoping it looked like she'd eaten more than she had.

Anne Armstrong beamed at her daughter. She believed her light talk and firmness with her daughter had made a difference. She felt Samantha's downcast mood shift upward and, after a brief pause, decided to pursue doing something with Samantha to keep that positive mood going. "What are your plans after school? I thought we might go on another shopping excursion. I need a new dress for the Bar Association cocktail party and dinner after the meeting your father and I are attending. I'd wait and buy a designer dress in New York, but I'm not sure if I'll have time, and I do so value your opinion."

"Mom, you know I have final exams in a few weeks. I was planning to study, but I could take a few hours after school and go shopping with you. I just need to be back early."

"Anne, Samantha's school work must come first if she is going to stay accepted in college. Michigan State University will still review her final grades and can relinquish their acceptance of her. Why don't you have that new dress designer come to the house and show you some of her latest fashions? Just order whatever you want."

"Travis, I appreciate that, but you know I don't like to spend that kind of money unless it is for a very special occasion; and I hardly think dinner with a bunch of lawyers qualifies. Really, you are too generous," Anne said softly, noticing the quiet pointed stare she'd received when she hit the word lawyer. She smiled coquettishly, grateful her husband still treated her so well after all of their years together, thankful he really did understand and forgive her.

"You're worth it. I'd buy you the moon if you wanted it, even if it meant spending every cent I made. Samantha, I hope someday you are as happy with your husband as I am with your mother," Travis said matter-of-factly, his eyes focused continuously on the *New York Times* stock exchange section. "But if the two of you do go into town, why don't we all meet for dinner at Pete and Mickey's. I hear they have a new chef, someone trained in Paris. He is the talk of all the inner circles. About seven?"

"That sounds great," Anne said, looking at Samantha, who nodded in agreement as she reached for the back of her chair and lifted her heavy backpack in a swift, calculated attempt to leave the table.

"May I be excused?" Samantha asked.

"Of course, dear," Anne said, smiling warmly as Samantha brushed a kiss on each of their cheeks and left the room.

"She looks so much better, doesn't she Travis?"

"Yes, she does. Something is bothering the girl. I hope

you will make an attempt, while shopping, to discover what it is."

"Why do you think I wanted to go shopping here instead of in New York? Of course that's what I'm going to do. You know how I love New York, and I'm counting on you to pick out something fabulous for me." Anne kissed his coarse salt-and-pepper hair, smelling the ever-present scent of his Ralph Lauren cologne.

"You're always a step ahead of me, dear. That's what I love about you," Travis said, as he neatly folded his paper. Briskly setting it aside, he grabbed his wife, pulling her back toward him so he could return her warm kiss before setting out for his busy day. Travis Armstrong was a proud, powerful man when it came to his clients and his own needs. He was confident and charismatic and very respected. Most of those he knew admired his directness and his ability to cut through red tape and get things done. He had taken over his father's law firm at thirty and now, at fifty, his was the most prestigious law firm and he the most influential attorney in the county, maybe even in all of Arkansas. He had hired twenty-five of the best attorneys he could find and together they had a cartel that could crush even the most carefully calculating enterprise, whether attorney, business or Mafia. Everyone thought twice before they crossed him, and everyone who asked for favors from him knew they owed him. Travis Armstrong took nothing for granted, trusted no one except his wife and children, and talked about personal issues with only a select few. Women enjoyed his company. He could easily choose among the finest beauties Arkansas had to offer, but he had declined each offer. Few of his male friends believed in his self-proclaimed sexual virtue.

Women still found Travis Armstrong attractive even though his jet black hair had begun to recede and become accented with white. Somehow that made him more attractive to the younger women he met. He was in awe of the attention he received. He wished that attention had been there for him in his youth. Maybe it had been and he had been too busy during the full days he put in working for his father. He had learned well the business of law and then after his father's retirement, made the business his own. Either way, he was grateful that, up until now, he had remained faithful to Anne

Bommerito, the Italian beauty in his English class, his wife now of thirty years. She was still as vibrant and exciting to him as the first day they met in college. In fact, he liked her better. They had grown together and had formed an alliance stronger than any he had known. She had always been there for him and he would do nothing to endanger their bond. His only regret was he hadn't spent as much time with his children as he had hoped.

His twin sons, Taylor and Tad, were in their first year of law school at Georgetown University. He was proud they were following in his footsteps; someday the firm would be theirs. Samantha, his youngest and only daughter, was in her senior year of high school. She was beautiful, with petite bone structure, pale skin, and long naturally curly brunette hair. She had his eyes, eyes that at times looked as stormy as the deep blue sea, but her mother's beauty was duplicated in Samantha's fine features. While Samantha had always thought herself too tall at 5 foot 8 inches, with her high cheekbones, long legs and tiny waist, she could have easily gone into acting or modeling. Travis thanked God her shyness and self-motivation had kept her feet planted firmly in the direction of college instead.

Travis constantly worried about his children. Lately he had become preoccupied with worry about Samantha. Something was clearly troubling her, but she refused to talk about it. She had become moody and self-isolated. Initially Travis thought he was worrying about nothing; it was his tendency to be overprotective of her. But as he began to watch her, she stopped going out on dates and didn't spend much time with her friends. They hadn't had a fight over her curfew in weeks. Her grades were fine, she had lots of friends, she had ambition. Maybe there was nothing to worry about; she was probably just growing up, realizing there are more important things than parties and boys. Maybe she was just getting a head start on being homesick. After all, they had always been a close family. Perhaps that's why she had been staying close to home and spending less time with her friends. His concerns about his only daughter raced aimlessly around his head on his way to work.

As he rounded the corner, engulfed in thoughts about Samantha, he slipped his silver Mercedes into reserved parking. Reaching for his briefcase, he let his thoughts stay in the convertible. Travis Armstrong had long ago made it a rule to keep his business and family problems as separate as possible. As the car door shut, his brain switched gears, prioritizing work on an upcoming trial.

Chapter 3

Samantha hardly noticed the drive. It wasn't really happening, so in her mind's eye there was nothing to remember. Her fluttering thoughts kept her occupied. Fear kept her still. The mounting lies kept her alert. It was dark now. She hadn't had anything to eat for days. Skyler said it was better to eat later. After it was all over.

She followed his orders, without thinking. Her mind could not think clearly on its own. When she tried to focus, her thoughts cut too deeply. They hurt.

Her thoughts didn't matter. His directions seemed rational. She trusted they made sense and everything would be taken care of. She would move forward from this; like a bad dream, it would soon be over.

The back entrance to the building was unlocked. They entered as if thieves in the night. It was still. Quiet. Sterile smelling. The doctor's office door was open, and he sat behind a large brown desk with stacks of files and x-rays. His grayed temples matched the overstuffed leather chair where he sat quietly observing them enter, stiff and wide-eyed in his starched medical jacket. As the introductions were made, he motioned her to a chair and motioned Skyler out of the room. The medical history was easy. She had always been healthy, up until now.

Skyler had briefed her on the necessity of claiming she would commit suicide if she did not have the abortion. The doctor believed her. She was convincing; she didn't have to act that part. She already felt dead.

The next steps made her feel as if she were reliving her first pap smear. The unisex gown, a vacant green color; the cold stirrups; the rubber gloves, the large instruments; and finally, the pain. She felt it. The pain. More than she remembered with the pap smear. And then the blood. It seemed it would never end.

And then it did.

As she stood up to get dressed, she fainted. When she awoke, she was alone in the room with Skyler bending over her, trying to get her dressed. He was holding two bottles; one an antibiotic, the other painkillers with a sleeping additive. The doctor had removed himself from the building.

Once again they were thieves in the night, walking through dark hallways and doors until they were finally outside. As the darkness absorbed their shadows, Samantha noticed how calmly Skyler maneuvered her. She looked at his briefcase. How could he be calm enough to work while she committed murder?

She wasn't thinking clearly she decided. After all, he was a lawyer, trained to handle difficult situations. She should be grateful, she thought, as the pills began to work and she fell into a deep slumber under the soft cotton blanket in the tiny back seat.

Skyler drove slowly. In his thirty-five years he had never felt so content. His plan was working better than expected. As he looked in the rearview mirror his tanned reflection smiled back at him. He admired his own cleverness. He had always been confident, and that was what had made him the successful attorney he was; but now he would have real success. Total control of another human being, one he had thought about being with since she was fourteen years old.

It was a long drive home, but he had reserved a comfortable room in a small motel not far from the doctor's office. It had two beds so he could watch her and make sure she was comfortable. He had in his pocket the home number of the doctor and a few other prescriptions she might need—in his name, just in case. He couldn't afford any mistakes or problems, and he wanted to make sure his investment paid off as planned. Five more months to go and he would have his prize. As he looked in the rearview mirror again he could see her sleeping peacefully. He hoped the whole night was peaceful and the double dose of pain pills he gave her would help.

Samantha didn't weigh much. He cradled her in his arms and carried her to the room. He carefully placed her in the bed, gently slipping off her jeans, shirt and bra. Opening the travel bag he brought with them, he pulled out an old college jersey that would be soft against her skin and keep her warm. The doctor warned him of chills and bleeding. He would change her pads throughout the night. He hoped the one box he bought would be enough.

As he watched her, he was in awe of her youthful beauty, even as she lay pale in semicomatose sleep, dark curls framing her delicate face. The drugs had affected her so strongly he wasn't even sure she was breathing, except for the occasional tiny hint of movement under her eyelids. What was she dreaming?

Soon the drugs would wear off and she would be in agony.

The doctor had advised him the first twenty-four hours would be the worst and the bleeding, although initially heavy, would subside in a few days. Skyler remembered the sullen look on the doctor's face as he explained she should not have intercourse for two weeks, her own family physician should check her, and she may need psychological treatment, due to her immature age. Both of them knew his warnings were to cover himself and to make sure Skyler knew he had better not touch her until after that time.

Skyler had placed the year's supply of birth control pill samples the doctor had given him carefully at the bottom of his travel bag. She had to decide to take them on her own; but she would take them, one way or another, Skyler decided.

As he prepared himself for a few hours of sleep before she awoke, he collected a glass of drinking water, the medicine, pads, and towels and placed them carefully on the nightstand. Skyler had referred many clients to the "extermidoctor, or Dr. Cide," the terms the local attorneys used to refer to him in order to protect his real name, but never had he participated in an abortion. This was new to him. The only thing he was sure of was he had never heard any complaints, and all of the women he referred had gotten on with their lives. That helped him feel guiltless. After all, if he didn't help these women, they would go to some guy who was only after the money and would ruin them for life—or worse, kill them. The way he saw it, the bottom line was he was doing all of them a favor, and he and Dr. Cide were able to obtain tax free play money. As he fell asleep, he counted the increasing number of crisp bills that lined his wall safe.

Samantha, though groggy, felt disoriented and she could not focus her eyes. She felt too weak to make a sound. Her throat was stiff and dry. As she began to move under the sheets, she could feel the heavy packing and the wetness between her legs. Her abdomen hurt and her attempt to reach for the lamp switch failed.

She remembered, as if a nightmare, the abortion. She looked around, her eyes now familiar with the night shadows, and saw Skyler sleeping soundly in the next bed. Quietly she pulled herself from the bed. She stepped onto the unfamiliar carpeting toward what looked to be a door, hoping it was the bathroom.

She wanted a shower. She needed a shower. She had to cleanse herself from that awful doctor touching her insides, ripping something away from her.

She wrapped her arms tightly around her waist and walked one painful baby step at a time. She did not feel like she was inside her own skin. Her body seemed old and unfamiliar. She did not like the feel of the unknown sweatshirt around her. It was not hers. It felt soft and warm, but it was too big and bulky. Where had it come from? Why didn't she remember? Tearing the sweatshirt off, she let it drop to the floor. Carefully she pulled her soiled underpants off and dropped them with the soaked bulky pads into the garbage pail. There were so many pads! She had lost a lot of blood.

Sitting on the stool, she looked down. She could see the fresh blood still trickling down her legs, and small clots of blood flooded into the toilet as she urinated. The mother of all periods, she thought. Mother, what a funny word; she was anything but that. The doctor and Skyler had seen to that.

The water felt good as she turned up the shower knob as hot as she could stand it. She felt weak and the water made her feel weaker. She didn't care. She couldn't feel anything else. Soon she would be back in her own clothes and her own bed. Soon she would be the good Christian girl her parents had raised. Soon she could put all of this behind her and one day maybe even learn to forget and learn to feel again; but not now. Now she had to get through the next few hours. Grimly she watched as the water, now pooled around her feet, reflected a transparent red color. A sudden ringing in her ears caught her by surprise as she faded into nothingness.

Skyler, hearing a dull thud, leapt out of bed, immediately noticing Samantha was not there. Hearing the shower, he dashed into the steamy bathroom only to see her collapsed form in the tub. Turning off the water and grabbing a large white towel, he scooped her up in his arms and laid her on the terry bath mat.

He could feel his own heart pounding as he listened for the sound of her heartbeat. Finally, hearing her breathing, he felt instant relief. Skyler moved her onto her bed, hoping she would wake up, but she didn't. A bruise appeared on her right temple, and he knew he needed to apply pressure and ice. Opening the room's small refrigerator, he found a white tray half filled with ice. Quickly, he popped out the little cubes and wrapped them in a wet washcloth. Touching the bruise slowly, he saw Samantha's brilliant blue eyes open and try to focus.

"What happened?" she asked in a low voice. "What are you doing in my shower?" she mumbled, looking around. She realized she was no longer in the shower.

"I told you I was here to help you. If you wanted a shower, I would have helped you. You are much too weak. The medicine I gave you is very strong and you took it on an empty stomach. You must stay in bed for a few more hours. Trust me, you'll feel better soon," Skyler said in his most convincing father-knows-best tone. Trying to be both strong and sympathetic, he was nevertheless irritated she had not followed his instructions.

"I've lost so much blood," she said sheepishly.

"Yes. The doctor said that's normal and will stop in a few days. We just have to make sure it keeps decreasing. You'll let me know if it gets worse won't you?"

Samantha nodded in embarrassment, biting her lip to keep from crying.

"Do you need help getting dressed? I've got extra clothes and pads for you."

"No, I'll be fine," she said, pulling the towel closer to her and the sheets over her half-naked body. "Could you just put a shirt and the pads on my bed and bring me my purse; I have extra underwear in it."

"Sure. Tell you what; I'll go into the bathroom for a few minutes so you can get dressed in private. Let me know when I can come out. You're sure you're all right? I could help you get dressed, if you're too weak, I mean."

"No, really," Samantha tried to smile convincingly. "I'm

fine. If I need help, I'll let you know."

"I've left your pain medication and a sleeping pill for you. I think it would be a good idea if you took them. You could use a few good hours of quiet rest. Also, I think you should eat at least a few of these crackers. If you need more water, I'll be happy to get you some from the bathroom."

"Thanks. I'm fine," Samantha repeated in as definite a voice as she could muster. She just wanted him to leave her alone. She wanted to get dressed, be alone and in her own bed. Just a few more hours, she thought, as she quickly dressed.

The dry wheat crackers were just what her stomach needed, and almost instantly she felt better. As the water enveloped the pills, she swallowed. Her exhausted, hollow-feeling body couldn't help but welcome the sleep. Sleep was a desirable escape from Skyler's annoying willingness to care for her. Her fingers clenched onto the warmth of the soft cotton sheets and she called him back from behind the bathroom door. By the time he came out of the bathroom, she was not only dressed but underneath the sheets so far only a few strands of hair were visible to him. She had burrowed so far beneath the sheets it was clear to Skyler she did not want to be disturbed. The pills he left for her on the nightstand were gone. He assumed they had already begun to work and there was little point in trying to talk to her. He decided to follow her lead and crawled into the other bed, quietly turning off the lamp on the bedside table, hoping for a few hours of uninterrupted sleep.

Morning moved quickly into afternoon and Skyler carefully woke Samantha with a hearty breakfast of coffee, juice, eggs, bagels, cream cheese and bacon. He told her he would not take her home until she cleaned her plate.

Samantha was grateful for the food. It tasted better than any other breakfast she remembered. It had been hours, days, since she had eaten. Her mouth was dry from the medication, so she swallowed cautiously, washing her food down with coffee and juice. Skyler watched her carefully. Color returned to her face. He loved to watch her eat. Her long dainty fingers fed her porcelain-like body with precise movement. She was a delicate beauty and he was tantalized by her.

Samantha remained unaware of Skyler's desire for her. He knew for the moment, he would have to curb his appetite.

As he began to put their things together for the ride home, he glanced at the briefcase beside his overnight bag and smiled to himself.

The ride home was uneventful. The bleeding had slowed, and Samantha was gaining her strength. The drugs made her a bit queasy but she knew that too would pass. The large breakfast she had eaten had absorbed some of the queasiness, for which she was grateful. Samantha's parents wouldn't be home until early evening. It was their day to play doubles at the club. They loved playing golf more than just about anything, and they traveled to some of the most famous golf courses around the world. The mantle in the den had many golf awards and trophies. Samantha hated the game, although she had quite a talent for it, according to her father. She had been dragged to too many golf outings when she was young and would rather have been with her friends.

Golf and piano. Two forced interests, both of which she hated. Now, she had a third. Sex.

Was her life to be one guided by events and other people rather than by what she desired and wanted? She fell into another heavy drug-induced slumber, despite the loud roar of the engine and the bright sunlight.

When she woke, Samantha saw the familiar surroundings: streets, buildings, trees. She knew they were the same. They couldn't have changed overnight, but somehow they were different and she wasn't sure why.

Over and over, Samantha kept repeating the story she would tell her parents about what she did last night, until in her mind's own eye she began to believe it. Skyler repeated the story, asking her every possible question her parents could come up with. He didn't want to take any chances. She was thankful for that. He was a fine attorney. He hadn't forgotten anything.

Privately Samantha decided what she really needed to tell her parents, if they asked what was wrong with her, was she felt like she was coming down with the flu. That would keep her father from asking a lot of questions and would keep her mother occupied making her chicken soup. That would insure she didn't make a mistake in answering any questions and she could delay conversation until her mind was clearer. She wished she were home right now. The thought of her mother's chicken soup made her feel homesick, even though they were only a few miles away.

Samantha looked down the street toward her house. It had never looked so good to her. She was grateful to Skyler, but was happy their allegiance was finally over. She couldn't bear the lies anymore. She didn't want to think about it; she only wanted to put it behind her. Skyler had been helpful; she wasn't sure what she should say or how to properly thank him as she gingerly climbed out of the car.

Skyler understood there really wasn't any need for further conversation about the abortion. He felt her uneasiness and didn't want to push himself on her. As he watched her exit the car, grabbing her backpack and purse, he nonchalantly saluted her and winked. Nothing more needed to be said. Samantha, relieved, simply smiled and said, "Thanks, thanks for everything."

Skyler watched her as she walked down the block to her home. She looked so young, so innocent. So beautiful. As she faded into the arms of her house, he imagined her wrapped in his arms. The thought was so powerful, so provoking, an erection bounded beneath his boxers.

As she entered the sanctuary of her home and the refuge of her own room, Samantha breathed deeply, relieved it was over. She could put it behind her. Carefully she unpacked her clothes and placed the bag of prescriptions Skyler had given her well at the bottom of her underwear drawer, confident no one would find them. Soon she could throw them out. Before covering the bag of prescriptions she decided to inspect its contents, not remembering it having been so bulky. Immediately her eyes spied a folded note. Carefully, she opened it and read the fine printing.

"Samantha,

The doctor thought it was a good idea you take birth control pills. He gave me a year's supply and said when you go to college the physician on campus would probably refill it. No one need know and you should only take them if you want to. If they make you sick in any way, you need to see a doctor – remember what is between you and your doctor is confidential. I would have talked to you about this, but it is your decision and you have had enough to deal with.

Feel better -- S."

Samantha stared wide-eyed at the note and then at the contents of the bag. She was uncertain why he would give this to her, but she was too numb to contemplate it further. She quickly stuffed all of the contents back into the bag, carefully covering it with an array of old underwear, nylons and socks.

Samantha was grateful her parents were not home yet. She needed time. Time to sort it all out. Uninterrupted time for herself. A shower. She suddenly craved a shower, not sleep, as she had desired moments ago. She looked at the Minnie Mouse clock, its innocent face, which had been on her shelf for over a decade. She had time for a shower, a change and some carefully applied makeup. They would never suspect anything, she decided.

When her parents arrived home they were obviously tipsy. They had decided to eat dinner at the club with their golfing partners. Samantha was grateful for their festive mood. They had obviously had a good game and, after thirty years of marriage, it was amazing to her how well her parents got along. She couldn't imagine being with anyone for all those years, still enjoying their company, let alone liking them.

"Samantha, we missed seeing you last night at dinner. How was your evening with Emily?" her father inquired in a jovial voice, which meant he wanted to talk and wanted details. Travis Armstrong, for all his belief in his own subtlety was as blatant as a desert flower.

"It was great, Dad. She has quite a collection of CD's and we decided to combine our collection and make tapes for college next year. She hasn't heard from any of the universities she applied to. I tried to talk her into going to Michigan State with me, but I think she wants to stay closer to home, you know, being an only child and all."

Samantha smiled at her father as he looked into her crystal clear blue eyes. She knew he couldn't tell she was lying. Really, she wasn't lying, Samantha silently reasoned; she had simply explained what happened, not last night, but two weeks ago, when she really had spent the night with Emily Osborne, her best friend. She prayed she could keep the sequence of her stories straight as she began to catalogue them internally.

"That's nice dear," her mother said. "You two must have stayed up too late though. You look so tired. Maybe you should take a nap, or go to bed early."

"I do feel tired, but I think it may be the flu creeping up on me. I felt flushed and feverish a few hours ago, so I did take a nap, and some Tylenol. I am feeling a bit better now though," Samantha replied, shrugging off a chill that surged through her entire body.

"Well then, I'm not taking any chances. I'll make some chicken soup for you and we can all have it tomorrow with dinner. You know how when one of us gets sick we all get it. Your father and I have a busy week ahead and we have no time to be sick. Why don't you go up and lay down and when it's done, I'll bring you a bowl on a tray. I'll make it with noodles and an egg, just like you like it. Okay?"

Samantha's mother, smelling of too many martinis, but looking as crisp as she did in the morning, smiled and kissed her on the cheek. She didn't release Samantha to her room without first feeling her forehead. Silently she shook her head in concern before retiring to the kitchen to inspect the cupboards for ingredients.

Samantha, grateful the inspection was over, retreated to her bedroom, kissing her father on the cheek. "Love you, Dad. I'm going to lay down for a while. A nap does sound good."

Travis Armstrong nodded, barely hearing his youngest, as he buried himself in the *New York Times*.

Chapter 4

The phone. Samantha hated the phone. It had become an intruder into her sanctuary. People wanting her to do things. Her parents checking up on her. Skyler, wanting to talk, to remain her confidant. She wanted silence. She wanted time and the safety of her room and her house. She wanted to live a sheltered existence with no surprises until she could go to Michigan and begin again. Reading novels took her to far away places and make-believe people; the only ones she wanted to deal with. But the phone kept ringing and ringing.

It was the housekeeper's day to go to the farmers' market for fresh fruits and vegetables. There was no one to answer the phone. She was alone in the house and there was no one to lie and say she was not there.

The ringing mesmerized her. It kept ringing, persistent. She knew finally she had to answer it.

"Hello," Samantha said indifferently into the ivory receiver.

"Samantha?"

"Yes. Oh, Skyler. Hello. I didn't recognize your voice. The connection is really bad; it's hard to hear you, " Samantha lied.

"I'm on my car phone. I'm just driving back from court. How about meeting me for lunch?"

"How'd you know I was home?"

"Your dad mentioned you had a half-day and then a four-day Memorial weekend, so I got to thinking I hadn't seen you in a while and we should get together."

"Oh. Well, actually, I've already made plans for the weekend. I'm going with Emily to her family's beach house. Maybe another time?" Samantha was relieved she had come up with an excuse so effortlessly.

"No problem. I'll call again. Have a great weekend." Skyler hung up the phone, clenching his teeth. She was not going to get away from him that easily. He had left her alone these past few weeks, understanding she needed her space to get over her ordeal. He wanted her to see him in a different light, not associated with the past she needed to forget. But now enough time had passed. He'd fix it so she had to spend some time with him. She owed him, and he would collect. His jaw line relaxed as he smiled to himself. Payback would be fun. He grinned as he pictured her luscious young curves.

Samantha had planned to decline Emily's invitation, but now she felt compelled to accept it. She had to get away from Skyler. He had become too concerned about her. She just wanted the whole incident to go away, but he wouldn't let it drop. Her appreciative feelings toward Skyler were being systematically eradicated by his constant invitations, phone calls and so-called friendly concern. She had become increasingly frightened of being with him. She wasn't even sure why. He never touched her. He had been only friendly, helpful and supportive of her predicament. Yet each time she heard his voice, she winced. She knew what they would be discussing. He wouldn't let her forget. His voice had become uncomfortable to her; it haunted her to the depths of her being. Unconsciously, she had tucked Skyler away in the same secret place in her mind she had exiled "the rapist". The rapist was no longer someone she thought of as Uncle Greg. She found it difficult to believe the Greg she knew was the rapist she feared, so she tried to forget them both. But Skyler's overbearing and continual concern for her made it impossible. They had formed an irrevocable contract and she was helpless to break it. There was no one she could turn to. His support and help had been great these past few weeks. She appreciated his calls to make sure she was fine and was glad the calls had almost diminished. She had thought he had almost forgotten her. And now this.

Reluctantly, she dialed Emily's number. She did not want to leave the quiet safe arms of her house, but she knew she had to.

Waiting for the line to connect, Samantha remembered she had been a bit curt to Emily when she had mentioned the long weekend at the beach house. She had some rudeness to make up for. But she knew Emily, whom she had known all of her life, would understand and forgive her. Emily would be happy she had finally accepted an invitation to do something other than spend the night at her house.

Samantha's parents felt relieved when she announced she had changed her mind and was accompanying them for the long holiday weekend. In habitual silence, they shared the journey to the country house, each consumed with their own mindful meanderings, comfortable they could convert their thoughts to pleasantries on cue; each confident they could masterfully hide what they were really thinking about. Their driver stared directly at the road, glad at the prospect of spending a few days in the country. He knew, even though the whole firm would be there, that there would be little for him to do. He didn't mind getting paid overtime. He enjoyed the silence in the small black limo, and it was nice to take it out of the garage on such a beautiful day.

Travis Armstrong sat with his soft leather briefcase open on his lap. His review of the current client list and the settlements brought in by each of the firm's members left him satisfied this short vacation was deserving. He felt relieved they were not leaving Samantha behind to sulk. He believed it was about time she recovered from whatever teenage problem she had that led to her recent depression. He knew teenage phases were a natural occurrence and his daughter would be in another phase before he blinked. It had been so much easier when she was younger, when all it took to make her happy was a kiss or a new toy.

Travis wished he could help his daughter with the things that bothered her, but since she had shown signs of becoming a woman, she confided more in her mother and was satisfied to be treated as a little girl by him. That was okay; he was comfortable with that. The boys were much easier to figure out. They were his "buddies," even now that they were in law school. He was happy his sons were grown and had always been cerebral and in control of their emotions, unlike the female gender. He loved his wife and his daughter, but over the years he had learned they would remain an emotional mystery to him. Travis was comforted in the knowledge his sons would faithfully be there working with him, ready to fill his footsteps as his age inevitably led him to retirement. He smiled, comforted at the thought of being able to leave his work behind him in the competent hands of the twins.

Anne Armstrong sat as still as a portrait, with *Scarlet* pressed between her fingers. She had intended to complete this sequel to *Gone With the Wind* weeks ago but her distraction and preoccupation with Samantha's moodiness and withdrawal made it impossible to concentrate. Even now, in the past hour, she had not been able to turn a single page. Anne wondered what thoughts were going through Samantha's mind as she sat still with her headphones, the volume on full blast, hiding her eyes behind shaded glasses. Her daughter's veiled expression had remained unchanged throughout the ride. Anne had been thrilled when Samantha announced her intention to join them, although she was quite taken aback. She wished she knew exactly why Samantha had changed her mind so suddenly, but decided to focus on the positive fact of her joining them.

In her final analysis, Anne believed it was her dotage over her daughter during the past several days that had made the difference. It was natural; clothes and shopping brought out the best in all teenage girls, and her daughter was no exception. She knew they were close enough if anything serious were bothering Samantha, she would have confided it. After having had two sons, she loved having a daughter. It wasn't that she loved Samantha more than she loved Taylor and Tad, it was that she had a special bond with her. A woman's bond; an invisible pact. She had, in an otherwise male-dominated house, a female to consort with. A female that one day would have the same conspiring heart with needs and dreams that could be shared in a way no man, however conscientious and attentive, could share.

Samantha listened as Karen Carpenter's words rang in her head, song after song, over and over again. "Day after day I must face the world of strangers, where I don't belong, I'm not that strong . . ." Each song had a meaning for her. And those that were too cheery, she skipped over. Thank God for CD players. Samantha identified with Karen. She wished she could talk to her. For the moment, Karen was the only woman she *could* identify with. And she was dead.

Sometimes, and lately more and more often, Samantha wished she could die; that she would die. It would be easier. No one would ever know what had happened. No one would ever be able to tell her how stupid it was to try to take the shortcut home from the library. Or how stupid it was to have stayed out so late. Or how stupid she was to have ever trusted anyone.

No one could make her feel guilty and stupid if she were dead.

No one could ever see how dirty she was; how soiled her insides were. Her death would somehow make up for the murder she had committed. If she were dead, no one could ever tell her congratulations on her first child, if she ever had one; and then no one could watch her crumble because it really was her second child.

Death would be better. Easier. But she couldn't do that to her parents.

All she wanted was to get out of this town and go to Michigan. Michigan State would be her place to heal; her place to study hard and spend time with animals. She would find a veterinarian who would hire her, even if it meant cleaning cages. It would help her forget. Animals didn't have the capacity to hurt, not with "malice aforethought" people did.

She knew she would find "serenity in solitude". She remembered her grandmother saying those three words over and over to her when she wondered why Nana didn't come downstairs and sit in the sitting room with everyone else. When Nana was alive, Samantha enjoyed being with her. Her first memories were of her smooth, powder-soft skin. She often wondered how such wrinkled skin could feel so soft and smooth. She loved the fresh scent of lilac-scented soap nestled in the grooves of her Nana's skin. She remembered feeling cheated when she was taken off to school. She remembered the pact they had made on her first day of nursery school when Nana promised if she were really good and brave they would have their time alone. Nana promised she would tell her a special story about real proper southern ladies and how they used to go to etiquette school. They kept their ritual time together on most days and whenever Samantha couldn't see Nana, she would tearfully apologize. Nana always kissed her, gave her a big hug and said "Dear child, I'll miss you, but there is serenity in solitude."

Sometimes Nana let her carefully hold yards of colorful yarn. She loved watching as her grandmother wrapped it into a fuzzy ball. Samantha loved watching it quickly grow from the size of a pea to the size of a grapefruit in minutes. And then, in days, Nana would produce a beautiful sweater or blanket, sometimes even doll clothes.

Samantha missed Nana more than she had ever missed anyone, especially now. She hadn't truly understood Nana's words, or why she enjoyed the quiet and the aloneness so much, until now. She knew if Nana were alive, she could have confided in her without worry, without fear. Nana would have known what to do.

As they rounded the corner, the car crawled up the long neat driveway leading to the large Victorian summer house. Its white painted pillars were stretched up, tall and proud, almost boastful as they led to a second-story veranda, outlined in long clay pots filled with pastel flowers of every shade. It looked so peaceful. Samantha's gaze filled her eyes with the smattering of vivacious colors in cheerful bloom. Stepping out of the car, she took in the house as if she were seeing it for the first time, quickly assimilating the layout of the front grounds.

Suddenly her gaze fell on their limo as it slowly moved away. The spacious parking area had several cars, looking freshly washed in the warm sun, and placed neatly in a row.

"Mom, why are there so many cars here?"

"Dear, have you forgotten? The whole firm has been invited."

"Emily didn't tell me; I thought it would just be us, like it used to be!"

"She may not have known. You see, since our summer house is being renovated, your father asked Mr. Osborne if he wouldn't mind hosting the firm. He wanted to reward everyone for doing so well during the first half of the year, and he has some announcements to make that are cause for celebration. Wasn't it a lovely idea?"

Anne, bright eyed, smiled at the wisdom of her husband. Then, looking at the sullen face of her daughter, she put her arm around her shoulders in an understanding motion as they began to walk toward the front door. Anne couldn't fathom what the problem was now. She thought Samantha would be pleased. Samantha had always been liked by the partners in the firm and Anne was anxious to show off her beautiful graduating daughter. Anne knew once Samantha went off to college, things would change, and there would be little time for Samantha to travel with them. She hoped Samantha would follow in the footsteps of her brothers and become preoccupied with school, career and traveling with friends. Anne knew it had to happen; her daughter had to grow up and move on. But she wanted to relish their last few months together and not think about all the changes that would occur once Samantha left for college. She'd deal with that tomorrow, just like Scarlet . . .

Samantha would just have to get over the fact the firm retreat was here, Anne thought, as she moved toward the entrance. She would still have plenty of time with Emily.

Samantha, aghast, could utter no response. She tried to smile. Her mother needed a positive response or Samantha would have no peace, no quiet, no serenity in solitude.

"Yes, it'll be great," Samantha murmured and then subconsciously added, "I just wish I would have known."

"I'm sorry you didn't know. I would have told you, but I thought you knew." Anne turned Samantha to face her, gently squeezing her shoulders in fond understanding and support of her feelings.

"Really, mom, it's okay. You're right. It will be fun. I'm going to go in and find Emily." And with that, Samantha walked into the house.

Anne turned away. She had lost Travis. Her eyes quickly found him across the lawn, looking over the cliff at the end of the rounded lawn. At the end of Oren Osborne's proud pointing finger lay the still, azure water.

The peaceful view was breathtaking. It was a unique piece of property, surrounded on three sides by water. The house itself was built with intricate vision, leaving every room inside with a panoramic view. The land had been passed down for several generations and was worth a small fortune. The building, with its large rooms, was priceless.

Oren Osborne had been a classmate of Travis' at Harvard. Travis had convinced his father that Oren would be a proud addition to the firm and argued vehemently that Oren "had a mind as close to F. Lee Bailey as he'd ever witnessed." His father agreed, based not solely on his outstanding grades and recommendations, but on his character and obvious temperament. Oren was a simple man with a charismatic personality that could melt ice, cut through metal or just glide through butter. There was no amount of legal training or any other training, with the exception of maybe acting, that could teach such double-edged finesse. Oren had proven to be decent and hard working, an asset well beyond their expectations. His eventual notoriety led the firm into some of the biggest criminal cases in the southern states, and the publicity of his success allowed the firm to bill four times as much for Oren's services than other firms could charge. Oren made sure he took cases pro bono, especially if the issues were newsworthy. Being in the press was well worth the free expenditure of time and the reward of dozens of new clients with ample ability to pay.

Travis was as proud and protective of Oren's success as he was of his own children. Oren had become a full partner after a few years and now after twenty-three years of working together, Travis felt about him as if he were his own blood brother. That was Travis' biggest fault. He seemed to "adopt" the siblings he never had. Now that his parents were both deceased, it was more important than ever to hold family and friends together, to keep them close.

Anne grabbed her hat and tied it atop her shiny mahogany hair, neatly bundled in a French twist, before marching to her husband's side to admire the familiar view. Anne felt at home here. They had visited so often in the past twenty years she felt as if they owned a part of it. Yet each time she gazed at the rippling water and the sea gulls, the view made her visit special and new. She felt young again and safe, the kind of secure feeling you have with those you know, who know you so well they approach you without judgment, whatever the situation. For just a few minutes, her worries about Samantha vanished and all was right with her world.

"Anne, what a pleasure to see you! You are as beautiful and radiant as ever. I trust things are well with you?" Oren redirected a sort of sincerity, often conveyed by clergymen.

"As well as can be expected when you have a teenage daughter!" Anne said laughingly, hoping Emily had been as moody as Samantha had been lately, so her worry could be alleviated.

"Yes. I know what you mean. If it's not one thing with

those kids, it's another. But I must say Emily has been so excited about going away to Europe for the summer and then attending a college away from home, she has been in almost too good a mood." Oren clenched perfect teeth on his cherry-tobacco filled pipe, giving her a wide grin.

"Well that's wonderful. Samantha has been just the opposite. She is so moody and depressed I'm nearly at my wit's end. Maybe spending these four days with Emily will cheer her up and get her back on the right track."

"Of course. They've always been close. I'm sure you have nothing to worry about," Oren said, crinkling a smile once again. His caramel-colored eyes added an exclamation to his simple response, subliminally caressing Anne into a feeling of reassurance.

"Why don't you go find Stephanie and bring her out here?" Travis interrupted.

"Oh, my wife is seeing to it the maids have set enough place settings and prepared the necessary rooms for the arrival of our guests—and that sort of thing," Oren responded.

"Well then, I'll go and see if there is anything I can do to assist her," Anne said. She was very well aware Travis wanted her to excuse herself. Many years ago they had set their parameters and she did not want to overstep those boundaries. She had too much respect for her husband to do that. Besides, she was anxious to see Stephanie.

Emily sat nestled in the window seat of her massive room, her speckled Jade eyes watching from behind sun-yellowed mesh shears as people pulled in and out of the drive. Patiently she waited for Samantha to arrive. She had hoped this weekend would be less formal than other office retreats. Emily was disappointed her father had agreed to the retreat. She wanted her last long weekend before leaving for Europe to be private and fun. Emily wanted some adventure, a last attempt at childhood gaiety, without any worry of having to act like an adult or a proper lady. Now she was eighteen, they would be too visible; and she and Samantha would be expected to be dressed for meals and make appearances at the evening parties. Samantha wasn't in the mood for parties these days, and Emily, genuinely concerned, had hoped over these next four days, she could help Samantha with whatever was bothering her. She had been so moody over the phone lately, and she never wanted to do anything. Samantha had assured her everything was okay and she wasn't mad or upset with her. Emily believed her; but she also knew her well enough to know Samantha was genuinely upset about something – something that wasn't going away easily. She had been moody and withdrawn for what seemed to Emily to be an infinite length of time. Emily hoped their four days together would be long enough for Samantha to feel comfortable enough to confide in her. They had always been able to confide in each other about everything. It couldn't be that parting for college would change things . . . or could it? Emily slicked her dense unruly auburn curls behind her lightly freckled ears.

Emily hated that she was going off to Europe for most of the summer and leaving Samantha behind. She wasn't sure she was ready to make new friends; she would miss her old ones. She would especially miss Samantha, her friend, her confidante and her closest cohort. Tears welled in her eyes at these thoughts, just as Samantha tapped meekly on her door.

"Hey, come on in! What are you doing knocking? This is practically your room," Emily said promptly, pushing her tears back with relief at the interruption.

"Hey yourself," Samantha smiled in retort at her best friend. "You know I always knock. What are you doing sitting there all curled up? You look too comfortable compared to the rest of the people I've seen around here so far!" Samantha rolled her eyes, relieved to be in the comfort of a room she'd been a part of as long as she could remember. It felt safe. It felt impenetrable; most of all, it felt isolated from the rest of the world.

"Yes, I know. It seems we've been preparing for days, instead of only hours, for everyone's arrival. So far, only five of the partners are here. Most brought their wives; you and I are the only kids."

"That's fine by me. I hope it stays that way," Samantha said, put at ease by Emily's announcement.

"It probably will. Mom told me not everyone is staying the whole four days because of other commitments, but everyone is staying at least until Sunday morning brunch."

"Great. That means there will be some free time away from 'the great charade'," Samantha replied, feeling more and more at ease.

Emily nodded in empathetic agreement. Samantha was comforted by Emily's unquestioning acceptance. For the first time in weeks, she didn't feel the pressure to act; to be something she no longer was. She didn't feel like she had to prepare her answers in advance and pretend. She felt grateful to Emily and wished she could explain everything to her. She knew her best friend must wonder why she had been so different lately.

Emily instinctively gave Samantha the time and space she needed, knowing eventually Samantha would tell her everything she wanted to know. That had always been the way things had been between them. They had mutual respect for each others' lives and feelings; they both knew even though they wanted different things out of life, they would always support one another. Samantha felt confident there would be plenty of time for them to talk. Even though she had decided not to tell Emily anything, at Skyler's insistence. She wondered if maybe she should confide in her anyway. She knew Emily was trustworthy and would help her. Samantha knew she needed to confide in someone, other than Skyler. Most days she felt as if she would explode. She needed to relieve some of the pressure, some of the guilt. She needed to feel normal again.

Suddenly Samantha felt tired, as if she hadn't slept in days. She probably hadn't. She couldn't remember a night since the rape she hadn't woken in a cold sweat. She longed for one good night's sleep.

"Sam? Sam? Are you all right?" Emily asked, staring at her friend's pale face, fearing she was about to faint.

"What? Yes, yes, I'm fine." Color replenished her cheeks. "I was just thinking about how many things will change after graduation. On one hand, I'm not sure I want to graduate, to have everything change. On the other hand, I'm excited for the change and sometimes think I need change now, more than ever. Know what I mean?" Samantha said, hoping Emily believed her, even though that had not been exactly what she had been thinking.

"You *know* I know what you mean. Sometimes I feel the same way," Emily replied, looking squarely at Samantha, as if she could see past the blazing blue eyes into her soul. "I can't believe we'll be graduating in a few days. Our lives are changing. We'll be moving in separate directions, but not forever; we will always be more like sisters, not just best friends. I'm really going to miss you, Sam."

"Me too. I don't know what I'll do without you."

"Remember when we were about nine and we decided the grown-ups played more 'pretend' than we did?" Emily queried, raising her thick arched eyebrows.

"Yes. It is amazing how perceptive we were at such a young age," Samantha replied, sighing thoughtfully.

"Well, I've been thinking a lot about that. Do you think we will go away to college and come back like them? I mean, do you think we will be afraid to say what we really feel and what we really mean? Do you think we will compromise ourselves for money and have to be nice to people we don't like? Do you think our friendship will survive it all?"

"I don't know about all of those things, but I know we will survive it. I know no matter what, I can count on you; and you know I'll always be there for you. I think a lot about growing up. I know I don't want to be . . . to be like all the phonies we see our parents deal with. I hope we don't fall into the same traps they have fallen into. But, there are some days I already feel that way. I mean I wish I would, I wish I could—" Samantha rambled, suddenly stopping herself short. She looked around the room at the light lilac paint and the floral lilac-printed border with matching spread and valance. She let her thoughts be absorbed into those lilacs and, as if she were watering them, they drained those thoughts from her.

"Come on, you what?" Emily said coaxing.

"Oh, I don't know. I just, I'm not sure I want to grow up. As much as I know what I want, I look around me, at all of the so-called adult role models, and I know I don't want to be like them. I want to be able to say what I want and what I feel and not worry about what anyone else will think or how they'll react," Samantha offered.

"Yeah, I know what you mean. I know half of the people in the firm, my mother doesn't like; but you'd never know it by watching her. She's the perfect hostess and she never says no to my dad. I can't imagine my whole life being run by a man and what he wants . . . and certainly not by my husband. I want a man who will let me be me," Emily said.

"Do you really think we can find men who will let us be

ourselves?" Samantha's brows were knitted as she looked up at Emily still sitting comfortably in the window seat. "I can't imagine that. I've watched my mother take orders from my father for so long and take care of my brothers, as if they were helpless, it's hard for me to believe my life will be different."

"It will. I promise it will," Emily said confidently smiling at her friend. "That's why you are going all the way to Michigan State University to go to school. You'll probably come back a totally different person."

"I hope so," Samantha said, silently crossing her fingers, hoping those words would come true.

"I hope *not*. You won't change so much you will forget me, will you? Who else could I talk to like this?"

"We'll always be best friends, no matter what. Blood or not, we are sisters and even if we grow up and move away, we will always be there for each other. I know we will," Samantha replied in a tone Emily could not challenge for sincerity. They both knew it was true, felt it with absolute certainty; they were sisters.

Samantha spent the next hour with Emily, unloading her clothes from the heavy wardrobe bag the butler brought up the rounded stairwell. Showing off the new wardrobe her mother happily bought for her on their latest shopping spree allowed Samantha to temporarily forget her problems. Her tortured thoughts were replaced for the moment with fashion ideas from Emily and her latest issues of *Cosmopolitan, Seventeen* and *Glamour* magazines.

Guests continued to arrive. One by one, they melded into the spirit of being on a retreat at a home away from home. The Osborne estate was comfortable and spacious. Each couple had as much privacy as they desired.

As the dinner bell sounded and resounded, the congregation collected around six glass-topped, antiqued green cast iron tables; each centered with a potted red geranium and strategically placed on the outdoor patio. Small red place cards, held in tiny silver geranium embossed holders, directed each guest to a seat. Those who had been members of the firm the longest sat in closest proximity to the Armstrong and Osborne table. The fragrant smell of barbecued steaks, chicken and ribs filled the air, complementing the piped-out elevator music. Mountains of vegetables, salads, fruits and breads were lined up in silver dishes, held in the outstretched hands of black servants, tidily dressed in nurse-white starched uniforms, black aprons and ties.

Samantha and Emily sat next to each other in comfortable silence, watching, as the adults in smiling sheep-like order, followed each other to their seats, cocktails in hand. Each of the women, dressed in their simple but obviously designer dresses and heels, were adorned with gold, silver or pearls. The men were more relaxed with open-collar golf shirts and casual slacks. The scene looked more like a private country club dinner than a relaxed retreat and cookout.

As the meal progressed into trays of desserts and after-dinner liqueurs, Samantha and Emily excused themselves as Travis began the highly anticipated speech regarding the success of the firm and the financial balance sheet that had been presented to him earlier in the week by Greg Maston, lifelong friend and accountant to the firm. The figures were so good that, in addition to the usual salary and bonuses, each would receive 10,000 shares in one of five stocks of their choice. Samantha had heard her father practice his speech and could not bear to hear Greg's name in praise. She *had* to leave. Samantha and Emily were almost out of earshot, cutting through the sliding glass door to the breakfast nook, when they heard Skyler's familiar voice.

"So, girls, what'd I miss?"

"Oh, Mr. Marks, hi! I thought daddy said you weren't able to join us?" Emily stated, unaffected by his sweeping sea-foam eyes and stare. "Really, you haven't missed much," she continued. "Mr. Armstrong is just making his announcements and everyone is still working on dessert. Would you like me to tell Cook to bring you a plate of food?"

"No, thanks. That's very nice of you to offer, but I'll just have coffee and dessert. I guess I had better get out there. See you two." Skyler winked at them and briskly walked out to the patio.

"See you later," Emily responded, not noticing Samantha's choked back surprise and sudden self-consciousness.

"So what do you want to do?" Emily asked. "It's still early, we could drive into town and see what's playing or go to the beach and see who is hanging out. I heard Tommy

Snyder is getting a group together for a bonfire."

"Oh. I guess we could do either. Whatever you want is fine. I'm really tired though. Whatever we do, I don't want to stay out late."

"Sam, it would be great for you to get out. You don't want to go out anymore. People have been asking about you." Emily stopped as they climbed the wide, rounded stairs. "You're not sick or anything are you? You'd tell me if something were wrong, wouldn't you?"

"Emily, why would you say that? I'm fine, really I am. I'm just tired from the long drive. Come on, let's get our stuff and go."

"Okay, just remember you can tell me anything. You know that, don't you?"

"Yes, Emily. Don't be a goof; I know that," Samantha said teasingly. Then suddenly putting her hand over her mouth, she made an urgent rush toward the bathroom.

As Samantha vomited violently in the powder room, Emily stood outside the door listening; wishing Samantha would stop before she became nauseated just from the sound. Decidedly, Emily moved towards the door. Quietly knocking and gently pushing the door open, Emily entered to see Samantha rinsing her mouth and face in the cool water flowing from the gold faucets on the marbleized gray and burgundy sink.

"Are you okay? Can I get you anything? Should I get your mom?" Emily asked, wide-eyed at the sudden change in her friend and fighting the urge to flee the sour odor.

"No, I'll be fine. I must have eaten something that didn't agree with my stomach. I think you better go ahead without me. I really want to take a shower, wash up and get into bed. Tomorrow we can do something?" Samantha asked apologetically, her arms clenched around her stomach as she walked back to Emily's room.

"No problem. I think I'll go watch television and stay in tonight too. I'll check on you later. Do you have everything you need?"

Samantha nodded and moved toward the pullout couch on the wall opposite Emily's bed. Fortunately, the maids had the bed already made up and the crisp grape-colored sheets looked inviting. Samantha reached in her bag and grabbed her nightclothes and toiletries. She needed a shower before she entered those sheets. Thankfully, since Emily's bathroom was attached to her room, it was easy to have a private shower. Samantha quickly entered the cleansing wet cocoon, she often retreated to. After her shower, Samantha crept between the sheets in relief at the solitude and safety of her best friend's room. Cleansing her mind of the buried thoughts that kept pushing forward from the sudden appearance of Skyler was difficult.

Sleep was not coming as easily as she thought it would, and she was relieved she had packed her sleeping pills. She had become accustomed to using them when her mind would not stop reeling. The pills gave her a few hours of peace.

Suicide she couldn't do; but escaping into a deep sleep, even for a few hours, was easy. And no one got hurt. Within minutes after swallowing three sleeping pills, she fell into a numbing sleep while counting the hand-painted floral porcelain beads on the brass head and footboards of Emily's queen-sized bed.

Sunlight awoke a cotton-mouthed Samantha to the sound of birds and a cool breeze from the early morning air. Emily slept soundly across the room. She was a late riser, Samantha knew.

Samantha heard the familiar stirrings of breakfast trays being delivered to the various rooms down the long corridor. She wasn't hungry and decided she would wait until brunch and eat with Emily. The men would be on the golf course by then. Most of the women would join them; the rest would be by the pool. The next gathering of the group would be dinner again, this time formal in the dining room; and then on Sunday, brunch would be with everyone, before those departing early left. Samantha would find a way to make it through. She would have to find a way to talk to Skyler without being seen. She couldn't risk anyone overhearing their conversation. Samantha was sure he would bring up everything; he always did. She couldn't chance that. She felt so uncomfortable around him, and yet she owed him a great deal. She didn't know what to do.

She wished she could talk to Emily. But would Emily understand what had happened and what she did? Would Emily keep her secret? What would happen if she told or if

Skyler found out Emily knew? No, Samantha decided, looking at Emily's peaceful face and steadily breathing petite body in sleep. She couldn't tell Emily, she had no right to upset her. This was her problem and she would handle it. After all, the worst was over.

Samantha felt alone, a feeling she had become accustomed to. She was losing more and more control over her own feelings and thoughts. She needed to forget, now more then ever. She did not want this house and this weekend to be swept in with the continuing horror she kept burying in the dim parts of her mind. Those parts grew every day and kept creeping like weeds into parts of her brain she had to use. She felt suffocated. She could not turn her mind from thoughts of Skyler. In anxious tugs, she removed the ponytail holder from her thick curls and grabbed her fluffy pink robe. A shower. Samantha had to have a shower. That would clear her mind.

Emily awoke to the sound of running water. It seemed as if it had been running for hours. She hated being woken up early on a weekend, especially a holiday weekend. It was impossible Samantha had to take another shower and it had to last a whole hour. There wouldn't be any more hot water left for anyone. What was she thinking, what was going on, Emily wondered. Samantha had been so preoccupied, not just yesterday, but for what seemed like forever. She would try to get it out of her today. She had to.

"Hey Sam, save me some hot water!" Emily yelled, as she opened the bathroom door just a crack. Emily could see Samantha's things thrown about the bathroom as if she had been in quite a hurry for her shower. That was odd, Emily thought as she waited for a response. None came. Emily opened the door another inch wider and heard whimpering.

"Sam, are you all right?" Emily asked loudly.

"I'm fine, I'll be out in a minute," Samantha replied quickly.

"I'm going to get in after you're out; then we can get ready for brunch and go down. Is that all right with you?"

"Sure. Just give me a second and I'll be out. I just finished shaving and I'm rinsing my hair." Samantha said as composed as possible, but frightened Emily had heard her crying. She calmed herself with the thought Emily would have pressed her for answers if she had heard her. No more. She would have to do a better job suppressing her emotions. She couldn't risk anyone finding out.

Emily gathered her things in anticipation of her shower. When Samantha walked in, wrapped comfortably in her robe, combing her wet hair, Emily looked straight into her face and directly at her deep blue eyes. They looked clear. Her face was not puffy, as if she had been crying. Maybe she was humming some weird song and Emily had mistaken it for whimpering. After all, Samantha didn't usually sing, and she claimed she couldn't hold a tune. That must be it, Emily rationalized as she entered the steamy bathroom.

"I'll be out in a few minutes. Just come on in if you need anything from the bathroom," Emily shouted as the water began to run.

"Thanks. I can't wait to eat, the shower made me hungry," Samantha responded, lying to throw Emily off. Samantha never felt hungry these days. And she felt like she could stay in the solitude of the shower all day; even when the water ran cold.

The girls went about their day as they had always done on the many long summer days they spent at their respective summer houses. They swam and ate and laid in the sun until their fair skin turned to a pale shrimp color. They pulled on their woven straw hats and took out the small paddleboat Emily's father had given to her on her twelfth birthday. They talked about boys, clothes, college and their future dreams. Eventually, they knew it was time to come in when they saw the adults pull up and the servants put away the colorfully adorned golf clubs.

Into the showers again, they dressed for dinner, carefully applying makeup. Each chose a sundress to wear to dinner, with sweaters covering their bare shoulders. Bare shoulders in the dining room were forbidden. They agreed they would make an appearance and then leave the table as dessert was being served. Tonight was Saturday. They were anxious to throw off their sweaters and head for the bonfire at the beach, down the cove where some of their classmates gathered nightly. Samantha, although privately reluctant, had promised Emily she would go with her to the beach. She was relieved it would take her away from any possible confrontation or discussion with Skyler, whose piercing eyes followed her from a distance. As much as she told herself that was not possible, with each passing hour she felt his presence more and more, without actually seeing him there.

Dinner was uneventful and Samantha was thankful, although Skyler was a very successful attorney in her father's firm, he was still one of the youngest and newest partners, so he was virtually at the opposite end of the long dining table. It was easy to avoid eye contact and conversation with him. Just as the girls had planned, they were allowed to be excused as dessert and coffee were served. Into the night they happily fled, driving Emily's blood-red graduation present, top down.

Samantha felt her soul release into the night wind as it ran through her long curls. She breathed deeply, feeling her lungs fill up and out. She felt a freedom she hadn't known in months. She wasn't sure why, but she hoped it would last. She looked at Emily, innocently driving while tuning the radio. She wished this feeling would not end.

As the car parked on a small stony area, the girls saw several familiar figures roasting marshmallows, and they quickly joined in. Bags of chips and pretzels and a cooler of buns, hot dogs and beer lay open in the sand. The night went quickly, and before they knew it, people started to disperse, either in couples to remote parts of the beach or into their cars. Beer in hand, Emily and Samantha made a toast to their friendships, said their good-byes and headed for their car. They were not used to drinking and they each felt the quiet tiredness the beer left them with, thankful they only had a few miles to go.

Returning to the house they found most of the lights off. Quietly, they retreated to their room. Emily opted to use the bathroom first, knowing she'd never get in once Samantha entered it. As Samantha waited for Emily, she suddenly felt a headache come on and wanted something with fizz to drink. Quietly she reached in her purse for some aspirin and then crept down the long stairwell to the kitchen for a cola. There, in the dark, she saw the tip of a lighted cigarette and smelled its repugnant smoke. Not seeing the face behind the cigarette, she excused herself for intruding.

"Oh, I'm sorry. I won't be but a minute, I just want to grab a soda," Samantha said quickly, opening the door to the refrigerator.

"Samantha, it's just me," Skyler said chuckling. "I startled you. I'm sorry. I couldn't sleep and thought I'd come to the kitchen for a glass of wine and a cigarette".

"Oh, hi. I didn't recognize you in the dark."

"Listen, I really can't sleep and I was wondering, would you take a walk with me?"

"I shouldn't really. I have this headache and I . . ."

"Nonsense, the fresh air will do you good. Swallow your aspirin and you can take the soda with you. I promise, we won't be gone long," Skyler insisted.

There was no way out, so Samantha agreed. "Okay, just let me get my sweater from my room," Samantha replied, really wanting to tell Emily she was going for a walk so she wouldn't worry.

"Nonsense. It's warm outside. Look, if you get cold I'll give you my jacket."

"But I've got to tell Emily I'm going . . . she'll wonder if I'm not back in the room."

"I don't think so. She's probably fast asleep. It smells like the two of you had quite a bit to drink."

Sheepishly, Samantha nodded in agreement. There was nothing more to say. She simply followed him out of the house, through the servants' entrance off the kitchen, and into the dark night.

"So, how have you been? I haven't heard from you for a few weeks, so I figured you were doing fine and getting on with your life," Skyler said, appearing sincere.

"Fine, I guess. I mean as fine as I can be. It's hard for me to forget everything, to keep lying to everyone. Worse, I fear seeing Uncle Greg. I haven't seen him since, . . ." Samantha's voice trailed into the darkness.

"Since the rape. Samantha, once you can say it, you can forget it and move on. You have to move on and forget everything. I'll help you in any way I can. You know I will," Skyler said sympathetically.

"I know. I've just asked so much of you already. I need to figure the rest out on my own. Really, I appreciate everything you've already done. I'm just anxious to go away to college and start over. I really believe that's when I will put it behind me. When I'm out of this small town." Samantha spoke softly, but her words were clear. She wasn't sure if the words were for Skyler's benefit or for her own. She really had grown to believe leaving was the only solution and only a new life would make her forget and keep those dismal memories locked tightly in cerebral storage.

"You probably are right. Change will do you good. Just remember I will always be there for you," Skyler stopped and looked at the petite girl in front of him. She was as beautiful in the moonlight as any woman he'd ever known. When he was with her, he felt miles high and as if he carried the wisdom of the ages. She was obviously too immature to know the effect she had on him. But he would help her grow and understand what he had really done for her, for them. She owed him, and it was time to make that known. "Look over there—the door on the boat house has come ajar. Let's go have a look. I hope it hasn't been broken into."

Samantha instinctively paused before following him.

"Are you cold?" Skyler asked, taking off his jacket.

"No. I'm fine. Actually, my headache is almost gone. The night air has made me tired. I think we should head back," Samantha said, looking at Skyler's sun-browned muscular frame.

"In just a minute," Skyler said, taking hold of Samantha's hand as he pushed the partially opened boathouse door with the other. Stepping in careful silence, the pair acted as if they were the burglars; quiet and cautious, taking care not to be seen. When their eyes adjusted to the shadowy room, it was clear they were the only ones in the building. Samantha thought someone might really be in the boathouse. Skyler shoved the door shut behind them. It was very dark, except for the stream of moonlight coming from the panes of thick uncovered glass.

"Samantha, there is something we need to talk about," Skyler said, pivoting Samantha in an about-face, placing both of his hands on her salmon-colored, almost bare shoulders. Samantha winced in the darkness; her heart pounded rapidly.

"I know this isn't fair to you, and you really had no way of knowing, because you are such an innocent; but I have become very attracted to you."

Samantha stared in disbelief, her young mind did not have a quick answer for him and, as it raced through reels of answers she'd read in books, none seemed appropriate. She was uncomfortable. She was scared. Flashes of Greg Maston's face appeared before her. Her pulse began to race, her body instantly beaded with sweat, her mind tried to steady her in her surroundings. Then, the instinct to flee seized her.

Samantha tried to push Skyler away and move toward the door. His muscular body lunged over hers. He grabbed her close to him as her arms instinctively hugged her clothes, trying to hold them next to her. He was too preoccupied to notice and began to rub her skin, his fingers slowly pressing into her milky flesh while he outlined her frame as if he were a blind man seeing for the very first time.

Samantha gasped and grabbed at his arms, trying to pull them off of her without upsetting him. She could not. Skyler moved, his hands grabbing her body whole, bending her down on the neatly folded boat covers and thickly woven wool blankets that lay in the corner of the room behind the door.

"Skyler! No! Don't, No! This can't happen!" Samantha said in a high-pitched scratchy voice intonated with raw fear. His powerful brawny body pinned her, as his hands continued to explore her body. "Why? Why are you doing this?"

"Just follow my lead, everything will be great. Trust me," Skyler whispered as he kissed her ears, her long throat and the crevice leading to her breasts.

Samantha felt the taste of blood trickling down her throat. She wasn't sure where the blood came from. It scared her. Her arms were pinned down. It was difficult to move. She felt dizzy and nauseous. She saw shadows in the boathouse moving slowly, dancing in the walls. She wasn't sure of reality. The face assaulting her faded in and out; seemed to be Greg . . . seemed to be Skyler. She wasn't sure. Why wasn't she sure, her mind questioned, as she tried again to free herself from under her captor.

Samantha was dumbstruck. The beer had made her tired and her body limp. It seemed to her they were moving in slow motion, this might even be a dream. She wasn't sure of anything. She watched his strong handsome face and saw his verdant green eyes moving over her body, his lips leaving traces of his warm breath all over her. The taste of blood in her mouth faded into a taste of sweaty salt in what now felt like a desert-parched throat.

Samantha's steel-blue eyes held no warmth for him, but

he did not notice. His anticipation of having her beneath him was no longer to be suspended, no longer to be held in abeyance. She was here now and he had for her a need, with a sense of urgency so deep within him he could not control himself. He found himself reaching for her with such an eruption of limitless desire it was as if he were someone else. He had never known such raw unabated want. He did not notice her horror. He did not notice her grimacing face or her contorted body. He did not feel her pushing away. Her sounds fell on his deaf ears. He did not notice when the sounds stopped. He only noticed when her body became compliant to his as she gave in with cool casual indifference.

Samantha knew she had to comply, just as she knew she had no choice when Uncle Greg held her down with the belt. To her horror, she felt her body bowing with his, as his sweaty anxious hands reached into her silken bra, fiercely pushing it up, swiftly taking it off as he unbuttoned her cotton sundress. With strident movements, he quickly removed the dress, lifting its skirt and lowering her lace-trimmed panties, inescapably revealing her smooth supple body to him. She felt him cup her small breasts, moving from one to the other, first his hand, then his mouth, swallowing her whole.

She stiffened; she wanted to scream. She tried. She tried again. She felt as if she were in slow motion. Her voice no longer worked at her mind's command. She had lost control. Finally, she let go of what was happening. She screamed an internal scream so loud and so deep it chilled her body into silent numbness. It no longer mattered no one else could hear her scream. She felt the swell of her breast and the nipples turning hard against his warm flesh. His fingers probed and pried at every line of her body, slowly, carefully, deliberately memorizing each morsel. He savored her warm flesh, being careful not to hurt her; being careful to imprint in her memory his touch, his kindness, the way he made her feel, despite the unusual circumstances.

She could feel his swell against her and she knew she pleased him. He was hot and his breathing became heavy. She used her inner turmoil and forged her movements by copying his. She unconsciously searched his body as he searched hers. Together they became impostors, and Skyler became the art collector buying with an untrained eye, as she feigned her pleasure, arching her back, moving her body with his to rhythmic crescendo.

As he finished, Skyler was genuinely enraptured with her performance. He believed it, and Samantha knew she had pleased him. Her slow deliberate movements had fooled him.

As he held her, his breathing became more even. Finally, stroking her breasts, he spoke in a soft thick voice, "That was wonderful. I'm so glad you understand. It has been you all along I have wanted. I know you feel the same way. We are two of a kind, you and me," he said into the sudden dead air.

It was over and he had believed her. He lay still, sprawled on her with eyes closed, waiting for a response. Samantha couldn't speak. Warm, uncontrollable tears spilled down the sides of her face, raining on her ears, almost signing her to respond to him. She simply smiled stiffly and nodded in agreement; in fear.

Samantha felt as if she were an intruder in her own body. She didn't want to be here. She didn't want this to happen. She didn't want to believe it. She felt her mind sinking and knew she couldn't let it shut down or she would never find her way back. She had to find her voice. She had to erase these moments. She had to fill the horror with strength so she could find a way out. Her eyes studied the boathouse.

Her mental transformation made it impossible for him to penetrate her soul as he had penetrated her body. She had been on the sidelines watching. She was not really the woman who had matched him movement for movement. She had placed herself outside of the situation her body was in and responded in a friendly, non-questioning manner, as she had for the past few months to everyone she knew.

Samantha had grown to know Skyler well enough to know she had to keep him in a friendly mood so she could leave and find a safe harbor to figure things out. Her voice came, soft and clear and deliberate.

"Skyler, I am thankful to you for all you have done for me, but this cannot happen again. It was just the alcohol I had. I shouldn't have had any. I'm sorry. It was my fault," Samantha said carefully, her voice breaking, cutting sharply into the silence. Her facade of composure and agreement continuing to fool him.

"No. You don't understand. This is the way it is to be, this is the way it has to be." Skyler said, grasping her arms so tightly she couldn't move. "You owe me. Why else do you think I've kept all your little secrets?"

Samantha quivered in the darkness. "You said you would help me because you were my friend . . . my father's friend . . ."

"Yes, but everyone has their price, and you are old enough to learn that. My price for my silence is you. I want you. And if you think I won't tell or I have no proof, you just try me. I have all of the medical documents and records from our little trip. Do you remember that?" Skyler said with quiet confidence. Then, reaching for a small envelope from his wrinkled pants, which lay in a tan pool next to their still-naked bodies, he handed it to her.

"What's this?" Samantha asked, holding the manila envelope in her hand, fearing to open it.

"Just my insurance. Don't open it now. Wait until you go home. The envelope contains a tape you'll want to listen to, which shows you just how serious I am. I have other copies, so I suggest you destroy this one to insure it doesn't fall into the wrong hands." Skyler stroked the long, tangled tendrils framing her face.

"You wouldn't do anything to hurt me." Samantha said slowly trying to take in what he was saying, unsure of herself. "You're my friend. I confided in you. You promised to help me. You wouldn't do anything that would hurt my parents."

"Sure I would. I work hard for your father and I have made him a lot of money over the years. I don't owe him anything. Besides, he would probably be grateful I helped out his daughter in her time of need. He won't believe Greg raped you, and I'll get a dozen guys to say they slept with you. And then there's the tape. You shouldn't make any hasty decisions until you have listened to it."

"You wouldn't. You couldn't do that!" Samantha held back her tears though she was crying inside as she spoke. Deep down she knew he could and he would. Samantha looked around for something to fight with. She saw nothing. She wished she could kill him and end it all, her whole nightmare could die with him. She had been a fool to trust him, and it was too late to do anything.

As she looked at him squarely with her fiery blue eyes and pursed lips, he heard her slow defeated sigh.

"I see you are getting the picture. Don't worry, I have a lot to teach you. It will be the best summer you've ever had. I can assure you, you'll go off to college a real woman." Skyler said in a jovial, almost laughing voice. He'd lost track of time. They had to get back to the house before anyone noticed they were missing, but not before he had his prize one more time. And with that thought, he felt his hardness and pressed himself against her, putting his mouth over hers, tasting her sweet acquiescence. His hardness now pointed the way to its desire. He felt her warmth as he parted her legs, like soft opening petals, needing the pollination of the bee.

Chapter 5

Samantha awoke from a stiff fetal-like position. Slowly she removed the covers from her buried face and blinked the sleep from her eyes, trying to focus and remember where she was. She had been in a trancelike dream where the motions she made were not her own. Her mouth was parched and stale. She ran her swollen tongue over her teeth, counting to ensure they were all there. Her cheeks still tasted of blood as she traced the coarse ridges inside them where she had bitten down in fear.

Thankfully, nothing visible was missing or injured. Her body felt stiff, sore and bruised from her insides out. She ached. Her head hurt. Faint pictures flashed from within her. She remembered. She closed her eyes tightly.

It was not a dream. Skyler had raped her repeatedly. She had gone along with it. He was blackmailing her. What was she to do now? Where could she go? Who could she tell? Suddenly, she remembered the tape he had given her. Where had she put it? Moving quietly around the room so she did not disturb Emily, Samantha grabbed her pink robe and reached deep into the large pocket where the tape lay hidden. She had placed it there after the shower she took before climbing into the safety of her bed.

She had to find a cassette player and listen. What could it contain? Pulling open Emily's desk drawers, she discovered the headset Emily used to run track with. Quietly she removed it before slipping into the safety of the bathroom. This time she remembered to lock the door.

Turning the shower water on to muffle any sound, Samantha sat on the stool, placed the earphones on, and carefully put the cassette in the holder. Hesitantly, she pressed play. To her shock, it was her own timid voice, explaining tearfully to Skyler how Uncle Greg had raped her. She listened for a few minutes and then heard Skyler's voice replying to her own. Suddenly she was reliving that awful morning after the rape. She couldn't listen. She pulled the tape from the case and held it with shaking hands and trembling body. How had he taped their conversation? She did not recall a tape recorder. Had someone else she was unaware of been in the room? Had he been wearing a tape recorder she hadn't noticed?

Samantha couldn't remember. She was shaking. Her whole body was trembling and tears burned in her unblinking eyes. Samantha wanted to destroy the tape. She couldn't do it here though; someone might find it. Carefully she placed it back into the deep pocket of her robe. Unconscious of what she was doing, Samantha walked into the shower and numbly slumped over. She couldn't feel the heat of the water and when it eventually turned chilly she removed herself. She didn't know how long she had been in the water. Her lips and fingertips turned a pale blue from the cold.

"Samantha, what is going *on*? You look awful. Did you fall asleep in the shower? Are you sick? Put this blanket on you. My God, you're blue!" Emily exclaimed, in honest concern for her friend.

"I'm fine. I did. I fell asleep in the shower; can you believe it? What a dumb thing for me to do. That beer last night really made me sick, and I took a few aspirins before I fell asleep. I guess they must not have mixed well with the beer." Emily looked unconvinced.

"Please don't say anything. I'll be fine." Samantha said, compounding her lies. And she knew each lie she told made the next one easier. She felt sorry for Emily as she stared at Samantha with genuine concern and worry.

"Fine. But you and I are going to get ready and we are going downstairs for some food. You probably threw up everything you ate last night, and you better eat something this morning before we see everyone and say good-bye to people. You can't let anyone see you looking like this; I don't want your parents thinking I did this to you. Your parents and mine will kill us both if they find out we were drinking," Emily whispered, as she rubbed the blanket over Samantha in an attempt to help warm her.

Samantha was happy to take orders. She was happy to feel a kind hand warming her, caring for her. She didn't have the mind to act or decide for herself, at least not right now.

What was she going to do? She would deal with it later. She had to. There was nothing she could do for the moment. She just hoped she didn't run into Skyler. She would have to talk with him, sooner or later. Not now, later. That was it. She could reason with him, later, when they both had time to think.

Surely she must have misunderstood him. After all, Samantha reasoned, she had been drinking and she had mixed medicine and alcohol. She knew there were side effects to mixing drugs and alcohol; maybe that's what happened. He couldn't be blackmailing her! He was handsome. He had a great body. He was funny and intelligent. He had everything going for him. He could have any female he wanted. Samantha had heard her father call Skyler the most eligible man in the county. So why did he want her?

She must have misunderstood him in her drunken state. That was it, she convinced herself. She must have given him the wrong signals and let him think she wanted him, when really she was only grateful to him; that was all.

Samantha's mind was reeling. It kept rationalizing. It gave Skyler the benefit of the doubt. It gave her a thin strand of hope.

As she cautiously walked down the staircase with Emily to eat breakfast, she felt her body release the warm semen; she felt it seep into her underwear, confirming last night's event. Quickly, without warning, she pivoted on the stairs and returned to the safety of the bedroom, clawing through her clothes looking for clean panties. She changed in the bathroom as she heard Emily knocking again at the door.

"Sam, are you sick again? Can I come in?"

Samantha flushed the toilet as if she had just vomited. She wished she could vomit, but she had vomited all that was left inside her after she returned to the room last night.

"Yes. I am sick, but I feel better now. I'll be right there; I'm just brushing my teeth."

Slowly they again descended the stairs toward breakfast. Samantha was well aware Emily was watching her closely. As they entered the breakfast room, they could see the table just being carefully set for brunch.

The girls agreed between them to sit in the kitchen and eat while Cook prepared the repast for the others. The smell of fresh cinnamon rolls and lemon muffins filled the air, comforting both girls. Cook smiled at them, understanding their need to be away from the adults for just a while. She put plates in front of them so they could help themselves to anything they wanted. Cook was used to the girls eating in the kitchen. They didn't like to be waited on, like the adults, so she never minded their presence in the kitchen. In fact, she was grateful for their youthful chatter and obvious vitality. Fortunately, the girls were not expected to join everyone for the final meal together before most of the group departed. Sunday was relaxing, and the girls were on their own until dinner.

The rest of the day was routine. The girls spent the day on the paddleboat and played a challenging game of croquet with the house rules they had made up on Emily's tenth birthday. They had wanted to prove the boys who had been invited couldn't meet the girls' course. They placed the wires in challenging positions, in the midst of flowers, rocks and roots. They still liked to play that course and, even now, the challenge of it gave them a sense of control, accomplishment and sheer relaxation.

Neither of them really knew why, but they would probably play croquet until they were so old they could no longer hold the mallets. They laughed and relaxed and felt like small children again. This time together was precious and they were determined to enjoy it to the fullest. Without discussing it, each of them knew their time together was growing short before Europe and college interfered with their friendship, as they had known it.

Samantha was silent most of the time, but Emily attributed her silence to last night's beer and the fact things were changing.

The girls went to join the remaining guests for dinner, only to find a comfortable place setting for six. Samantha was relieved everyone else, including Skyler, had departed earlier. Samantha and her parents were the only ones who remained, and they would leave with the Osborne's tomorrow.

Samantha was heartened Skyler had left without any attention directed toward her. She must have been right, she thought, hopefully. He felt as bad about what happened as she did. Surely it was a mistake; a misunderstanding.

As the evening progressed, Samantha rigidly controlled

her face and answered each question with an instinctive delicacy that carefully mimicked happiness. Everyone who had worried about her, including Emily, quietly marveled at her sudden transformation. Each took silent credit for the positive change.

Samantha, unconsciously, was mastering her world. Her world as she now knew and understood it. Her quiet manipulation of those closest to her reinforced what little strength she had remaining. She couldn't control what was happening to her, but she could control her own behavior. Her first and most important goal was to reassure her family and friends she was okay. She would deal with the rest later. She had no choice. Her silent determination left her with more fortitude than she'd had in months.

"Dinner on the patio was a marvelous idea, Stephanie," Anne said lightly. "It is such a beautiful evening and the perfect way to spend our last night. "

"Thank you. Really, though, I must confess it was Oren's idea. He said he has a surprise for us all," Stephanie beamed, looking around the table at the faces now turned towards Oren.

"Later dear. Later. I don't want to spoil it," Oren said, chuckling, as he raised his elegantly stemmed wine glass from the table in a toasting motion. "I'd like to make a toast," he said, now standing. "A toast to good friends and time well spent. A toast to Travis for his kindness and fairness to the firm. And, finally, a toast to the future; to our safe journeys home and continued good health, safety and prosperity until we can meet again."

Everyone raised their glasses, clinking them in unison. Then Travis, beaming, spoke in a boisterous tone, "I couldn't have said it better and we would like to thank you for your kind words and your hospitality." Travis raised his glass and again the six glasses clanked. Samantha and Emily remained silent watching their parents repeat kind gestures back and forth, as they had on so many other occasions. The girls sat patiently watching and waiting. When they were younger, they loved the toasting the best because they always got to taste the sweet red wine, dry white wine or bubbly champagne. Now, they simply followed along, raising patient eyebrows at each other and secretly sharing the same wish to be excused from the table.

Colorful crisp salads entered on a large silver tray. As they were being served with fresh ground pepper, dressing, French bread, sweet butter, apple butter and honey butter, no one noticed the three men dressed in black and white with red ties and instruments in their arms. The tallest man, with a deep olive complexion, pulled from behind an evergreen a microphone on a stand while the others simultaneously pulled out two small speakers. The music began softly, blending in with the soft summer breeze, the vibrant setting sun and the succulent aromas.

Oren's wide dark eyes looked at his wife for approval. She grabbed the floral napkin from her lap and wiped the corner of her eye. "You are a dear man," Stephanie said, patting his hand. "What a wonderful surprise!"

Travis raised his glass once again and exclaimed, "First class!"

The evening continued with small talk and praise of each other. Little business was discussed. The men rarely spoke of business in front of their wives and children. Long ago they had made a pact that meals were for family and digestion. The women appreciated that their husbands were so thoughtful. The children didn't care either way; but both silently wished this meal would end so they could enjoy their last night together.

Finally dessert was cleared. Emily spoke up first, asking that they be excused to pack for tomorrow and to go for a walk. Samantha remained silent but nodded in agreement as she heard Emily's explanations and apologies for being too tired to stay at the table any longer. Both sets of parents instantaneously agreed as they moved to the garden gazebo to sit and sip their after-dinner drinks.

"So give, Samantha!" Emily said, as the girls walked barefoot on the shoreline, their shoes tied and slung over their shoulders.

"Give?" Samantha said. "What do you mean?"

"Come on, you know. You're holding something back. You were too quiet at dinner. For God's sake, you have not been yourself all week. I know something is up."

"Okay, you're right. Everything is changing. It's depressing me. I don't want to lose you, and even though I know you'll always be there, things will be different. I can't bear the thought of—"

"Come on, Samantha, you're lying to me! We already discussed all of that. What's really going on?" Emily confronted Samantha with all the passion she had. "Remember me? I *know* you. The real you. *You* are not you!"

"I, I . . . " Samantha started, dumbfounded at Emily's straightforwardness.

"No, Sam. I want the truth."

"I can't tell you right now. I swear I will. But right now, I just can't. There is something, something awful, but I have to work some things out before I can tell you" Samantha said, tears streaming. "I'm going to be fine. I haven't told you because I don't want you to worry."

"Sam, I'm your best friend. If you can't tell me, then who can you tell? Whatever it is, you know you can trust me; you know I can keep a secret. I'll help you no matter what."

"That's just it. I can't tell you. I can't tell anyone. I haven't told anyone. I will, when I'm ready. Then you'll understand why. Please don't be mad at me." Samantha's voice was shaking, her breathing uneven. She felt sweat on her brow and under her arms. Her whole body was warm and faint, but talking with Emily, even admitting there was something wrong and she would talk about it someday, gave her inner strength. A current of that strength ran through her mind, calming her rampant thoughts and stopping what had been a steady stream of tears. "Trust me, please, just trust me. You know in your heart I would tell you, if I could. I just need some time."

"Okay, I will trust you. I will give you that time, not because I want to, but because you've asked me to. Just remember I will help you with whatever I can. Even if you just need me to listen, I'll be there," Emily said, with a strength and determination in her voice Samantha never knew she had. "I'm going to call you from wherever I am in Europe, too. You'll have all my numbers, I promise. Then you can call me if you need to. Call me anytime. I'll be there for you."

"Thank you, Emily. Thank you for everything. I know I can count on you. I know you'll be there." Samantha said, locking Emily into a sisterly hug.

For the next hour before the girls returned to pack their things, they continued their walk along the beach, mostly in quiet thought and reminiscence of their past together.

In the remaining hours before their departure, and after a delicious brunch, Samantha kept her mind occupied calculating her options. She knew whatever happened and whatever she did, she would have to spend not just the next few hours or days, but the next several months with a smile plastered on her face so as not to give a clue to the realities she had to face. The long journey home would allow her to think things over, as she shut her parents out with her headset blaring or a feigned sleep.

Chapter 6

Graduation came and went without incident. After a week Samantha still hadn't heard from Skyler, except for eighteen beautiful pink roses sent from the entire firm and accompanied by an oversized card with many signatures, including his.

Samantha opted not to have a graduation party and had been presented with a check from her parents for $25,000 in lieu of a car and a party. Undergraduates could not drive a car on campus at Michigan State University. Since she was living in a dorm and shopping was close by, it didn't make sense to have a brand new car that sat at home. Her parents, surprised at her maturity, decided she could handle a large check and could take her time and decide what she wanted to use it for later. Samantha, touched at their trust in her—undeserved trust in her she thought—decided to put the money away and forget about it. The bank her father used was more than happy to suggest it be placed in long-term certificates of deposit. Samantha agreed, disinterested in the money. She knew it would not solve anything, but it did comfort her to know that she had her own independent holding, just in case she really needed anything she did not want to ask her parents for.

As each day passed, she became more and more sure everything was fine and her involvement with Skyler was just a bad mistake, a misunderstanding. Samantha was convinced Skyler must think so too, otherwise he would have called her, he would be pursuing his threat of blackmail. But why, then, the tape? Why had he been so clear and descriptive about his desire for her? Samantha tried hard not to think about it; but she could not control the flood of fears that continued to wrench her. Desperately, Samantha second-guessed the whole incident in her need for self-comfort. She let her mind indulge in momentary fantasies and; wishful thinking. She didn't know what else to do.

Samantha was grateful she had been taking her birth-control pills since the abortion. She wasn't sure why she had decided to take them, except she had followed Skyler's instructions to the letter. At least she didn't have to worry about going through another abortion, another murder. Her short pregnancy and constant thoughts and nightmares about the abortion held her mind hostage with guilt and kept her body thin and undernourished. She felt more guilty about the abortion than the rape. Inherently, she felt everything that had happened was all her fault. The rapes were her fault. The abortion was her fault. Skyler threatening her family was her fault. Somehow she had sent out the wrong messages—unconsciously flirted with danger—so the outcomes were her responsibility; her fault. The abortion involved an innocent victim. A victim she would never know or touch or hold; but she would always remember. She had no explanation for it to herself, for her family or for God. And though she longed for one, none came.

Samantha regretted not talking with Emily; not telling her when she had the chance. Emily could have been her reality check. Maybe she could have even helped.

But it was too late. Emily was gone to Europe for the summer to learn German and gather bits of culture she would share with the future husband she intended to find at college. That was her plan; that was the plan of her parents. Soon Emily's name would be found on the society pages and she would be pictured on the arm of an up-and-coming man from a well-known family.

Samantha was glad her parents were allowing her to pursue her dream of becoming a veterinarian before thinking about finding a husband and being a proper southern lady, like her mother and her mother before her. Having two eligible brothers, who were soon to be lawyers, helped her parents be preoccupied with finding *their* potential and proper mates. Not to mention their own preoccupation with their friends at the state capitol, as well as in the White House. Thankfully, her parents were having too much fun with their own lives to seriously interfere in Samantha's. Still, she wished she could talk to someone. Her thoughts were driving her crazy and she was sleeping less and less. By the time Emily returned, Samantha would be leaving for Michigan.

There would barely be time for good-byes. She decided she wouldn't burden Emily with her mess. It was probably for the best. No one deserved to carry the burden she was carrying.

Two more weeks passed. The phone rang and Samantha answered it without her usual caution, comfortable in the belief Skyler's intimacies had been a mistake.

"Armstrong residence," Samantha said into the receiver, wishing her peace had not been intruded upon by its ring.

"Samantha, it's so nice to hear your voice. I trust you have been doing well," Skyler's deep friendly voice said.

"Uh, yes. I'm fine." Samantha went numb. She felt dizzy and her knees began to buckle. Sitting on the Persian carpets that had been strategically placed on the white marble foyer floor, she went on. "What can I do for you? My parents are in Washington, I can give them a message for you."

"No. I know where they are. That's why I called. I wanted to talk to you. You know what I want. How about we meet for dinner around seven?"

Samantha froze. She could not respond. She felt flushed and faint and couldn't find her voice.

But Skyler's voice continued to echo in to the receiver. He did not care she did not respond to his question. "I'll pick you up. Wear a dress," he commanded.

"But, I—" Samantha stopped as she heard the dial tone. Skyler had not waited for her response. Obviously there was none needed. It was an order, not an invitation.

The clock moved slowly, but it could not move slow enough for Samantha. She dreaded the evening. She loathed Skyler's voice and everything else about him. She no longer saw him as a person, just as an object of pain. She tried to cheer herself up, telling herself she was going out with a friend; it was just another date. Trying to pretend he was someone else. Yes, that was it. If he didn't listen, she would have to change him, in the recesses of her mind, into someone she liked and wanted to be with. Then, she concluded, she could focus on how to get away from him. Her first mission, above all else, was to find any other tapes he had and destroy them. She also had to figure out how he taped their conversation, so it couldn't happen again. What if he had other evidence? He had told her he did. She didn't believe him, but she had to behave as if she did so she could find out the truth.

The doorbell rang at exactly seven. Samantha opened it. Her thick hair shone, even though she had it wrapped in a tight French twist secured by two Chinese sticks. She wore a long-sleeved, high-collared dress, despite the heat. She did not want him to imagine she had any attraction toward him. There was none.

"Hi there. You look great," Skyler said, taking in every detail. "You'll be a bit warm in that dress."

"Oh, I always get cold in restaurants," Samantha said, avoiding his eyes.

"Well then, let's go. Your carriage awaits!" Skyler teased lightly, holding out his arm for her as if she were his princess.

Samantha, although noticing the gesture, ignored it as if she hadn't seen his arm or heard the comment. Quietly she climbed into the front seat of his freshly polished green Jaguar, keeping close to the door, unlocking it after Skyler locked them in.

"Don't worry, I won't hurt you. You can keep the door unlocked. You can even get out any time you wish. I'm just in the habit of locking my car doors," Skyler said, peering over at Samantha, trying to put her at ease.

Samantha said nothing. Fear filled her with silence. Fear made her alert. Fear made her spend this time with him.

Taking deliberate care not to scare her, Skyler began making small talk about Memorial Day weekend at the Osborne estate. He rambled on and on about how great it was being part of a firm that liked to be together, that handled things as a large family. He made several comments about how much respect he had for each of the partners, especially her father. He said nothing about the boathouse. He said nothing about the tape or the blackmail. And, for the first time, he said nothing about the rape or the abortion.

Samantha was taken in. Confused. He seemed so normal. He seemed to forget what had happened between them. She knew better than to believe him, to buy into his lies and his professional demeanor.

But the longer she listened to him, the more confused she became. He was almost interesting to listen to—in an adult, sort of boring way. If it weren't for what had happened, she could probably like him, she rationalized. Then she bristled at the thought of liking him at all. There was an undeclared war between them. The incident at the boathouse had begun the battle. But really, hadn't it begun earlier, when she needed his help and he taped her confidences?

Samantha opened her car door the moment Skyler turned the engine off. She'd be damned if he'd treat her like a date, like they were a couple, when she was there under protest. She waited for him a few feet from the car, clutching her purse. She was glad he had not used the valet parking. She needed these few moments walking in the fresh air before she had to eat across from the man she despised, in a public place where she had to act as if she were in good company.

Dinner was a diversion from the discomfort of being alone with Skyler. She had admirable restraint considering the resentment and hate that was quietly seething beneath her calm composure.

Samantha was a desirable and an enjoyable break from Skyler's busy work schedule and heavy caseload. He knew she was there only under threat; but he would change that, he rationalized. She needed him, whether she knew it or not. She would eventually want him, once she realized all the female desires stirring within her.

Skyler carefully studied her, feeling an undercurrent of agitation. It had to be his way. It wouldn't take long for his labor to bear fruit. Looking across the table at her, he was absolutely convinced she would be his. Already he felt her mounting confusion about him as he moved from wearing the "white" hat to the "black" one. Her confusion as to whether he was the Good Samaritan or the devil.

Soon what he had planted could be harvested. He was anxious in anticipation of his harvest. Skyler was a watcher of women, a connoisseur. He knew women. All women were, for the most part, the same. Women were naturally curious creatures who liked to nurture and control and yet they liked to be taken care of and needed. They liked challenge and strength. Women lived for paradoxes. He lived to create them. Skyler, like the puppeteer, planned, carefully plotted to pull each string just right.

Samantha would need him and desire him. In fact, it would be her decision from now on. He was sure of that.

Samantha observed Skyler curiously. His behavior was

oddly normal. He was kind and considerate. He spoke to her with a gentle caring tone. She felt oddly at ease and unhappy he could make her comfortable.

"What would you like to drink? Champagne or perhaps some wine?" Skyler asked.

"No. No thank you. I don't drink," Samantha said, then blushed at the thought of the last time she had a drink at the beach.

"Fine," Skyler said, also not acknowledging her last drinking episode. "I'll have a dark beer, something German perhaps."

The waiter nodded and looked at Samantha.

"I'll just have a lemonade, if you have it, otherwise a diet soda," Samantha said.

"To eat Madame? Are you ready to order?"

Instinctively, Samantha looked at Skyler for advice.

He returned her questioning look with approval.

"Why don't you give us a few minutes," Skyler replied.

"As you wish."

Samantha wished they had ordered. It would have filled the time. It would have given them something to talk about. She wished she could sink into the floor as she felt his eyes burning through her.

Skyler didn't notice how discontent Samantha was. He acted as if they had been dating for years; as if they were teacher and student; husband and wife. From the far recesses of her mind, Samantha found the tolerance to sit with him and eat as if she were fine. She had already been through the worst, or so she thought. What was left, once your body had been taken and your actions controlled?

"Come now, it can't be that bad. Am I such boring company you have to wince?"

Samantha looked surprised. She did not realize she had let go of her feelings so he could read her expressions. She would not let that happen again.

"I . . . we shouldn't be here at all," Samantha whispered, lowering her sullen eyes.

"Yes we should. You'll see, the food will be great. We'll relax together. You'll see I'm not the ogre you think I am," Skyler replied, his tone dark and serious. "You just need to try, to give me the benefit of the doubt, like I gave you when you needed me and were in trouble."

"And, if I don't?"

"Samantha, you are intelligent enough to know no one would believe you if you said anything. I have the evidence that proves you got pregnant and you chose to have an abortion. I know every part of your beautiful, sensual, body and I will be happy to testify you got drunk and you wanted me. That you seduced me." Skyler paused, looking squarely at Samantha before he continued. "Emily was a witness to your drinking, was she not?" He looked at her and watched as his words penetrated. Brutally, Skyler forced his point. "In this town, your family and your reputation would be scarred, if not ruined for life."

"But I was raped."

"But you have no proof and you didn't report it."

"You told me not to."

"No, I told you that you had washed away the proof by taking a shower and it would be difficult to prove. I told you the media would get a kick out of putting your family in all of the newspapers. All of those things are true. Are you telling me they are not? That the facts are somehow different?"

"No. But . . ."

"In court, there is no 'but'. It is either 'yes' or 'no'. 'Maybe' doesn't count."

"I'm not in court. We're not in court."

"You will be if you report the rape. You would be put on the witness stand against Greg. You would have to answer a lot of personal questions."

"And you would have to do the same. You helped me. You found the doctor and set up the abortion. You took care of everything."

"As I remember it, you agreed with everything. You demanded my help and my silence, for your own protection. And I'll be happy to testify to that. Of course, you could use alcohol as your defense, maybe even incapacity or insanity. Is that what you want? If so, be my guest! And by the way, you should think about the fact that abortion, for someone your age, without parental or judicial consent, in our state, is illegal. It is a crime."

"Against the doctor; against you for arranging it. Not

against me. That's not possible. I'm the victim!" Samantha felt like jumping up and hitting him. Her flushed skin was hot and she felt as if spiders were crawling over her flesh.

"There's no evidence except what I have in my possession, locked up for safe keeping. As far as anyone will know, you did it yourself. Any physician will be able to testify you have had an abortion. You may not go to jail, but jail would be easier than what you will be faced with in the media and within the small community we live in. You'll find people love to gossip." Skyler stopped and went in for the kill. "As to the issue of rape, men will believe you wanted it, you even enjoyed it. They'll seek you out."

Samantha turned cold and pale. She couldn't think. He had thought well beyond what she had even considered. She had been too wrapped up in the individual acts to see the whole picture. He was right. Everyone would look at her as the guilty one.

The waiter, returning for their order, did not see the tension between them. Samantha ordered as little food as possible, only a main course, grilled garlic shrimp. Skyler added a soup and salad for her, ignoring her protest as he ordered the same for himself with prime rib as his main course. She would eat everything in front of her, no matter how long they had to stay there, he advised her candidly. Skyler would see to it their meal was as normal as possible and she ate a decent meal. She had gotten almost too thin. He wanted her healthy. He needed her healthy and strong to keep up with him. It wasn't just sex he wanted. He wanted her companionship. He wanted to take her sailing, hiking, skiing. He wanted to teach her to love him, as he had grown to care for her.

Skyler paused. He could see she was distraught and hiding back tears. In the momentary silence, he decided he had better ease up on her before she fell apart.

"What evidence do you have from the doctor?" she quizzed, her eyes like round blue pools; the calm before the storm.

"The file. The medical file on you. Your history. The procedure, medication, instructions; everything pertaining to the procedure."

"He gave that to you? That's confidential; that's mine!"

"Sorry. The file is missing. Of course, no one knows it

even exists, at this point. Even if someone were to find out, no one will know where the file is, or what happened to it," Skyler said quietly.

"Except you," she said indignantly.

"That's right," Skyler acquiesced.

Samantha shifted the tricolor fettuccine noodles under the grilled garlic shrimp back and forth thoughtfully, artfully separating the colors in piles. Silence descended over their table, roared in her ears.

"Are you all right? I truly am sorry. I had no intention of bringing all of this up. But it is better you know the facts as they are."

"I am fine. Really. You are right. I've gotten myself into quite a situation. I should probably thank you," she lied, riddled with guilt and anger. Samantha was anxious to find some time alone so she could sort out what he had said. Anxious to look in her father's law books to see if any of his statements were true. Samantha was impatient to know what he wanted with her, eager to know why it had to be her. She knew he had so many other women available to him.

"You had gotten yourself into a dilemma. You required my help. We got you out of a bad predicament by working together. You are fine. Everything's fine. Together we make a good team. Things will be better from now on. I promise." Skyler said, now smiling easily, gently patting Samantha's hand across the table. His composed, seemingly sincere expression was meant to be disarming, eliciting approval and belief.

Samantha was beginning to feel comfortable with his game. She smiled, curving her mouth up just enough to remove any sign of doubt or disapproval from her expression, and the spell was cast.

Dinner finally cleared, Skyler ordered dessert and cappuccino to end the evening. As she slid a delicate spoonful of chocolate mousse between her full lips, she mentally braced herself for the evening that lay ahead of them. Engrossed in her own thoughts, she slowly slid the spoon out of her mouth, returning it to the delicate parfait glass. Almost as an afterthought, she looked into Skyler's watchful face. She was daunted as she saw a flicker of uncertainty, his bright eyes intent upon her.

Skyler was impressed with himself. He had pulled it off! She trusted him. She understood his rules and his reasoning. She would play along. She would be his.

The couple left the restaurant side by side. Samantha felt apprehensive about the hours that followed, yet she said nothing as he opened the car door for her. She sat as she had before, as close to the car door as possible, so there was little chance of accidental contact between them. She wanted him in no way to be encouraged by any action on her part.

Skyler, watching her closely, felt her anxiety about the rest of the evening. Neither spoke about it. Skyler made as much small talk as he could and as he exited the ramp leading to her home, Samantha became weary.

Not here. Not at my house, not in my room.

"Where are we going?" She quizzed him.

"Home. Where else would you like to go?"

"Not here . . . You're not . . . I mean we can't . . ." Samantha was reduced to stuttering. She tried to find the right words to dissway Skyler from touching her in her home, in her place of silence, serenity and solitude.

"Well, I have an early day tomorrow, and I have to make it an early evening," Skyler said gently, looking at her with apologetic eyes. "How about Friday? Can I pick you up on Friday, say six? Dinner and a movie?" Skyler's tone was one of adolescent friendship, sincere and unsure of her willingness.

"Oh, I . . . Well, okay," Samantha responded, confused and stuttering again. She was shocked he had not touched her in any way. He was almost a perfect date. Something had to be wrong. What had happened? Had she done something wrong? Slamming the door shut, she watched him slowly drive away, a playful grin on his boyishly handsome face.

Quietly, Samantha climbed the staircase of the dark, still house, contemplating the evening. She felt grimy in her dress. Taking it off, she carelessly flung it over the soft fuchsia velvet loveseat. Her only thought, at this moment, was the deep cleansing of a shower, the comfort of the loud spraying water and the soft sudsy perfumed soap.

For many hours after her shower, she lay awake trying to sort it all out. She was now sure she had not misinterpreted the blackmail. She was sure he wanted sex from her, not money. He made more money than he knew what to do with. But why had he not attempted anything with her after dinner? Samantha rolled over again. Minnie Mouse's hands responded to her glance. It was 3:00 a.m. Her heavy eyes told her she was immensely tired, but they refused to stay closed.

Dreams floated in and out like passing clouds, not soft and white, but gray and stormy. Streams of reality cut deeply into her subconscious. She kept seeing faces, shadowed like works by Picasso—likenesses of Greg, Skyler, the doctor, her father. All the men in her life, in pieces, part of a whole, but not one was a complete face. They were all in recognizable pieces. She couldn't talk to anyone. They couldn't hear her. The floating pieces did not include ears, yet many had three eyes. She tried not to look at them. She tried to get away, but they were everywhere.

Samantha awoke in a sweat. She oriented herself to her dusky room and then again looked at Minnie Mouse. Her hands were not moving very quickly; 4:17 a.m. She was afraid to close her eyes again and see the faces. She felt as if they loomed above her anyway. With a quick sharp throw of her sheets, she hauled herself into the shower. She had to relax and feel the freshness of the water running onto her skin. Maybe then she could get some real sleep. Start the night's sleep over. If she started her night over, maybe she could get a few hours of sleep.

Morning came quickly after she slid back into the soft sheets, relaxed with her skin lightly powdered and covered with a fresh silky peach nightgown. Samantha felt rested and shrugged off the incoherent dreams, ready to move forward with her day.

Rummaging through her clothes, sorting what she was giving away, what she was leaving home and what she was taking to school in the fall, Samantha anxiously focused on moving away to college. She created checklist after checklist of the things she needed to do and the items she needed to buy. The lists would keep her busy, both mind and body. She was more and more anxious to leave and begin her new life in Michigan. She was determined to focus on college and do one thing in preparation for her departure every day until she left. From this day forward, she vowed, she would live one day at a time and fill her days with positive accomplishments, even if they were small.

Samantha decided she had to use every ounce of energy she had to focus on the positive, using it to push away the negative thoughts and energy she had experienced over the past months. She needed to prove to herself she was a survivor. Then, maybe, she would find the strength to put her struggles behind her or find someone to help her. After last night, she knew she had to rely on herself and trust herself, at least for now. There was no one else. They were uncomfortable thoughts, but in an odd way, they gave her strength.

Samantha had two days until she saw Skyler. She had decided to ask the housekeeper to tell everyone who called she was out. When no one else was available to answer the phone, she would leave the answering machine on and screen the calls. She did not want to talk with Skyler before he picked her up on Friday. She needed this time to search her father's study for any law books that might answer her questions. She couldn't risk going to the office, but she could go to the state's law library if she had to. Samantha could tell people, if they asked about her sudden interest in law, she might consider law school after or instead of veterinarian school. Given her family, no one would question that. In fact, that would give her an opening to ask her father and brothers questions about hypothetical situations. Of course, she decided, she would only do that as a last resort.

Samantha didn't trust lawyers, not even the ones she was related to. Growing up, she had seen and heard too many unpleasant things. Lawyers thought differently. They examined every word and phrase too closely. They noticed reactions and asked questions that led you to say the wrong thing or too much of the right thing. There were no lawyers Samantha could trust, not even her father.

The leather-bound law books were intimidating, the language threatening. They smelled old and musty. As she ran her inquisitive eyes and fingers over the titles, she decided the *Black's Law Dictionary* was the place to begin. It sat open on its golden book perch, propped conspicuously on the corner of her father's oversized antique cherry desk. The dictionary would explain to her the legal words she did not understand. Then she could go from there. Samantha was thankful she had done well in school and she had taken the college-bound writing and research English classes. If she ever needed those skills, she needed them now.

Samantha's long fingers flipped the crisp pages until she reached the B's. Expectantly, she ran her finger down the margin, finding quickly the second word on the page, just under "Black Lung Benefit's Act" was "Blackmail". She read it carefully, her eyes scrutinizing every word, every line, every sentence. She reread the part that could pertain to her and said the words out loud as if they would mean more to her that way. As if she could memorize them.

> **Blackmail.** *Unlawful demand of money or property under threat to do bodily harm, to injure property, to accuse of crime, or to expose disgraceful defects . . . See Extortion; Shakedown.*

Nothing. Blackmail for sex. There was nothing about blackmail for sex in the definition. Skyler wasn't demanding money or any property. He had all the money and personal possessions he could ever use.

Samantha knew she couldn't panic. She tried hard not to, even though she felt the lump grow in her throat and saw the words in the thick book turn blurry. The tears that stung her eyes acted as pearls of strength and fortitude as she forged ahead, flipping crisp pages until she found "Extortion."

> **Extortion.** *The obtaining of property from another induced by wrongful use of actual or threatened force, violence, or fear, or under color of official right. 18 U.S.C.A. Sec. 871 et. seq.; Sec. 1951. A person is guilty of theft by extortion if he purposely obtains property of another by threatening to ...*

Samantha grew frustrated as her eyes skimmed over the itemized list, the corners of her mouth unconsciously drooped.

> *... (1) inflict bodily injury . . . ; or (2) accuse anyone of a criminal offense; or (3) expose any secret tending to subject the person to hatred, contempt or ridicule . . . ; or (4) take or withhold action as an official . . . ; or (5) bring about or continue a strike . . . ; or (6) testify . . . ; or (7) inflict any other harm which would not benefit*

the actor. Model Penal Code, Sec. 223.4. See also Blackmail; Hobbs Act; Loan Sharking; Shakedown. With respect to "Larceny by extortion," see Larceny.

Samantha saw the words blur into a whirlpool of letters, jumbled into foreign lines, leading circularly into infinite ramblings. So many more words to look up. She had counted on an exhaustive list, but she hadn't counted on so many words—so many she didn't understand within the definitions. Samantha had been taught the dictionary was to clarify words and their meanings, not to confuse them.

Relentlessly she pursued each word, which led to more references and more bewilderment. Her inner turmoil grew deeper and deeper. None of the definitions fit. Not one definition talked about sex, about rape or about blackmail of any kind relating to those things. Blackmail and extortion led her to the Hobbs Act and racketeering, which were totally off the track. Larceny and larceny by extortion seemed to help her, but again, neither mentioned sex.

Could it be it was legal to blackmail for sex? It was illegal to blackmail for money or to threaten someone.

There were dollar amounts on larceny, and the definition mentioned property, but not stealing a person by rape or forced sex. Samantha was baffled. It *was* legal, she surmised with deep dismay. Skyler was smart. Her father always said he enjoyed trying cases with Skyler because "if there was a loophole in the law, Skyler was the one who had the nose to find either the loophole or the way around it." Well, she reluctantly concluded, he had found the loophole and it was she who would pay.

Although Samantha continued turning the crisp, slightly yellowed pages, she had lost hope. The growing list of words she had written down on her notepad multiplied, expanding her fruitless mission into unending dead ends. The text spun Samantha in a whirlpool of useless verbiage. It sucked her in, captured her piece by piece, layer by layer, filling her with despair beyond what she had ever known. Her body melded with the sea of words, floating her down into dark spiral crevices, while the useless definitions remained sealed in the pages, forever holding their secrets.

She forced herself to continue, needing time to digest the

words. Of course, she thought, as she looked up, her father's old copying machine! Turning it on, she flipped the pages of the weighty stiff-backed book, back and forth, until she copied every possible definition she needed. Carefully, Samantha clipped out from the copied pages only the necessary definitions and pasted them on one page, making a final copy. Then, gathering even the tiniest paper scrap, she shredded all of the remains, except for one legal-sized sheet, which she carefully folded and placed in her pocket. She would read it later. She would read and ask questions until she learned what it all meant. She would find out why she seemed to be a "loop-hole in the law." She would uncover the hidden meaning in the words. She vowed she had to save herself and this would be the start. It was up to her. She felt stronger than she had in days.

Samantha inspected her father's office to insure all was as it was before she entered. Her father was particular about his office, and even her mother dared not enter. When Samantha was growing up, her father's office was as scary to her as the principal's office, still and pristine as a graveyard, challenging her sensibilities, marking her fears. Samantha wanted to move past those fears now. She was in a living nightmare. Facing the principal's office, her father's office or a graveyard would be easy in comparison. She looked at her father's office as a safe harbor where she could gain her strength, at least until she had another solution.

Climbing the staircase to her bedroom, with a sandwich and soda in hand, she felt confident the neatly folded paper in her shirt pocket was the first clue to her solution. For the first time she felt she had begun to fight back, to try to take back what she had lost. As she sat in the comfort of her room, she pulled out the words and began to study them. The definitions were frustrating. For the most part they made sense, but they didn't help her. It didn't stand to reason there was no protection for her. Her father seemed to help, protect and defend so many people with the law. Was it possible, as Skyler said, there was no help for her—that she would be the guilty one? That, without care for the truth, everyone would assume she was the guilty one? For the first time in months, she fell asleep in her clothes without the need of a long cleansing shower.

Early the next morning, Samantha awoke and felt like a mummy opening her eyes for the first time in years. She had had the same floating dreams, but this time she wasn't as frightened. Although she still could not speak, this time she was able to bring her hand up to her throat and rub it, smoothing it gently, as if to heal and coax the voice.

Listening to the birds chirp, she focused on her white ceiling. It was as if she were hearing and seeing for the very first time. She still felt as if she was dreaming, and yet her mind told her she was alive and awake and well.

And then she remembered, and reality came flooding in. Today was another day. It was her last full day before she would see Skyler again.

Samantha felt anxious. She had to go back to the library. She had to find more clues. She needed to reread the definitions. Maybe she missed something. Maybe she forgot to look up a word. She moved from the comfort of her sheets, slowly, into her private bath and slipped yesterday's clothes off. The water felt good, splashing and spraying over every part of her thinning body. It gave her life.

Wrapped in a comfortable navy sweatshirt with matching overstretched sweat pants, Samantha walked into the kitchen and grabbed a large mug of creamed coffee and a piece of dry toast before sliding silently into her father's study and the arms of the burgundy leather chair planted at the head of his desk. She placed her hand again on the worn gold-embossed *Black's Law Dictionary*. She needed a new angle, different words, maybe a different book?

She thought of Skyler. Fretfully, she brushed her fingers through her curls, still damp from the shower. She remembered how she used to look up to him. She remembered his caring selfless tone when he first befriended her. She remembered his cruel impatient tone when he raped her. She remembered his kinder, more reasonable tone at dinner. Her skin became instantly warm and then icy cold, shivers overtook her. Her mind recoiled with recrimination; with guilt. Her brain was unable to function under the confusion she felt.

The cool, worn leather chair turned warm and sweaty under her. The dull squeaking of her sticky flesh pulling from the chair woke her up, like an alarm, out of her trancelike state. The numbers on the digital clock had turned minutes into hours. Her eyes moved over the mesmerizing rows of books. She stared at them all, more confused than ever. The dictionary had been the first step; although not much help, it was a beginning, a start to finding her way out of the maze. She needed more information, a clue as to where to look next. The rest of the books were puzzling, the words obscure. She needed help. She needed answers. It was unlikely any of her father's books contained the answers—any answers she could understand without an interpreter.

Samantha knew she had to find a way to help herself. She had to find someone to help her. But who and how? She couldn't trust anyone. She couldn't risk any questions. She couldn't act suspicious. She needed to think. She needed a nap. She wanted a long, bubble bath to clear her mind. Today she had only a few hours remaining, before dinner, to take another step toward her goal.

She had begun her fight to move forward with her life. Maybe it didn't really matter what else she did for the hours that remained. Tomorrow was another day and as much as she hated the thought, she would be seeing Skyler. He might touch her; he might not. Whatever happened, she would think of her new-found words and copied definitions. It was *some* comfort. She would concentrate and learn and fill herself with the words. The words would wrap a protective shield around her; inside her. Samantha knew as long as she kept the words in her head, Skyler could not reach her core, her soul. She could hide behind them and they would protect her. No one could touch her. No one would, she vowed silently.

Chapter 7

Samantha was apprehensive as she dressed for her date with Skyler. It had been two stress-filled, but mentally productive days, since she went out with him last. The plunge into her father's law books had been more confusing than helpful, but she vowed to herself that she would continue to study law books until they made sense. She would continue to digest information until she discovered a solution, no matter how slowly it went. It was the only chance she had. The only way she could keep her sanity. Learning the legal language—a collection of words, which to her were foreign—helped keep her shifting mind occupied. It kept her too tired to let in the daily fear and the nightly ghosts.

Samantha wanted to read some of the cases in the law books, but she hadn't figured out how to find the right ones. Her father's books contained thousands and thousands of cases. She could spend her lifetime reading them. *Black's Law Dictionary* was a comfort, in that she could understand at least parts of the definitions. Understanding the cases would be difficult, but she would keep reading and looking in the dictionary until the words and concepts made sense. Samantha decided she would go to the public library and every bookstore in town to find books that explained what the cases and their words meant. She also decided she would have to find someone who could help explain things to her. Her father. She would begin with her father. That made sense to her more than anything else. After all, he would be proud to explain to his only daughter what he did. She would begin by asking discreet questions about using legal references and law books when her father arrived home and then would push on at dinner when he was captive. She would go on-line with his computer to find a law library. Samantha relaxed at the thought that the internet might help. Maybe she could find an online buddy that could help give her information. Tomorrow she would begin, but tonight she had to deal with Skyler.

The Armstrongs were not returning until Saturday afternoon. Samantha had to insure Skyler did not come into the house when he brought her home and, if he did enter the house, he did not touch her. She had to make sure he did not decide to spend the night. She wanted to leave the house as soon as he arrived so she could spend the evening with him manipulating how the date would end.

Samantha still wasn't sure what had happened after the last dinner. As much as she hoped he was no longer attracted to her, in the dark recesses of her ego, she wondered whether he no longer found her sexually attractive. Once she had given in to Skyler's sexual desires. Had she done something wrong? Had she not pleased him? What was wrong? She knew she should be glad, regardless of the reason, that he hadn't touched her the last time they were together, but still she pondered. Samantha prepared herself for an hour before Skyler's arrival. Everything was in place. Her shiny brown hair flowed down her back, secured by an art deco barrette her mother had given her on their last trip to Long Beach. She wore a longer than mid-calf, washed-out blue, puckered skirt and a matching denim embroidered shirt, buttoned up all the way. From under the shirt collar she hung a silver Native American string tie. In her delicate lobes hung matching silver dangle earrings. On her feet were thin white socks and blue and brown cowboy boots.

She looked good, she thought, but not available. Samantha decided she would dress creatively each time Skyler forced her to go out with him. She would hide as much of her body as possible with clothing that was not easy to take on and off. Surely that would deter him, she thought, with a grim smirk. She did not want to give Skyler any opening to believe she was agreeing to his desires. She knew she must agree to see him, not just because he was blackmailing her, but because she had to find the evidence he had—the tapes, the file and anything else. What else could he possibly have? Desperately, Samantha hoped there wasn't anything else.

The bell chimed just as Samantha inspected herself for the last time in the hallway mirror. She opened the door, purse slung over her shoulder.

"Hello," Samantha said blandly, avoiding Skyler's eyes.

"Aren't you going to invite me in?"

"No." She stepped out, shutting the heavy white door behind her.

"Okay. There's no need to go inside. I just thought we could talk for a few minutes. I thought the show started at seven, but it begins at half past," Skyler said cheerfully, opening Samantha's door for her.

Samantha remained silent. She had no response for him and she didn't want to offer any excuses. She wasn't sure what might set him off so she wanted to be on her best behavior.

Skyler turned on the engine and then reached into the back seat. Samantha felt a chill as his arm brushed her shoulder.

"Here, I got this for you. I hope you like it," Skyler said smiling.

Samantha looked at the yellow cellophane. It held a perfect yellow rose surrounded with babies breath and greenery. She stared at it, wishing it would disappear. The rose was beautiful and under any other circumstance, Samantha would have been thrilled. She uttered the only word she could.

"Thanks."

"Look at me, Samantha," Skyler said, placing his first two fingers under her chin, turning her face towards him. "Come on, look at me," he coaxed playfully.

Samantha looked at him shyly, quizzically.

"Yellow. One perfect yellow rose, for you. A symbol for us," Skyler said sincerely. "Yellow is the color for friendship. I want us to be friends. Best friends. Close friends. You'll see, we are perfect for each other. I'll give you all the time you need. I promise."

Samantha could hear her pulse pounding loudly in her head. She looked with disbelief at Skyler, remaining mute.

"Don't worry, it'll be great," Skyler said, patting her hand gently. Pulling the running car out of the driveway onto the road, Skyler nodded his head to convince himself. "I thought we'd see *The Awakening Hour.* It seemed an appropriate film for us, and I figured you hadn't seen it since it opened only this week."

"That's fine. I haven't seen it," Samantha said coldly, looking out her window at the rows of houses they passed, trying to occupy her mind, wondering about all the other lives in those houses.

"So what have you been doing to keep busy while your parents are gone?"

"Not much. I've been staying home getting my things ready for school."

"Haven't been going out with any of your friends?"

"No. Emily's in Europe. She left a few days ago."

"When will she return?"

"Just before I leave for Michigan State."

"Too bad. I know what good friends you are, but you do have other friends—"

"Not like Emily," Samantha said, cutting him off.

"Yes, but boyfriends. You must have a boyfriend or two calling you to go out?"

"No. I don't have a boyfriend," Samantha said plainly, still looking out the car window.

"Not one? Your father used to talk about all of your friends and dates. Are you telling me he lied?"

"No. I do have lots of friends. I haven't seen them. School just got out and everyone is busy with family, vacations, getting ready for college and stuff. Some of my friends are working for the summer, too."

"Come on. You mean to tell me not one of your boyfriends would make the time to take you out on a date?"

"I don't have any I'm dating. If I go out with anyone, we all go in a group. I'm not interested in seeing anyone so close to leaving for college."

"But you had a boyfriend. . . Jason. That was his name wasn't it?"

"That was ages ago."

"But you really liked him and you went out with him for over two years. You must still like him."

"No. It's over. I'm glad it's over," Samantha said, for the first time taking her eyes off the window, looking directly at Skyler's driving profile. "I don't want to talk about him and I don't want you to bring him up. I told you it's over."

"I'll bring up whatever I need to bring up and you'll answer me. That's what friends do. That's what we'll do. Do you understand?" Skyler said, clenching his teeth, speaking in a low but fierce tone.

"Yes."

"So, did you have sex with him?"

Samantha remained silent, seething at the invasion of privacy and the inference of the question.

"It's Okay. You can tell me. I won't be mad. I just would like to hear about it. Just pretend I'm one of the girls."

"No. We didn't have sex. He wanted to; I wouldn't. We broke up. End of story."

"That's a shame. For him, I mean. I can understand how he would not be able to resist you. But I can also understand you wouldn't want him. A boy, I mean. Why have a boy when you can have a real man?" Skyler flashed his white teeth in a grin that contrasted with his tanned skin, satisfied finally with her answers.

Instinctively, Samantha protested, "It wasn't like that. . ."

"It doesn't really matter. I'm just glad it's over. I don't want you to have any distractions from our relationship."

"We don't have a relationship." Her voice was sarcastic.

"Oh, but we do," Skyler said, reaching over, stroking her forearm, patting her hands. Samantha winced, but remained silent. She did not want to aggravate him.

"Samantha, really, you have to trust me. Everything will be fine. Haven't I been good to you? Haven't I been there when you needed a friend? When you needed help?" Skyler asked, his eyes piercing, as if he could see through to her soul. Samantha could do nothing but hide her anger in her balled fists under the wrapping of the perfect yellow rose that lay innocently on her lap. From his tone, Samantha knew the conversation on that subject was ended. His questions had clearly answered her worst fear. She was to be his, only his, until he said so or until she got the evidence from him. She was glad when they finally arrived at the theater. The prospect of two hours of silence was a relief. Once in the theater, Samantha felt more at ease. She did not want to feel too comfortable, though, because comfort might lead to putting down her guard.

They were surrounded by people on all sides. It appeared not a seat in the house was vacant. They might be seen. What would she say if they were seen together? Surely Skyler had thought of this. Why would he want them to be seen together? She would have to ask Skyler, but she would wait until there was some dead air to fill.

All through the movie Samantha waited for his hand to creep over to her in the darkness. It did not. The anger and apprehension she felt earlier receded and she enjoyed the movie, munching on buttered popcorn and a large diet soda.

"Great movie," Skyler said as he lifted himself from the uncomfortable pop-up seat, standing closely behind Samantha, while waiting for their row to clear.

"Mmm," she agreed.

"What? You didn't like it?"

"I didn't say that. I did like the show. I mumbled, but I was agreeing with you. I'm tired."

"Not yet. It's too early. What about a bite to eat or going to Riba's to dance?"

"I'm full from the popcorn, and I can't get into Riba's. I'm underage, remember?"

"You can get in with me. I just won't let you drink," Skyler said, as he winked conspicuously at her.

Shrinking back, Samantha replied, "Okay, I could go for a burger or chicken fingers."

"Great. Let's go to Whitney's. They have great food and we can go into the back room and dance if you feel like it after dinner. Have you ever been there?"

"No. I have heard about it though. I've heard people come from all over to go there. Do you think we can get in on a Friday night?" Samantha let her curiosity overshadow her fear for the moment. She had always wanted to go to Whitney's. Maybe she could salvage something positive from the evening.

"Of course. They know me. They'll let us in."

The crosstown drive was filled with Skyler's interpretation of insights into the movie. Samantha listened to him talk, nodding occasionally. "So what'd you think about the movie?" he asked, realizing she hadn't uttered a word in several miles.

"Listen, I've been thinking about the movie. About, well about . . . what if we were seen together? What if we are seen together? What do I tell people? What do I tell my parents?" Samantha quizzed.

"You simply tell them you were keeping me company. There's nothing more to tell."

"What if they want to know more?"

"Trust me."

"But—"

"Trust me."

When they reached Whitney's they were told that there was a wait of over an hour. Samantha watched as Skyler tipped the host a crisp fifty-dollar bill. They were let in as if they had a reservation and within minutes shown to a table. Samantha was impressed, but didn't let Skyler know that. It was too bad they were together under such extreme circumstances. He would probably be the perfect guy for her otherwise. She shuddered. This was a man she'd once respected and trusted. A man she now hated.

"Great timing, wouldn't you say?" Skyler asked, winking.

"More like great tipping," Samantha replied sarcastically, ignoring the wink she had grown to despise.

"So what's your pleasure? Everything on the menu is grand," Skyler said in a gallant tone.

"I really just wanted a burger, a veggie burger, if they have one," Samantha replied, ignoring his playfulness as she folded her menu and placed it aside, unimpressed.

"Whatever you want, you can have. They have a wonderful late night menu on the back."

"Fine. Then I'll have a veggie burger," Samantha said, not picking up the menu again.

"As you wish, although it's called a garden burger," Skyler said, ignoring her uncooperative mood, as he ordered for both of them.

Samantha listened as he ordered the food, making mental notes of topics she could raise to prevent the subject being her.

"So, do you come here often? It seems like a fun place."

"You care where I go? That is a good sign. Yes, I have been known to frequent this place. What about you? Where do you go for fun?"

"Nowhere. I spend my time getting ready for school."

"That can't be all you do."

"Like I told you before, that is what I do now. How do you have time to take me out with your workload? Dad says right now you have the heaviest caseload in the office."

"That's true. I like to keep busy. I want to be more than

just the youngest partner. I want to be the best. I want the firm to recognize me as the best."

"But dad says you are one of the best."

"That's the point. I want to be *the* best. I want a raise and a bonus that says I'm the best. I deserve it, and I always get what I deserve. It's not a choice. It's a promise I have made to myself. I never let myself down—or anyone else, " Skyler said with such intensity Samantha dared not challenge his words.

"This garden burger, as you call it, is probably the best I've had," Samantha said, relieved to change the subject.

"Well, good. I'm glad you like it here," Skyler said with a grin.

"I really should get home. My parents will worry if I'm not home when they call. I didn't tell them I was going out."

"Why didn't you tell them? You knew in plenty of time to tell them."

"What would I say? I didn't want to lie. I've lied enough to them. I couldn't tell them I was going out with you. You know they wouldn't like it."

"Sure they would. You could tell them I offered to take you out; to keep you company while they were gone. Your dad would probably thank me," Skyler said, winking at her again.

Samantha winced at his wink, at his tone, at his comments. She hated him. She had to get out. Instinctively she grabbed her purse, knowing every man knew that meant his date was ready to leave. But, Skyler did not move. He wanted her to ask.

Exasperated, Samantha took a deep breath. "Really, Mr. Marks, we must go. I can't worry my parents. They will ground me if I'm not home when they call. I'm sure of it."

"Mr. Marks, is it, after all we've been through?" he asked, winking yet again, his green eyes laughing at her, waiting for the proper response.

"Okay, Skyler, we really have to leave." Samantha said softly, patiently pleading. It will be after midnight by the time I get home. I don't want to upset my parents. They'll ring until I'm home."

"Fine. That wasn't so difficult was it? Your wish is my command, my dear lady," Skyler said, slightly bowing, as if he were her prince charming. Then looking up at her he added,

"Next time we come, we're going to Whitney's Back Stage. You'd love it. The music, the dancing; you would be queen of the dance floor."

Samantha cringed, but remained silent. She didn't want to think about any other dates with Skyler and she refused to give him any hope she would look forward to a date, to a dance, to anything.

Samantha's silence didn't bother Skyler. He enjoyed her company regardless of her mood. She had to be there, so they might as well make the best of it. In time she would see. In time she would want him as much as she hated him. Her confusion was already apparent and right on schedule. Skyler smiled to himself, proudly.

The ride home was peaceful. Neither spoke, each in their own quiet and separate worlds. Again, Skyler dropped Samantha off, walking her to the door. She fumbled with her key, trying to put it in the lock and get quickly into the safety of her home, alone.

"Don't worry, Samantha, I'm not coming in. I don't want you to miss your phone call, so I'll talk to you later. And here, your rose. You wouldn't want to forget it, would you, friend?" Skyler said, again, winking on the word "friend."

"Oh. No. Thanks. See you," Samantha said, without looking at him, as the key finally turned.

"Save me next Friday night. I'll pick you up at eight. Wear something casual. Jeans and tennis shoes would work well."

"Work well," what did that mean, Samantha wondered, as she shut the door carefully locking it behind her and swiftly setting the house alarm. What did any of it mean? He claims to want me, but then he doesn't touch me. What was going on? Samantha pondered her usual questions, posed her concerns, and then pushed the thoughts away. Samantha was too tired to think about anything. She played back the messages on the telephone and was comforted by the recorded voices of her parents wishing her a good night. They told her they would be home early in the afternoon. Samantha took her nightly shower and went straight to bed. Just as she was on the brink of sleep, she heard her phone ring. Not her parent's line, but her private line. She reached out, pushed the button and sleepily grabbed the receiver. With an unsteady voice, she said, "Yes?"

"Is that any way to answer the phone? What happened to hello?"

"Oh, hello," Samantha said, startled by the voice.

"I had a wonderful time tonight. You're not only beautiful, smart and fun to be with, you're also a great companion. I'm looking forward to our next date. I just wanted you to know I'll be thinking about you in my dreams."

Samantha did not respond and, in the silence, she heard his breathing. She could feel its warmth through the line. It made her shiver. In an instant, she flushed. Then he spoke again.

"Pleasant dreams to you, too," Skyler said in a deep, erotic voice, as if he was answering something she said. And with that, he was gone.

Samantha felt cold chills crawl through her. Her temples flushed and her breathing was uneven.

Skyler! How had Skyler gotten her private number? She'd have it changed. Maybe not—suppose he got mad? She'd think about it in the morning, not now; she had to sleep. She had to erase him from her thoughts. Tossing a pillow over her head to shut out the world, she tried to silence his voice as it echoed inside her. Within minutes, she disembarked in her private domain of dreams, wherein she was desperately trying to decipher her world and regain control of it.

In the morning, Samantha awoke, startled by another nightmare of floating faces. The faces were again, in pieces and without ears. This time they were wearing armor and bowing and rhyming in deep sullen voices. But she couldn't make out what they were saying. And the only thing she was sure of, in her dreams, was she wanted to go home and she would, in fact, get there. There was a warmth in her dreams, despite her obvious confusion. Yet the dreams still scared her; the unknown in them frightened her. She knew she needed to decipher them and eventually she would.

She no longer woke up in a cold sweat because of them. She knew they would always take her back home and she would awake in her bed. But she also believed the dreams were trying to give her answers, messages. She just couldn't hear them or figure them out yet. Maybe it was Nana coming down from heaven to help her. Samantha felt there was a kind presence around her. She hoped the presence was Nana.

Nana had always told Samantha if she needed her she would be there. Samantha was comforted by the thought, even if it was just wishful thinking.

Despite her long sleep, Samantha felt exhausted as she climbed into her morning shower.

"Samantha. Samantha?" Anne Armstrong called. "Are you here dear?"

"Yes Mom, I'll be right down."

"Where is everyone? Why is there no one to take our bags? And I do not see Cook anywhere. What have you done with them?"

"Mom, really! I didn't need anyone around me. I wanted the house all to myself, so I gave the staff time off and asked everyone to report back for duty by noon today. I didn't expect you till this afternoon. I cleared it with Dad. Didn't he tell you?" Samantha's eyes pleaded with her mother not to be angry. Anne could not resist her daughter when she had that pleading childlike look.

"Of course he did, I just forgot," Anne lied to her daughter. Travis had probably just forgotten to tell her.

"I brought the bags, dear," Travis said, looking apologetically at his wife, knowing he had deliberately forgotten to tell her of Samantha's decision to let the staff go while they were gone. "I'll carry them upstairs."

"You'll do no such thing. Samantha says Mr. Tammy will be here at noon. The bags can wait till then. Why don't we freshen up, and by then Cook will have arrived. We can all have lunch out on the veranda and catch up. Okay with you, Samantha?"

"Sounds great, Mom," Samantha said, brushing a kiss on her parents' cheeks before retreating into the family room.

As Samantha flipped through the magazines sitting next to the comfortable oversized leather chair, she only mimicked interest in the pages. Her mind, racing in all directions, categorized and catalogued the questions she wanted to ask her father about his study, the law books and the computer. Samantha had carefully hidden her dictionary list of words with the tape Skyler had given her; but she reviewed it daily, memorizing more and more each day. She wanted to learn. She had to unlock the mystery and free herself.

As the luncheon bell rang, Samantha casually walked onto

the veranda and seated herself in between her parents. An array of club sandwiches, salads and fresh fruits were set around a bouquet of freshly cut roses from the garden.

"So dear, how was your week?" What have you done with yourself to keep busy?" Anne asked, looking conspicuously at Samantha, watching every move she made and each morsel she placed on the china plate in front of her.

"It was fine. I don't mind being alone. I've been going through my room and making lists of what I need for college, and I've set aside a few bags of clothes I no longer need." Samantha casually put a fork full of melon in her mouth. "I also received my room assignment at Michigan State. They placed me in Hubbard Hall. I remember seeing it when I visited. It has two towers; one for the men and one for the women. I'm on the tenth floor. I've written, asking for the names of my roommate and suitemates, so we can coordinate who brings what."

"What a wonderful idea, sweetheart. You are so organized! You get that from your father." Anne smiled, looking at her handsome husband, buried in the stock reports.

Travis sat reading the *New York Times*, sipping his tall glass of iced tea, half listening to the chatter. Years ago he learned he really only needed to know half of what they said.

"Dad. Dad?"

"Yes, Samantha?" Travis replied, peering up from his bifocals, his thick salt-and-pepper hair perfectly layered and combed straight back, framing his golf-tanned face.

"I was wondering if there was something I could do at the office this summer?"

"A job? You want to work? Why not enjoy your last summer before college? You don't need to work."

"I know that, Dad. I just thought, well I thought . . . what if I decide to be a lawyer, instead of a vet . . . or maybe do both? I've thought a lot about animal rights and I might want to go into law to protect animals, so I thought—"

Travis cut his daughter off, impressed she had put so much time and thought into her future plans. "You thought you might like to learn a little bit to see if you are interested in the field. That's smart thinking, Samantha. I'm proud of you. I just don't know what you would do. You know we usually only hire third-year students to clerk. Unfortunately, you really don't have much to offer."

Oh, you don't have to pay me. I just want to learn. Couldn't I watch some of your trials, and then maybe you could explain what happened later? Kind of a father-daughter project?"

"I suppose that would be all right. There's no harm in that."

"I was also wondering, well, I might need a computer at school and I thought maybe you could teach me how to get on yours. I could do research for you, on-line. I swear I won't touch your documents. I just want to figure out what kind of computer I want to take to school. We used the Macintosh at school, but yours is an IBM and I'd like to see the difference. Besides, I'd have to learn how to use it."

"Fine with me, but not until I get one of our interns to come over and explain how to use it; or maybe you'd like to stop by the firm one morning."

"No. Actually, I'd prefer it be here," Samantha said, beaming at her father. She couldn't believe it had gone so well. "Thanks, Dad."

"For my girl, anything. And before you even ask, yes, I'll buy you a computer when you figure out which one you want. We were planning on that anyway, because the twins have used theirs so much. Whatever you decide. I think you should consider a notebook with an internal fax-modem and cd-rom; and, of course, a portable printer. You can take the portable computer with you to class, like your brothers did."

"Great idea, Dad."

Anne Armstrong looked at the two of them. She would miss Samantha's bright energetic face at the table. They had their problems, but she was sure a part of her would be missing the day Samantha left for college.

"Can I see your list for college, dear?" Anne broke in. "We'll need to plan some shopping trips and we must be careful about space. I don't think you'll have much room in the dorm."

"I thought about that too. Do you think we could pack trunks according to seasons and then, as I go back and forth, we'll trade; or we can send them back and forth?"

"You really are getting ahead of yourself. Michigan is cold. You'll have to buy some things when you are up there."

"I don't know my way around the university. I have to study, not shop."

"You don't have to worry about anything. Shopping will be a nice distraction for you. You also need to see what the other students are wearing. We want you to feel in place. Your father and I will give you a sizable allowance and place it in your checking account every month. And remember, you have the Gold Card for emergencies, so you won't have anything to worry about. We only want the best for you."

"You're right, Mom. I'm just anxious, and with Emily gone I just haven't thought about anything else but college."

"Have you heard from Emily?"

"Not really. Just the few postcards she's sent. She said she'd call soon."

"I'm sure she will. You two have always been like sisters."

As the conversation progressed and the lemon meringue pie and coffee were served, Samantha's mind was already on the next part of her plan. She had to make sure the court cases she saw of her father's were ones Skyler was not assisting in. She was fearful to ask who was working on the case with her father. She was fearful to even mention his name. But for the first time in weeks, Samantha felt things were in her favor. She was taking charge for the very first time. She had made a plan and had followed it. It would be her salvation. Even if it didn't work, it would keep her mind occupied. Her spirits were lifted for the moment and nothing could break her serenity as she mused over the list of 'foreign' words back in the solitude of her room. Listening over, and over, to the comforting voice of Karen Carpenter that filled her room with words she understood and felt with every breath.

Chapter 8

Skyler called Samantha every night around midnight to make sure she was home and in bed. Subconsciously, even when she tried to sleep through the ring, she waited for the call. Skyler had been the only person she had talked to, other than her parents, since their last date almost a week ago. Initially, the conversations started out small. Samantha listened to his comments and his wishes for her to have a wonderful sleep. She didn't say much. After several phone calls, she began to respond to his questions. She told herself she didn't want to upset him, and talking to him on the phone was better than being subjected to more dates with him. Samantha still hadn't told her father they had gone out. She feared it was only a matter of time before he found out. Their town was too small and gossipy for her parents not to find out.

The phone rang on cue, like an alarm.

"Hello."

"Well, you're still up."

"Just barely."

"How was your day? What did you do?"

"Mom and I shopped all day. Getting things for my dorm room and pricing computers."

"Sounds like fun. Did you see anyone?"

"Like who?"

"Anyone, anyone at all."

"No one. I keep telling you, most of my friends are gone, working or busy. I've been busy too. No I haven't seen or talked to anyone except my family."

"Well then, what's new with your family?"

"Not much. My brothers won't be home until August. My Mom is planning a combination welcome home, good-luck-at-college and birthday party. It'll be just family and close friends." Samantha said. "It will be great to see the family together. I really miss the twins," she added wistfully.

"Sounds like fun. Whose birthday will it be?"

"Oh, mine. My eighteenth birthday," Samantha said, suddenly sorry she had mentioned it.

"We'll have to be sure to celebrate. Eighteen is a big birthday. It must be celebrated like no other you've had up until now. It marks the sign of many wonderful things to come in life."

"Really, it's just another day. We don't have to celebrate it. I've never enjoyed celebrating my birthdays," Samantha lied, yawning.

"Every year is special and must be celebrated."

Samantha kept silent. She wanted to hang up, but she knew it was up to Skyler when the conversation could end. She punctuated the silence with another yawn. This one was real. She was very tired and could hardly keep her eyes open.

"All right, I'll let you get some sleep. But first, tell me when your birthday is."

Samantha hesitated. She did not want him to know but she couldn't lie. He would find out. "August twenty-third," she replied simply.

"Sweet dreams, sweetie," Skyler said softly as he hung up the receiver.

Samantha was too tired to care. Sleep was what she needed, what she craved. In the morning her father promised she could accompany him to the courthouse. Wednesdays were motion days. He said she would probably be bored, but she could sit in the courtroom and watch as attorneys were called, case by case, to make their motions and oral arguments. Her father said it would be a good beginning for her. She agreed enthusiastically. Her father couldn't be with her. He had two pretrial conferences. She actually preferred it that way. There wouldn't be anyone to monitor her reactions. She didn't have to feel self-conscious.

Samantha decided to write down her questions and ask them at dinner. She was thrilled it had been so easy to manipulate her father. She planned for a good night's sleep, forgetting to turn the ringer off on her phone. Skyler called, with his usual forceful style and seductive tone.

The interruption to her sleep cycle made her restless. She couldn't get comfortable afterwards. Crawling out from her warm soft sheets, she walked into her bathroom and reached into the medicine cabinet. Finding the half empty bottle of sleeping pills, she uncapped it, swallowed three and slipped back into the solitude of the covers. Before she knew it, she was fast asleep. This sleep was so deep and dull no dreams crept in.

An hour before the alarm went off, she was wide-eyed, disappointed that even with sleeping pills, she could not sleep a full eight hours. Her long hot shower revived her. She chose a simple navy dress, sheer stockings and navy pumps. Gold knot earrings and a plain gold chain with a locket completed the outfit. Samantha had watched her father dress for court appearances many times. She knew her navy attire was appropriate.

Samantha was calm as she slid a fresh notepad into its leather cover and slid the long chain of her purse over her shoulder. She would appear at breakfast as if she were an enthusiastic pre-law student. No one would guess she was on a mission to solve a mystery; her own mystery.

"Samantha, you look so professional! I'd hardly guess you were just about to enter college. I'd think you were a law student, maybe even a young lawyer," Anne Armstrong said, staring hard at her daughter, wishing she could mold her back into the shy little girl that used to hide behind her skirts.

"Good. Then I've succeeded. I really want to fit in."

"Why wouldn't you fit in, dear?"

"Oh. I don't know. I just think there will be a lot of people there, and they will all know I'm not supposed to be there. Watching, I mean."

"Samantha, anyone can watch court proceedings. They are open to the public. Don't you remember your brothers going to court to watch your father?"

"No. Well yes, maybe. I guess I never really paid much attention," Samantha said, hoping her mother wouldn't make any deeper inquiries.

"What haven't you paid attention to?" Travis Armstrong asked as he sat down at the breakfast table. A small black maid moved silently about, pouring him a freshly brewed cup of coffee from a silver pitcher.

"Samantha was just saying she didn't want to be conspicuous in the courtroom. That she thought everyone would know she shouldn't be there," Anne said, as she brushed a kiss on his cheek and sat beside him.

"Nonsense. We are all taxpayers. The courtroom, unless it is a closed hearing, is open to the public. More people should take the time to watch the proceedings." The strong voice came from behind the *New York Times*, as he dunked his cherry Danish in his coffee.

"Will you be home for lunch?"

"I don't know. Ask Dad."

The two women looked at the newsprint barricade and then at each other with raised eyebrows. Now was not the right time to ask anything. They would have to wait until the quick few seconds when he leaned over to kiss his wife goodbye before making a dash for the car. In that instant he was vulnerable to a question or two.

"Lunch, dear? Will she be home for lunch?" Anne asked as his lips touched her forehead and she patted his familiar large hand on her shoulder.

"Um, no. I'll take her out with me. Then I'll drop her off before I return to the office." He smiled at his wife. Always thinking, always planning. She hadn't changed in years and he was glad. He liked the familiar. "Will that do?"

"Of course. I just wondered where everyone would be today and what I would do with myself."

"I'm sure you'll keep busy," Travis chuckled, as he opened the door for his daughter to enter the garage ahead of him. "I'll take good care of her." Travis assured Anne with a smile before he let the door close behind him.

Samantha loved the smell of her father's car. It smelled of his cologne and leather. The music was always soft and relaxing, and even if the radio wasn't on, the car was comfortable and familiar. It reminded her of her father and the safe environment he had always kept her in. She clutched the leather notepad in her hands so tightly her knuckles turned white.

"Samantha, there is nothing to be nervous about. You're only watching. Honestly, you look the way I feel just before trial."

"Really? Even now?"

"Yes. Trial work is difficult. You have to be prepared. You have to remember everything and be prepared to counter any argument from the other side. You have to be ready to answer questions from the judge. You have to be able to justify to your client what you are doing. You have to be believable to a jury. There's a lot involved. That's why I'm so happy you've taken an interest. You may choose not to go to law school after vet school—after all that's a lot of schooling, a lot of years, a lot of time! Maybe you'll decide to go to law school instead of vet school. It is your decision alone. But I think it is wise to explore your options. It shows maturity. I'm proud of you for that."

Samantha remained still as her father spoke. He was so genuine. He was finally talking to her as an adult; something she'd always wanted. She wanted to revel in it for just a few seconds, all the more because she felt like a heel. She was not worthy of his trust; of being treated as an adult. She was a liar. She was a murderer. She was imprisoned in a life she didn't want, a life she couldn't even talk about. She didn't want to hurt her father. She kept silent. That was better than the lies. At least silence was easier to keep track of.

"Here we are. I'll show you around quickly and then, after you're seated in the courtroom, I'll go to my pretrials. When I'm finished, I'll come get you. If I'm not out by noon, or by the time the judge takes a recess, you can wait in the courtroom or meet me in the attorneys' lounge. No one will say anything. If they do, just tell them you are my daughter and you are waiting for me. Any questions?"

Careful not to trip on the wide cement stairs leading into the building, Samantha nodded her head. "I'll be fine Dad. I don't think I'll get lost in here. It doesn't look that big."

"You're right. It's not."

"I remember when I was a little girl, meeting you here with Mom. I thought it was so huge! It scared me then."

He remembered and laughed. "You don't have to be a little girl to be scared of this building. Whatever size it appears to be, believe me, there are many adults who fear it."

"Oh Dad, you know what I mean."

Travis smiled thoughtfully at his daughter. "Yes, I do. I remember. Sometimes I miss those days." A bemused smile crossed his face as he remembered the twins running in the solemn building, hiding behind the wooden courtroom pews, while Samantha hid in the long woolen coat of her mother.

"Here's the courtroom where motions are heard today. The attorneys' room is at the other end of the hall, and the women's restroom is in the basement. Just take the elevator and you'll see it as you get off. Okay?"

"Dad. Honestly, I'm not five years old. I'll be fine." Samantha put her hand on her father's arm and gave him a loving squeeze. She did appreciate him. She wouldn't admit she felt like five, regardless of her outward facade.

"Have fun, dear. We'll make you a member of the Bar yet! I'll see you in a few hours." Travis was proud of his daughter. She was growing up to be an intelligent adult. He hoped she would learn to appreciate the field of law as much as he did. He had always hoped he could turn the firm over to all of his children. Samantha could be the first female lawyer in the firm! That would be quite an accomplishment. The partners would have no choice but to accept her. Yes, it was time they had a female in the firm, even if she was a relative. Hell, *especially* if she was related.

As he turned a few steps beyond her, Travis put aside all thoughts of his daughter and proceeded to rehearse his arguments, turning his full energy over to his cases.

Seated on a hard wooden pew in the second row, Samantha looked around the courtroom at the oil paintings of the justices, the long oak attorney tables and the cushioned wooden jury chairs. She looked at the witness stand and the tall judge's desk. She pictured herself there in the judge's chair. She wished she could control lives and make important decisions. Most of all she wished she could pass judgment on Greg and on Skyler. Samantha wanted to throw the book at Greg, and even more at Skyler. But first she'd have to understand more about the law. She winced at the desire to control her own life again. It seemed an impossibility; a futile ambition. But this was a beginning. She was starting to feel stronger, as if she were a battery and the courtroom were her charger. She wasn't worried about how long it took to figure things out. She had time. Skyler hadn't seemed to want her any more and, actually, the only time she left the house was when she was with him; until now. As long as he kept his distance from her physically, she could handle the rest, she speculated. Begrudgingly, she had to admit, once she relaxed, she had almost enjoyed their dates, although she would never admit that to him—or to anyone else.

"All rise," the deep voice said as the white haired man in a long black robe entered. He took his seat in the black leather chair behind the dark oak desk, where a large worn gavel was angled on a beaten piece of round wood.

Samantha marveled. She felt as though she were in church—watching not a priest, but God himself. This was powerful. This was moving.

"Booth versus Booth, case number . . ."

Samantha watched intently as the attorneys rose, made their motions, argued their briefs and then answered the judge's questions. No one got upset at the judge's decision. She watched the attorneys leave and, as she viewed them through the glass in the door, they talked as if they had been friends all their lives. They made it seem so easy.

Everyone knew what was going on—everyone but her. But, she refused to get discouraged. She watched case after case. Much of what she saw looked familiar from watching *"Family Law"*, *"The Justice Files"*, *"L.A. Law"*, *"Matlock"*, and *"Ironside"* on television. Still, she really didn't learn anything.

The cases were interesting, but many were the same thing over and over; probation violations, divorces, broken contracts. No case was like her case. None of the words she wanted to know, to further understand, were used. She needed to see criminal motions or hearings. How would she explain that to her father? How would she ask? Well, she'd gone this far. She had to take the next steps. One step after the other. As she continued to listen, absorbing every detail, Samantha convinced herself it would get easier and her search would produce something that would help her. She'd find a way.

As Samantha continued to watch, absorbed in her own thoughts, she did not see the large figure slide in beside her. Her sense of smell recognized him first; his cologne, his warm breath.

"Samantha, how beautiful you look," he whispered.

Samantha turned, surprised. "Skyler. What are you . . .?"

"I saw your father in the hall and he told me you were here. Just thought I'd stop by and see how you're doing on your own in here."

"Oh. I thought it would be fun to watch what lawyers really do. I may decide to go to law school."

"So, I see you do listen to me."

"Well, I listen to everyone. My father taught me to listen to all views before I make my decisions."

"I'm just glad you listened to me," Skyler whispered, so close to her ear she felt his soft, warm lips brushing against her. It gave her goose bumps.

She hoped Skyler didn't notice. She remained silent, intent again upon the motions, hoping her absorption in the proceedings would clue Skyler he needed to leave her alone.

The row got more crowded, and Skyler moved closer to her. She looked up at him ready to tell him not to sit so close to her, when she noticed he had moved because her father had taken the empty space on the other side of him. Samantha watched as her father unknowingly betrayed her by shaking Skyler's hand. The men whispered between them for a few minutes, moving papers back and forth. Finally, she heard her father's voice as he leaned forward over Skyler toward her.

"Are you ready? How about lunch?"

"Yes, this was great. I'm ready, but I'm not hungry. You can take me home if you want."

"Nonsense. You need to eat. Besides, I want to hear all about what you thought of your morning," Travis said, beaming at his only daughter. "Skyler has agreed to join us." Turning to Skyler, Travis handed him a file and said, "These need to be filed downstairs with the respective clerks. Call the office and let them know where we'll be. We'll go on ahead and get a table before a crowd gets there. You can meet us at Bernie's in about twenty minutes."

Skyler grabbed the files and placed them in the top opening of his pliable-long handled leather briefcase. He nodded. "See you there."

Samantha was silent as she followed her father down the long marble corridors, down the cement steps into the tarred parking lot. Travis felt his day was off to a good start, and he was happy to be spending some quality time with his daughter. He did not see the look on her tearful face as she stood waiting for her door to be unlocked.

Climbing into the car, Samantha said, "Dad, really. I'm not hungry. Would you mind dropping me off at home?"

"Yes, I would mind. Is there a problem? Don't you feel well? Or is it just you don't want to be seen with your old Dad?"

"Dad, really. I'm just not hungry. And," she hesitated,

"I'm not going to be comfortable with Skyler there and the two of you discussing work."

"Promise," he looked at his daughter, "I promise we won't talk too much about work. I thought you liked Skyler. He told me he entertained you while we were away last week. A movie, I thought he said. I just thought we'd thank him by taking him out with us."

Samantha was stunned. Skyler had told her father they had gone out, and he hadn't told her! Now she really felt like a liar. "Okay, Dad. I'm sorry. Of course I want to go."

"So you didn't tell me, did you have a nice time at the movie? He said you saw that new Grisham film. I thought maybe that piqued your interest in the law."

"The movie was just something to do, Dad. It was great. I had read the book a few months ago. It was nice of Skyler to call and offer to take me."

"Oh, I thought you two ran into each other at the mall and that's when he offered to take you."

"Oh, yes. I . . . Well, I was in shorts. I thought I would be too cold at the theater and Mom would've had a fit if I had gone into a theater dressed in shorts, so I told him I needed to change and I'd meet him there, but he offered to pick me up. Then he called first to make sure I was ready before he came over," Samantha said, her insides fluttering with the new lies she had just told. How was she going to keep them all straight? What would her parents think of her if they ever found out what a liar she was?

"Mmm," Travis murmured, as he pulled into the restaurant, unsure as to why he felt unsettled about Samantha's explanation. Skyler had made it seem so innocent and plausible. Was there more? Was there something he should be paying attention to? Samantha was so moody, it was difficult to read her. He wished Anne had heard Samantha's voice when she explained attending the movie with Skyler. Anne would be able to sense if there was more to the story. So much for his lack of parental intuition; there was little he could do about that. But, his lawyer's intuition kept nagging at him. Well, he reasoned, he knew his daughter. She had not given him cause to doubt her. Confused and emotionally drained, he shook his head. He'd given Skyler the benefit of the doubt as well; should he have, was the question he'd have to answer.

Bernie's Pub & Grill was just getting crowded as they sat down. Samantha looked around. She recognized some of the other attorneys as her father raised his hand to them in greeting. She felt almost grown-up sitting in a restaurant where most of the people, including her, were dressed in business attire. She wished she didn't have to be here waiting for Skyler to appear, but she knew she would handle it. She had no choice.

"Well dear, did you learn anything?"

"It was really interesting. You and Mom were right; once I sat down I felt comfortable. Everyone ignored me. For the most part what the attorneys were doing was repetitive; different cases, similar arguments. I'm not sure if I were a judge I could sit and listen to it all day. Judge Stanley seemed to ignore some of what was said, but then all of a sudden he'd ask a question or announce a decision, and it made sense."

"You have to understand he's been on the bench for almost twenty years. He's heard it all, and most of the motions you heard were probably routine, with noncontroversial points of law. But you are right; from a non-attorney point of view, it probably seemed redundant and like he didn't pay attention."

"Yes, well, I was thinking I'd really like to watch a trial or maybe criminal motions. I bet criminal work is fun."

"You watch too much television. It's not like what you see on television—even the criminal motions are routine and somewhat boring, although procedurally different. If you're really interested, I'll check the criminal court docket and see what's on the calendar that you might find interesting. Maybe Skyler would take you and explain what's going on."

Samantha gasped inwardly. "No, please. I've bothered him enough."

"I'm sure he'd be happy to do it. He seems to have adopted you, like a sister. There's no harm in asking."

"Dad, I want to go on my own. If he goes with me I'm not going. Please, don't even mention my interest to him." Samantha panicked under the watchful eye of her father. Her face flushed. She took a deep breath before she continued. "I want to make an independent judgment about whether I want to be a lawyer, about whether I'm really interested, or whether

I'm just curious because it's what you and Taylor and Tad are doing. You've always said Skyler is made for the law. I don't want that kind of influence. Really Dad, please."

"Okay. It was just a thought."

Samantha looked at her father, pleading with her large vibrant eyes to underscore her points. Travis nodded. Samantha was just as stubborn as Anne, and there was no arguing with either of them when they made such a plea to him.

Their conversation lagged for only a few seconds before Skyler appeared, briskly pulling out his chair and tucking back the paisley tie that fell onto the white china bread plate in front of him as he sat.

"So, what have I missed? You two seem awfully quiet."

"Oh, I was just telling my father about the Michigan State campus and how beautiful it is. I'm hoping he'll find the time to come and visit me."

"You know your mother and I will visit you."

"I've been to Michigan State. My younger brother went there two years before transferring to Michigan Tech. Then he transferred back to Michigan State for his Master's Degree. He has another term or two before he finishes. I don't know what the draw is to Michigan. The sky has been gray every time I've been there, and the winters there are quite nasty. Me, I prefer our beautiful blue cloudless skies and southern sun."

"I didn't know you had family that went to M.S.U.," Samantha said, turning pale. "Actually, I don't know anyone who went there. I chose it for the pre-vet program."

"Would you like me to ask my brother to give you a call? He might have some pointers for you."

"That would be a great idea. Wouldn't it, Sam?" Travis asked comforted by the fact someone would be able to assist his daughter.

"That would be nice, but I don't think so. I want this to be an adventure—going to school, I mean. I don't want any expectations. I just want to be surprised."

"Samantha, I don't understand. How could Skyler's brother ruin your expectations? Maybe his help could make the difference as to whether or not you like it there."

Samantha didn't want to pick any fights. She couldn't handle this issue and win against both her father and Skyler.

She decided to simply agree and deal with it later. Skyler's brother couldn't be like him. Or could he? "Okay, you're right. He could be a big help. Do you think he'd know what kind of fashions they're wearing on campus these days in Michigan?"

"My brother? Tom?" Skyler raised an eyebrow and chuckled. "Probably not, but I bet his girlfriend, Stacey, would know. I haven't met her, but I believe she will be a junior this fall, so she's much closer to your age. You could give her a call. In fact, I'll call you later with their numbers, or I'll give them to your Dad. That way you could call them at your convenience. I'll let them know you'll call. In fact, maybe we could all get together, if Tom comes home during his summer break."

"Why wouldn't he come home on break?" Samantha asked, genuinely interested.

"Right now he's working at General Motors, in the engineering division, as a student intern. That pays for most of his tuition."

Travis was pleased. Getting his daughter prepared for college was, for the most part, left up to Anne. Getting Samantha acquainted with a few people in Michigan she could call on if she needed anything would relieve him. It was something he could help Samantha with.

"You know, Samantha, Tom tells me there are wonderful ski slopes in Michigan. You might want to take an elective ski class. If you like it, you could buy some skis. It would be a great way to meet people," Skyler said, trying to coax a positive response from Samantha.

"That's a wonderful idea. If you like skiing, I'll be happy to buy you your own skis for Christmas. You wouldn't want to wear skis that didn't fit properly," Travis said, trying to elicit an honest smile from Samantha's face—one without the grimace behind it he'd witnessed several times throughout their lunch. "Say, maybe we could *all* vacation in Colorado, and you could show us some of what you've learned?"

"Really, you two are putting the cart before the horse! I'm not even sure I want to ski. I'm not sure I'll like the cold and winter enough to want to ski. Can I take a rain check, Dad?"

"Sure," Travis said, laughing. "You haven't even started your first semester and I've planned out your free time. How's your lunch? Are you ready for dessert?"

"I'm really full, Dad—too full to eat anything else. I'll have my dessert at home. Cook said she was making cherry pies this afternoon."

"Skyler?"

"Thanks, Travis, no. I've got to get back to the office. I've got back-to-back meetings with clients," Skyler pushed back his chair. "It's always a pleasure to see you, Samantha. Good luck in school, whatever you decide about skiing."

"See you at the office. Don't worry, I've got the check," Travis said, nodding agreeably to Skyler.

As Skyler got up from his chair he let the burgundy cloth napkin fall from his lap onto the floor. It covered the purple crystal that had fallen from one of Samantha's necklaces. Samantha was religious about wearing it. He'd never seen her without it, even when it didn't match her outfit. He watched her on each of their dates clasp it as if it were magic. He was surprised she was not aware it had fallen. She hadn't noticed, nor had her father. He scooped it up inconspicuously into the napkin, then into his pocket like an expert thief. Thank God he had done enough criminal defense to have learned the tricks of the trade from the criminals themselves. He turned and left.

"Are you ready, Samantha?" Travis asked, as he downed his last drops of coffee.

"Yes. But could we wait just a minute? I just want all this food to settle. I shouldn't have eaten so much," Samantha said, wanting to insure they didn't run into Skyler in the parking lot. She'd had all of him she could take. Just wait until he called. She would give him a piece of her mind. She was furious with his interference. Telling her father about their date, wanting to inflict his brother and his girlfriend upon her, interfering in her new life at college. She had had it. She was fed up, and would let him know.

"Nonsense. That's as much as I've seen you eat in weeks. It's good for you. If taking you to court gets you to eat, then maybe I should take you everyday."

"Oh, Dad! Let's go."

Samantha enjoyed the rest of her day, shopping with her mother for her trunks. She had hoped to spend some time alone and try to find a moment to slip into her father's study before he got home, but she was just as happy to put that off.

She had renewed faith in herself, despite Skyler's interference.

She went to bed, but waited as the fluorescent face of the clock shone in the darkness. Minnie's arms moved to midnight and then to one. No call from Skyler. Why hadn't he called? It was not like him. Had she offended him? Why would he be upset with her? She was upset with him.

Sleep was what she needed. Sleep was what she wanted. Sleep. The bottle in the cabinet. That would bring her sleep. She needed to tune out, to turn her mind off. She didn't take them often, she told herself as she swallowed. Just when she needed them. Sleep. She faded into sleep and into the boundless mirage of faces. The kaleidoscope of immeasurable pieces, undefined parts of a whole, interchangeable features. The ears were still missing, the eyes unblinking, staring at her as if waiting for an answer. She couldn't respond, her voice was still lost as she stood and watched the pieces floating all around her. The drugs no longer insulated her from the dreams, from the pieces. It was sleep, but restless sleep. Somewhere from the depths, the dark places in her mind where the faces loomed, a small voice whispered, "You should've taken more, more pills would have kept us from creeping in."

Chapter 9

Two days and nights passed without a call from Skyler. What was he up to now? Samantha worried. It was too quiet. She couldn't sleep when he called, she couldn't sleep when he didn't. What was she to do now? She shouldn't worry; she had to take care of herself. Tired of thinking about it, she reached into the medicine cabinet and pulled out four sleeping pills. Surely she would sleep soundly with four. Two or three just were not enough.

Looking into her mirror, she swallowed the pills. It was odd. She looked at herself in the mirror as she took the pills. She used to spend hours sitting on the sink, inches from the mirror, investigating her face, her hair, her body. Now she stole glances at herself. That's all she could handle. She repulsed herself. Her face, her body, her hair, they held fingerprints. She could feel them. They held lies. She had made all of those lies real by going along and lying more and more as each day passed.

Samantha didn't want to see. She didn't want to feel or to think. She was about to fall into a deep and wonderful sleep, a dead sleep. Her dripping hair left droplets of water running down her lotioned body. She didn't want to dry it. She was tired of drying it. The shower had relaxed her too much and the pills would soon make her drowsy. It was summer. Surely her wet hair wouldn't take long to dry. As she put a towel on her pillow and crawled beneath the sheets, she looked at the phone. It remained silent. Soon her thoughts would be silenced too. She was almost unconscious when she heard the familiar sound, as if in the distance. Her limbs were weighted; it was difficult to move them. Finally, from a will that came from far within, her limbs moved toward the ring.

"Hello?" she mumbled, picking up the receiver, her eyes closed.

"Samantha? Is that you? Did I wake you?"

"Mmm, uh huh."

"Are you sick? You don't sound well." Skyler said, then added, "You weren't drinking again, were you?"

"Mmm, no. I'm tired." She tried to make the words sound normal but, even in her state, she recognized the slur in them.

"Okay, so I don't call for two days and you don't even miss me. You should've waited for my call. You know I couldn't stay away for too long. But you also know you were a bad girl the other day. You'll have to make it up to me," Skyler said playfully, but sternly. "You will, won't you?"

Samantha tried to pay attention, but it was difficult. She couldn't move her mouth to form words. Her grip on the receiver could no longer be maintained. She didn't care what he was saying; she just kept agreeing with everything, figuring he wouldn't know the difference. She knew all he really wanted was her to agree with him.

"Mmm."

"I'll see you tomorrow. Sweet dreams, baby," Skyler said in a naughty voice, before hanging up. He was pleased she had been so agreeable, unlike the other day, at lunch with her father. Maybe things were changing. He entered the bar for last call and his evening rendezvous with his favorite waitress.

Samantha drifted off to sleep, the receiver buzzing in her arms, cradled there as if she were five, holding her favorite doll. For a time she was numb. No dreams. No tossing or turning. No movement at all.

The dreams finally began to creep into her drugged unconscious. The pills had almost run their course, and her eyes fluttered for a time looking in the darkness. She closed them, knowing she could not get up. It was not yet time. She saw the pieces again; the faces. They lined up in front of her, placing themselves in a careful circle around her. They were no longer above her. They were organized around her. She saw herself reaching up, high up to a lever jutting out from the piece that resembled her own face. She pulled it. The circle turned, spinning round and round. Pieces passing her. She stood still, watching, unafraid. The pieces were familiar. Hair. Long hair, short hair, thinning hair, scalps. White hair, black hair, brown hair, blonde. Eyes, almond-shaped, round-shaped, brown, blue, green. They stared at her as they passed her.

The faces were familiar.

She had to piece them together. Instinctively, she knew the game. She had to build the faces; piece by piece, part by part. Eyebrows, cheeks, mouths. No ears. Where were they? How could she complete the faces in the time allotted? She heard the ticking of a timer. She began to perspire, her hands shaking as she continued to pull the lever. Round and round it went stopping on piece after piece. She collected them. They didn't fit together. Like an uncoordinated child, she forced them. They disappeared, one by one. She tensed; she would lose if she didn't finish. She didn't want to give up her time. She heard the buzzer. Time was up. The parts disappeared. She looked up. She saw a mirror. Heavy and gilded. An antique, it looked to be. She stared at it. Was she to step through it? Why was it here? She walked closer, toward the reflective glass. Her eyes opened wide. She saw no reflection. She reached out to touch it. It disappeared.

She awoke, startled. Her mind sputtered. Where was she? What was wrapped around her? She tugged at the sheets and felt it. The phone. What had happened? Slowly her eyes focused and she remembered. She had a vague impression of the phone call, the ringing, Skyler. She was supposed to see him today. Where were they going? She didn't remember what he had said, only that he was to pick her up.

Grabbing her pillow she pulled it over her face to blot out the world. It didn't even work temporarily, she thought with exasperation, as she heard her mother rapping softly on her door.

"Are you up?"

"Yes, Mother. I'm just laying here, thinking."

"Well, I thought I'd better check on you. Your father is at the office and I'm going to meet him for lunch at the club." Anne paused momentarily before entering her daughter's hushed room. "It's time you got out of bed. Skyler called saying something about needing a golf partner today and, since your father and I are already playing with the Pumerfords, he wondered if you'd like to join him. Your father told him you'd been wanting to get out there and practice."

"With him? Mr. Marks? How boring, Mother! What did you say?"

"I told him you'd call him at the office when you got up."

"Gee, thanks," Samantha said sarcastically, putting the pillow back over her face.

"Come now, Samantha. It will be fun. Besides, your father tells me he offered to introduce you to his brother in Michigan. It wouldn't hurt to be nice to him. Anyway, Skyler is an excellent golfer."

Samantha was furious. Couldn't her parents see what he was doing? Why weren't they their usual overprotective selves? Why did they choose to meddle in her life now and throw Skyler Marks at her? He had fooled them, just like everyone else. No one would ever take her side or believe her against him. It was impossible. She had to go along—for now.

"Okay. You're right, Mom. It'll be nice to get outside in the sun. It looks like a great day for golfing."

"You'll have to dust off your clubs and shoes. Remember the ones we gave you for Christmas last year; the ones you haven't used," Anne said teasingly, grabbing Samantha's pillow from her, casually tossing it at the end of her bed.

"I get the hint already. I'll get in the shower and get ready, then I'll call him."

"Maybe we'll see you two at the club for lunch?"

"I doubt it, Mother," Samantha said, now out of bed, closing the bathroom door behind her.

Wet hair still dripping, Samantha dialed the office number. It rang so long she almost hung up. Then she heard his voice at the other end of the receiver.

"Yes? How may I help you?"

"Mr. Marks please," Samantha said, not wanting him to know she recognized his voice.

"Well, well, the sleepyhead wakes up. I'm so glad you finally called me. I thought you had forgotten me."

"Skyler? Why are you answering the phones?"

"Because your father and I are the only ones here. I let it ring long enough so any client would have hung up, so I knew this was a personal call. I'm glad it was you. It's so nice to hear your voice this early in the morning."

Samantha remained silent. She did not want to talk with him any more than she had to. Every time she opened her mouth, she accidentally told him things she didn't want him to know. It was difficult for her to act. To try to be someone she was not. To lie all the time.

"Mmm," She finally said to fill the emptiness.

"Did your Mom tell you about golfing? Would you like to go?"

"I guess. Whatever."

"We don't have to go. I'm just here to please you. We can do whatever your little heart desires."

"Really, I don't care."

"Fine, then. I'll pick you up at ten. Bring your clubs, a change of clothes, and be dressed in whatever women golf in these days. We'll decide what we'll really do when I pick you up. See you then," Skyler said in a low voice, pressing his fingers onto the bandaged shoulder that remained from last night's encounter. He hadn't been rough. She had irritated him, the waitress with the inviting legs and fiery hair. He bought her drinks and a late dinner. She had no reason not to go along. No reason to scratch him. He'd been with her before and she'd said she liked him. She knew what he was about. She was old enough to know—old enough to have experienced the raw sex his body ached for, the passion of the animal inside.

Samantha would make him feel better. He was sure of it. He packed up his worn black briefcase to make an exit for the day. Destiny was with him today, and having an insurance policy didn't hurt. He chuckled as he pushed the elevator buttons.

Samantha winced when she saw the hall mirror, remembering her dream. She did not look at the full view of herself. She only glanced at her silhouette, from a distance, making sure her attire was in order. She smoothed her hand over the buttons of the polo shirt, insuring each tiny button was securely fastened. She would give no hint of flesh that did not need to be exposed. Her long khaki pants, almost blousy on her since her weight loss, did not flatter her thin lanky body, but they were acceptable golf pants. She brought jeans, a t-shirt and a sweatshirt for later. He said casual. She kept it very casual. She refused to make any extra effort, as if this was a normal date. Samantha was skeptical she would ever go on another normal date anyway. Besides, what was normal, she pondered?

As the doorbell rang, she grabbed her bag and let herself out. She did not want to let him inside. Samantha did not want the small talk with her mother or the scent of his cologne lingering in her house, her sanctuary.

"Samantha, is that Skyler?" Anne called out from the top of the stairs. Hearing only the faint sound of the vacuum cleaner, she walked down the staircase, looking around for her daughter. "Sam? Sam?" Anne knitted her brows in puzzlement and then opened the front door, only to see Skyler's black Mercedes pulling out of the rounded drive.

How odd. Anne closed the door. Samantha is not usually so rude. Maybe Skyler had set an early tee time. That must be it, she determined, as she ascended the staircase to prepare herself to meet her husband.

"Well . . . ," Skyler said, taking a sidelong glance at Samantha. "You look great, as always."

"Thanks."

"So." He paused. "Did you decide what you want to do?"

"No. I told you I'd do whatever you wanted. I don't care," Samantha said. Noticing his unconvinced stare at her and fearing his wrath, she added in a less irritable tone. "Really, it doesn't matter to me. What else did you have in mind?" She glanced back at the blanket and covered picnic basket in the back seat.

"I thought we could go for a hike. There is a wonderful trail that leads to a beautiful sandy point and private cove. Not many people know about it. I used to go out there and study when I was preparing for the Bar exam. It's the most peaceful place on earth I know about."

Samantha was momentarily caught off guard by his sincerity. She could almost visualize the cove as he continued to speak. Lost in her own vision and in need of a peaceful place, she forgot for an instant he was the enemy.

"You passed the exit to the club," Samantha said, startled.

"I know. I thought by the expression on your face you'd rather see the cove. Shall I turn back?"

"Oh. No. That's fine. Whatever."

Skyler, a seasoned man, had enough other dealings with women to know there, in the silence, was a sudden wordless quarrel between them. He would not give in to her emotionally tangled mind. Soon she would figure it all out and succumb to him without question. Soon she would find the emotional battlefield a desolate place. She would learn not to harbor such negative emotions against him. Intentionally, Skyler raised the volume on the radio and for the next several minutes they listened to the "Lite" station, as they played the top forty hits.

Samantha hated she was listening to her favorite radio station and her favorite songs with Skyler. How dare he invade the music she liked best? How could she bear to associate those songs, her favorite songs of the year, with him and this captive date?

She felt claustrophobic. Her life seemed to be completely out of her control now. Her body had been invaded, her soul cornered. Her parents were being brainwashed into believing Skyler had good intentions towards her. And now this; her music. The music she marked time with. The music she listened to in the solitude of her room. The music she'd now remember him with. Samantha winced as her ears filled with the voices of U-2, Sting, Sade, Phil Collins and the Backstreet Boys. They were no longer her private songs intertwined with her feelings, wishes and dreams. They were part of her horror.

As they neared the number one song in the countdown, Skyler carefully turned off the highway onto a service drive that led to a dirt road and an orchard like area. Dust and small rocks sputtered around the car, but Skyler did not mind. He drove slowly, enjoying his private thoughts. The music had put him in a positive mood. In the mood for good company, fine champagne and food. Everything was perfect. Skyler didn't care what kind of mood Samantha was in. He'd fix it, whatever it was.

That's what he did best, or so his women told him. He smiled, looking at the pale youthful beauty next to him. He smelled her clean scent. She didn't wear cologne or perfume. Its absence suited her innocence. She was unlike the others he had been with and she would learn to appreciate him as they did. He wanted to smell her and only her. Her warm soap cleansed skin, soft against his own.

Samantha watched, her eyes alert, filled with the majestic view of the trees. Small ones, tall ones, broad and tangled ones. They all looked so happy staring in the sun. She looked beyond their green peaks to the blueness of the sky and the marshmallow-like clouds suspended beyond. Was God up there? Would He help her?

"Too much thought for such a beautiful girl," Skyler said, breaking the silence, and turning off the radio. "Just beyond those trees, we're almost there."

"Where?" Samantha quizzed him, not seeing any water.

"Patience. It's a virtue," Skyler teased her.

"I've got plenty of patience. You're just pointing to air and expecting me to see something."

"And see you will. It's a beautiful sight. And it will be all yours. Ours to share for the afternoon."

Samantha suddenly felt more uncomfortable than she had in weeks. Surely he wouldn't touch her out here in the open? He couldn't. Someone would see them. There would be others that would be there on a day such as this. There had to be, she convinced herself.

"Here we are," Skyler said, parking the car toward the large boulders that acted as a wall at the end of the road. "We walk from here."

"Fine. Can I put my sneakers on? They're in my bag."

"Sure. I'll grab lunch," Skyler said, opening the back door and removing a large cotton blanket, a cooler and a picnic basket.

As the doors slammed, Samantha took a deep cleansing breath. She could smell the fresh air and the scent of running water and fish. "Where are we?"

"I can't tell you. You can try to find this place on your own, but it is difficult, even if you have an excellent sense of direction. There are some tricky turns and forks that look so similar you could literally drive around in circles for hours."

"How did *you* find this place?"

"I was a good little boy scout," Skyler teased, taking her hand into his, steadying her as she walked down the hot, sandy path. It was lined with uncomfortable rocks, as if, in another century, someone had built a primitive road. Samantha tried not to lose her footing as they maneuvered down the hill toward the water. Then it came into view. A clear blue expanse of water met the sky on the other side. There must be land near where the water met the sky, but at their angle and distance, her vision could not focus on it. It was truly beautiful. Just like the Renoir oil painting her father hung above the black baby grand piano in the living room. They had simply walked into the painting. Nothing like this really existed, at least not so close to home. And yet, here she was with Skyler. At that thought, her warm flesh chilled in the heat.

Samantha watched Skyler spread the large fluffy picnic cloth. She was mesmerized as she watched him meticulously place on the corners, the items he had carried, insuring a breeze would not lift the blue checked cloth from its carefully placed position. Rubbing her hands together, Samantha muttered over and over in her mind, "You're fine, you're okay. Everything will be fine, you can do this . . ."

The birds squawked as they noticed the intruders. They were not used to the sight of humans. They did not like it. Instinctively they fled. Samantha gazed in awe at the flock, silently wishing she could be one with them.

"Come on, sit down. Kick off your sneakers. Get comfortable. Can I pour you some champagne?"

"No. You know I don't drink."

"So you've said." Skyler poured her a glass, despite the protest. "I've brought soda for you as well, but we need to have a toast with this. It'll taste great in this sun. It's chilled to perfection."

Samantha took the glass compliantly and sipped it. She liked it. It tickled her nose as it went down, and yet it warmed her insides. She sipped again, not thinking of Skyler, but of her own sensations, trying to divert herself from what she worried was the inevitable. Casually, as she continued to empty her glass, she looked around, as if interested in the view. Truly it was spectacular, but what she wanted to see most in the picture—people—there weren't.

"I see you like it," Skyler chuckled, refilling the tall glass. "We still have our toast to make."

"Oh? And what are we toasting?" Samantha asked blandly, masking her curiosity.

"To youth and beauty, and to a wonderful summer for the two of us." Skyler clinked his glass against hers.

Samantha didn't sip. She couldn't. She felt like running away, like when she was a little girl playing hide and seek. But she wasn't little and she couldn't run. There was no place to hide.

"Drink it down or it won't come true. The toast is for

you. Don't you understand how lucky you are? Most girls would be thankful to be here with me."

"Sure, I understand. What's not to understand? Toast, make a wish, take a sip, it comes true; like magic." Samantha replied sarcastically, her eyes downcast, now looking into the champagne as if it were poison. Then, shrugging her shoulders, she drank it all down in one swift, fullmouthed gulp. She hoped somehow the alcohol would drown her feelings, her pain. But it didn't.

"Hey, slow down! There's plenty more," Skyler said, laughing and pouring her another, intentionally ignoring her flippant remarks.

"Whatever," Samantha replied, raising the glass in a toasting motion toward him. Then lifting it to her lips, she again tried to drown herself in its sweet taste.

Skyler watched as the little girl tried to hide behind the actions of a lush. He had seen this many times in the women he'd picked up casually in bars. They all had a story, and they all drank. Well, not his Samantha. He wanted her sober. He wanted her to remember. He wanted no excuses. The champagne had loosened her. That's all he would allow.

"Hey, why are you putting that away?" Samantha looked at him with raised brows.

"You've had enough. I'm not going to have you get drunk on me. Your parents wouldn't like that."

"Speaking of my parents, why did you tell my father you took me to the movies last time we went out? He mentioned it to me and I'm sure my surprise gave me away. I couldn't believe you would do that to me. That you would tell him. You promised you wouldn't say anything."

"Samantha, no one tells me what to do. I thought it best to mention it in passing. Trust me, your father thought it very gallant of me to rescue you from another night at home, alone." Skyler paused.

"In fact, he tells me you spend too many nights alone at home." He lifted one of her long curls from near Samantha's face and twirled it round and round his fingers, feeling it's softness compliantly twist in his hand. He studied her expression. She was angry with him. He didn't care. She would learn to get along. All women did.

"Still, you should've told me."

"Fine. Next time I'll make it a point to tell you; to warn you of every move I make with your family." Skyler's voice mocked her sarcastically.

"Now you're making fun of me. You're being mean. Why?"

Skyler chuckled, shaking her petite shoulders. "That's what I love about you. Your complete innocence."

Samantha thought about this for a minute. She didn't understand. She didn't want to understand. She wanted to go home. She thought of the safety and serenity of her room. Despite where she was, she put her mind in that room. It was safe there. He could not enter.

"Let's eat. I brought ripe brie and crackers, a variety of mini-sandwiches, grapes—green and red, pasta salad and, just for you, a raspberry mousse torte for dessert, with a whole can of whipping cream, specially purchased from the ice creamery." As he removed each container, Skyler listed their feast as if he were an accountant itemizing the woven wicker basket.

Samantha watched Skyler as he carefully began distributing plates and silverware around the colorful array of food. "It looks great," Samantha said. And it did look good to her. She hadn't realized how hungry she had become. She loved eating outdoors in the fresh air. She always had. Food tasted better outside. Had this been under any other circumstance, this would have been the most romantic date she'd ever had, Samantha thought with dismay.

Skyler watched her eat, her dainty mouth biting morsel after morsel. He thought, as he watched her, he had never seen another woman in his whole life eat so slowly or so daintily as Samantha. He could watch her all day. He loved the way she savored each bite, as if it were her last.

Samantha ate more slowly than she had ever eaten. The longer she spent eating, the more likely she could make the excuse it was getting late and her parents expected her home. She was unaware of the effect she had on Skyler. Unaware her slow deliberate movements only made him want her more.

Samantha looked around at the array of food. She had eaten more than she had eaten in weeks. Although to most persons, it would seem she had only picked at the display. She didn't want to become so full she became tired or ill. Therefore, her only option for delay was to talk companionably with Skyler.

She began making a mental list of subjects she could raise to keep him talking. Finally, she broke the silence.

"So, what have you been working on? Anything interesting?"

Skyler smiled, flattered she had asked, flattered she wanted to know more.

"I've got a case going to trial in a few weeks. You've probably heard your father talk about it . . . Johnny Castriano?" Skyler said, obviously proud.

"No. I haven't heard Daddy talk about anyone with that name, although the name seems familiar to me. Isn't he the guy they always talk about with big Mafia connections?"

"Very good. So your father has mentioned it," Skyler said, his compelling green eyes now alive with pride; his ears alert for secondhand compliments.

"No. I've read the name in the papers and heard it on the news. I do read, you know," Samantha said, responding cautiously, sensing she somehow had given him the wrong answer. "My father made it a rule many years ago not to bring his work home with him, and for the most part, I don't really know what he's working on. That's why I went with him to the courthouse."

Skyler believed her. As Samantha made idle chatter about her father, Skyler nodded as if he were attentive and interested. He didn't care about her words. They held no information for him. It angered him that Travis Armstrong had not recognized he had landed such a big client. If he won the case the state had against Johnny Castriano and kept him out of jail, his client list would grow immeasurably within months, maybe even weeks. And there was the $80,000 retainer the firm had been paid up front.

Skyler didn't believe Travis didn't talk about work at home. After all, he had two sons in law school and now Samantha was thinking about law as a profession. The fact his children wanted to become lawyers must have been from Travis' influence, Skyler surmised. That meant he talked at home about his work, the firm and the cases they handled. Even if Travis didn't regularly speak about work, Skyler never underestimated the power of pillow talk. There was no way he didn't talk about the firm to Anne. She was too involved in his life to not know what went on at the firm. There had to be conversation beyond the bedroom.

Was it possible Samantha was lying? Why would she withhold information about what her father talked about at home? No, she was not smart enough to lie to him. It was more than likely, in fact more probable, Travis Armstrong had again failed to recognize his importance and his contribution to the firm. Skyler swallowed his mounting anger. Its taste was bittersweet. He knew his time would come.

Samantha watched Skyler as a flush spread up from his neck to the tip of his ears. Was he ill? "Is something wrong? Are you all right?"

Startled by her concerned voice, Skyler looked at Samantha. As if for the very first time, his eyes focused on her quizzical face.

"I'm fine, I suddenly feel too warm in these clothes," Skyler said, flashing his perfect white teeth at her as he removed his shirt. "That feels much better. You should try it."

Samantha darted a look at the bare muscular chest that faced her. It looked like something right out of the muscleman contest her father and brothers liked to watch on weekends when they were all together. She looked away quickly, but the perfection couldn't help but be noticed. Also noticeable was the white bandage taped to his back and shoulder. Had he had surgery? Samantha averted her eyes from the stark white gauze. "What happened? Were you in an accident?"

"No. It's nothing. I was doing yard work; clearing bushes. I got scratched up pretty badly. It'll heal in a few days," Skyler said casually. Then, smiling, he teased in a soft playful voice, "Thanks for asking. You really do care! It's really great to see you're concerned about me."

"Just curious," Samantha replied blandly, her eyes lowered, her hands searching the ground for a four-leaf clover.

"Would you like to go swimming now, or later, after our food digests?"

"I can't. I didn't know we were coming here so I didn't pack a suit."

"Here, bathing suits don't matter. There's no one for miles." Skyler chuckled, carefully studying her face. "Besides, if anyone else is around here, they're not paying any attention to us."

"I think I'd like some of that dessert you said you packed. Where is it?" Samantha asked looking around as if she cared, as if she were still hungry.

"In the cooler, right on the top."

Samantha felt relieved as she slid her body carefully toward the cooler, putting her several inches further from Skyler.

"Don't bother serving it. Just bring it here with two forks and we'll dig into it whole. In my estimation, some foods—and all desserts—should be eaten just for the fun of it, without ceremony."

Samantha looked at him quizzically. She wasn't sure what to make of his peculiar editorial, but she knew better than to inquire or probe for further commentary. She simply did as she was told, carefully unwrapping the raspberry mousse torte and placing it between them. Avoiding his eyes, Samantha handed Skyler a clean dessert fork.

Skyler watched Samantha avoiding his gaze. She watched him, regardless of how she tried to hide it. He loved her guarded, yet intent, attention to him. She did care about him, whether she realized it or not. Skyler remained captivated with her as he mounded whipped cream all over the torte before plunging his fork in for huge bites of their raspberry feast. Carefully, he balanced his fork, intermittently moving it not to his lips but to Samantha's. She opened her mouth in silence, watching him take what remained on the fork to his mouth.

"Mmm, mmm, I'm not sure which is sweeter—you or this wonderful torte," Skyler said in a playful voice, pausing for just a second, as if pondering the question. He continued, in a soft sensuous voice, as if he were a cat ready to pounce. "I think it's you Sam, all you. You are the sweetener I need in my life."

Samantha lowered her eyes. She felt embarrassed. She felt scared, and her breathing became shallow. What was he doing now? She held her breath in fearful anticipation, as she watched him take another bite to his lips. She, too, took another bite. She had to delay. She had to get home. She needed the safety of her room, the room he couldn't touch her in. Stay focused, she thought to herself. I am in my room. No one can touch me.

"Champagne?"

Samantha looked at him, purposefully not responding as he filled their glasses.

"We've just about finished the bottle. I guess it will soon be time to go home." Skyler watched Samantha as if she were under a microscope.

"Yes. I told my parents we'd be home early," she said matter of factly, then added, "They'll wonder why they didn't see us at the club."

"No. No they won't. I told your father if we didn't see them, it would be because we went out to the driving range. And that is what you are to tell them," Skyler said in a stern voice. "So you see, I've got things covered."

Samantha sipped her champagne. She liked the way it made her feel. She allowed her mind to drift in and out of her room; her safe harbor, where he couldn't be. Skyler removed the torte from its place between them.

"Turn around Samantha. You are so uptight. I brought you here to relax. You need to be relaxed. All this pent-up tension is not good for you."

Samantha looked at him as he motioned her to turn around, positioning her by placing a hand on her arched shoulder.

"That's it, now relax," Skyler said, as he began to rub her shoulders, working down her neck to her back, then up to her temples. He was gentle. He wanted her to relax. As his firm hands felt her muscles relax from the massage, he whispered over and over, "Relax, relax. Let yourself go. You are floating now. Can you see yourself? Relax. Relax. That's it, your body is floating."

Samantha felt distressed when he touched her. But his hands were kind and warm and gentle. Not the hands that had assaulted her. Not the hands of the man she loathed. They felt good, they released tension. As he rotated and rubbed, her body loosened. This was not the man she despised. She began to float. No, no! That was not what she wanted! She could not let herself relax. She had to stay alert. But, Samantha began to feel very tired, very limp, almost lifeless. She wanted to close her eyes, but she refused to. She tried hard not to blink, for fear of slipping away. Despite her well-intentioned efforts, she felt herself floating, relaxing. No, no! She couldn't let go! She couldn't release herself into any sleeplike state with this evil man! She should not have had the champagne.

"Relax! Relax. You're safe. You are with me. You will always be safe with me. Relax. Relax. Release yourself from all tension. Relax. Let yourself float . . ."

And for a few moments she did. She did not want to relax, but her body had been fed. The sun and heat had warmed her, sapping her strength and the champagne had relaxed her will.

Skyler could feel Samantha relax. He was content for the moment, as he felt her mind drift and her tight muscles loosen, releasing her from unnecessary stress. He kept his voice smooth, deep and low, at a slow hypnotic pace. He had practiced. He had quickly learned to mimic the voices on the training tapes. He knew what the power of suggestion could do. After all, hadn't he quit smoking by hypnosis? It had been over a year, and he remained a nonsmoker. He was fascinated, even with his strong will and determined mind, he had succumbed to the power of suggestion. If it could affect him, it could affect almost anyone, he rationalized. He had studied it intensely, and now his efforts would be paid off in full.

Samantha's mind continued to drift in and out of her room. She felt herself back within the safety of Nana's arms. Back in the safety of her room. Serenity in solitude. Nana's words kept repeating in the waves of relaxation. For a moment, the current of the chant was so strong, Samantha thought she actually saw Nana; she knew she felt her presence. She felt safe in her illusion. She felt unsafe with reality. She knew Nana wasn't there really, but she lived each day on the brink, wanting to believe wishful thinking would come true. And yet, she knew it would not. She knew, as her waves of hope crested, she had to sail her mind back to reality. A reality which meant she had to get Skyler's hands off of her. She was clear about that, but she found herself fighting the words over and over again. "Relax, relax . . ."

She felt as if she were floating on a riverboat, relaxing, dozing in the sun. Suddenly she awoke, startled she had let herself mellow so deeply, escaping into the shelter of her imagination.

"Hey. Remember me?" Skyler whispered softly into her

ear as he leaned forward over her shoulder. "You should get massaged regularly. You take to it so well."

Samantha heard the familiar voice and shuddered internally. She felt the weight of her head. She felt her dry mouth. She wanted to take a nap, away from Skyler.

"Shall we go?" Skyler asked, his hands carefully placed on her shoulders, his head so close to hers she could hear his even breathing.

"Hmm? Oh, I guess. I'm really thirsty. Is there another soda?" Samantha asked, leaning forward toward the cooler. Moving awkwardly away from Skyler, Samantha tried to move far enough so she was out of Skyler's reach. Out of his grasp. As she moved, she felt his hands slide slowly down her back.

"There should be a few cans left," Skyler remarked, surprised she hadn't immediately sprung to her feet at the mention of their leaving. She'd hesitated. She might want to stay. She might want to be close to him. Her uncertainty was a revelation to him; an opening for him to believe what he wanted to believe, not what was. He watched, savoring her. He didn't notice her sluggish champagne-drugged movements. He saw only a petite woman chugging a soda, innocent of her effect on him.

Samantha wiped dripping soda from her mouth. She wasn't sure of anything except she needed to get away from this man. How could she do it, she wondered, pondering her circumstance as her fingers brushed over her face. Slowly his body moved to hers. She felt tense immediately. Her body rigid. Her mind more alert.

"Samantha," his soft strong voice pierced her. "I need you next to me. Let's spend a few quiet minutes together. We need to let the champagne settle a bit before we leave. I don't want your parents to suspect I let you have a taste." Skyler lowered her onto the blanket, his hard tanned body so close to hers their hearts beat as one.

Samantha froze. Her body felt stiff, yet strangely comfortable. She needed a nap. She needed to shut her eyes, if only for a moment. Why had she tried the champagne? Never again, she thought, as she tried to stay alert. No, no! Her mind raced, screaming. Yet it seemed a dream to her as she faded into a state like sleep.

"You and I are meant to be. We fit, you'll see that." Skyler whispered softly, kissing her hair as if she were a child being put down for a nap. He was as careful with her as if she were a baby. Gently he laid her in the crook of his arm and began stroking her soft dark curls. Skyler loved the texture of her hair, the fresh soap scent of her warm flesh, her perspiration. It tasted good to him. He wanted her. He needed to touch her, inside. To feel her fully. He would wait. She needed her strength. A nap would do them both good. He wanted her to remember her time with him.

As they nestled on the blanket in silence, the gulls returned to view their spot, still habitated by the intruders. They squawked. They dipped and circled. Then, just as easily as they had appeared, they exited.

The faces appeared, and Samantha was sure she had made it to her room safely, without harm or encounter. The faces, still in pieces, floated in and out of her sight. The dream was different this time. The pieces, always familiar, had parts she looked at every day. They were her own this time. Her brows, her high cheekbones, her eyes, her full lips. No ears. She didn't have ears either. The pieces floated and she tried to catch them. She could not. They floated onto the wheel. The wheel of . . . of . . . She had never been able to read it before. Maybe she had never noticed the sign. It was at the top. The wheel of destiny. She squinted. She saw the figure of a woman. An old woman. Nana? Nana? She called out. She tried to reach her, but she couldn't. She tripped, her body fell forward. She was awake.

Where was she? Where was her bed? What was this scenery doing in her room? She lay confused, reality slowly filtering back, as she felt Skyler's arms around her tighten. "It's about time you woke up, sleepyhead."

She wondered how long she had dozed, her mind still muddled, perplexed by the sleep she had fought so hard against. Her dream seemed like it had taken place over a span of hours. Her eyes focused on the still beautiful scenery. The sun had only moved slightly. Time couldn't have moved far during her unconsciousness.

"I . . . I have to get home. I don't feel well. My parents. They'll be worried."

"No. I told you they won't. I took care of that already. You have nothing to worry about," Skyler said, forcibly rolling her from her side to her back. "I have something that will make you feel better."

Samantha's eyes grew wide and uncontrollably filled with tears as his face came within inches of hers. "Please, I really have to go."

"Relax," he said in a soft hypnotic voice. "Relax."

Samantha's head pounded. She was alert; her body stiff. Her insides trembled with fear. She knew it was time. She knew he would take her, out here, for all to see. What could she do? She felt helpless.

Skyler ignored Samantha's agitation. Her tears were not new to him. She was just one of those women who cried at the drop of a hat.

He reached into the cooler for the bottled water. Her eyes remained locked on the clear blue water, using its rippling to calm her, to help her think her way out of her immediate plight.

"Here, Sam. Take these. You'll feel better."

Samantha stared at him. "What?" She didn't understand.

"Come on. It's only aspirin. I forgot what a lightweight you are when it comes to drinking. Aspirin. Take two. It always works. Trust me."

Samantha had heard those words from him too often. She didn't trust anyone these days and she didn't want him continually asking her to do something she shouldn't. She looked at him closely. He seemed sincere. Slowly her fingers reached into his soft lined palm and took the aspirin.

Skyler was silent as he watched her put them in her mouth, one at a time, drinking down the water in large gulps. Soon she would feel better. Soon they would both feel better. He was feeling powerful. The day had gone well and she seemed to trust him more and more each time they were together. Removing the emptied glass from her hand, Skyler again began to massage her neck, back and shoulders. He was silent for a time and then again he whispered, in almost silent prayer, in tune with the rhythm of the massaging circles, "Relax . . . Relax . . . I'm here . . . You can trust me . . ."

Samantha, though confused, was momentarily comforted by his caring movements, his attentiveness, his soothing voice. She felt almost foolish she had thought the worst of him. Guilty she despised this man who was being so kind to her. His voice was soft and tranquilizing. With a deep cleansing breath, unconsciously released, she wanted to sleep again. She could feel it coming on. Her lids were heavy. She was so relaxed. How did he know how she felt? He seemed to anticipate everything she felt, every move she wanted to make. She had never known anyone quite like Skyler. The perfect . . . the perfect . . . devil. That was it, she thought, relaxing into his trance. The perfect devil, that was who she was with.

Skyler let her sleep as he quietly packed up their meal. He watched her. He loved watching his captured beauty. So unaware. So easily manipulated. So much needed to execute his plans. The shade from the tree had moved over them. He watched as the lines of shade devoured the sunlight that spilled across her body. Her cheeks had a natural pink glow, now red from the sun. He watched the thin gold wire hoops dangle from her small ear lobes. He liked them on her. He shrugged as he carefully lifted them from her lobes. She wouldn't miss them. After today, she'd probably think she'd forgotten to put them on, or she'd lost them. Either way, he knew she'd never ask him about them, so he wouldn't ponder the question. He didn't have to. He cocked his head and smiled, folding them carefully into the white handkerchief he had pulled from his pocket.

She moved, startled again by the sleep she had taken. What was wrong with her? She had made a pact with herself to remain alert, to stay distant from this man, this devil. She felt his hard body against her. His firm strong fingers, his muscular hands were on her. His soft mouth touched hers. She felt it, so natural—no, no! Her mind raced. *Not* natural! Yuk! Ugh.

He kissed her long and hard. He kissed her again, deeply this time, stroking her hair away from her face. Kissing her cheeks, her neck, her mouth again. She looked up, her clear blue eyes wide. Here it came. Here he was. Please God, no. No. Her mind raced, screaming in the depths of her inner reality. But no one could hear the screams except her own mind . . . and maybe God. Yes, that was it. God. Only God can help me fight the devil. God, help me please, silently she begged.

"Get up," he gently ordered. "I've packed, and as soon as we fold this blanket we're ready. Come on, time to go."

Samantha gaped at him, stunned a few kisses were all

he wanted. Quickly she got up to help him fold the blanket. Putting her shoes back on and grabbing her purse, she walked carefully toward the path leading to the car, not waiting for Skyler to lift the picnic basket and cooler, wanting to keep her distance from him.

"Hey, don't worry. We'll get you home on time," Skyler said, quickening his stride to catch up to her.

"I just want to get home. I'm sure my parents are worried, and I was supposed to get a call from Emily this weekend. She wrote and told me she'd call. I hope I didn't miss it. It got late so quickly." Samantha was surprised as that lie flowed easily, believably, from her mouth. Emily hadn't written and she wasn't going to call. She just needed another reason to get home, something else that would make her missed—besides the parents Skyler had fooled with his charm.

"I'm sure with the time difference, it'll be the middle of the night here by the time she calls you. Her father says she's having a wonderful time."

"Oh. Yes, that's what she says when she writes."

Silence passed between them as they made their way to the car. Samantha felt as relieved as she did confused. Again, he hadn't forced himself on her. Why? What was he doing? What did he really want? Hadn't he made himself clear weeks ago? A few kisses. That's all. Maybe that's all he needed—she hoped. She thanked God.

Samantha continued to ponder as she watched the moving cars pass them. Maybe he didn't like her inexperience. Maybe she was as repulsive to him as she was to herself. That was fine with her. She should be grateful, she rationalized, as she stole a glance at his dark handsome face. His eyes, from the side view, looked like speckled green limestone. He had the longest lashes she had ever seen on a man. In an odd way, she ventured, without his heavy whiskers and thick brows, he could be a beautiful woman. Oh, what a thought! She almost laughed. Then, clasping her hands together tightly, she reminded herself no woman would be as cruel as this man. This devil man.

Still, why didn't he want her?

"Samantha, I really had a nice time. I hope you did too."

Samantha looked out the window. She didn't want to look at him. She was so confused. Her mind. Her feelings.

His voice. His presence. His actions. Nothing matched. Nothing made sense. She steadied her voice and narrowed her thoughts before she responded, simply. "It was nice. The view was beautiful. Thank you for sharing it with me."

Her response pleased him. She was coming around, whether she wanted to or not, whether she would admit it or not. He sensed her acquiescence and believed she understood their need to be together. His need to have her. His desire for dominion over her. Soon, she would be ready. Soon, she would want him; would request him over and over again.

As they pulled into the driveway, Samantha forgot about her golf clubs and shoes. She grabbed her bag and her purse and reached for the door handle. "Bye."

"Not so fast, sweetie. Tuesday's the fourth. I want very much to take you to dinner and the fireworks. How about I pick you up at seven?" Skyler said, smiling as he winked at her. "Remember, if they ask, we went to the driving range and dinner at the Eatery."

Did she have a choice? She opened the car door, nodding as she slammed it shut. She loved fourth of July fireworks. She would not let him spoil them. She would be safe, she reasoned. Too many people would be around for him to even kiss her. She would have a good time, because she wanted to, she decided, with shaky conviction.

The house was silent and empty. Samantha was relieved to discover her parents were not yet home. That meant, with any luck at all, she would not see them until morning. As Samantha turned the golden doorknob and anticipated the solitude and serenity she'd find in a hot shower, she silently wondered if she had anything to wear on Tuesday night.

Just as she dozed off that night, the phone rang. Samantha picked it up without thinking, believing it to be her parents checking up on her.

"Hello?"

"Well, you seem to be feeling better, love. That's the nicest greeting I've received in ages." Skyler said, unaware Samantha's heart sank immediately and warm tears welled in her tired eyes.

"Oh, it's you. I was just going to sleep," Samantha said, her body quaking slightly. She wanted to explain to Skyler she had answered the phone anticipating one of her parents would be calling. But she didn't dare, for fear he would take the liberty to come over and he would never again believe her when she said she had to get home.

"I just wanted to hear your voice before I go to sleep. I hope you had as nice a time as I did. I really think you are someone special, Samantha. I hope you know that." Skyler said, with the sincerity of a priest.

Samantha blinked in the silence that followed. She knew she had to respond, but his comments had frozen the connections between her mind and her mouth.

"Samantha, you do know that . . . You have to know by now how much I care about you."

"Yes. I do." Samantha reluctantly admitted.

"Good. Just relax. Everything will be fine. I'll take care of everything. Pleasant dreams, love."

Samantha lay awake for what seemed hours before her mind fluttered into dreams. The familiar faces, still in pieces, floated round and round. They seemed her friends, but for the lost ears. She became engrossed in fitting them together, in finding out how they fit together so she could be with whole people, not just parts of faces. But how could she find those ears and why didn't her own pieces stay together? Like Alice in the looking glass, Samantha continued to test the mirage, exploring every detail.

Chapter 10

Skyler was pleased with his day. He had enjoyed Samantha's company, and her parents were at ease with their friendship. He would be the friend she needed. Eventually she would trust him completely, even learn to rely on him. He loved hearing her voice before she fell asleep. It was comforting to him. She made him feel powerful and in command; as if he could accomplish anything, even take control of another human mind.

Everything was going as planned. He grabbed the thick stale smelling book he had checked out at the library earlier that day. *Hypnosis For Better Living* was a nice addition to the other books he had read about hypnosis and relaxation. The mind was a remarkable tool, easily manipulated, for all its complexities. As he began to read the telephone rang.

"Hello?" Skyler queried, hoping at the other end of the line wasn't a client in jail.

"Mr. Marks?"

"Yes?"

"Mr. Castriano understands you had trouble with one of his girls," the deep voice stated, as if for the record.

"I took care of it. It was fine. Everything's fine," Skyler said knowing he could not ask any questions, wondering what had been said; how they knew. Skyler's mind was as alert as if smelling salts had just been placed under his nostrils.

"Mr. Castriano wanted me to tell you the problem has been taken care of."

"But, there is no problem."

"You're right. He just wanted you to know from now on there won't be any more problems. Oh, and next time you're to let him know about any problem directly. Right away. He doesn't like to find out these things on his own. Mr. Castriano likes to take care of his friends."

Skyler looked at the phone as he heard the click. What had the girl said about him? Puzzled, Skyler closed the book, replacing it on his nightstand, before slipping into the king-sized, navy paisley designer sheets. As he drifted into sleep, his mind played over and over the scene of the young girl's refusal to comply with him. The deep scratches from her final fearful compliance were still healing under his still-bandaged shoulder. The recollection loomed in his dreams, frame by frame, lurking in the darkness, as if reruns of an old film. What had the caller meant? He pondered in restless slumber.

Chapter 11

Samantha's head pounded as she lifted it from the soft feather-filled pillow. She couldn't complain. It was self-induced illness. She shouldn't have accepted the champagne. When would she learn her lesson? Drinking seemed to be taken for granted by most people, and yet her body could not handle it. She would have to accept that alcohol only made her sick, regardless of what kind it was. It couldn't really make her forget or accept her problems. It couldn't make her at ease or calm her nerves.

Decidedly, Samantha vowed she couldn't lose control of herself, her body, or her mind. Whatever happened, she needed to stay alert in every sense of the word and in every instance, under every circumstance. It was all so confusing. She wasn't sure what Skyler was doing with her, what he wanted, but she was more certain than ever her unwanted devil partner did not have her best interests in mind. Samantha kept reminding herself not to trust him. It was odd, she had these nagging questions about him and yet sometimes, she found her unconscious mind fantasizing about him. If only things were different!

She must really be sick to think about any positive aspects of Skyler. There were none.

Samantha rolled back the covers and prepared for brunch. Sunday clothes were expected, regardless of what she had planned for the day. That's just the way it was. It had become an Armstrong tradition. Brunch was served every Sunday, and everyone in the house must be seated promptly at eleven o'clock in the breakfast room. The tradition became entrenched once her brothers became teenagers. Sunday brunch was the only time the family could meet and catch up as a group. Since the twins had gone off to college, and now law school, she generally had her parents to herself. Samantha used to enjoy her time alone with her parents. Now it had become almost unbearable.

She carefully dried her showered body and applied enough makeup to hide the dark circles formed from her unsettled sleep. The dreams were becoming real to her and she saw them more and more clearly, even in her conscious hours. Even though she thought she was able to sleep deeply, the dreams always kept her on the border between sleep and waking and she did not feel relaxed, even after a full night's sleep. Samantha knew she should have taken some sleeping pills, but she was afraid of the mixture of pills and champagne in her system and had decided against it. Now she wished she had taken at least one. What real harm could it have done?

Carefully tying her wraparound skirt and smoothing its soft cotton fabric, she swiftly checked herself in the mirror, her eyes avoiding her face. She was fine. Her parents, more self-absorbed of late, wouldn't notice. She was sure of that.

"Samantha. You look nice. How was your afternoon yesterday? We didn't wake you when we came in. You looked so peaceful." Anne Armstrong beamed at her daughter, happy she was more content than after high school graduation. A month had done her a world of good. She was sure her daughter would be back to herself by the time she left for college.

"How was the golf lesson? Skyler is quite a golfer," Travis exclaimed, eyeing his daughter.

"Fine."

"Did you like the new clubs?"

"Yes, Dad. They're fine."

"Then why so glum?"

"I'm not. Just tired, I guess."

"The fresh air did you well. You even look like you got some color in your face."

Samantha looked at her mother and tried to smile. "I guess I did. I didn't really notice. I was trying to concentrate, but it was so hot outside yesterday," she replied, with a pasted-on smile. "What's it like outside today?"

"Another perfect day. The news this morning said it is supposed to get to 95. Is that the doorbell?" Anne asked, raising a questioning eyebrow at Travis.

"Hyrum will get the door. I didn't invite anyone," Travis said, trying to clear the accusatory eyebrow his wife had given him. He knew she hated guests on Sunday morning. Her motto was "any day but Sunday."

Anne liked her private time and, years ago, she insisted on Sunday brunch with the family. She would acquiesce if she knew in advance there was a possibility someone might stop by. While she always said it was to insure there was ample food and fresh-cut flowers, Travis knew the real reason was so she could dress to perfection—a quality he actually liked about her, but didn't fully understand. If people dropped in unannounced, they should be happy with what they found, not critical. Women! As much as Anne loved people around her, she hated them. He'd never understand women.

"Yes, Hyrum?" Travis asked, his eyes shining with curiosity.

"It's Mr. Marks, sir. He has something for you, I believe."

"Oh? Excuse me for a moment," Travis said to his wife and daughter, putting down the Sunday paper. "Why don't you ask Maria to set another place. I'll see what he wants and ask him to join us."

Anne shrugged and nodded. She knew she didn't have a choice. Meticulously, as she motioned to Maria, she mentally inspected her floral dress, jewelry, and nails and then patted her hair with her hands, insuring every strand was in place. She was too proud to go look in the mirror. It was not proper for one to leave the table once the food had been served. It was her mother's rule, and she had never disobeyed it—at least almost never.

"Mom, you're fine. You look great," Samantha said noticing how uncomfortable her mother had suddenly become and silently gripping her own fingers together, hoping Skyler's presence had nothing to do with her.

"Thank you, dear. I know I worry too much. It's just, with your father's position, I don't want to give anyone cause for talk."

"May I be excused?" Samantha was hopeful.

"No. You've hardly eaten and it would be rude to both your father and Mr. Marks," Anne said, not surprised Samantha wanted to leave the table. It had been a constant struggle to keep her anywhere near food. She had hoped things were better with Samantha. Just as she thought Samantha was fine, there was another problem lurking about.

Skyler comfortably followed Travis into the breakfast room sitting in the vacant chair beside Samantha. Skyler winked at Samantha just before she lowered her eyes. He watched her face flush.

Samantha felt warm as the familiar lump formed in her throat.

"Skyler was kind enough to drop off Samantha's clubs and shoes. You left them in his trunk," Travis said to his daughter in an apologetic voice aimed at Skyler.

"Oh. I guess I was so tired I forgot. I'm sorry, Mr. Marks."

"No problem. It was as much my fault. I forgot. And please, call me Skyler."

"I asked Hyrum to clean the clubs and shoes and put them in your cubby in the garage. From the looks of it, you need some more balls and tees. I'll pick some up this week."

"Samantha's swing has really improved. There's nothing like hitting a few buckets of balls on a beautiful day. I thought the driving range was as relaxing as a full game. Didn't you Samantha?"

Samantha looked stunned. Her clubs and shoes had never been used. What had he done now? They never went golfing, so how could they have gotten dirty? Her silent questioning rage prevented her from listening attentively to Skyler's lies. She didn't want to say anything. She didn't want to respond. She simply nodded in agreement and murmured a "yes" as she intently broke apart her blueberry muffin, buttering it as if she had every intention of eating it.

Samantha surveyed each of the adults as they became engrossed in a conversation of their favorite golf ranges. Even at her age, she knew there were more important things than golf, yet they spoke about golf as if it was the most important aspect of their lives. She knew better. She knew peace of mind was important, being safe was important. Most of all, she knew getting away from Skyler was important—and necessary.

Samantha's thoughts strayed from the conversation. She could not focus. Noticing her silence, the adults tried several times to bring her into the conversation. She simply nodded. She hated golf, especially now that her clubs had spent the night in Skyler's car. As she moved the food around on her plate, occasionally appearing to place crumbled morsels in her mouth, she artistically made the remaining edibles look as if she had eaten most of the original portions.

"Miss Samantha, you have a phone call," Hyrum said,

embarrassed to have interrupted them for the second time.

"Oh, I'll be right there. May I be excused? I really couldn't eat another bite." Samantha looked pleadingly at her mother, relieved, not caring who was on the phone.

"Fine. Maybe later we can finish showing your father the computer information so we can get that ordered in time for school?"

"Sure, Mom," Samantha agreed, grateful to whomever was on the phone.

"Oh, Samantha! Before you go, I wondered if you'd like to join me on Tuesday for the fireworks? My brother and his girlfriend will be up for a few days from Michigan. I thought you'd like to talk with them," Skyler said, flashing his white teeth at her, locking his lips into a friendly smile. "In fact, your parents are welcome to join us as well."

"Whatever," Samantha said rising from the table. Then, seeing the stern look from both her parents, she quickly added, "Thanks. Yes, I'd love to join you."

Samantha chose to answer the call in her father's study. Even though the study was off limits, it was private and she could use the excuse the study had the closest private phone. Besides, whomever her caller, she had already waited too long.

"Hello?"

"Samantha! It's so good to hear your voice! Can you hear me?"

"Emily? I can't believe it. It's about time you called!" Samantha was so relieved she sighed deeply, as if to release all of the bad air she had bottled up since the last time they had been together. She didn't realize, until she heard Emily's familiar voice, just how much she had missed her friend. She wished she had confided in her before she had gone to Europe. She couldn't tell her now. It would have to wait.

While the girls exchanged stories and promises to write and meet before they each began college, Samantha's parents declined Skyler's invitation for the fourth of July, but agreed it would be an ideal opportunity for Samantha to meet his brother and learn more about Michigan.

Before leaving the study, Samantha pulled from her skirt pocket the list of legal phrases she had copied from *Black's Law Dictionary*. She had folded and unfolded the list so many times the creases had already worn severely into the paper.

She looked around the room at the books that held the key to her release from Skyler. She would find a way to unlock the knowledge she needed. She had to. But not now. Footsteps told her that her mother was approaching. Samantha slipped out the door.

"Samantha? Where are you going? Why were you in your father's office?"

"Mom, you'll never guess who was on the phone! Emily. She sounded great! I'm going to go upstairs and write her a letter." Samantha kept her tone upbeat, intentionally ignoring the question.

"That's wonderful, dear. Will you be able to see her before you leave for college?"

"I think so. She gave me the date she's coming back so I'm going to check. In fact, I've got to write her today. I want to make sure she gets the letter."

Anne was pleased to see her daughter so excited. It had been a long time since she saw such sparkle in her eyes, heard such happiness in her voice. It was like momentarily having her back to her old self, before graduation got so close. As she watched Samantha bouncing up the stairs, grabbing onto the polished banister, she shouted, "Oh, by the way, we've accepted Skyler's invitation for the fourth for you. Your father and I can't go, but you should have a great time. I'll tell you about it later."

"Fine, Mom. Is he still here?"

"Dad walked him out to his car. I think they're still talking about golf. That was really very nice of him to take you out. You should have been more polite."

"I was, Mom. I didn't . . . I don't really know him enough to say anything. I wasn't rude or impolite."

"Of course you weren't, dear. You're right," Anne replied with a kinder tone than her previous comment, noticing the sudden forlorn look on what, seconds ago, had been a bright cheery face. "I'll be going for a drive with your father in about an hour. We want to look at some investment property. You are welcome to join us. Otherwise, we'll see you later for dinner."

"I don't want to go for a drive. I've got too many things to do," Samantha said beginning again to climb the stairs. "I'll see you later."

As her mother retired to her own office, address book in one hand, steaming coffee teetering in a china cup in the other, Samantha retraced her steps back to the front door, knowing her mother would hibernate for at least an hour. Peering out onto the driveway she could see the back of her father's body, his arms flailing to accentuate his words. Skyler stood there listening, his hands hanging out of his pockets by his thumbs, his mocking grin making her father believe he was listening to him. She grimaced. She had grown to recognize that look. Why didn't others see it? Grown-ups! They weren't as astute as they thought. She felt older than they did; yet she felt so young and naive for having believed Skyler, for having fallen into his trap.

Samantha hated her parents for holding Skyler up to her, for trusting him. If they only knew what he was capable of! Samantha felt a headache coming on as she watched Skyler and her father breaking into gales of laughter. Their gaiety triggered deep remorse, as she swallowed the massive catch in her throat the size of the ever growing mountain of lies she had to live with. Back in her room, she sat on her bed with the unfolded list again in front of her. She could feel her head pounding, louder and louder as she reread the words, the definitions, trying to find the missing link. What had she missed? Her body became stiff as minutes unknowingly turned to hours. Her thoughts became muddled, vacillating between reality and fantasy. She lacked the control to remove herself from the bed. Time stood still and she with it. She was safe, comfortable, alone. Serenity in solitude. Her Nana was here with her. She didn't want to move, afraid the sense of safety would again disappear. The long Minnie Mouse arms moved around and around, crawling from one number to the next. Finally, her mother's concerned voice woke her up.

"Samantha? Are you in there? May I come in?"

Instantly folding the paper, quickly placing it back into her skirt pocket, she answered, "Yeah, Mom? I was just reading."

As the door opened revealing her mother, fresh in her new pantsuit, and pristine makeup, Samantha tried to dispel her own downcast mood.

"You've been up here for so long. Are you all right?" Anne asked, looking conspicuously at Samantha's face before eyeing every detail in her room. Nothing seemed out of the ordinary. Her daughter's face seemed sullen and withdrawn, despite her obvious attempts to hide it. She had watched her eat a healthy brunch, and yet her clothes hung on her as if they were still on their hangers. She had gotten so thin. Her color was pale except for the tinge of pink on her cheeks from golfing with Skyler. At least he had successfully encouraged her to get out of the house! Maybe going out again so soon for the fourth of July and talking with people who knew about the college she would be attending would put her in better spirits for a longer period of time. They were lucky the firm had such a close knit group and Skyler was willing to take the time from his busy schedule to help Samantha. Anne watched Samantha rearrange the pillows against her headboard.

Fondly, Anne kissed the top of Samantha's head as she turned to leave, not wanting to bring up any topic that could lead to a quarrel. "I can't believe you spent the entire afternoon in your room. That must be some letter to Emily!" Anne smiled before she continued. "Don't be long. The grill's on. Dinner is just about to be served. We are having a wonderful salad, barbecued ribs, chicken, and your favorite—corn on the cob and diced potatoes."

Samantha looked into her mother's face. Why was she reciting the menu? Usually, Cook decided what was for dinner and Samantha ate whatever it was. They all did. Except on her birthday. Then she was always consulted for her birthday dinner. What would she ask for this year? What she wanted right now was dinner in her room, in her bed, surrounded by the comfort of her pillows. Samantha liked the way her pillows felt next to her, soft and cool against her skin, always there to hold when she needed them. Then, there staring at her, was her mother's face. A face that had always been there for her. A face that had always represented safety and protection. And now a face of concern. Silent questions penetrating through each fine line.

"Who's coming to dinner?" Samantha asked, looking squarely at her mother, watching her expression intently. Lately, there had been so many things Samantha hadn't been clued in on she didn't trust even the smallest change in routine.

"No one, that I know of," Anne replied, puzzled. "Why

do you ask that?"

"Just wondered. Sounds like a lot of food to me."

"A lot of food? I don't think so. What difference does that make anyway? Your father requested barbecue and that's what we're having. Do you want Cook to make something else, is that what this is about?" Anne said gently. What was brewing in her daughter's mind now?

"No. Whatever. I'm just going to wash up and I'll be right down," Samantha said in a dismissive tone, shrugging off her mother's kiss and attempted hug. These days Samantha did not like anyone touching her, no matter who they were. Each time her parents kissed her, hugged her, or even patted her shoulder, she winced. She hoped they hadn't noticed. She couldn't help it. She did not want to be touched. It was as plain and simple as that; being left alone was good. Touching was bad.

Samantha's mind raced angrily as she watched her mother withdraw. When will they ever treat me like an adult? "She makes me feel like I'm two," Samantha uttered under her breath, as her mother closed the door.

Samantha stared at the warm water splashing fiercely onto the facecloth in the burgundy basin. The water mesmerized her, as the splashing droplets flung themselves in every direction; the intense sound rushing in her ears, clearing her mind, calming her fears. Samantha grabbed the cloth from the water and wrung it out, watching as the droplets fell in a stream, rendering the cloth limp. That's how she felt inside—like someone had squeezed her into a lifeless rag, after filling her with poison.

Samantha felt her knees weaken as she wiped the cloth on her face, looking in the mirror and seeing her face in pieces, parts at a time, covered partially with the cloth. She couldn't look at herself. She hated seeing her full reflection. She wanted to forget it.

As she scrubbed her face harder and harder, she did not notice her skin turn red, she only felt the shower. It was next to her. Before she knew it, she had her clothes off and was under the pulsing of its warm spray. She had lost all concept of time and had no hunger. She only wanted the quiet hibernation of her room, the absolute solitude of her shower.

"Samantha? What are you doing in there?" Anne asked

her daughter in a stern yet concerned voice, her knuckles rapping loudly on the bathroom door. "Can I come in?"

"Mom?" Samantha said, briskly turning the crystal and gold faucet, watching as the water dwindled into droplets, forming a tiny rivulet that made her feel alive; well.

"Yes. Samantha, come out of there or I'm coming in."

"Really, Mom, you are so dramatic! I was just taking a shower. I told you I'd be down soon."

"Soon has passed dear. It's time for dinner. You should have been at the table twenty minutes ago." Anne paused momentarily to listen. "Are you feeling all right?" She opened the door.

"Yes. Quit asking me that!" Samantha said, sharply, uncoiling the towel from the turban form she had wrapped around her dripping locks.

"Sam, honey, I only ask because I care. I see you suffering and I don't know why. You're alone all the time. I worry. You're my only daughter. I always thought we could talk; we had each other in a house full of men," Anne looked directly at her daughter, hoping her words, even a few of them, had made some kind of sense, some impact on Samantha. Seeing her emotionless face, she knew they had evaporated immediately.

"Mom, you worry too much. I am fine," Samantha said, too stiffly, in a stretched voice with each word carefully annunciated. Catching her tone as it rang inside her like a harsh bell and seeing her mother's face looking as if it would break into tears, she added in a hushed childlike tone, "If you must know, I'm having my period. I didn't realize it right away, and I had a little accident." Samantha looked at her mother, one tear sliding down her cheek. Samantha hoped her mother would think her wet face was from her dripping hair. Seconds passed in what felt like moments to Samantha. She watched as her mother's face instantly changed from concern to understanding; woman to woman. Samantha could feel it, her mother's inward sigh of relief. It had worked. Anne, with every sense of motherhood and womanhood, bonded with her at the instant she heard the word "period". The fate of every woman and an experience only another woman would understand without further explanation. Anne felt relieved, and understanding immediately crossed her face. Ruined panties, cramps and nausea! She was grateful it was nothing more than her monthly cycle. Anne remembered not being able to talk about things like her period with her own mother.

Immediately, Anne understood Samantha's awkward embarrassment about her cycle and having had an accident, not knowing when it would come. She herself had been irregular at Sam's age. She wondered why Samantha had never mentioned being irregular before. Oh well, at least she hasn't asked to go on the pill like so many other girls her age! For that, she was grateful. Then, compassionately, despite her agreement with Travis to make Samantha eat with them and monitor her moods and intake of food closely, she found herself saying, "Would you like a tray of food sent to your room?"

"Really? That'd be great. I'd really like to get into my nightshirt and crawl into bed," Samantha said meekly, with honest sincerity.

"Just this once, it'll be fine. But you better eat everything Cook puts on your plate! And if you feel better, after you eat, get your robe on and come down and have dessert with us, okay?" Anne patted Samantha's robe-covered shoulder, gently kissing her before turning to leave the room.

"Thanks, Mom."

"Hope you feel better, dear."

Samantha quickly pulled on her nightshirt and crawled into bed. She took with her the list of legal words from her skirt pocket before she placed her skirt into the dry cleaning hamper. The list, however nonsensical to her, was a comfort. She needed to keep it with her, near to her. It was her insurance policy for getting herself back.

"Miss Samantha?"

She heard a deep voice from outside her door followed by a quiet rapping.

"Yes, Hyrum. You can come in."

"Thank you miss. Where would you like your food?"

"Here next to my bed."

"Hope you feelin' better." Hyrum said in his usual gentlemanly manner.

"Thanks. Uh, would you mind if I bring down the tray in the morning? I want to sleep after I eat, and I don't want anyone to wake me. I'm really very tired."

"As you wish, miss. I'll tell Cook not to expect the dishes

till mornin'. She won't like it one bit, but I can handle her fur you."

"Thanks. Tell her the meal is just what I needed." Samantha said. She felt as if she were five, staying home sick from kindergarten, requiring sympathy and care from all those in the house.

"Don't worry, miss. Now, you get yourself better!"

And, with that, she was alone. As much as she wanted to eat, the aroma of freshly barbecued animal flesh made her feel sick. Lies were always hard to swallow. She picked at the food, still steaming from the coals. She made an honest attempt at eating it. When she could no longer look at it or smell it, she took the shredded morsels of food and flushed them down the toilet in large clumps, watching mindlessly as they spun, disappearing into a whirlpool. Clean water refilled the basin, as if the food had never been there. Everything fit but the bones and the corncob. It looked as if she had eaten almost everything. Quickly, she gulped down the large glass of chocolate milk, as if to wash away the lump of guilt. Then, carefully placing the silver cover back over the emptied plate, she removed it from her view.

Downstairs, Anne was having a difficult time explaining to Travis why their daughter refused to join them for dinner.

"I don't care what's wrong with her! She could just as easily sit at the table with us. What's the difference whether she sits in bed and eats or at the table and eats? If she's so sick she can't make it down the stairs, then we should take her to the hospital. Maybe they could tell us what's really going on."

Anne sat still, watching her husband's face turn red with anger. She knew better than to argue or respond right away. Pausing for a moment, acting as if she agreed with him, she quietly nodded her head. "I agree with you. I'd like to know what's really going on, but we can't push. As much as we want to keep her as our little girl, she will be in college in a few weeks and on her own. We have to respect her privacy and give her room to make her own mistakes and handle her own problems." Anne paused with an arched brow. "Believe me, it's as hard on me as it is on you. We were always so close. You had the boys and I had Sam."

Travis listened patiently as Anne's voice trailed. He hadn't meant to be so hard on her. He just wanted everything to be in its place. He liked order and discipline. He liked to know where he stood. He didn't like games. He didn't like silence. Sam's silence was deafening. It was a cry for help, but she continued to ignore their attempts to help her. She looked so pale and forlorn all of the time. What had happened to his sweet, innocent, outgoing daughter?

"I know. I'm sorry. I just feel helpless, watching her put you through whatever teenage problem she's having. Haven't we always been there for our children, for Sam?" Travis said, looking at his wife, putting his hand over hers.

"Yes. That's why it is so frustrating. But really, this time she wasn't feeling well. I didn't think it would harm her to stay in bed. She promised to eat and maybe come down for dessert."

"That's why I love you. You give everyone the benefit of the doubt. She won't eat. She won't come down for dessert. But if you say she is sick, then I'll believe you. I trust your assessment, and God knows, I don't know anything about female cycles and problems, so I really shouldn't judge her. Boys are so much easier," Travis sighed, speaking softly, not wanting to upset Anne and ruin their evening together. As they continued to discuss Samantha, he calmed down enough to eat his own dinner.

"What about Skyler?" Anne quizzed him suddenly, a light in her eyes as if she had an idea.

"What about him?"

"He's been wonderful with Samantha. At least he can get her out of the house, dressed in matching clothes and makeup. Could it be she just needs another adult to talk to? Maybe you could talk to him? Find out if she's said anything?" Anne's voice sounded hopeful as she appealed to him with a smile.

"Skyler has a busy caseload and a few trials coming up. He doesn't need to entertain our temperamental adolescent daughter in his free time or act as our spy!" Travis said knitting his brows as he carefully rolled his corn in butter. Skyler had quite a reputation with women, and Travis didn't need his daughter being adversely influenced by him. It was something men didn't talk to their wives about for fear of implication. Women didn't understand these things. It wasn't that he lied about Skyler to his wife, he just omitted parts about him that were private. As long as Skyler's behavior and choice in women didn't affect the firm, there was no reason for anyone to talk about it. In fact, he believed some of the partners held Skyler higher in their esteem because of the women he caroused with. Skyler reminded them of their potent youth, and it made for interesting conversation and harmless speculation. After all, Skyler wasn't married. Up until now his friendship with Samantha had seemed harmless and it did seem to do her some good for whatever reason, but beyond Samantha meeting his brother on Tuesday, Travis's instinct said no. Looking up suddenly from his plate, he saw his wife's face turn cold, her mood somber.

Pushing aside his own bias against Skyler, Travis sighed and added, as if to convince them both, "Okay, if it makes you feel better, I could assign someone to help him out for the next few weeks so he could get Samantha out of the house and maybe introduce her to some people her own age at the club. He knows everyone, and that way, it wouldn't be like *us* forcing people upon her. Maybe that's what she needs, to meet new people."

"Exactly. Thank you, dear." Anne said, again smiling warmly at her husband. She knew him. She just hoped her plan worked.

Samantha couldn't sleep. As she thought about the fourth of July, she remembered she had to find something to wear or else go out and buy something. She didn't feel like shopping these days and had been complacent about letting her mother pick out her clothes whenever they went. She didn't even bother to look in the fitting room mirror, but simply judged by her mother's expression. What mother liked, Samantha bought. Usually her mother's taste was pretty good. She was always on top of fashion and was careful about Samantha dressing conservatively. Too conservative for Samantha's taste, usually. But lately, Samantha preferred it that way. Clothes didn't matter to her now as much as they did in high school, before . . . She couldn't think about it. She wouldn't think about it. She'd simply try to find something to wear in her massive closet.

Samantha pushed aside one hanger after the next. Nothing seemed suitable. She couldn't bring herself to try anything on. She didn't want to look at herself in the mirror, and she couldn't even admit it to herself. She just summed up her mood as going through what Emily would have called "the uglies"—and then, with that in the open, they would have laughed and made hair and nail appointments and maybe scheduled a massage to cheer themselves up. Their mothers had passed on a pampering tradition they learned to take full advantage of at an early age.

Those days felt like a lifetime away. Samantha shut her closet door. She needed Emily. She couldn't wait for her return. Only six more weeks. She would talk to her then. Emily would be there for her birthday party. She would have to hold out until then, until Emily could help her out. She couldn't trust anyone else.

Frustrated, Samantha again sat in bed, against the fluffy pillows, filing her nails so short her hands looked like those of a young boy. She didn't care. She didn't want to fuss with them anymore. The rhythmic scratching of the emery board against her nails mesmerized her, pacifying her anxious worry over meeting Skyler and his brother. Slowly her thoughts turned to his voice. When would he call? When would she hear his voice? That voice. It was somehow relaxing she had to admit, but why? It had been frightening to her just a few days ago. Even now she should be frightened, and instead she heard his words over and over; "Relax, relax." They soothed her.

Samantha closed her eyes, repeating the words. She wanted to relax. She needed to relax. She was in the safety and solitude of her own room. No one could harm her here. She repeated the words again. "Relax, relax . . ."

Relaxing on cue, now on the verge of sleep, she waited for the faces. The pieces of faces. The pieces that comforted her; that kept her mind occupied night after night, playing the game, trying to match them up. Where were they? She wanted to play.

The illusion kept flowing, funneling in all directions, pooling into a paralyzing confusion that led Samantha finally into a black sleep that was anything but contented.

She was alone. She didn't want to be alone. Where had they all gone? She looked, squinting her eyes to make her vision sharper; to find the hidden details in the dark. Was this a new game? She turned slowly around and around. And then she felt it. His touch, warm against her flesh. It was kind and gentle and protective.

No, no! No one could touch her. She watched herself and shuddered, but he did touch her again. Cold. She felt isolated and so cold. Where had all the people gone? Where were the familiar parts, the parts she could make whole? The ears. Were the missing parts somewhere with the missing ears?

She didn't want to be alone. She needed to be close to someone. She wanted to be touched, to be desired. Isn't that what every girl wanted? Shouldn't she want it too? *Seventeen, Glamour, Cosmopolitan.* The cover girls rushed by her. They didn't stop to see her. They didn't stop to talk. They didn't notice her, not one bit, not at all. She was alone again. And then she felt it. The familiar touch. The warm voice. "Relax, relax . . ." And she felt warmed, like the sun was rising, but it remained dark. And in the darkness, the sun cast a shadow; a familiar shadow. A likeness known to her.

Relief. She wasn't alone. It was him. Her skin flushed warm, but with goose bumps. Her mind raced, trying to remember the bad things he represented; what he was. She stood alone, looking for another familiar face. But there was no one else, just him. Skyler was there, smiling, staring as if looking right through her; as if he could feel all of her emotion and erase them all at once. The bad things he had done to her. She suddenly understood them; they had a purpose. She looked closely at him. Was he near or far? She could not tell. She squinted. He was waving her towards him, and then he stopped. She knew it was her move; her turn. She knew he wanted her to make the move forward toward him. Her move, her choice. Samantha stood still, fear and pleasure running together through her body. Which was which? She couldn't decide. Her feelings were undistinguishable from one another.

She reminded herself he was the devil-man. But the flow of negative thoughts weren't fast enough to keep up with the glow of his speckled green eyes, laughing, smiling admiringly at her. His perfect white teeth flashing against his full lips and tanned, flawless skin. The eyes somehow encapsulated her, made her like him more. To want him? She saw herself reflected in those effervescent green eyes. She hadn't seen her own full reflection in such a long time. She seemed older and prettier. She felt confidence glide in and out of her, feeling as if she could somehow read his mind. She liked what she saw in his reflection of her. She had no other reflection. She saw herself as a woman in his eyes. He treated her as an equal, as an adult. No one else had. No one else did. Had she misjudged him?

Wasn't what happened between them partially her fault? She shouldn't have been drinking. She led him on; she must have. This beautiful man couldn't really have hurt her. No wonder he got angry and blackmailed her.

He vanished.

She looked around and around. She saw a tape, parts of a tape, then the whole tape. What about the tape? Had he taped her to protect her; to show her he cared? What did it all mean? Why was she alone again?

The faces suddenly appeared, the familiar parts. But they were different—colder somehow. They were not smiling, the parts floating by. The ears were still missing and the pieces were smaller than she had remembered, except for the mouths. They were too large, too stern. She did not like them anymore. She did not want to play. She ran, but her feet did not move. She couldn't get away. Oh, no, it was happening again . . .

"Samantha? Wake up, you're dreaming. Samantha? Dear what is it? I'm right here." Anne said, holding her daughter's shoulders down until the tossing stopped.

"Mom? What are you doing here? I didn't hear you," Samantha said abruptly, her vision not focused yet, surprised to see her mother sitting on the edge of her bed.

"What in heaven's name were you dreaming about?"

"Was I dreaming? I don't remember. I don't know," Samantha said, closing her eyes again, speaking so softly her mother wasn't sure she had answered. Samantha didn't want her mother to worry, but she needed her to leave. She wanted to be alone. Staying as still as a possum, she didn't respond to any further prodding from her mother. Anne, seeing Samantha was calmed and asleep again, straightened the covers and left the dark room, closing the door quietly behind her. Shaking her head in contemplation of her daughter's continual nightmare, she headed for bed and the comfort of her husband's shoulder.

Samantha immediately opened her eyes in the darkness after hearing her mother retreating to her own room. What time was it? She peered up at Minnie's fluorescent face. The arms pointed to 11:47. Had she really slept so long? She tried to recall her dream. No, it was more like a nightmare. Piecing as much of the dream together as she could remember, Samantha unconsciously moved her hand toward her head and began rubbing her temples to ward off her pounding forehead. Samantha never had trouble with headaches. Now she had them daily.

Tossing the straightened sheets from her warm flesh, she retrieved the box with her ample supply of sleeping pills, aspirin and other assorted medication she had pilfered from her mother's medicine cabinet. Sleeping pills and something with codeine in it ought to do it. As she swallowed the pills, she felt momentarily as if they would come back up whole. Clenching the ceramic counter, she averted her eyes from the mirror and felt the nausea go away almost immediately. Her eyes darted away from her own reflection, despite the nearness of the looking-glass. Even her unconscious knew she was repulsive and ugly.

At that thought, the dream came flooding back. Skyler. What did he see in her? Why would he want her—a pretty girl who had faded into an ugly duckling. A grim truth, she snickered, not a Grimm Tale.

Now, back in the safety of her own bed, she struggled not to close her eyes. She was uncomfortable with the dreams. They no longer felt safe. The phone rang dully. Her head still pounding, the pain moving backward, she felt her hand grab the receiver. As the medicine took a hold of her, she felt she was inside a stranger's body. She could cope that way. It was a nice feeling. She put her lips close to the receiver.

"Yes?"

"Hi, baby. How are you tonight? You sound awfully sexy with that tired raspy voice. Were you thinking of me?"

"I . . ." She didn't want to admit she *was* thinking of him, sort of. But her mind didn't feel like her own. It felt dull and heavy, oddly relaxed. She couldn't filter the right words. Slowly Samantha heard herself utter, "I was just going to sleep."

"Alone, I hope." Skyler said in a low muffled voice, almost as if he wasn't supposed to be on the phone.

"Mmm." Samantha answered, barely hearing the question, slowly relinquishing her body to sleep.

"I'll see you Tuesday. Dream about me, sweetie, because I'll be in your dreams as you are in mine."

Samantha didn't consciously hear what he said, nor did she feel her hand instinctively hang up the receiver. Her head lay heavy on the pillow, her mind in total blackness, the pills blotting both reality and pain.

Skyler quietly hung up the receiver too, his lips reaching to the deaf ear on the pillow next to his. His mind remembering Samantha's soft voice. Feeling his quiet warmth, the girl awoke and rolled over toward the handsome man who had paid for the room, providing her a roof over her head a warm shower in the morning. It was the first night in a week she would sleep all night in a bed. He promised he would leave and she could have the whole room to herself. Her body was a small price to pay for clean sheets and water. She shouldn't have run away, but there was no turning back. She couldn't go home, she told herself, as she again opened her body for the man who paid for the room.

"Samantha, my Samantha." The runaway heard the name whispered softly in her ear over and over again as his hands groped and probed her flesh. She didn't care what he called her, as long as he paid for the room and left her breakfast money on the nightstand. As her streetwise body willingly reacted to his, she wondered who Samantha was and why he was not with her.

Chapter 12

Pushing away the warm sheets with determination to have a better stress-free day, Samantha bolstered herself with positive thoughts. She wouldn't let anything get to her. She would be pleasant and smiling and happy. She would make it through breakfast and then retreat to her room, without any problem. She had to convince everyone she felt much better so they would leave her alone. She would have to eat and smile and laugh and talk. But, standing in the shower, it seemed an impossible task to her. Over and over, her mind kept repeating the words "you can do this. Relax, relax."

Samantha's hands moved slowly over her body, rubbing the thick cloth hard into her skin, creating a camouflage of lathering white bubbles over any part of her within her vision. The lather made her white and pure. It made her smell new and fresh and clean, unlike herself. Relax, relax. And then she turned under the spray and instantly the whiteness disappeared, without her wanting it to.

Stepping into her familiar robe, she snatched a towel, deliberately letting the cloth hide her reflection in the steam-covered glass. She didn't care what she looked like. She looked fine. She looked as she had always looked. As much as things had changed, much had remained the same.

Dressed in a lightweight cotton sweater and a long denim skirt, Samantha bounded down the stairs, her hair, still damp, bouncing at her back behind a thick headband. Her gait was carefully designed to be an outward demonstration of her improved mood and overall healthy feeling meant to fool her parents and maybe even herself. She'd been acting happy, or at least contented, a lot lately. She could do it for a while longer. She needed to stall, to buy time. She could be herself in seven weeks, after she left for school and her new life. Leaving would be a relief!

"Samantha. I'm glad you decided to grace us with your presence," Travis said sternly to his daughter, as he inspected her face.

"Oh, Dad. I just didn't feel well. I'm sorry I missed you at dinner," Samantha said. She averted her eyes and bent to brush a kiss on his cheek. "I'm fine now, honestly." She couldn't meet his eyes. He'd know she was lying. Avoidance was the solution. She kissed him as much as it churned her stomach to touch his cheek.

"I want you to go for a physical. You've been sick too often this year. I want you to have a full check-up. If you don't call the doctor first thing Monday, I will. Your mother has a first-rate doctor. You are to see him."

"Give me a break! I feel fine. Really it was nothing."

"Samantha." His voice was strong and stern and frightful. Samantha looked at her plate. All she could do was agree.

"Fine. I'll call first thing. But I want to see a woman doctor. Not a man." Samantha was surprised to hear her own voice use such an assertive tone. Anne and Travis looked at their daughter in astonishment. The silence was uncomfortable and, in it, Samantha's mind floundered for a reprieve under the discomfort of their stares.

"I mean, okay. I'll call," Samantha said softly, filling the silence, feeling like an ungrateful, scolded three-year-old.

"Fine, you do that. Anne, see that she does." With that, Travis removed himself from the table, throwing his stiffly starched napkin from his lap onto his half emptied plate with such force his English muffin was pushed onto the brightly flowered tablecloth.

As the women listened to the heavy footsteps moving briskly away, becoming faint, and then disappearing through a door, Anne looked at her daughter as if she had been slapped by her. "Well, what did you want him to do? He is very worried about you. We both are. We don't know what to do anymore. You don't eat. You have nightmares. You don't go out unless we force you. We don't know what is wrong."

Samantha stared at her mother. She wanted to cry. She wanted to tell her. Most of all, she wanted to feel. She waited for emotion to filter through her body. It did not come. She heard only the pounding of her head. Another headache. She had become accustomed to having them. They were familiar and reminded her that even though she could not find the emotion she had once had, she could feel pain. Wasn't a headache a feeling? Wasn't a feeling an emotion? Samantha, lost in her own thoughts, continued to stare blindly at her mother.

Anne stared back at her daughter, hoping to evoke a response, some emotion. Any emotion! There was none. It was as if Samantha had gone away and her corpse had remained behind, decaying visibly in front of them one cell at a time.

"You will make that appointment. Dr. Sugars has a new partner, a woman. I don't recall her name. She's about thirty-five and I think you'll like her. In fact, you don't have to make the appointment, I will. I want to go with you."

"You can't! I'm too old to have you in with me. I'll call. I'll go. But please, don't go with me," Samantha pleaded, her mind racing.

"You heard your father. You are going. And," Anne looked squarely into her daughter's face, not letting her avert her eyes, "I am going."

Samantha watched her mother's face, not wanting to hear the words, not wanting to fight. "Fine, but I see the doctor alone or I'm not going."

"Fine. But we will talk to the doctor together after the checkup. That's final, or I'll ask your father to clear his schedule and join us."

"Fine." Samantha knew there was no further point in negotiating. Her mother had cut her best deal, and if she didn't take it now, she would lose and lose badly.

"Fine." Anne knew her daughter would obey and not challenge her further. She had trained her well in the art of female negotiations, and the unspoken words between them settled the issue.

Like mother, like daughter. They sat still in silence, as servants occasionally moved in and out, clearing dishes, adding fresh coffee. A lot of movement for nothing. Samantha stared at her plate; a lot of waste for nothing. She felt nothing—nothing good anyway. Her only conclusions were distrust, betrayal and dismay. She felt like a cornered animal with nowhere to turn. She had to eat a few bites, or she would encounter her mother's bitter mood again. Twice in one day was more than she could take. "Relax, relax." The words kept humming in her mind as she pictured a massage in the tight places in her body. Her muscles began letting down just a little bit. Just enough to move her hand from her lap, to her fork, to her plate, to her mouth and back again. She didn't really taste the food. She just swallowed hard and repeated. She acted as she had done so many times before, as she had become accustomed to.

Her mother watched and followed suit, eating small bites in unison with Samantha, silently counting the forkfuls, watching her swallow. Anne didn't really care how long it took, she would watch Samantha eat until she finished her plate, until they finished their plates together. Anne felt it was in her daughter's best interest that she take notes and look for patterns of behavior, piecing them together like a detective. She had to try to help her daughter; whatever was bothering Samantha. It must be more than just normal teenage blues and more than leaving home for college. Like a spy on a mission, Anne operated with a secret agenda as she added Samantha's behavior to her mental notebook, as she had become accustomed to.

Like mother, like daughter.

Chapter 13

Anne, increasingly alarmed, headed for the phone in her home office earlier than she would have liked. She flipped through her personal rolodex of family, friends, business and personal associates until she found Dr. Gerald Fulgrum Sugars, Obstetrics and Gynecology. She punched in the phone number.

"Good morning, Community OB/GYN."

"Yes. This is Mrs. Travis Armstrong—Anne Armstrong. I'd like to speak to Dr. Sugars."

"Is this an emergency?"

"Yes. I mean, well, no. No, it is not an emergency . . ."

Impatiently, the seasoned secretary interrupted. "Dr. Sugars is at St. Mary's. He had an emergency delivery. Is there something I can help you with, or would you prefer to discuss the matter with the nurse?"

"I—we need an appointment. As soon as possible, for our daughter."

"Is she having a problem where she would need to be seen immediately? I could see if another doctor could fit her in."

Anne was not in the mood for word games. After the long weekend with Samantha's mood swings and Travis' tantrums, she just wanted what she wanted without questioning.

"Well yes, actually, I do want her to be seen by another doctor. Dr. . . . I'm sorry, I can't remember her name. The female doctor who recently joined the group."

"Yes, that would be Dr. Tessa. What did you say your daughter wanted this appointment for?"

"She hasn't been feeling well. She also needs a yearly physical, as soon as possible."

"We are booking yearly exams about two months—"

"I'd like to get her in as soon as possible. Is there anything today?"

"Is she sick? Usually we don't schedule yearly exams—"

Anne cut in. "I'm very worried about my daughter, and I can't wait for her to be seen in two months. She hasn't been feeling well lately and she'll be moving out of state to go to college. Please, if I could just talk to Dr. Sugars, I'm sure he would agree she needs to be seen."

The secretary, experienced in dealing with patients, knew Anne would not take no for an answer. "I'll let you speak with the nurse, and she'll see if your daughter can be fit into the doctor's schedule."

"Thank you," Anne said relieved to be transferred to someone who would help.

As she placed the ivory receiver in the cradle, she stared at the date and time of the appointment written in her appointment diary. She had accomplished only part of her goal. The next step was to tell Samantha it had been made, and the hardest step was to take her there. Even as concerned as she was, Anne felt uncomfortable forcing her daughter to go to the doctor, especially a gynecologist, at almost eighteen years of age.

Where had the time gone? Anne sat quietly, remembering the years. She would miss her daughter. She knew instinctively their relationship would never be the same after she left for college, after the world gave her innocent child an education her parents could not. She stared at the family pictures on the shelf above her desk, remembering, relaxing, finally smiling. Her coffee had turned cool. Slowly, deliberately, she poured a fresh stream into her china cup. She had done her job as a mother as best as she could. She hadn't been a perfect mother, but she'd tried her best. A sudden sadness pierced her. She sighed deeply. Reality grasped her as it had not before. At their ages, her children had to take some responsibility for their problems and their own happiness, and she had to give Samantha the same room she gave the boys. She owed that to her. Maybe Travis forcing her to see the doctor was wrong. Maybe they should trust Samantha. After all, she would tell them if she was sick. She always had in the past. Why shouldn't they trust her now? Maybe they should give Samantha the appointment information and let her decide if she needed to go, without their pressure. Her reflections soothed her. Maybe that was the right decision. She knew it was the decision she felt most comfortable with.

She wanted to trust her daughter and her own intuition.

# # #

The house was quiet; it was almost nine. Samantha lay still in her bed. She had been awake for hours, listening, wishing she could sleep. How would she avoid the doctor's appointment and her parents? She didn't want another day like yesterday. She was short on excuses. She couldn't tell them she was sick. She couldn't stay in her room packing or reading or cleaning. She couldn't think of any excuse she hadn't already used too many times. She could not be seen by a doctor and, if she was, she could not have the doctor talk to her parents. Surely the doctor could tell she'd had an abortion. Surely the doctor would tell her parents. Then what would she do? She shuddered at the thought. She couldn't let it happen.

As she pulled her thinning body from her sheets, she blindly grabbed her robe and headed for the shower. She had another headache. What next? She asked herself sarcastically, as she swallowed a handful of white pills and stepped under the hot shower. Her mind raced as she pictured the worst scenario. She couldn't let anyone see her. She couldn't let anyone find out. She couldn't tell Skyler her parents wanted her to go to the doctor. She would have to take care of this. But how? She calmed as she repeated the words, "Relax, relax. Breathe deeply. Relax."

Then, almost at once, it came to her. If they wouldn't change, she would. She could be the perfect daughter they missed. She'd gotten used to acting. She could be bright and chipper and, most of all, believable. She could blame her moods on leaving for school and missing her family and Emily. Emily would soon be home, so her mood shift was perfect timing. Yes, that was the solution. Be perfect. That's what they want. That's what they expect. And that's what they'll get.

Samantha desperately reviewed her behavior and her parents expectations and made a conscious effort to change everything at once. As she dressed, she made sure her clothes were the new ones her mother had picked out and her hair was perfectly brushed and sprayed into long impeccable curls, teased around her face and shoulders to give her a fuller look. Her makeup was flawless.

She forced herself to look in the mirror with a critical eye. She noticed every detail. She saw in her mind's eye what they wanted. The perfect daughter. The perfect illusion. She reached into the familiar drawer containing her makeup. She applied it all, just as she had been taught; foundation, powder, blush, eye shadow, liner, mascara. Her makeup looked natural. It hid her sallow, thinning skin and dark circles. No one would know. Her carefully clad body would be the perfect facade. As she headed for breakfast, she knew she was entering the first of many roles she'd have to play and the proof would be in achieving the result she wanted. No doctor's appointment.

The breakfast table, usually set and perfectly arranged, had already been cleared. The room was empty. It looked more like a showcase room for the cover of *House Beautiful* magazine than a place where people gathered to eat. Samantha looked around the familiar breakfast room. The only thing she liked about it was the tall bowed window looking out onto the rose beds and flowered shrubs. It was a peaceful view, quite the opposite from the meals they ate together as a family.

Samantha walked quietly into the kitchen to ask Cook where everyone was. Cook usually knew everything about her family, although Samantha didn't know much about her. In fact, she pondered, what was her real first name? She couldn't remember. For as long as she had been able to sound out words, she had called her Cook, because that's what she did. She didn't mind everyone calling her Cook.

"Good mornin', Miss Sam. I expect you want your breakfast?" Cook said, looking at the thin girl.

"Sure. But first, can you tell me where everyone is?"

"You know your dad is at the office and your mother, she ate her breakfast in the study this mornin'. Said she had some work to catch up on."

"Oh. I'll eat a little later. I'm going to go talk to my mother."

"No, Miss Sam, I'm under orders to make you breakfast and watch you eat it. How 'bout some coffee and juice to start?"

"Great," Samantha said sarcastically, not meaning to insult Cook, but feeling as if her parents had invisibly slapped her by asking the servants, who usually hung about in silence like wallpaper, to interfere and monitor her.

"What else can I fix, Miss?"

"Cereal, toast. I don't really care, whatever you have," Samantha said, as she pulled out a bar stool from underneath the long kitchen counter and sat staring into the juice and coffee that had appeared instantly.

Samantha sat in silence, eating everything on her plate as she had been instructed to. If she had been asked what she had eaten for breakfast, she couldn't have responded honestly, because she didn't remember. The food all tasted the same to her. All she knew was it was hard to swallow and she had to keep shoveling each morsel into her mouth and down her throat, without the slightest hint of pain or dislike on her face. Well, she thought, as she listened to Cook hum a gospel tune, the acting had already begun and her first viewer had believed her so much, after she had swallowed only a few small bites, Cook barely gave her a watchful glance. Absentmindedly, after Samantha had played with her food long enough, Cook, still humming, whisked her plate away, swiftly cleaning it and loading it into the dishwasher.

It was time to approach her mother, although the idea made her feel somewhat queasy. It must be nerves. Relax, relax, she told herself, as she quietly tapped her knuckles on her mother's office door.

"Mom? Can I come in?"

"Yes, dear. Come in. Have a seat."

Anne watched her daughter enter the room and sit. She was very thin, but she looked different, better somehow. Anne wondered what had changed.

"Mom," Samantha said, drawing a calming breath, "I'm sorry about yesterday. I didn't mean to be a brat. Is Dad still mad at me?"

"No one is mad at you. We care about you. We're worried about you, that's all." Anne looked sincerely into Samantha's eyes as she spoke. "If there was something really wrong, you'd tell us, wouldn't you?"

"Mom, haven't I always told you everything? There's nothing wrong. Really. I'm feeling much better, and I think it's because of all that sleep I've had in the last few days. Maybe

I had a virus. I even woke up hungry this morning, and I ate everything Cook put on my plate. You can ask her," Samantha said, not letting on she knew Cook was acting as her parents' spy.

"That's great, dear. I suspected as much. But, I did make you that appointment with the new female doctor in Dr. Sugar's office. Everyone likes her. She's young, and being that she is a female, maybe you can talk to her, if you need to. You know what I'm talking about here. In case there ever really is anything you aren't comfortable talking about with your father or me."

"But Mom, I'm fine. I don't need to see any doctor. Besides, I'm going away to school in a few weeks. Can't I wait till then? I'll need to have a doctor in Michigan anyway, in case I get sick. Couldn't I wait until I go to Michigan? I really don't want to see two doctors and I'm old enough to go by myself." Samantha tried to sound sincere with a casual tone of voice but she couldn't help feeling nervous inside and transparent on the outside. She tried not to sound as if she were pleading, begging. Samantha looked at her mother's disconcerting face and instantly felt as though her breakfast had landed in her chest, not in her stomach.

"Well, you have a point. The appointment is in one week. If you can convince your father, and if you feel good all week, then I'll cancel it. If not, we go," Anne said sternly, in a tone her daughter would take as final and would not challenge further. Staring at her as if she could see right through her, she continued.

"And that includes eating. I want to see you eat good meals. And, if there are any more episodes of illness of any kind, you are going that same day to the doctor. I don't want you off in another state, far from home, sick. Is that understood?"

"Yes, Mom," Samantha said jumping to her feet, relieved. Bending over, she kissed her mother lightly on her cheek. "Thanks."

Skipping up the steps to her room as if on top of the world, Samantha entered the solitude of her room and headed straight for the bathroom. Her breakfast was too much for her shrunken stomach. One look into the toilet basin forced her instantly to bend, as her mouth deposited her breakfast into the wet porcelain. Afterwards, she sprayed the room with disinfectant to cover up the odor, brushed her teeth and reapplied her lipstick. She couldn't take any chances. She had to look and act perfect from now on. She had to act as if every movement was being recorded and scrutinized. Samantha felt like a puppet whose strings were being pulled by two masters. Her parents and Skyler. There was no room for what she wanted, for what she really felt. Everywhere she turned, she was being directed, told where to go, what to eat, how to act. She didn't like it, but she was beginning to master it. She almost believed in her charade herself. A few more days and maybe she would totally believe her actions to be of her own free will. That wasn't all bad, she shrugged. At least she wouldn't be lying.

Chapter 14

Turning in front of the mirror, Samantha was pleased with her appearance. In honor of the fourth of July and in careful preparation for the evening fireworks, she chose royal blue shorts with a matching red, white, and blue polo shirt and flat white canvas shoes. In her hair, she wore a wide red headband pushed forward enough to give her hair a fluffy loose look, letting animated curls hang in a delicate but abundant frame around her face. Her makeup was applied carefully, as if a professional artist had painted the face of a porcelain doll. She looked radiantly beautiful, yet like a delicate flower that would wilt if one touched it.

Samantha tried to pay attention to every detail. She put herself in her parents' roles and imagined all of the things they would inspect about her. Her mother would check her clothes and makeup. Her father, her mood, tone and mannerisms. She had to avoid being forced to go to the doctor, regardless of what she had to do, even if it meant being nice to Skyler. She had been lucky her father usually gave in when both she and her mother wanted and agreed to something. And, although he had put up a fight, they had convinced him she didn't need to go to a doctor, she had a virus, coupled with female problems and she really was fine now.

Travis begrudgingly agreed, but told her he would keep a careful eye on her. Samantha knew that meant more spying on her. Her father would ask Skyler for a detailed report of their evening. She didn't want to give Skyler even the slightest opportunity to complain about her. Besides, she rationalized, they would be spending the evening with Skyler's brother and girlfriend. It would be fun to talk about Michigan State and how different life was in Michigan. She wouldn't be alone with Skyler, so why worry, she rationalized, swallowing more pills for the headache she felt coming on. She slipped a few more pills in the small white bag slung over her shoulder, just in case. Samantha rubbed her temples, repeating the words that had become second nature to her. "Relax, you can do this. You can pull it off. Relax, relax."

Samantha had begun to worry about the frequency of her headaches. She had to get rid of these headaches. They came out of nowhere and they were getting more intense. She couldn't tell her parents about her headaches because of her mother's ultimatum. Maybe, she rationalized, when she was on her own at Michigan State, she would see a doctor. A headache doctor wouldn't need to check the rest of her. Besides, a doctor in Michigan wouldn't know her family or her family doctors and, once she was eighteen, they couldn't call without her permission.

It was almost eight when Samantha heard the chime at the door announcing Skyler's arrival. Travis and Anne were seated in the den reading, waiting for Skyler to pick Samantha up so they could leave and join their group for dinner. Hyrum, in formal white gloves, showed Skyler into the den and left to summon Samantha from her room.

"Skyler, how are you this evening? We appreciate you taking Samantha with you. I hope we didn't intrude on any other plans you might have made," Travis said very graciously, in an apologetic tone.

"It's my pleasure. Samantha is a charming girl, and my brother loves to talk about Michigan. He'll appreciate a captive audience, and it will give me a chance to get to know his girlfriend. Are you two going out? I hope I haven't kept you waiting," he said in a friendly, businesslike tone.

"No. We're having dinner at the club. We'll be just on time. How's the Castriano preparation going?"

"Fine. We go in on Wednesday for preliminary motions. It looks really good. I think I can challenge much of the evidence against him before we even get into trial. The prosecutor is beginning to see it my way. In any event, I'm not worried," Skyler said, composed, exuding confidence.

"Skyler, you're a damn fine lawyer, and I know I don't have to say this to you, but remember, take nothing for granted. They've been after him for a long time, and I don't think they'll let go of any evidence that easily," Travis said, with just enough of a hint of father-knows-best in his tone to pull the comment off as advice from a friend rather than a boss.

"I'll keep that in mind. Samantha! You look very patriotic in your red, white and blue," Skyler said, dismissing Travis' well-intentioned comment and casually putting his hand out as all eyes turned to Samantha.

"Thanks," she said, shaking his hand. "Are you ready to go? I'm ready whenever you are. Sorry I wasn't downstairs when you arrived. I hope I haven't kept you waiting." She kept her voice bubbly and smiled widely, as if she were greeting one of her best friends.

Not waiting for Skyler's response, Travis inspected his daughter, relieved to see her so lighthearted for a change. "Nonsense. We've just been discussing Skyler's big criminal case, and I was thinking you might like to watch it. You had an interest in the criminal system, didn't you? And you know I would like you to consider law school." Travis' wishful thinking showed in his face and he knew it. He'd much rather convince his daughter to go to law school and become the first female partner in the firm than to see her cooped up all day with sick animals as a veterinarian. But, of course, he knew in his heart he would be happy with anything she chose, as long as she was happy. But then again, couldn't anyone find happiness with a law degree? She could marry a lawyer who could join the firm. The very idea made Travis smile.

"I'd really like to watch a criminal trial, but I've been so busy planning for school, I'm not sure I can right now. Can I let you know later, Dad?" Samantha turned to Skyler and smiled, not wanting to show the horror she felt by her father raising her request for information in front of Skyler. Well, that ends my ability to pursue knowledge of criminal trials. How would she explain her interest to Skyler? Surely he would ask her about it. Maybe he would insist she go. She didn't want to see him in action in the courtroom. The thought left her cold, coating her flesh with bumps like that of a freshly plucked chicken. How appropriate, she thought, looking down at her bumpy forearms, the chickenhearted becomes chicken-fleshed. She smiled at her own humor. That was all she could do. She didn't dare give away her feelings. From now on, anything that bothered her would be met with a smile. No one would guess. No one would know.

"I think you should make the time to go. Skyler is a brilliant defense attorney. He is the kind of attorney every aspiring lawyer should have the opportunity to watch."

Samantha stood silent, letting her smile answer instead of her voice as her eyes looked from Skyler to her father. She didn't know what to say, and nothing she could think of would solve her dilemma.

"Thank you for the compliment. I appreciate your confidence in me. It's getting late and we really had better get on our way. It won't be dark until around ten, so we're meeting for dinner before the fireworks. Ready?" Skyler said, turning to Samantha familiarly, as if they were siblings.

"Sure," Samantha said kissing her parents. "Bye! See you later. I have my keys."

"Have fun, dear," Anne said affectionately. Then turning to Travis, she added, "We'd better follow them out, dear, or we'll be late."

The ride to meet Tom and Stacey was pleasant. Samantha waited for Skyler to speak, to start a conversation, to look at her—anything. But he didn't. Samantha hated the silence between them. It gave her too much time to worry. She wanted to slip back deep into herself. She wanted to stay completely tucked away, hidden from view, hidden from anyone who could guess her secrets, who could expose her. But, the newly committed Samantha needed to fully take over; to exist in a carefree world that would accept her without question, without expectation. The new Samantha needed to take control of the situation now. Right now, before she slipped back.

Skyler was lost in his own thoughts. Samantha glanced at him out of the corner of her eyes. By rotating her eyes so far left her headache threatened to come back. She could see his profile without moving any other muscle, without him noticing her look. She had to think hard and find just the right thing to say. But what could she say? She pondered. Instead, she remained quiet, watching the bustle of the evening. People were everywhere. They seemed happy, contented. They belonged in the moment, a part of the universe around them. Samantha wanted that feeling. She was trying hard. To continue her charade, she had to keep up the facade. She had to submerge any negativity. Samantha was fearful any wrong mood, move or statement would get back to her father. She knew there would be an inquiry from him to Skyler. She was uncomfortable with what Skyler's response would be. She did not want him to know her parents wanted her to see a doctor. She did not want to explain anything to him, especially something that was between her and her parents.

Finally, she spoke, almost without thinking. "Where are Tom and Stacey? I thought you'd bring them over to meet my parents? I know Mom and Dad wanted to meet them."

"I thought about it, but I decided I didn't want to get delayed at your house. Earlier today your father mentioned to me they would be leaving around the same time I picked you up. It would have been rude for me to bring people over, knowing they were leaving, don't you agree?" Skyler said earnestly, not taking his eyes from the road.

"Oh. Of course, you're right."

"We are having lunch tomorrow with your father. You can join us if you like. I'm sure your father won't mind." Skyler said, still preoccupied.

"Who is we? Tom and Stacey and you and my father?"

"That's right."

"I don't think I can. I begin my computer classes on the new computer I just got for school. Father insisted I learn to use it properly, even though I did well in my computer classes at school. I don't think he'd appreciate it if I missed class to go out to lunch with the same people I saw the night before," Samantha said as if she really wished she could go. "You know how strict he is about commitment and follow-through on projects. I want to avoid any of those lectures; I've memorized them."

"I know what you mean. I've received a few of those lectures myself," Skyler said with a half-smile, turning to Samantha and, winking.

"He means well," he added, returning his eyes to the road.

Samantha looked at Skyler, surprised. She waited for him to continue, but Skyler again became silent and self-absorbed until they arrived at the restaurant.

Samantha watched as Skyler tipped the host for a better table on the upper patio. He really knew every place and person in town. She followed him outdoors, to a table so close to the railing, they had a view of the city below and the forest beyond. It was exquisite and unlike any place Samantha had ever been. The white linen tablecloth with the floral napkins and delicate centerpiece reminded her of home. She felt immediately comfortable, yet hesitant at the same time. They were confusing feelings for her and she was unsure what to say. How young and weak she felt next to this man who was so worldly, so knowledgeable, so strong. And yet, she knew he was also so evil. The devil-man. She had to remind herself of his bad qualities. She had to remind herself to relax. Relax, relax. She repeated the words over and over until her fluttering mind was awakened by the sound of Skyler greeting his brother.

"About time you two got here," Skyler said, grinning and standing up to shake the hand of his brother and kiss the cheek of the tanned, petite blue-eyed blonde attached to his arm.

Samantha stared as if she were seeing double, barely listening to the introductions. A smile pasted on her face, she couldn't get over the obvious resemblance between the brothers. Despite the decade of age difference and despite Tom's bleached blond hair that waved and hovered around his thick neck in tiny curls, the resemblance was remarkable. Tom's hair, though not pulled into a ponytail, looked as if it was frequently worn in one. His deeply tanned flesh, perfect teeth and laughing green eyes were cookie cutter copies of Skyler's. Tom's physique was that of an avid outdoors person. His hands, though well groomed, were not soft or perfectly manicured and buffed like Skyler's. They were instead those of a man who worked with his hands everyday.

Samantha began to fantasize about what Tom did with his hands. Tie knots on rope for sailboats, hunt wild game, build furniture, sculpt wood? She was taken with her curiosity. Tom was not what she had anticipated. Even his mannerisms were nearly identical to Skyler's. But as she listened to the brothers talk, she saw the real differences, not just in their hands. And she was relieved by the differences in the brothers. Tom was easygoing and effortlessly, immediately made everyone around him feel comfortable. This was unlike Skyler, who seemed so mature in his speech and mannerisms that, except for his good looks, people were not immediately open to him—unless they were as confident as he was, unless they were his equal. Samantha had always thought that was due to his training as a lawyer, something she was familiar with because of her father and brothers. In contrast, Tom was so casual and easygoing, Samantha immediately liked him. He acted as if he were within her age group, despite his being nearly twenty-four and having completed four years of college. He had one term left before attaining a master's degree, Samantha recalled.

In the presence of Tom and Stacey, Samantha was easily able to submerge her troubles, letting her new happy, bubbly self emerge. For a time, she almost forgot her hatred of Skyler and her problems. She loved listening to the differences between the northern and the southern states. Tom and Stacey had traveled quite a bit together, and they had wonderful stories about Michigan State and cross-country skiing, camping and hiking.

Stacey was as much an outdoors person as Tom. Her natural beauty allowed her to be free of makeup, and her clothes had clean, simple lines that underscored her open personality. She didn't wear a bra and had no self-consciousness about it. Her blonde hair was thick and straight and long, with a blunt cut that accented its movement around Stacey's finely featured face and lean body. She reminded Samantha of the flower children she'd seen pictures of from the sixties and seventies. Her long neck gracefully held a wide black ribbon that displayed a hanging gold peace sign. None of Samantha's friends dressed like Stacey; it was really different. It was really like college, like the pictures she and Emily had seen in *Cosmopolitan* and *Seventeen*. She hadn't really believed people were wearing those clothes the models wore because no one she knew would even think of wearing them. That was as good a reason as any to consider them. She looked at Stacey's sandaled feet and perfectly painted cherry toes. Now people she knew *were* wearing them. And so would she, she decided in an instant, smiling proudly to herself.

Her transformation to a college student had begun. Samantha found herself memorizing every feature of Stacey, making mental notes about the new wardrobe she needed to put together for school. She wanted a less conservative look than the clothes she'd purchased so far. Samantha, entranced in the conversation, marveled at how well Tom and Stacey understood each other, one being able to finish the sentence of the other on almost any subject. Samantha felt as if she had known them for a long time. She loved the way they touched each other gently and caringly. She began to be so comfortable with her new self, even if it was make-believe. Samantha reminded herself the old Samantha was alive and real and just below the surface. For the moment, she was able to push the old Samantha farther and farther below. Hiding the old Samantha felt safe and became easy and natural. Samantha let her instinct take over, forgetting her fears. And, as the evening progressed and dinner turned into dessert, she let her subconscious take over. She didn't have to think about the old Samantha. It felt right to feel safe and happy and to let her problems go. Relax, relax. She repeated the words as she pushed her old self still deeper and deeper into her soul, into the caves that held prisms of unpleasant memories locked in total darkness.

All too soon they had to leave the restaurant. Samantha was sorry the fireworks had to interfere with these precious moments. Inexplicably, she felt more during dinner than she had felt in a long time. She didn't want to explore it, she just wanted to let it happen, whatever it was. She felt comfortable, and the circumstances felt right and normal and natural. Whatever the reason, she wasn't going to jinx herself by examining the situation too much. She wanted so desperately to be happy. And, now, talking about her future, her college, her Michigan, she felt overwhelmingly relieved.

By the time they drove to the fireworks, Samantha looked at Skyler as she would have at any other date. She had finally felt comfortable at dinner. She wanted the feeling to last. She had not felt it in so long. She hadn't felt anything in so long. Yet, somehow, this felt right. Everything would be fine.

Turning her head back to ensure Tom and Stacey were still following behind them, Samantha turned toward Skyler and said, "Tom is really nice. I like Stacey too. What did you think of her?"

"She seems to care about my brother. I think she must be the real reason he went to Michigan State to get his Master's."

"What do you mean?"

"She was only a first-term freshman when they met. Tom never talked about getting his Master's until recently." Skyler paused, his tone reflective. "He also never mentioned Stacey in a serious tone until recently. That tells me there's more to the story."

"Lawyers. You're all the same! That sounds just like something my father would say. Honestly, you are all too suspicious about everything."

"Not suspicious, just careful. We are always on guard, so no one outmaneuvers us; so we are not blindsided. Is there anything wrong with that?"

"I guess not. It's just a strange way to live, that's all," Samantha responded folding her arms together as she gazed out of the window.

"No, it's the right way to live. If you do decide on law school, the first lesson you'll learn is C.Y.A., or 'cover your own ass' first. That's what it's about. Protect yourself, because you are the only one who can and who will. It's also the first lesson I teach my clients. Haven't I taught you that much this summer?" Skyler asked, turning off the engine and reaching into the back seat for a blanket and cooler.

"I guess I never thought about it like that," Samantha said, mulling over "C.Y.A."

The fireworks were spectacular. Samantha watched Stacey settle back and nestle into Tom's shoulder in the darkness. The pair, in unison, looked up into the blazing sky, listening intently to each other's whispers and the whistling of the firecrackers. They looked as though they were one bronze art sculpture, posed for all time to be admired. Samantha didn't dare interrupt them. She enjoyed watching them as much as she enjoyed the brilliance of the glowing sky.

Skyler stayed close to Samantha, close enough for her to feel his warm breath, close enough for her to hear his whispers about how beautiful she looked under the brilliance of the colorful sky. Somehow Samantha didn't mind. She was lost in herself, lost in the sky, lost in the beauty of the couple she saw next to her. She longed to be a part of someone, to feel the closeness, the tenderness, the comfort. She longed to feel content. She wanted that more than anything. In the darkness she felt Skyler's hand rubbing her back and shoulders, slowly, gently. She didn't mind. She focused on the loving couple next to her. She felt as if she were a part of them. She fixed her thoughts on them as she felt Skyler's warm soft hands on her.

Then, too soon, it was over. The finale sounded in their ears, and smoke from the many fireworks that soared up and exploded, filled the nostrils of all those viewers who were close. Samantha smiled. She felt warm and content. She stayed silent and still for what seemed many moments; yet it was only seconds. And in those few seconds, Samantha was able to penetrate into the depths of her most inner self and bury the old Samantha. She felt cold and then warm. Her body tingled and then it was over. She felt new and reborn. She no longer remembered the hurt, the pain. She was untouched, fresh, alive. She had no fears.

Hundreds of people stood up at once and retired happily to their cars and their homes. Samantha watched the people as if they had just arrived. She didn't object as she felt Skyler take her hand in his and lead her back to his car. She remained silent, watching as Tom and Stacey walked to their car, their arms locked around each others waists. Samantha, reverently silent, absorbed it all.

As they said their good-byes, Samantha wistfully watched Tom and Stacey drive off, after promises they'd keep in touch and check in on her at Michigan State in the fall. Samantha wished she could be Stacey, with a man like Tom; someone with a jovial personality who spoke freely and honestly, a tender man considerate of the female point of view and feelings. Maybe she would find a man like that in Michigan. Maybe she could get to know Tom better.

"What are you so quiet about?" Skyler asked in an animated voice, resting his hand lightly on Samantha's thigh.

"Tom and Stacey. They make a nice couple."

"That they do."

"Where are we going? I promised I'd get home early."

"Yes, but your parents will be out late, and they know you're safe with me. You know that too, don't you?" Skyler asked, as he began to rub his hand up and down her thigh.

Samantha did not respond. Her mind fluttered back to Tom and Stacey, sitting as one, watching the fireworks. She still felt part of them.

"It's time. You know that, don't you?" Skyler stated.

Samantha's brows knitted, but she did not respond. She didn't want to. She didn't want to think or move or feel. She didn't want to do anything that would break the magical spell Tom and Stacey had left her with. She remained silent, her eyes fixed on the road ahead.

As Skyler pulled off onto a pebbled road that led to a dirt lane, Samantha's senses became alert. She was caught, trapped in her own mind. Unable to unleash the old Samantha, the new one took over. Samantha took a deep soothing breath and reassured herself. Gradually she felt calm, comforted, as she heard her mind chant over and over, "relax, Stacey, relax . . ."

Skyler drove down the dirt lane for a few minutes before pulling the car over into a clearing and shutting the engine off. It was dark and quiet. Only the brilliant crescent moon lighted the ground. Skyler grabbed Samantha and pulled her close. Putting his mouth over hers, he grabbed her curls hard, pulling her neck taut and her head back. Samantha held her breath, trying to grip her fear, trying to take control.

Finally she did. Samantha took control. She relaxed. She talked to herself, found herself. After all, there wasn't anything to fear. She was home. She was in her bedroom. She was in the comfort and solitude of her bathroom. As she took off her clothes, she felt herself step into the comfort of the water. She relished the hot pounding water on her flesh. It felt good and clean and right. She stayed there for what seemed hours.

Until she turned into somebody else. . . . Stacey gave into him, kissing him back deliciously. Running her hands around his face, her fingers through his long hair, the curls twirling around her fingers.

Skyler unlocked the door next to him and grabbed the blanket he had tossed in the back seat earlier. Then, grabbing Samantha in his arms, he swiftly carried her to the smooth grassy clearing in front of the car. As they huddled together on the soft plaid blanket, Skyler found his way around Samantha's body, memorizing each curve, slowly, gently parting soft supple crevices that moistened at his touch.

Samantha closed her eyes to keep the water from getting in them. Stacey reveled in his touch.

Skyler couldn't see her face in the darkness, only the shadows allowed by the moon's glow. Samantha didn't feel his body against hers, she didn't feel his hot breath against her, only the steam from the shower. But Stacey did, she felt it all. Stacey took it all in, enjoying each of his fingers prodding every crevice, entering her body, moving within. Stacey took him deeper and deeper. Stacey moved with him and felt him grow inside her until he swelled into an explosion that left her body limp, her insides wet. Skyler was gentle with her. He loved watching her slim, naked body, as the sweat that had pooled between her breasts and on her neck began rolling off, as her chest rose and fell with each breath, in and out. She was so beautiful. And she was his now! His as he had always wanted her to be. He had finally captured her. She was his. He watched her calm breathing as he dressed. Then he touched her shoulder. Her eyes fluttered open to find his body over hers. He was touching her gently, lightly lifting her, dressing her, slowly, carefully, as if she were a china doll that would break.

The ride home was silent, as it had been earlier, each lost in thought. Skyler kept Samantha's hand in his as he drove, stroking each finger, his thumb sensually rubbing her palm. Samantha felt revolted by his touch, but glad it was only her hand he wanted. Samantha wondered if her parents were home and how her computer class would be. She had to get up early. She pictured her closet and wondered what to wear to class. Stacey felt Skyler's hand and wondered if he really liked her. If she had pleased him.

Pulling into the driveway, Skyler brushed a kiss on Samantha's cheek as Samantha quietly closed her eyes. Stacey crept from the car and smiled at him.

"Sleep well, sweetie. I won't call tonight. I'll let you get your rest so you can dream about me without any interruption. You were great. I'll talk to you tomorrow." Skyler said, flashing his dazzling grin at her, his deep voice soft and lustful.

Samantha didn't hear him. She was alone in her dreams, searching through the blackness. Stacey looked back and smiled, a flirtatious smile, watching the car pull away.

After her shower, Samantha slipped into bed and into a disturbing dream. In her dream, she walked and walked. She turned her head from side to side, her eyes going round and round looking, searching. Why was she alone? Why had they left her? She looked down at her feet. There was a box. It was pretty and pink. The faces were gone. The parts were gone. She couldn't find them. There was only this box. She picked it up and held it. It comforted her, she felt herself roaming about in empty rooms of darkness. Darkness was everywhere. She couldn't see anything clearly in the dark except the box. Nor could she see any of the rooms she was in; but she knew she was wandering in rooms, moving from one to the next. The rooms had no doors, no windows, only entrances and exits. Samantha couldn't see anything definite. She wasn't scared, but she did feel more alone than she ever had in her dreams. There was no longer safety in her dreams, only silence and darkness. She was truly alone. A tear fell, traveling over her thick lashes, noticed only once it spilled onto her hand—the hand that held the box. She blinked. She paused for an instant before she pulled it open. Then she heard a familiar tune play and the timeless words rang through her mind: "Humpty Dumpty sat on a wall, Humpty Dumpty had a great fall, all the King's horses and all the King's men couldn't put Humpty together again." Samantha shut the box. It frightened her. Quickly she shoved the box into her pocket. She wanted to keep it. She didn't know why. She was afraid to leave it in the darkness, lurking in the shadows. And then there were no more shadows. Only stillness and darkness. She was peaceful once again as she sank further into quiet oblivion.

# # #

Morning startled Samantha. The brightness of the day filtering through her drapes blinded her. The darkness was gone. For that, she was relieved. She craved a shower. She didn't remember how she had gotten home. The last thing she remembered was tiptoeing up the staircase and slipping into her room. She wasn't sure if her parents had been home, and she didn't want to find out. She didn't care. She remembered having had an overwhelming urge to take a shower before she crawled between her sheets. Raising her arm to her hair she ran her fingers through her curls. They'd be damp if she had showered. Was it possible she only dreamed about having taken a shower? It seemed so real. Again, she tried to retrace the evening. She had been glad the evening was over. She remembered her relief it was over. She remembered she really liked Tom and his girlfriend. It was worth spending the time with Skyler just to meet them. She couldn't wait to move to Michigan and be on her own.

Why couldn't she remember getting home? She must just need to wake up. Looking at Minnie's hands, she knew she had better hurry and get out of bed. She couldn't miss breakfast with her parents. She'd promised she'd be perfect. If she failed, it meant the doctor. She couldn't fail. She wouldn't fail.

Beyond her room, she would be everything they wanted her to be. Inside the serenity and solitude of her room, inside the privacy of her mind, she would be herself. At least she had the solitude and safety of her room, she consoled herself. At least she knew Nana was watching her and understood. Nana's continued words in Samantha's mind showed the strength of Nana's presence. It showed her she wasn't really alone. And on days like today, when acting was so important, Nana's presence was what kept Samantha moving forward.

Samantha was determined. She was also proud of herself. She had made it through her date with Skyler. In fact, she had enjoyed herself for the first time in a long time. She liked being with another couple. There was safety in numbers. And she truly liked Skyler's brother and girlfriend. They had been so nice to her. So nice she could even tolerate Skyler. She could even learn to like him. He had been a perfect gentleman to her. Maybe she had been wrong about him. Maybe he really was her friend, or could be her friend.

"Samantha, you look bright this morning. Why are you up so early?" Anne asked as she inspected her daughter. Samantha still looked thin and pale to her but her hair was pulled back with a cheerfully colored art deco barrette, she wore matching earrings and jewelry, and her makeup was carefully applied. Samantha had taken care with her outfit, and her mood was bright. Anne felt an immense relief as she heard the excitement in Samantha's voice.

"My computer classes begin today. I want to get there a little early so I can set up my computer and see if there are any other programs I might need to buy. Skyler's brother told me I should buy a program that creates outlines."

"There is plenty of time to decide what you need to buy. Be sure to buy only what you need. There are new computer programs developed every day."

"Oh, Mom, I know. Tom just told me it would really make a difference if I bought a program that would put my class notes in order. He said it really helped him get organized and saved him study time. Don't you think that's a good idea?"

Samantha asked her mother, averting her eyes as she poured milk into her cereal.

"Of course that's fine. If you need it, you can buy it. Just make sure you'll use it. Maybe you should ask your instructor."

"How did you like Tom?" Travis asked Samantha from behind his morning paper.

"Tom is great. He looks like Skyler, but they aren't alike. Tom is much more easygoing. He is very nice. He was very easy to talk to; not what I expected. I liked him and his girlfriend. They make a cute couple, and they told me lots of things about college."

"What's Tom's girlfriend's name?" Anne asked.

"I think it is . . . you know, I can't believe it—I've forgotten. I'm sure I'll think of it in a minute," Samantha said, knitting her brows while running a list of names through her mind, sifting them out, discarding them one by one. Shrugging her shoulders, she decided not to give it any more thought, sure it would pop into her head as soon as she stopped thinking about it.

"I'm having lunch with Tom and Skyler. You are welcome to join us."

"No, I can't, Dad, but you can say hi for me," Samantha said, with her mouth half full of cereal. "I've really got to run. I'll be home for dinner." With that, Samantha was off with her notebook computer, packed carefully in its padded black briefcase, slung over her shoulder.

"Samantha really looks great, doesn't she? I think she's over whatever illness or whatever else was bothering her. You'll have to thank Skyler for spending time with her and for introducing Tom to her. Focusing on college has really done the trick," Anne said, sipping her coffee and smiling at her husband behind his paper.

Travis, sensing his wife's need to talk, relinquished his paper, folding it and slipping it into the side pocket of his soft leather briefcase. "You were right. You are always right when it comes to Samantha. I try, but I really don't understand her like you do. The boys were so much easier."

"You do a fine job with her. There are just some things that are meant to be between mother and daughter. That's all."

"Are you ready to go to Washington this weekend? I thought we'd leave on the red-eye Friday morning so we get in a full day on Friday. I could use the whole day for meetings, and I have to file a case at the Supreme Court building. I thought you could entertain yourself with shopping. I've had Estelle book the flights. Any objection?"

"Now that Samantha is doing better, I think it's a splendid idea. I'll call Estelle and ask her to make us a reservation at Dominique's for dinner. Is there anyone else joining us?"

"Not that I know of. I'll leave that up to you. It'll just be the two of us, since we'll be with so many people at the Saturday brunch fundraiser for the Women's Foundation. Then in the evening, we have the presidential fundraiser." Travis put his napkin on his plate with one hand and grabbed his briefcase with the other.

"With Samantha on my mind, I had forgotten that was this weekend. I've only got two days to shop and pack."

"You'll make it. Whatever you don't find here, you can buy in Washington. You've never had a problem finding something to buy," Travis chuckled at his wife.

"You are such a thoughtful man, even after all these years," Anne said, beaming at her husband as he kissed her cheek and rubbed her back with a gentle pat.

"I try," Travis said cheerily as he headed down the hall to the garage door.

Chapter 15

Samantha stretched out on her bed. Her elbows dug deep into the feather comforter where she had been concentrating for hours on the list she was making on her computer. The list contained every item she was taking to college and everything she still needed to buy or do before she left. It made her feel college was sooner than the many calendar days that appeared before her. It helped her escape. She couldn't wait to leave for college! Using her computer made her feel she was already there.

Samantha loved the computer classes and stayed late, learning every function she could. It was easy. She had a knack for it and the computer was something she could submerge herself into for hours at a time. No one bothered her while she was with her computer. If she placed a plate of food, a soda and a mug of coffee next to her computer while she worked, her parents were satisfied she was eating and they were impressed with her serious commitment. In the few weeks she had taken on her perfect personality, she had mastered fooling their watchful eyes. She no longer felt guilty for lying to them. Lying had become easy. Being perfect was difficult, but she knew she would eventually master that too.

Deciding she'd better get ready for bed, she slipped off her clothes and stepped into the shower. It felt good against her skin. It made her flesh pink and hot. It filled her nostrils with warm moist air. Every sensation that coursed through her told her each minuscule muscle had totally relaxed. She felt pleasantly exhausted as she slipped into her robe, brushed her teeth and crawled beneath her sheets without drying her hair. She didn't mind that her wet hair made the pillow cold and wet; she was too relaxed to care about anything. As she lay, pleased with her work, her head felt very heavy. She felt content for the first time in as long as she could remember. It was true if you buried yourself in work and kept your mind occupied, time passed quickly. She placed the computer near the edge of the bed.

Closing her eyes, she smiled to herself as she imagined how content she would feel with the heavy class load she was taking. It would feel great to use her mind and air it with fresh new thoughts. Samantha could feel her body relax, sinking deep into peaceful limbo. Time and space merged into one. Her body, like a space capsule, floated away as she glided into dreams of darkness.

In the familiar blackness, Samantha knew she was dreaming, but it was different somehow. She felt uneasy; her once-limber body stiffened. Where was she? Samantha was confused. Was she awake or dreaming? Perhaps she was awake, watching herself dream. That didn't make sense. Or did it? Samantha pondered her surroundings. She felt uncomfortable and scared. She wanted to wake up. But she couldn't. There seemed to be someone else there, but she couldn't see who or what it was, looming in her darkness. Who could it be? The familiar faces, even in their parts—that's what she wanted to see. That's what was comfortable for her to see.

She walked, ran, twirled around. Then she sat down. For all of her movement, she still stood in the same place. It was as if she had been moving in someone else's body. It was not comfortable.

There, off in the distance, she heard the nursery rhyme tune. The box! Where was the music box? She couldn't see it. It was not in her pocket. The tune got louder and louder. She felt more and more alone. She wanted out of the dream. She wanted to wake up. Then she looked down. She saw her hands. Slowly she moved them. She pinched herself. Ouch. She must be awake. It wasn't a dream? She saw the faces again. But this time they weren't familiar. She looked closer. They were familiar. There were just so many new parts, new features. Were there any ears? Still no ears.

The music was gone. She strained her ears. She heard silence. No, there was ringing. She heard ringing. Where was it coming from? As she turned around and around to look for its source, she felt her eyes spring open. Into reality.

Startled, she felt her heavy body. Samantha blinked. She had fallen asleep, she had had a nightmare. Her phone was ringing. As she picked up the receiver, she looked up at Minnie. It was 12:35. It had to be Skyler. Samantha frowned and sleepily responded into the receiver. "Yes?"

"Is that any way to greet me? How about a friendly hello or a 'hi honey, I missed hearing your voice all day'? Is that too much to ask?" Skyler said, in an obviously hurt tone, as if he was genuinely insulted and irritated.

"I didn't mean anything. I was sleeping. You woke me up."

"Aren't you even going to say you're sorry and you've missed me?"

"Okay."

"Okay what?" Skyler said forcefully.

Samantha heard his tone and froze. She wanted safety. She needed to be alone, unencumbered by the ever-present fear of Skyler. She wanted to hide, to sleep and not wake up until he went away. Her hand gripped the receiver tightly. She closed her eyes; she had to. As Samantha went into the safety of her slumber, another voice spoke out into the darkness, into the receiver leading to Skyler.

"I missed you. I'm glad you called. When will I see you again?" The voice coming from Samantha said. It was vibrant and direct. It was soft and sensual, and her words purred from her lips as if she'd said them so many times before. She *had* said them many times before. She loved Tom. He was kind and gentle and fun and, best of all, he loved her too, just the way she was.

Skyler sensed her acquiescence. He wanted her and he wanted her now. "Do you think you can get out of the house and meet me? I'll park down the street about a block. I'll meet you in fifteen minutes. Are you game?"

"Really? You mean it? You're serious?" Stacey responded as if she were hungry and in love.

"Yes. See you then. Don't get caught. If you do, tell them you're going for a walk around the block." Skyler kissed the phone, slamming the receiver with a grin. She was his. He had mastered her.

Stacey jumped from her bed and peeked out into the hallway. No one was there. Nothing to worry about. No one will know. She quietly shut the door and dressed as if there were a fire in her room. Stacey smoothed her long locks. She was pleased as she looked in the mirror at the long blonde hair, smooth around her face. She washed up and didn't put any makeup on. She didn't need any more color than the sun gave her, and she hated to fuss with makeup. Tom hated makeup. He wanted the natural woman and always said she was a natural beauty who didn't have to fuss. Quickly, quietly, she put on a summer jumper without the matching shirt underneath. The jumper barely covered her bra-free chest, giving a strong suggestion of her free mounds and natural cleavage. Bare feet pushed into thinly spiked high heels made the skirt on the jumper look shorter than it was on her tall legs. Quickly, dropping her keys into the jumper pocket, the imposter slipped down the staircase into the midnight air. Her brisk gait down the street emitted an aura of extreme confidence.

Just as he had promised, Skyler's jade Jaguar was waiting for his date. His eyes sparkled as he gazed at her youthful face. He was pleased with her appearance, although it was a different Samantha than he had seen before. Finally she dressed to please him, or at least she tried. Her pale face, usually adorned with makeup, was bare, making her look years younger. Her clothes, put together as if she were much older, as if she were in a bar soliciting, were unlike her. At least she appeared to be trying, he mused. Skyler was so pleased with his accomplishment he didn't notice when she referred to him as Tom as she greeted him.

"Tom, you're here. I thought I would be early," Stacey whispered.

"I wasn't far away when I called you from my car phone. As promised, I'm here just for you," Skyler said, pulling the car from the curb, keeping the lights off until they were another block away.

"Where are we going?" Stacey said, staring at Tom's handsome features.

"You'll see. It's a surprise." Skyler said, smiling as he rubbed his hand up and down Samantha's thigh, reaching higher and higher with each stroke until he found the top of her cotton panties and yanked them downward. They remained still in the moving car for the next few minutes. With tacit understanding of what was before them, their eyes remained silently on the road.

In what seemed to be a blink, Skyler turned off the car lights and pulled into a dark, deserted alley. Stacey watched silently as Skyler turned off the engine, leaving the keys in the ignition.

"Push the knob so your seat goes back." Skyler ordered.

Stacey did as she was told. She remained silent and followed instructions, opening her door, getting out of the Jaguar as Skyler slid from his seat into hers.

"Come on back in. Not on my side, on me. Hurry up."

Stacey slid into the cramped seat onto Skyler's lap, facing him, her panties stuffed into her pocket, her heals slipped off, thrown onto the back seat, her arms around his neck.

Skyler closed his eyes as he felt himself inside her. It was what he liked best these days. Control over another human being, over the daughter of his ungrateful boss, over a beautiful girl he could mold for his own personal pleasure. Samantha exceeded his expectations. Sex with Samantha was unlike that with his other women. She would remain his for a very long time, he thought, as he moved inside her. Her body was made for his. Even in this small space she was able to please him.

As he moved her off of him, he motioned to Samantha to crawl into the tiny back seat to get dressed. As Stacey got dressed, she didn't notice the tears that dropped through her lashes. She didn't see the tiny red droplets staining her underwear. She felt dazed and forgot where she was for the moment until Skyler spoke.

"How'd you like it? We are good together, aren't we?" Skyler said grabbing a lock of Samantha's hair as she pulled up her pale blue panties.

Stacey looked up at him as if she were lost, confused. His voice in the silence startled her back into reality. Stacey wasn't sure how to respond to Tom. She didn't remember him ever treating her so roughly before. She felt tired and bruised and sore. Stacey looked up at him. She saw his beautiful face and she softened in an instant, her mouth curving into a half smile.

"Don't worry. You don't need to say anything. I can tell from your expression it was good for you too. I'll have you home in a minute. You look like you need a few hours of sleep," Skyler said, smiling to himself, not paying any attention to Samantha, treating her as if she wasn't really there.

Stacey got out of the car a few houses away and walked to the familiar house. She was glad she'd had a few minutes with Tom before he had to get back to his books. He must have been rough with her because he was worried about his exams and he wanted to hurry back to his books.

That must have been it, she decided, as she hurried up the stairs of the sorority house with silent movement so as not to disturb the housemother.

Chapter 16

As the summer progressed, Samantha kept busy with her computer and with carefully packing her things for college. She counted the days until Emily came home and until they celebrated her eighteenth birthday. She couldn't wait. Her parents were, much of the time, in Washington, planning fall fund-raisers. While her father spent the remainder of his time with his clients and with running the firm, her mother spent all of her free time—or so it seemed to Samantha—working on the Foundation for Women Candidates and their never-ending candidate search and fundraising efforts.

Samantha didn't mind that her parents made themselves absent during her last summer at home. They had left her alone more and more since she had turned fifteen. Now, they seemed at times to forget they had a daughter, unless she was other than perfect. Then they had an excuse to gang up on her. At least their absence gave her freedom. She loved her time alone in the spacious house and in the solitude of her room.

Before she knew it, she felt the hot August sun beating down on her wherever she went. The smell of September's impending arrival filled her nostrils as she walked in the evening air. Samantha had never thought much about walking alone in the dark until she was raped by Uncle Greg. Now, she was afraid to be in the darkness, outside, alone. And yet somehow, in the past few weeks, she found herself frequently in the night air, walking as if she didn't have a care in the world, unafraid. She wasn't sure if she should be thankful she was over her fear, or fearful she didn't remember wanting to get over her fear. A nagging voice inside her told her not to be afraid of it, not to question it. So she didn't. Yet sometimes the night startled her. Sometimes she didn't remember having gone out. Samantha worried about not remembering; but it was just the stress she was under, just the emotional need to go out into the world instead of remaining inside the cloistered silent house. She vowed she'd try to do better, take things more slowly, so she would remember more, so her dreams wouldn't seem so much like reality. She was, for the most part, ready and packed for college. She wanted to direct her energy and spend her remaining time at home concentrating on relaxing and focusing on her computer and herself.

As she reached under her pillow to retrieve the August issue of *Cosmopolitan,* she felt the worn paper she had written on so many months before. She pulled it out with the magazine, unfolding it carefully so it would not tear at its severely worn creases. The words were familiar. They had become part of her permanent memory banks. But the meanings, still foreign, had not merged with the words, nor had they offered any solutions.

What had happened to her desire for knowledge? What happened to the search for the key that would unlock the mysterious words? Had she been so preoccupied with other things she had let go of her search? Dismally her fingers smoothed over the words as if they were braille and could answer her thoughts. She stared at them, remembering Skyler's voice, hearing between his words the insidious power he held over her. His voice assured her he meant what he said, as she felt his hot breath on her. And still, with all she knew, with all she felt, she hadn't pursued the promise she had made to herself.

Samantha sat on her plush rose carpet and sighed as her body wilted against her bed frame. Skyler had terrified her at first, but he had now at least toned down his desire for her. Yet he still called nearly every night and kept close tabs on her life and what she did almost every minute. Other than that, did she have to worry about anything else? Could she put the past behind her? Wasn't she soon going to be leaving everything behind her anyway? Samantha pondered never having to deal with it again—any of it; the rape, the abortion, Skyler, her parents. She closed her eyes, crossed her fingers, and made a wish like she had when she was a child. It made her feel better when she was little. It was hard to feel anything now.

Samantha frowned as she explored her options. At first she had maintained the ritual of carrying the list of phrases with her, even to the point of sleeping with it close to her, under her pillow. Now, preparing for college, lost in thoughts of starting over, hadn't she neglected following through on the commitment she had made to herself? Wasn't it still important to discover a way, any way, around Skyler's threat of blackmail, just in case he really followed through with his threats?

Silence usually comforted Samantha. Today she couldn't help but feel disturbed by the silence. She felt some intangible, unrecognizable voice calling out to her to leave everything alone. To stop thinking. To stop searching. The shrill voice, loud and haughty, called her from within. Her head ached. As she crawled onto her bed, she placed the pillow over her face, clasping it tightly against each ear. But the voice, now wispy, didn't stop. It laughed at her. It called her a wimp, a child, a baby. Nothing quieted the voice. She was losing control. She clasped the pillow so hard her hands and fingers ached.

The dreams; they had now entered her reality. What could she do? She was sure she was going crazy. There was nothing to do, she decided. She could talk to no one. There really wasn't anyone who would believe her, who wouldn't blame her. There wasn't anyone who would really listen.

Samantha sprang to her feet and headed for the medicine cabinet. She couldn't find anything strong enough for her headache, her pain, in her cabinet. Her parents; their cabinet. Surely they would have lots of things she could take. As she entered her parents' spacious Victorian bedroom, she felt a chill of loneliness and raw sadness rip through her veins. She felt homesick for her parents. Homesick in her own home.

Samantha had felt waves of homesickness before, but never like this. Tears welled in her eyes. Samantha wouldn't let them fall; she couldn't. She ordered her tears back where they came from as she tilted her head back, biting hard on her lip to refocus the pain. She was old enough not to need her parents. She was old enough to take care of herself.

She stared into the medicine cabinet. It had been reorganized—new bottles added, familiar ones gone. Still, it was filled with all sorts of medicine; tubes and jars, vials and bottles. Lots of bottles. Clear ones, green ones, brown ones, white ones. Lots of orange plastic ones. But she wasn't sure what each of them did or why there were so many prescription drugs.

Samantha lifted them, one by one, carefully replacing each exactly as it had been placed by her parents. She had to find one with her mother's name on it. Her mother suffered from migraines so she would have the right drug to cure headache pain. Pulling open her mother's makeup drawer, she spotted several rust-colored plastic bottles. Xanax, Tylenol 3, Vicodin, Darvon. What should she take? Tylenol 3. It always worked before. She would take two. She needed two. Maybe she should take three, she contemplated, grabbing the plastic vial, removing it completely. She needed the whole bottle. Her mother would never miss it, she decided, swiftly retreating to her room.

Swallowing the pills quickly, Samantha grabbed the list of words from the floor, carefully folding it. She could hear the voice inside her laughing louder and louder. Music encircled her. Where had it come from? Her hand clenched the folded paper underneath her pillow. As she sank into a state of numbness, she vowed to pursue her search. Skyler's words engulfed her. C.Y.A. Cover your own ass, protect yourself, stay a step ahead. Maybe that was as good a reason as any to pursue the words. Protection, just in case he followed through.

As sleep captured her, she heard the loud music of the nursery rhyme drowning out the voice, as her hands slipped from the pillow onto the music box in her pocket.

Chapter 17

The morning sunlight sent Samantha staggering to the blinds to close them. She had gone to sleep early and, except for the interruption from Skyler's call, she had over ten hours of sleep. Still she felt tired and weak. Her mouth was dry, her throat sore. Her body felt tender and bruised. Maybe she had fallen out of bed and didn't remember, she thought, light-headed as she crawled back into her warm inviting sheets.

With her eyes closed, Samantha tried to concentrate and piece together what could have made her feel so tired and so rotten. She listened to the chirping birds. Her parents were up. They hadn't woken her up. They've been gone so much this month, they must have gotten out of the habit of waking me up. Surely her parents weren't off their kick of watching her eat—or were they? Samantha felt too ill to worry about it. She didn't feel like eating. She felt too tired to lift a fork, let alone chew and swallow. From her parents' voices, it sounded as if they were eating their breakfast. She would have to make her excuses later. She couldn't go down. She'd been good. Missing one breakfast wouldn't upset them, even if they still cared about her eating habits, she thought, as she continued to try to piece together her night.

What was it Skyler had said to her on the phone? Something about her birthday and his gift to her. She didn't want him to give her anything, but she remembered he insisted she'd love it. She didn't know it yet, but it was something she wanted. What did that mean? She didn't want to figure it out. She wished he'd leave her alone.

What happened next? What did they talk about? Samantha squinted trying to remember the rest of their conversation but she couldn't. Had she fallen asleep while they were talking on the phone? No, that couldn't be it. She looked at the receiver placed neatly on the pink princess phone hook. Wouldn't the phone be off the hook if she had fallen asleep while talking on it? Samantha became restless. She couldn't stay in bed any longer. She needed a hot shower, maybe a cleansing bath. She was too tired to stand in the shower. Yes, a bath would be better, she determined, as she poured bubble bath into the already collecting tepid water.

As she pulled off her pajamas, she felt a pool of wetness drop into her underwear. Her period wasn't due for a few days. Had it come early? She wondered if it could come early, even though she was on birth control pills? Looking into the cotton crotch of her panties she saw the wetness. It had no color. It was clear. Maybe it was urine. Samantha puzzled over it. There was no reason for the liquid that made any sense to her. She smelled it. It smelled foreign to her. No, it smelled like . . . like sex. She hadn't had sex. How was this possible? Suddenly Samantha felt nauseous. It must be an infection. Had Skyler given her one? Did she get it from Greg? What should she do?

Quickly climbing into the bubbled water, she leaned her head back onto the plastic air pillow and closed her eyes. What next? The letters STD flashed into her mind. She'd read about them; sexually transmitted diseases. And now she had one.

She couldn't tell anyone. She couldn't go to a doctor, and she refused to tell Skyler. The thought of telling Skyler, of asking him, gave her goose bumps even in the heat of the water.

Samantha pushed away her thoughts. They weren't real to her. She didn't want them to be real. Relax, relax. Samantha had gotten used to clearing her mind, to pushing reality far below the surface. She lay still in the water, letting her thoughts drift under, letting her mind concentrate on planning her day. It seemed as if she'd been in the water for only moments; but as Samantha picked up the gold bar of soap, she saw her severely wrinkled fingers and hurriedly finished washing her body.

Wrapped in her robe, Samantha was surprised at how much better she felt. She didn't get dressed for several minutes but, after she did, she spent the next hour checking her underwear every fifteen minutes. There was no more wetness. Maybe it was a fluke. She was right to bury her fears. She didn't want to deal with it. It was probably nothing. What could she do about it anyway? She shrugged. Who would help her? No one. There wasn't anyone to help her.

As she heard the jingling of the phone, she stared at it.

She didn't feel like talking to anyone. She wanted to play with her computer. She'd let it ring. When her taped voice on the machine answered it, she was surprised to hear the familiar voice she'd missed so much these past few months.

"Samantha! I can't believe you're not in! I have so many things to tell you. Most important, I'm home! Give me a call. I've got to—"

"Emily!" Samantha shrieked into the receiver. "I can't believe it's you!"

"Great timing. Did you just get in?"

"No. I was in the bathtub and I didn't hear the phone over the radio," Samantha said, easily lying to her best friend. Then, shrieking with girlish glee, Samantha added, "I can't believe you're back!"

"A week early. I couldn't stay away another day. Everything was great, but I was more than ready to come home. So, can I come over or do you want to meet me somewhere? I'm dying to see you!"

"Sure! How about Maxine's? We can have lunch and talk and maybe go shopping? Unless you spent all your money in Europe!" Samantha said, laughingly teasing her friend. She felt renewed and suddenly aware it was another beautiful day, and she would soon be outside and part of it.

"Hurry up. I'll see you there in half an hour," Emily said, before hanging up the receiver.

Samantha had become an expert at averting her eyes from the mirror in order to avoid a full view of herself. And yet, with precision, she was able to apply her makeup and fix her bouncy brunette hair into a beautiful framework of abundant curls around her face. Her eyes, vibrant blue in contrast to the pale blue cotton peasant blouse, matching long crinkled skirt and white flat sandals, carefully masked the turmoil she felt inside. She looked fresh and young. Looking at her, no one would guess the trauma she shouldered every day. Samantha arched an eyebrow acrimoniously at the thought of playing such a trick on the rest of the world. Then she closed her bedroom door and bounded down the staircase to her mother's study.

"Mom? Can I come in?"

"Yes, Samantha? I'm here, come in. We missed you at breakfast," Anne said to her daughter, as she inspected

Samantha's appearance and coloring.

"Sorry. I got talking with Emily. She's back and I'm going to meet her for an early lunch! Just thought I'd let you know we'll probably spend the day together, and I might not be home for dinner. I'll call and let you know," Samantha said lightly, trying to avoid her mother's eyes, for fear she'd see through her white lies.

"That's fine, dear. I'll be here most of the day. I'm planning to spend my day making phone calls for the League's auction," Anne said, thumbing through her rolodex.

"Thanks, Mom," Samantha said, patting her mother's shoulder. "Don't work too hard!"

"See you later. Say hello to Emily for me; and please, at least have a glass of milk and toast or a bowl of cereal before you go. Put some food into your stomach."

"Mom, I'll be eating a burger in less than half an hour! I eat. Don't worry so much. If you don't believe me, call Emily later and ask her," Samantha said, shutting the door behind her as if to add an exclamation point to her words.

At the restaurant, Samantha was surprised to see a grown-up, sophisticated Emily. Samantha felt like a child as she took in Emily's French twist, low-cut clinging burgundy dress, and matching pumps.

As they hugged, the girls' conversation immediately began to run together nonstop. To any stranger listening, the conversation would have been nonsensical, even gibberish; yet they understood each other as if they were of one mind. To each of them, it felt as if they hadn't been apart for more than a few days. Samantha was relieved Emily hadn't changed, despite her appearance. At least Emily could be counted on. But could she be confided in? So much had happened. Would she understand? Would she be mad she hadn't told her before? What should she do? As the conversation began to slow down, Samantha thought of several ways to approach the subject, but none seemed right. And then suddenly lunch was over. Neither girl could eat or drink anything else. Happily, they headed for the mall.

As Samantha followed Emily in her car toward the mall, she turned the volume of the radio up to a deafening pitch. As the radio poured out ". . . summer breeze makes me feel fine blowing through the chasms in my . . .," Samantha tried to collect her thoughts and drown out the whispering voice inside her that began to speak as soon as she decided to confide in Emily. Why couldn't she drown the voice out? Why was she having nightmares in the middle of the day? It must be the stress of holding everything in. She pursed her lips together. Emily would help her. She had to confide in her. Regardless of what Emily's reaction would be, she'd help her, even if it was late, even if she was angry with Samantha.

There it was again. The voice was low and deep. It called her a weakling, a baby, a wimp. It dared her to tell anyone. It told her not to trust anyone but Tom. Tom she thought. Who is Tom? The only Tom she knew was Skyler's brother. It couldn't be him. She barely knew him. With the thought of Tom the voice disappeared as quickly as it had appeared. Samantha looked at Emily's happy face as they parked their cars side by side and strode lazily to the mall entrance. She couldn't tell her friend now, not on their first day together after so long. Tomorrow. She'd tell her tomorrow, she assured herself.

It was almost midnight when Samantha entered her darkened house. Her parents had either gone to sleep or had gone out. Samantha didn't care to find out. She didn't want to talk to anyone. She wanted to hold the day she'd had with Emily in her head, privately. It had been so long since she'd felt such contentment and security! She was amazed the simple fact of Emily's presence could make her feel that way. As she carefully relived the day in her mind, as if it were a motion picture she could play over and over at her leisure, she smiled in the silent darkness and tossed her clothes carelessly onto the velvet chair beside her dresser. Just as she was about to head into the bathroom, the phone rang. She stared for a few seconds, wishing it would disappear. She moved toward the phone in the darkness. Her answering machine was blinking.

"Hello?"

"Well, what is this? The traveler comes home. Was he interesting?" Skyler asked sarcastically.

"What are you talking about?" Samantha said, mimicking his sarcasm.

"The man you were with all day. Was he as good as me?"

"I was with Emily."

"Emily? I thought she wasn't coming home for a few more

days. I can check, you know."

"I have no reason to lie. Emily called me this morning. She decided to come home early."

"Really? What did you do?"

"We met at Maxine's for lunch. We ate burgers and fries and chocolate malts. Then we went shopping at the mall. The shops closed at nine, so we went to T.G.I.F. for dinner. I just got home." Samantha sputtered detail after detail. What she wore, who was there, who she talked to. She was used to accounting to Skyler for her time. She hated it. She really didn't have a choice. As she leaned onto her pillow, Samantha decided nothing would ruin the great day she'd had. Not even Skyler and his rude comments. Samantha wished she could scream at him. She barely listened as he told her how well his trial was going and bragged about how he would get Mr. Castriano off easily on a technicality. Mr. Castriano would owe him big, he said.

Samantha didn't care what Skyler did all day. She hated his bragging. Half of what he said, she didn't understand. She didn't want to understand it either. She rested her cheek against her soft pillows and let the receiver rest unattended on her ear as she murmured an occasional disinterested response.

"Samantha? Samantha!" Skyler shouted, enraged, into the receiver. She'd fallen asleep when he needed her. He slammed down the phone. The dozing pubescent girl between his paisley green and burgundy sheets heard his angry voice scream, "Bitch!"

Opening her eyes, she saw the man that rescued her from the brutal hands of her pimp. She had showed him earlier just how grateful she was and hoped now she'd be able to get some sound sleep in his huge bed before he tossed her back to her keeper. She thought, as she entered the apartment earlier, she had gotten lucky with the handsome stranger. He was rich too. She could tell from the way he lived and the nice clothes he wore. His car looked brand new. He smelled of scented soap and expensive cologne. But now, as she looked up and saw him ripping off his t-shirt and robe angrily, her eyes grew wide. Frightened, her heart raced.

"Roll over, bitch. You're just like the rest of them! You take from me and you don't give me anything back," Skyler said in a harsh whisper as he climbed onto the naked girl's back.

The girl, shaking, followed his orders. She couldn't refuse him anything. Mr. Castriano would not like it if this man was unhappy with her, like the last girl. Where was the gentle man she'd been with only an hour ago? The one that fed her and bathed her and had sex with her as gently as if it were his first time. Since she'd been on the streets the past few weeks, she'd been lucky. The others she'd met told her about things like this. Mr. Castriano threatened her with worse if she failed to deliver. She hadn't believed anything bad would really happen to her. And now it was too late. She promised God she'd go home if she lived through this. She began to pray.

As he entered her in a place that had always seemed forbidden, she cried out, "No! No! You're hurting me!"

Wincing as he grabbed a handful of thick russet hair from the back of her head, she heard his fiery voice say, "Now tell me you love it. Now, bitch, right now! Tell me how you love it . . ."

Chapter 18

"Emily cut her trip short? Did she say why?" Anne asked her preoccupied daughter at breakfast.

"No, she didn't tell me why she came home early, but yes, she did. We got talking. I don't even think I asked why she came home. I was just so glad to see her. You should see her new look! She looks so sophisticated and so much older. She helped me pick out a few new outfits—"

"You girls shouldn't be in such a hurry to grow up! There's so much ahead of you. Enjoy yourselves," Anne said, sipping her coffee while checking off her list of donors for the League auction.

"Oh, Mom, really," Samantha said, exasperated with her mother's negative comments and little girl lecture. "Where's Dad? Isn't he having breakfast with us?"

"No. Skyler called him early this morning to go over some big case they've been working on. Somehow Skyler found new evidence, and the prosecutor was giving him a hard time about allowing it into evidence. He wanted your father there for backup."

"Oh." Samantha said, tuning her mother's voice out at the mention of Skyler.

As silence clouded the breakfast table, Samantha moved the cool uneaten scrambled eggs and soggy toast artfully around her plate. "Mom, could I be excused? I'd like to see what Emily is up to today," Samantha said meekly.

Anne's attention turned toward her daughter again. As she looked into her daughter's crystal blue eyes. What was really hidden behind them? It seemed inconceivable Samantha would ever be able to tell a lie. Since she had been born, Anne had always been able to read her daughter's face. Instinctively now she knew there was something wrong. Something about Samantha still made her feel uneasy, despite the positive mood and appearance change over the past several weeks.

"You've hardly touched your breakfast. Have a few more

bites and then call Emily. Really, dear, you are still too thin for my liking."

"Oh, Mom. You worry too much! You've seen me eat lots of food. Pretty soon you'll have me outgrowing all my new clothes," Samantha said, popping another obligatory bite of eggs into her mouth, washing it down with warm orange juice.

"Fine. Just promise me you girls will take time out to eat, whatever you decide to do. Take some money from my wallet and treat Emily to a nice meal. Tell her it's my welcome home to her."

"Thanks, Mom. I'll let you know what we're doing after I call her."

"Don't forget your birthday party this weekend. Take my charge card if you need another dress."

Samantha grinned at the thought of turning eighteen. She didn't want the party, but it was an Armstrong family tradition to have a full family gathering with friends and all the trimmings to share in what was supposed to be the newly turned adult's first alcoholic drink. The eldest male in the family always made a short speech ending it with the traditional birthday toast with a wish for success and happiness in the adult world. Samantha always thought it was a strange tradition. No living Armstrong remembered how it got started, but every adult Armstrong had fond memories of his or her coming-of-age party. Now it was her turn, she felt indifferent. She remembered her brother's party. It was enormous. There were so many people no one noticed when she crept into her father's study and took her first drink. She didn't know what it was, but she remembered it tasted bitter, and she didn't want another.

As she dialed Emily's line, she thought about the kind of sensation she would make at her party. She wanted to be like Emily; sophisticated looking, but still herself. She also wanted to be soft and natural like . . . like . . . her thoughts fluttered. Why couldn't she remember the name of Tom's girlfriend or, for that matter, her face? Maybe she shouldn't remember; after all they'd only met once. But, she reflected, she remembered Tom down to the very last detail.

"Hi, Emily. What are you up to? I was thinking if you're not too busy, maybe you could help me pick out my dress for my birthday party?"

"Sure . . ."

As the girls made their plans for the day, Anne stood outside her daughter's door listening to the details. She was genuinely worried about Samantha and thought it her duty to reassure herself nothing was wrong or else to find out what was wrong and fix it. It was the right thing to do. She stood as quiet as a church mouse with her ear to the door. Surely Samantha would confide in Emily, Anne convinced herself, as she eavesdropped. Maybe she should have a chat with Emily? As Anne pondered her options, she heard Samantha hang up and begin the shower water. Retreating to her own room, not any wiser than before she listened at the door, she felt a pounding headache coming on fast. She reached into her medicine cabinet for her medication. Very few pills were left. Had she really gone through the prescription that fast? She couldn't have; time was just moving too fast, that was all. She closed her eyes . . .

# # #

The next few days went quickly for Samantha. Not even Skyler's phone calls and inquisitions could break the spell. Emily was home, and Samantha didn't feel so alone. Her brothers were expected to arrive in time for the party, and the house was buzzing with preparations. Slipping into her black spaghetti-strapped dress and satin pumps, she felt goose bumps of anticipation. It was time to go down. She could hear the guests arriving. Had her brothers arrived? Surely they wouldn't wait downstairs. She opened her door; they must be running late. It would be like the twins to make an entrance all their own. Even at their age, they still garnered all the attention they could get; and when they didn't get attention, they created a situation to divert it from others. When Samantha was younger, she was jealous of the twins and the fun they shared. She was the baby; she should get the attention, she rationalized. But she had to admit she admired their antics. She even tried to copy the twins when she was younger, but the qualities she duplicated had the opposite effect. After several punishments and scoldings, she gave up trying to be like her brothers.

Excitement laced her nerves as she went downstairs and saw her family and friends. She hadn't realized just how much she'd missed them until now. For those brief seconds, for that interlude in time, she felt normal. She felt as if it were Christmas, as if the past months were nonexistent. As if she'd been freed of the nightmare. When she looked around the room, she felt warm and happy. Safe. Her parents, her aunts, uncles, and cousins, even her brothers were there. The twins raised their eyebrows at Samantha, making her blush. She felt like a small child as they motioned her in between them. As they kissed her on the cheek, she noticed how much older and more mature they seemed.

"Hey, Sammy cat, you look great!" Taylor said, grinning at his baby sister, realizing for the first time she had grown into a beautiful woman. "Did you see the mountain of gifts you got? It'll take you till Christmas to open them all!"

Putting his arm around her shoulder, Tad said, "We didn't put our gift on the table. You know us; we didn't wrap it—"

"But you'll love it," Taylor interrupted.

"Tell me what it is, pleeeeaze," Samantha begged, as if she were five again.

"What d'ya think?" Taylor teased, looking at Tad.

"Why not; it is your day, Sammy cat; your wish is our command!" Tad said. "Pull it out Taylor."

Samantha watched as if her brothers were the only ones in the room. Taylor pulled out a small box from the inside pocket of his suit jacket.

"Happy birthday!" The twins said in unison. Then Tad added, "We thought you could use it at State and then later in law school or vet school."

"A micro cassette recorder. This is really cool! I can tape my classes. I can't believe you two thought of it. It's perfect. Thanks! Samantha exclaimed, hugging each of her brothers fondly. "I'm going to show Mom and Dad."

Samantha saw her father wave her over to him as he gathered the crowd into a unified group. She decided to show her parents her gift later. Slipping the tiny tape recorder into the small hidden drawer of the antique hat rack, Samantha swiftly grabbed a glass of champagne from a passing waiter and took her place next to her father. Everyone she loved had lined up to prepare for the toast. Her father finished filling any emptied glasses he saw, and he motioned to the waiters to continue filling glasses in every part of the room. Even her young cousins had glasses of apple juice or soda. So many crystal glasses, all filled and raised in honor of her. As she looked around the room smiling, tears of thankfulness and happiness swelled inside. She couldn't let the tears out. She had to concentrate. The toast was about to begin, and all eyes were focused on her father. As he cleared his throat, she wished her grandparents were alive. She comforted herself by visualizing them in the room, smiling at her. She raised her eyes toward her father as she saw him raise his glass to her and speak.

"It seems like yesterday I held a tiny pink baby girl in my arms . . ."

Samantha listened to the raw silence as her father, commanding his usual attention, spoke about her. So many kind things, Samantha thought. So many things about her he'd noticed, things she never knew he knew. Samantha looked around the room at the smiling faces, caring faces. She looked around the room self-consciously, suddenly uncomfortable with the attention. She wondered if anyone could see through her. She felt naked, as if they could see she was not the fine innocent woman her father described. She looked again around the room, this time more intensely. She noticed facial features and expressions, checked each face for a sign they knew she wasn't worthy of the elegant toast; she wasn't worthy of their acceptance of her as a woman in the community. And then she saw them. The parts, the pieces from her dreams. They were here. They were whole. They were real. She no longer heard the words of her father. She only saw the familiar features with their raised fluted champagne glasses and their artificial faces. She also noticed suddenly Greg Maston and Skyler were present. Her heart sank. Her body stiffened. She forgot how to breathe. An instant flood of fear embraced her body as her insides fluttered and then went limp.

Knowing she had to act normal, perfect, she stood still, a smile pasted on her face. Silently she watched in stunned fascination as if the voices, the people, the room, were in slow motion. She didn't have a firm grasp of what anyone was saying. Even the clear clinking of the crystal, chiming her praises and well wishes, weren't enough to wake her from her daze. Her emotions took over the rational, comprehending part of her brain. Anyone paying close attention to Samantha could see she was struck with an inexplicable inner sadness.

But no one noticed. They were mesmerized by Travis's speech. Years of trial work had made him an excellent orator, and his words touched all those who heard him. Except Samantha, whose ears had grown deaf to his words, despite her desire to hear them. Spellbound by the shock of seeing Greg and Skyler together, in her house, at her party, with her family and friends, even the commotion and well-wishers in the room could not jolt her from the emotional upset she felt.

Samantha's parents were proud of her, as they watched her raise her glass, take a sip of her champagne and say thank you to the group. They did not see that Samantha guzzled the remainder of the gold bubbly liquid and grabbed another from the tray. As family and friends wished Samantha happy birthday, she simply smiled, holding her champagne glass so tightly her knuckles turned white and her nail beds blood pink. She couldn't utter a word. She sipped and nodded and smiled over and over again. Finally she was left to her thoughts; left to find an escape hatch while everyone occupied themselves with appetizers and cake.

Samantha was so self-absorbed she didn't notice the two men approach her from behind.

"I thought you'd never be alone," Skyler whispered. "You look wonderful. Happy birthday, my sweet," he said, handing her a small silver-wrapped box.

"You . . . I can't accept this," Samantha said, stuttering, unsure of what to say, feeling as if all eyes were upon her.

"It's yours. You will take it. You will wear it everyday and think of me. Open it, you'll love it." Skyler ordered, his teeth clenched as he spoke.

Samantha quickly unwrapped the gift, hoping no one was watching. She felt Greg's presence and his uneasiness as he stood on the other side of Skyler, silently observing, as if he were a paid bodyguard. She hated Skyler for bringing him, after all of the things he knew, after what she had told him! As she released the gold necklace from its box, Skyler grabbed it from her hands and quickly clasped it around Samantha's neck.

"It's a broken heart, Samantha. See, it has an 'S' on it. Everyone will think it stands for Samantha, but we'll both know it stands for Skyler. I have one just like it, the other half—your other half." Skyler whispered from behind her neck. "The halves belong together."

Samantha turned to face him, her face flushed with anger; her eyes like daggers in his. She could not speak for fear Skyler would tell her secrets. After all, he had promised her a special surprise on her birthday. Was it the necklace, or was it Greg?

"You don't have to say anything. It's your day, you should enjoy it. I brought your buddy, Greg, so you remember to behave in college. Remember you are mine, and you'd better stay that way. If I find out you've even thought about being with someone else . . ." Skyler knew he didn't have to finish the sentence. Her eyes told him she understood.

"By the way, before we leave, I want you to know I played your little tape to Greg. He won't be bothering you again; unless you want him to," Skyler whispered, snickering a sarcastic "happy birthday" as the pair turned and walked away.

In her silent anguish, Samantha saw the room and the faces melt away like a kaleidoscope of burning plastic. She wanted to close her eyes. She wanted to erase them from her vision. She wanted to run, to hide, to take a shower, to scream.

Samantha took a few steps backward, fully intent on retiring to her room to collect her composure. Instead she felt a headache that overwhelmed her with instant pain, stymieing both her desire and her ability to leave. Suddenly, though, she was separated. Magically, mystically, her will had come true. She could hear the others, but she could not see them. It seemed to Samantha she'd somehow floated away, far away to her safe place, her private place.

She looked around uncertainly before settling in. The serenity in the silence of her room was magical; her bed, comfortable. Relax, she told herself. Relax.

Where is Tom? Stacey thought, looking around the room, as she was handed a fresh glass of champagne. That was odd, he was just here talking with someone she didn't recognize. He'd better not be cheating on me with her. No, Tom would never do that to me, she reasoned. As she looked around the room, she felt lost without Tom by her side. She needed to be near him in this large crowd with all of these people she did not know. As independent and confident as she was, she knew she didn't fit in with this phony crowd trying to impersonate real people. She wanted to find Tom and leave this masquerade. She felt claustrophobic. As she turned and swallowed her last drop of champagne, her eyes cast themselves upon Tom, another man, and the unknown girl. Slowly, inconspicuously, moving toward them, she strained to hear their conversation.

"So I hear you and Samantha have been doing quite a bit of shopping lately. Did you leave anything in town for the rest of us to buy?" Skyler asked, laughing.

"Just the big ticket items we couldn't carry," Emily retorted. "We found some great things for school. It's been great being with Samantha these past two weeks."

"Yes, she is a lovely girl. I'm sure she'll do well in college. Her father tells me she is leaning toward a pre-law major. He's very proud of her" Skyler paused. "Can I get you anything to drink, champagne or a cocktail? Perhaps a few more appetizers?" he said flirtatiously, moving closer to Emily.

"No, thanks, I've already had too much to eat and I really don't drink. I—"

"Come now, that's not what I hear," Skyler said teasingly, in a low sensual voice, his lips almost touching her ear.

As he winked and walked away, Emily felt like a naughty child who had done something very wrong. She wasn't sure what to make of it. Surely, she had interpreted his actions in the wrong way. Maybe it was the champagne getting to her; two glasses wasn't much, but then again she was not used to alcohol. Emily wasn't sure what Skyler's comment meant, and she didn't want to find out. She saw Samantha walking toward them as Skyler drifted, Greg meekly at his heels, toward the appetizer table.

"Sam? Samantha!" Emily called out as she watched her friend walk right past her. "Sam? Is something wrong? Are you mad at me?" Emily asked, turning Samantha around to face her. "Where are you going?"

"What?" Stacey said, looking at the stranger who had touched her. "I'm looking for my boyfriend Tom, Tom Marks. Do you know him?"

"What are you talking about? Tom . . . Skyler 's brother?

Skyler told me Tom is away at school. Is he here?"

"Of course he's here, he brought me."

"What are you talking about? Are you all right? You're not making any sense. I think you'd better let me take you upstairs. You really shouldn't drink. It always makes you strange," Emily said with sisterly concern, forgetting completely about her troublesome chat with Skyler.

"I'm perfectly fine," Stacey said, looking around the room only to see she had lost sight of Tom and his companion. Stacey looked perplexed as the strange girl pulled on her arm and motioned her out into the foyer and up the stairs.

"No, I don't think so. I don't think you're fine. Come on, let's get out of here for a while. It'll be quiet upstairs," Emily said quietly, trying to avoid any attention as they left the room.

Opening the door to Samantha's room, Emily turned on the light and ordered Samantha to lay on the bed. Stacey saw the concern in the girl's eyes and curiously followed her orders. After all, Tom was so preoccupied talking with people he knew, he didn't even notice I was there; he probably won't notice I'm gone.

"Here is a cool cloth. I think you should lie down for a few minutes with this on your forehead. You look really flushed. It'll make you feel better." Emily placed a cool damp cloth on Samantha's face.

Stacey started to argue but decided the sooner she went along with this girl, the sooner she'd be free of her.

"I'll be back in a few minutes. I want to make sure you're not missed. Your parents will make a federal case out of you being sick," Emily said, shutting off the light and closing the door behind her.

Emily checked her watch every few minutes. She had decided to give Samantha half an hour to sleep and then she'd wake her with a cup of coffee. It would be easy enough to walk out of the room with the coffee, but covering for Samantha would be difficult if her parents asked where she was. They'd never believe she didn't know. They wouldn't like it if they knew Samantha was in her room. Emily decided the best idea was to stay clear of Samantha's immediate family.

Stacey closed her eyes in surrender. Samantha slept soundly, except for the music box. She couldn't find it; she couldn't close it to stop the sound. But she could hear the words that went with it. She couldn't get them out of her mind. "Humpty Dumpty sat on a wall; Humpty Dumpty had a great fall; All the kings horses and all the king's men couldn't put Humpty together again." Who was chanting those words? She felt as if the words were coming out from inside of her; yet her voice was not her own. Whose voice was it? Was someone there? Samantha tried to speak, to call out. No words came. The music was coming closer and closer, louder and louder. Samantha twirled round and round, faster and faster. Still she could not see the music box. The room was spinning . . .

"Samantha? Samantha?" the voice whispered. Samantha opened her eyes. She focused, confused. Where was she? Why was Emily standing over her?

"How are you feeling?" Emily asked.

"What are you doing here? Why am I here? Is the party over?"

"You don't remember? I haven't been gone that long. Here, have some coffee." Emily said, sitting on the edge of Samantha's bed and staring at her friend.

"I feel fine," Samantha said, as she sipped the hot coffee.

"You weren't making any sense when I brought you up here. You didn't even seem to recognize me. You really shouldn't drink. Alcohol gets to you too quickly."

"I only had two, maybe three glasses of champagne. I didn't even finish them. Every time I sat one down, some maid came along and took it. Besides, since when do you tell me not to drink? Who made you my mother?" Samantha said, squinting her eyes at Emily, studying her carefully, cautiously, as if she were seeing her for the first time.

"I'm sorry. It's just you weren't you; you scared me. You were saying strange things."

"Like what? I don't remember saying anything. In fact, I don't remember you coming up here with me. Actually," Samantha added in a low contemplative tone, "I don't remember coming up here at all." She was embarrassed to admit to Emily she didn't remember leaving the birthday party and coming to her room. The last thing she remembered was having a headache and wanting to get away from Greg and Skyler.

"You were talking about having a boyfriend named Tom. You said you came to the party with him. Trust me, you weren't making any sense. You don't have a boyfriend you haven't told me about, do you?"

"Get a grip. You know I don't have a boyfriend! And, I can't think of anyone named Tom at my party— Oh my God, Emily! How long have I been up here? We've got to get downstairs. My parents will kill me if they think I ditched my own birthday party. You just don't know how they treated me all summer," Samantha said, suddenly frantic, shaking her head. "Trust me, this is not good."

"Okay. I know. You've told me. Don't worry, I'll cover for you. If they say anything, we'll tell them I wasn't feeling well."

"Thanks. Let's hope it works!" Samantha said, rolling her eyes in apprehension.

After descending the stairs, they immediately inserted themselves into a large conspicuous group of people. The party was so large, spreading throughout the house and the backyard, no one had missed the girls. The Armstrongs, always the perfect hosts, kept their company busy; each relative holding up their end of the entertaining, as was expected.

Soon the three siblings and Emily found their way to the game room with their cousins, as was their tradition at every family function. Anne summoned her three children, when people began to leave, so they could stand united as a family and properly thank their guests as they slowly departed. Samantha, Taylor and Tad had always hated this part of any family gathering; and, as each guest left, one of the siblings invariably smirked some rude comment underneath his or her breath that sent the trio into gales of laughter. It was a tradition the twins had begun and taught Samantha as soon as she could learn to speak. It was private, it was fun and it was theirs. They knew it was childish, but it was a tradition they vowed never to break. It was their exclusive stress reliever.

Anne and Travis were relaxed. They had both had too much to drink, each drinking for their own reasons. Anne because her house was about to be empty, another child's room vacated. Samantha leaving for college made it final; she was old and alone, except for her husband and her work. Where had the time gone? She wondered with each glance at her grown children and with every look in the mirror. Even with three adult children and years of learned wisdom, she still in her heart and soul felt like a young bride.

Travis, happy each of his children seemed content, was not ready to let go of a daughter he'd spent the past eighteen years protecting. Maybe he'd overprotected her, but she'd needed it. Then he winced. The thought of her alone and so far away made him crazy. The picture of her dating, staying out late, and . . . It was the "and." He couldn't even think about any man touching his daughter. His children were gone, he was a success; now what would he do? Retirement? Never. He was still in his prime. It wasn't that he was afraid of it—he just wasn't ready for it. What was next for him? He'd achieved everything he'd ever dreamed of. Travis shuddered at the fleeting thoughts, pushing them aside. Today was his daughter's day. Some other day he'd worry about himself.

Chapter 19

As the remaining days at home blended one into the other, Samantha grew restless for her escape to freedom, to college. Even Emily couldn't keep her occupied and content at home. Samantha worried a lot. More often than not she would find herself not remembering what had happened or would find herself dressed in clothes she didn't remember putting on. She blamed it on the stress she felt all the time, in all directions. There was no other explanation she could think of. After all, she remembered the important things. It was the small things she couldn't remember, couldn't explain. Things like, what time did she fall asleep, why wasn't she at home when she told Emily she would be, why did her legs ache and cramp up like she'd been running, and when did she change her clothes? It was haunting her that she couldn't remember or explain.

Samantha remembered Nana forgetting things and telling her "forgetfulness was the result of a busy mind". Nana also said "when people became preoccupied with life, the small things would slip through the brain; but the big, important things would be there forever to be retrieved when they were most needed." Samantha liked thinking of Nana and her words. They made sense to her; they were comforting to her. Most of all, they kept Nana close to her. Vividly she remembered Nana asking, "Will you remember me when I'm gone?"

And Samantha remembered her coined response was, "You'll never leave me."

And then one day she did. And in an instant, Samantha was left alone, forever. But Nana's words, her voice; they were always with Samantha, and for that she was grateful.

Without her thoughts of Nana these past months, she would have been left without hope and really alone. Nana's presence in her memory gave her a strength she hadn't known she'd had. Thank you Nana, she whispered in the silence, smiling up at her picture on the shelf next to Minnie. Grabbing it, she carefully packed the picture between her sweaters.

Samantha's headaches had increased, and she decided as soon as she had settled in her dorm room and her classes, she would see a doctor. She couldn't believe Labor Day was this weekend and she'd be in Michigan in four days. As she packed the last of her boxes and labeled them, she left out only those clothes she needed for the long weekend, carefully placing them in her overnight bag. At the very bottom of the bag, underneath the padding, she placed containers of pills she had pilfered from her parents' collection. Some of the prescriptions were outdated. She was able to retrieve them from the small gold garbage bin next to her mother's night stand.

Emily was about to pick her up. The girls, with their parents' permission, had decided they would spend the weekend at Emily's summer home. Their parents would join them on Monday and help close up the house for the winter months. They assured their parents they'd be fine and they wouldn't really be alone because the staff would be doing the final cleaning for the year. Reluctantly, both sets of parents had agreed, sensing the urgency and need for the girls to spend the last days of summer together.

Samantha looked around her room, confident she wouldn't miss it once she was gone. Her brothers didn't miss anything from home except a few of the favorite dishes Cook spoiled them with. She wouldn't miss the food; she wouldn't miss anything.

The twins' stories about college and law school were so exciting. She was sorry to see them go, but they said they couldn't stay away for more than a week from their clerking positions, even though they were on summer break from school. Samantha suspected their reason for leaving was more due to the fact their father kept quizzing them every chance he could and their mother treated them as if they were nine again. She wished she had gotten a chance to ask them questions about the words on her list. But she didn't. She couldn't. She felt guilty bugging them as her father did, so instead they spent their time giving her advice on how to survive college. The house really felt empty when the twins left. She knew her parents felt it, but Samantha was surprised at how lonely she felt without them. Samantha had never before felt that strongly about their departure. This time was different. Different because all of their lives were changing; she wouldn't always be there when they came home, and they might not be home when she visited. Life at home was about to change, for everyone, in every aspect, whether they wanted it to or not.

"Samantha? Are you up there? Are you ready?" Emily asked excitedly, as she climbed the stairs to the familiar room.

"Get up here! Of course I'm ready. I've just got one bag and my purse. Cook made us a basket. She wouldn't tell me what she packed, but she guaranteed me we'd like it. Cook said she packed our favorites so we wouldn't want to stop along the way and get fast food," Samantha said. She smiled fondly as she repeated Cook's words, imitating her voice. "Never can tell who ya meet in them restaurants and wha'cha eat along the road. Better you eat my food and stay put."

Emily smiled, understanding Cook's words were to show she cared about the girls. She was always a second mother to both of them.

"That sounds like our Cook. I'll go with you to the kitchen to thank her. Just don't tell her I stopped at the Stop, Gas and Go to buy junk food. She'll take it right out of the car!"

Samantha laughed lightheartedly. She loved the way Emily understood, not just her, but her family. "Shall we?"

"I'm ready whenever you are," Emily said, looking around the room for what would be the last time in a long while. It looked as it always had, but familiar things—Samantha's personal things—were missing. It saddened her.

"Are you going to get that?" Emily asked as Samantha shut the door.

"It figures the phone would ring the minute we're leaving. Okay, I'll get it," Samantha said, talking more to herself and the phone than to Emily.

"Samantha? Your father just told me you are leaving for the weekend and then you'll be leaving for Michigan right after. Why didn't you tell me?" Skyler said angrily.

"I didn't think about it," Samantha said breathlessly, her heart pounding. Emily took a seat on her bed. Could Emily hear the conversation? How would she explain it?

"That's abundantly clear. Who are you going with?"

"Just Emily."

"And who else?"

"No one. We just wanted to be alone before our folks

come up."

"And how many parties are you planning?"

"None. That's not why we're going."

"Why should I believe you? If there was nothing to tell, then you would have told me; there'd be nothing to hide."

"I didn't hide anything. I just forgot. It didn't seem important."

"Everything you do is important to me. Haven't I made that clear to you?" Skyler said, through a tightly clenched jaw.

Samantha hesitated. Emily stared at her, wide-eyed. She began to sweat and felt a headache coming on. She closed her eyes and concentrated on getting Skyler off the phone.

"Yes, I'm sorry. Can I call you when we get there?" Samantha said, in as calm a voice as she could find.

"You'd better. Are you wearing my necklace?"

Samantha, unconsciously and out of fear, reached inside her polo shirt and, without pulling it out, felt its presence. "Of course. I said I would."

"Good. That makes me feel better. I'd better not find you without it."

Samantha remained silent. She did not want to respond. She had nothing left to say.

"Have fun, sweetie. You have my numbers, call me. Regardless, you know I'll call you!"

"Bye," Samantha said, not acknowledging Skyler's last words.

"Who was that?" Emily asked. "Are you seeing someone you haven't told me about?

"No. Let's get out of here! I swear, I'll tell you later. I just can't talk about it here, now," Samantha pleaded. "Please?"

Emily was frightened for her friend. Mute and puzzled, she followed her. Emily's thoughts retreated to the Samantha she'd left a few months ago. She'd never seen her like this. At least not since last spring when they had a little too much to drink. Was this related to drinking? She contemplated the correlation, looking earnestly for another nexus to explain Samantha's behavior.

Lost in their own thoughts, averting each other's eyes, the girls climbed down the stairs, retrieved Cook's basket and headed for the beach house. Samantha hated to drive without music blaring and, for now, the loud music was just as good an excuse as any to avoid questions and deep conversation with Emily. She felt bad keeping Emily at bay without even a hint, but she just couldn't find the words to explain. How much of that phone conversation had she heard? How much could she explain to Emily without lying—without telling her everything? How much *should* she tell her? Samantha needed someone with objectivity to talk to. She had been through a lifetime of growing pains with Emily. They really were sisters. Maybe telling Emily would relieve some of the stress she felt. Maybe she would be able to stop forgetting so many things if she felt less stress; maybe her headaches would stop. So many maybes . . . Samantha bit the inside of her lip to keep it from quivering and to keep herself from crying. She wished she had definite answers. Maybes scared her.

Emily wasn't sure what to say to Samantha, what to ask. She was glad the music was too loud to talk. Who had Sam been talking to? It didn't sound as if she liked the person on the other end of the phone. Had she been hiding a boyfriend? Why didn't she tell her anything about him—they'd always shared everything. At least until last spring. Had Samantha been mad at her since last spring, so mad she stopped telling her things? No. That didn't make any sense. Emily replayed as much of the conversation as she could remember in her mind, slowly, hoping for a clue. And then she remembered one. Samantha had referred to her; she'd said "Emily, we wanted to be alone." She didn't explain who I was, Emily thought. That must mean she'd told the person a lot about me, or I know the person, Emily rationalized. Who do I know Samantha would date she wouldn't want me to find out about? Emily wrinkled her forehead as she made a long list of possibilities, beginning with their high school classmates. She pondered the question for a long time, but she couldn't come up with anyone. It just didn't make any sense to her.

# # #

Skyler hung up the phone and stared at the files in front of him. He was in the last stages of the Castriano trial. He would offer final proofs next week, then make closing arguments. He had to come up with a brilliant closing argument;

Mr. Castriano would pay him well beyond his fees. Skyler smiled. There are more ways than one to get ahead in this town. Where was Samantha when he needed her? She skipped out on him. She left him! She would learn not to do that again. He creased his forehead and squinted his eyes intently. She would remember her lesson.

As Skyler pictured Samantha dancing, flirting, in the arms of another man, his brow began to moisten. He unbuttoned his collar and loosened his tie. He couldn't concentrate. He shouldn't have to be in the office working on the long holiday weekend. But he would work as long as he had to. He had to win this case. His mind kept wandering to visions of Samantha. Her touch, her taste, her smell. Enraged, he threw his papers angrily across the long oak desk and crumbled his notes. Shaking with outrage, he dialed the summer house. There was no answer. Had she lied? He dialed again. And again. Surely the maids would answer if they were there. He hit redial.

Skyler reached into the drawer and grabbed a small scroll topped brass key from the back of his file drawer. Without looking at it he instinctively walked across the room and removed the heavy statues from in front of his small black office safe. As he turned the tumblers, he heard the dull click that opened the heavy door. Reaching in, he grabbed a large shot glass and fresh bottle of Royal Crown Whiskey. Pouring one, then another, straight into his chest in two swift motions, he took a long deep cleansing breath. He felt warm and relaxed. Using the small key, he opened the contents of a carved dark cherry box. Guarded, Skyler reviewed its contents and smiled a sinister grin. Samantha was his and he had all the proof he needed to make her his for a very long time. Carefully, he pulled out a micro cassette tape. Next, he retrieved the meticulously labeled evidence bags. All memories of Samantha; strands of hair, an earring, a broken fingernail. He grabbed the large sealed manila envelope and opened it; the doctor's file. It was beautifully detailed. It was all there, and it was all his, just as she was.

Let her enjoy her weekend! Let her go to school. Let her live her life. He would be there with her throughout it all! She was his. And his insurance would see it stayed that way. He gulped another glass of the gold liquid confidence. Carefully he put away his memorabilia and dialed the beach house again. As he heard the echo of the ring, he clinked the phone onto speaker and listened to it ring and ring and ring. He again began working, all the while making mental notes of each ringing minute that passed.

# # #

During the long ride, the girls made their peace, as if the incident earlier hadn't happened. Neither wanted to spoil their last weekend before college separated them. Instinctively, they knew they would discuss it. Later.

As the girls entered the long driveway leading to the beach house, they were silent. Each lost in her own thoughts, mindlessly they exclaimed surprise at how full the green oak trees were. Emily would miss watching them slowly change into a burst of colors against the background blue of the water. The picture of southern autumn would stay etched in her mind for eternity, she decided, letting go of her suddenly sad feelings.

The trees would soon transform into an autumn colored rainbow. They were indicative of the change she hoped she would experience in college. She could feel it so strongly it filled the silence. Emily understood Samantha's silence and for a long time did not interrupt it.

"So what do you want to do first?" Emily asked. She kept her tone light, but she was studying Samantha's every movement.

"Let's unpack. I'd really like to wash up and maybe go for a walk along the shore. We could talk there. Okay?" Samantha tried to sound casual, but her heart was beating fast. She was sure Emily could hear its rapid pounding. She was also sure she had better talk with Emily before Emily got it into her head to mention anything to her parents or anyone else.

"That sounds great. Let's take the rest of Cook's food," Emily said calmly, trying not to sound as anxious as she felt.

Setting down her bags, Emily unlocked the front door. Immediately, the girls heard the phone's beckoning ring. "Must be one of our parents," she laughed. "You'd think they didn't trust us to get here in one piece!" Picking up the receiver, expecting her mother to be on the other end, she said, "You've got great timing! We just got here."

"That's strange," Emily said, turning to Samantha as she replaced the receiver. "I guess whomever it was didn't like my comments. They hung up." Noticing Samantha's silence, Emily asked, "Don't you find that hang-up a little strange?"

Samantha remained silent. She knew the caller had to be Skyler. He hadn't believed what she was doing; now he'd know. I'm glad I didn't answer it. She followed Emily up the winding staircase. After they took their bags to Emily's room to unpack, Samantha made the excuse she had forgotten her purse in the car. She made her way to the breakfast room, found the phone and dialed Skyler's car phone number, knowing he wouldn't answer.

"I'm not available, please leave a message . . ." Skyler's recorded voice said while Samantha decided what she'd say.

"You asked me to call. We're here and we're going for a walk. I hope you get this message. No one answered at the office when I tried your line, so I thought you'd be in the car. Bye," Samantha whispered in the stillness of the immense house.

"Samantha? Are you down there? Come on up. I can't wait to get outside," Emily yelled anxiously down the staircase.

"Coming," replied Samantha. "Just wanted to leave a message at my dad's office that we got in and we would be out for a while. You know how they worry."

The girls unpacked and freshened up in silence, each again, lost in thought. Each filled with anticipation and disappointment. Emily still couldn't believe her best friend had hidden something from her. Samantha couldn't believe she'd been taken off guard by the phone call and caught. More than that, she couldn't believe her best friend was now suspicious of her.

Emily stared at Samantha, trying to anticipate what she would be told. Judging by Sam's behavior, it must be really bad. But what did that mean? What was the worst thing she could be told by Samantha?

Samantha tried to concentrate, preparing herself for what she was about to tell Emily. How much should she tell her? She still hadn't decided. Emily's reaction filled her with alarm, despite her now calm and cheerful mood. She could feel Emily's eyes following her every movement, analyzing every vibration. It was almost as bad as being at home with her parents, she thought sullenly.

The pre-autumn weather was brisk near the water, although the sun gave no hint of relinquishing its control. As the girls strolled along, picnic basket and cooler in hand, they moved slowly, casually, letting the wind comb through their wisps and carry their long manes into the breeze behind them. The silence between them brought the need to speak to an urgent head. They knew it was time, yet neither spoke. They were afraid. Emily, of what she would learn; Samantha of what she had to tell.

"So, Sam, are you gonna talk to me or what?" Emily said, taking a deep breath and letting out an exasperated sigh.

"Okay, I'm sorry. You're right. Let's go over to the rock pile near the weeping willow," Samantha said, trying to buy just a few more minutes.

Samantha knelt on the grassy area and spread a large cloth. Carefully, strategically, she placed the basket and cooler on its corners so the wind would not disturb them. Emily studied her. This was not Samantha. Samantha never straightened anything. Samantha always said exactly what she meant. Quietly, Emily continued to watch Samantha. Someone had stolen her; invaded her body and snatched her soul. This person before her being so careful, so meticulous about everything, was not Samantha. What could be that bad? She waited in silent trepidation.

Fear grasped Samantha's mind. It infiltrated her nervous system. She felt faint and unsure of herself. As she opened her mouth to speak, she heard an unfamiliar rasp in her voice. Surely she wasn't so nervous she couldn't speak? Take a drink of soda and try again, she told herself. Relax, relax. As she listened to the pounding of her heart and her own rapid breathing she was sure Emily could hear it too.

"You were right, Emily," Samantha began, avoiding direct eye contact with her. It was the only way she could maintain control enough to speak. "I was talking to a boy, but he's not a boy. I mean, he's a man." Samantha looked up at Emily's wide-eyed stare and tightly clenched jaw and took a deep cleansing breath before continuing.

"You know him. It was Skyler."

"Skyler Marks from the office? Why is he calling you?"

"He helped me out a few months ago and now he . . . well, he doesn't want to see me get hurt and so he keeps a close eye on me."

"Sam, that doesn't make sense. How did he help you? Do your parents know?"

"No. And you can't tell them. You can't tell anyone. You swore you wouldn't." Samantha grabbed Emily's arm firmly, without concern about the strength of her grip.

"And I won't. You know I won't tell. I can't believe you haven't told me this before. Does this have anything to do with how you were acting last spring?"

"Kind of."

"Well, then, c'mon Sam—spill it. I only want to help you—unless you really don't trust me after all these years."

Samantha closed her eyes and began, clenching her woven fingers together tightly while her body rocked forward and back, slowly, evenly, in rhythm with her voice. "My parents weren't home. I wanted a change of scenery, so I went to the public library to study. I was there longer than I should have been and it had gotten dark, really dark. My parents were supposed to call from Washington and I was worried I'd miss their call. You know how they worry when I'm not home on time. So I . . ." Samantha hesitated, as tears spilled through her lashes with such great speed the droplets glistened on her wringing hands. "I cut through the alley way. And there he was. And he grabbed me and he—"

"Who grabbed you, Sam? Skyler?" Emily asked softly, gently patting her friend's shoulder, still unsure of what had happened that could have brought on such inner turmoil and tears. Samantha had never been one to cry easily. It was usually just the opposite; *she* was usually the one to cry.

"No. A man . . . it was. . ." Samantha stopped and then hearing a familiar voice crying from somewhere deep inside, quickly continued, "I didn't see him. He pinned me. I couldn't move. He was too big and heavy and I couldn't move. His belt was around my neck. It was hard to breathe. I thought I would pass out . . . and then he. . . he raped me." Samantha sobbed loudly, clenching her hands to her face, her ears, her stomach. Tightly she wrapped her arms around her waist, her eyes closed tightly, trying to constrict her words from her ability to visualize. Remembering. Warm, wet, salty tears, streamed steadily. Rocking back and forth in the silence, she waited for Emily to speak. She couldn't look at her.

"My God!" Emily gasped. "Samantha, did you tell the police? Why didn't you tell your parents? Or me? We all would have helped you. Sam, you have to report it; give the police a description! What if he comes after you again—or someone else?"

"No," Samantha said. "It's too late. I can't tell anyone. I'm sorry I didn't tell you, but I just couldn't. It was so awful. Too awful to believe. Too awful to talk about."

"I still don't understand what Skyler had to do with anything."

"He, well he was there at the door in the morning. I looked so bad—bruised, and I was shaking, and I just sort of blurted it out."

"But he's an attorney. Why didn't he take you to the police?"

"You don't understand. I was hysterical. I had taken a shower. I cleaned off all the evidence, and it would be just my word against the attacker. That's what Skyler told me. And my parents, the media would have had a field day with the story! I didn't want my parents to be upset."

"Samantha, this doesn't make any sense. Why would you think they would be upset with *you*? You were the victim."

"I wasn't supposed to be in the alley. They always told me to stay away from the alley. They would have blamed me."

Rubbing her hands over her face in futility, Emily looked at her friend. Now what? Frustrated, she fought away her own tears. What do I say? What do I do? She stared disbelievingly at her friend.

"I'm sorry," a tearful Samantha whispered in a raspy voice; then biting her lip, she said it again.

"Sorry? You have nothing to be sorry for. It wasn't your fault! But, you should have—I mean I wish you would have told me. I would have found a way to help you."

"No. Really, there was nothing anyone could have done. It's over and I just want to forget about it."

"Were you tested at least? Are you all right, really? What

about AIDS?"

Samantha took a deep breath, trying to calm herself so she could calm and reassure her friend.

"Yes. I had an AIDS test right after it happened, and I went for another one last week. I went out of town for the test. I didn't use my real name. But they say I'm fine. I'm going to go for another in six months, just to make sure."

Emily listened carefully as these incredible words came out of her friends mouth. The words didn't fit; they were out of character, out of place. But here they were. Reality at its finest, she thought bitterly.

"I still don't understand about Skyler. Why is he still calling you? What does he want?"

"He started calling me and checking on me, and he even got me out of the house a few times at first, right after it happened, when I was too frightened to leave. Somehow he just got really possessive of me, and he's always checking up on me." Samantha paused, studying her friend's face, then added, "He's worried the guy will come back. I just get tired of his phone calls."

"Really? I couldn't tell from the tone of voice you used when he called," Emily quipped sarcastically, trying to make her friend laugh.

Samantha looked at her through tears and suddenly turned up a corner of her mouth. "Yeah, I guess I was a little bitchy to him. Okay, a lot bitchy. But the guy deserves it. He won't leave me alone."

"Just tell him to." Emily said matter of factly.

"It's not like that. He just doesn't listen. I think it's the lawyer in him. He's just like our fathers. They must teach it or something in law school or at the firm. All the lawyers in the firm act the same. Skyler is no different. He has his opinion, his side of the argument, his needs. And he won't listen to me. What I think or want isn't important to him. "

"We'll make him listen," Emily said defiantly.

"No. No, you can't. You promised. I don't want to make him mad. He really means well. Besides, I'm leaving on Monday. What's a few more days?"

Samantha's eyes pleaded with her friend. Emily knew her friend meant it by the tone in her voice; it actually gave Emily a fleeting thought Samantha was desperate—desperate enough to commit suicide, run away, do something really crazy. No, Emily unequivocally decided, she would have done those things already. She'll be fine, she mentally comforted herself.

"Swear you'll tell me everything. Swear you'll tell me if he doesn't leave you alone?"

"I swear, Emily; I'll tell you. Just please don't say anything to anyone. I just couldn't bear anyone else to know."

Samantha hadn't lied. She just hadn't told the whole truth. She couldn't tell her friend the rest; she was clear about that. She didn't want to put either one of them in any danger. She'd be gone in a few days and then it wouldn't matter; it would be all over. It would all be behind her.

Emily was happy Samantha finally confided in her. So many things finally made sense. Emily was sorry for her friend, but she understood. What would she have done in her situation? She shuddered. She couldn't think about it, she didn't want to. She had to think about Samantha. Could she find a way to help her?

They talked for hours. They had so many things to catch up on. Real things. Real thoughts and dreams. Feelings they hadn't shared with anyone else; feelings they couldn't share with anyone else.

The sunset was beautiful, peaceful and magnificent. It gave the girls a new beginning. Their friendship had been reborn; a new, more potent relationship had been created. Now, in sync with nature's silence, a stronger pact between them, they strolled up to the house. The lights had been turned on in every room in the house. They understood, without discussion, the servants had arrived for the busy task of closing the beach house. They retired into the house with the empty remnants of Cook's basket, comfortable with the promise they had made to have the most enjoyable, most relaxing weekend they could have, before college and adulthood separated them.

Chapter 20

The trip to Michigan was the longest drive Samantha had ever made by herself.

The knowledge she had made it without any problems boosted her confidence in herself and in her own abilities. Settled in the bottom bunk of the small dormitory bed, she looked at the initials carved into the hard wood over the years. She wondered who they were, what their lives were like now and if their spirit would bring her luck.

As she climbed out of her comforter into the morning, she smoothed the worn, oversized green and white college football jersey her brothers had given her on her twelfth birthday. She felt independent, emancipated, truly liberated. Most of all, she felt autonomous. She wanted to shed the clutter that had become part of her mind, now, while she felt powerful. This must be what it is like to be newly born. She wished she could totally transform into a new life, not just a new beginning. She was determined to take one day at a time, moving forward positively each day.

Standing in the morning breeze that drifted through her open dormitory window, she stretched. The campus was beautiful, from the little she had seen in the dark of night. She was grateful she had a third-floor room. Not only did she have an expansive view of the campus, but she already felt safe there. It was a long hike to carry all of her boxes, but her room was at the end of the hall, more private than the others, and a bit larger as well. Smiling contently, she looked around at the maze of boxes she had piled into the small open area between furniture. She still had a few in her car to carry up after breakfast.

She stretched. When would her roommate arrive? She decided to find her way to the cafeteria, even though she wasn't hungry, because she wanted to learn her way around the dorm and the campus as quickly as possible. Samantha felt lucky she was let in last night, since the dorm didn't officially open until this morning. The handsome Resident Assistant she had awoken just a few hours earlier, told her that traditionally the dorms didn't open until the Thursday morning before classes began, except for the R.A.'s (as she learned they were called), since they had the task of settling everyone in. Fortunately, he already knew the room assignments for the entire dorm and was either too tired or too nice to turn her away. Samantha would thank him later for helping her unload most of her things. He was so kind she'd felt at ease with him almost the instant he spoke. Samantha wondered, as she got dressed for the day, if all of the people would be as nice as he was. John Scott. Even his name had a nice ring to it. It was simple, yet poetic sounding, she decided, as she said it out loud.

Where was the R.A. for her floor? She opened her door and looked down the long hallway. Taking a deep breath, she stuck her room key into her back pocket and headed out to search for the cafeteria. It wasn't hard to find. She followed the aroma of food and the trail of people. Although everyone ignored her, as though she didn't exist, she felt at ease as she grabbed a tray. She did not want to feel visible, or even be visible. She simply wanted to be left alone in her new cocoon so she could make her metamorphosis without criticism. So far, everything was as she'd imagined, as she had hoped.

When Samantha looked at her filled tray, she was surprised at the hunger she was feeling. It had been a long time since she'd actually thought favorably about eating. She sat down and removed the heavy, glazed plates from the tray. A newspaper had been laid on the seat next to hers. "The State News." How cool! The university had its own newspaper. She lifted it curiously and smelled its freshly inked pages.

Suddenly she stiffened. Every nerve froze as she felt the firm hand on her shoulder.

"Hey, first you wake me out of a deep sleep, then you work me to death, and now you steal my paper? What's a guy to do with you?"

The deep voice frightened her until her brain, frantically, cohesively, put the face and the voice together. She let out a sigh of relief. Startled, speechless, Samantha looked into the large Tootsie Roll-brown eyes of the Resident Assistant. She blushed as if he'd precisely read her earlier thoughts about him.

"John! Hi. You startled me. I didn't mean to take your paper. I mean, I didn't know it belonged to anyone. I'd like to buy my own. Where can I get one?"

"Calm down. You look like you've seen a ghost! I didn't mean to break your concentration. I'm just kidding about the paper." John set his tray down across from hers. "The paper is free. They are delivered to every dorm early in the morning. Someone else left it here."

She watched in amazement as his long legs bent to seat himself comfortably at her table. He was so casual. He was so confident. Was he always like this?

"Can I join you?"

"Of course. I'm actually glad you found me. You're the only one I know, and I hate to eat alone."

"Has your roommate arrived?"

"No, I don't think so. I'm kind of anxious to meet her."

"Don't worry. I'm sure you'll make lots of friends. Would you like me to introduce you to some people? I—"

"No!" Samantha said, with more force than she had intended. She looked up at his raised brow and puzzled expression. Samantha had cut him off too quickly, and she knew it the second she had opened her mouth. He must think I'm a ninny, she thought, biting the inside of her cheek as her downcast eyes focused on her barely eaten scrambled eggs.

"I'm sorry. I didn't mean to imply you couldn't make friends on your own. I just thought I could give you a head start. Sometimes it's not as easy to make friends as you might think," John said, studying the face of his beautiful breakfast companion for any clue as to how deeply he had upset her.

"It's okay. I mean, I should be the one who is sorry. I didn't mean to snap at you." Samantha paused and, as if she were Scarlett O'Hara, batted her long dark lashes before looking directly into his eyes. "I just want to take one thing at a time and stay focused on my school work. If I meet too many people right away, I might not study."

John paused for a moment, almost forgetting what they were talking about. In the instant this fair-skinned, dark-haired, blue-eyed beauty looked at him, it was as if he recoined the phrase, "don't it make my brown eyes blue." He was filled with her look of innocence and frailty, her sweet mouth and most of all, her piercing eyes. They consumed him with emotion, and cut right through him. They were the most vibrant eyes he'd ever seen, or maybe just the first eyes he'd really noticed in such detail. Suddenly, understanding she was waiting for him to respond, he revived himself and spoke.

"Oh, I get it. You've heard Michigan State is a party school, and you are afraid you'll party too much. That's smart. Most freshman don't think like that. Every term I know someone who gets put on academic probation and another kid who leaves school because they can't get off probation. I admire your commitment," John said, smiling. Picking up his hot coffee he silently toasted her approvingly with the mug before putting it to his full broad lips. He saw her expression immediately relax.

Samantha liked John. He was so easygoing and kind. He seemed honest and trustworthy. But could she trust him? Samantha had to smile at herself. She barely knew him! She would see what happened in time. Maybe after today, when the dorm was filled, she wouldn't ever see him again. Surely he had a lot of friends: it was hard not to like him. Looking up at him, she watched him clear his plate. His handsome face revealed a strong jaw, kind eyes, and thick, barely black brows framed by a short, casually styled, sportsmanlike haircut. Did he play sports? Should she ask? No. She needed to wait. She had to be careful, had to make sure he was what he appeared to be. She'd been fooled so many times. Besides, there was a lot to do. Sighing, she surmised she had a lot to learn too.

Lost in her own thoughts, she half-listened to John as he described the process of dropping and adding classes, as if she were a sponge soaking up his every word. Her hand unconsciously reached into her pants pocket, and her fingers grabbed and clasped the folded paper with her uninterrupted words.

"Not hungry? Don't worry, you'll get used to dorm food," John laughed, as he watched her scan her plate one last time before letting her fork crash loudly onto it.

"Sure," she said sarcastically, making a sardonic face. "It has to get better. Doesn't it?"

"Yes. Really, it will. There is always a great salad bar and wonderful ice cream cones-soft swirl. Guaranteed to make you forget whatever it is they served."

"I've really got to organize my room. My roommate will hate me if she see's the mess I've left it in. Thanks for sitting with me."

"My pleasure," John said, grinning. "We'll have to do it again. Soon. Let me know if you need any more help moving boxes or even the furniture in your room."

"Thanks," Samantha said, staring into his deep eyes with her best southern smile.

There was no word Samantha could think of to describe how she felt except "elated." It was an unusual feeling for her. It was a feeling John unknowingly helped her recover. Samantha grinned, rolled her eyes, and ran her fingers through her hair. She felt it was possible to walk on air. It seemed only seconds had passed and she was back in her room. Kicking her flats off and flinging herself onto the stiff bunk bed, she looked up, half expecting to see her own white ceiling. She laughed at the coils staring back at her from the upper bunk and relaxed instantly. Closing her eyes she began to picture John. Meeting him had unleashed dormant adolescent romantic feelings that had been forcibly repressed by the horror of Greg and Skyler. It felt good to find normal emotions; to feel them activate. She wanted to memorize John's strong, comforting voice. She tried to capture the way he spoke. She liked his Michigan accent.

Emily. She couldn't wait to tell Emily about him. Even if she never saw him again, it was a good experience and one Emily would enjoy hearing about. She had to call Emily. She'd get out of bed in a few minutes.

Instead, she fell into a deep sleep. Samantha felt her body being lowered down, down, down, into quiet darkness. No faces, no music. Nothing was in the darkness. It was still and peaceful. Then she woke up with a start, at the sound of a loud noise not remembering where she was. The door stood open and one of her stacked boxes had crashed to the floor. Her eyes took this in as she focused on the small figure entering the room.

"Oh, I'm sorry," the strange girl said. "Are you Samantha?"

"Yes. How did you know?"

"Our names are posted on the door. Everyone's names are on their doors. Didn't you see them?"

"No. I got here late last night. I was lucky they let me in. I got up really early and went down for breakfast and then I laid down for a minute. I guess I fell asleep." It was getting dark outside. How long had she slept?

"What time is it?"

"Almost six."

"I guess I really must have been tired! What's your name?"

"Melissa Senger. Everyone calls me Missy. When I arrived, I noticed a lot of people were headed toward the cafeteria. I thought I might go and eat before I empty my car. Do you want to go?"

"Sure. Let me just wash up. It'll only take a second."

As Samantha ran the water, she smiled. Missy looked like a nice girl. She looked like someone she could get along with. She was excited about getting to know her at their first meal together.

"Samantha?" Missy knocked on the door. "You have a phone call."

"I do?" Samantha asked, spitting out the toothpaste, unconsciously raising her eyebrows. "How strange! I didn't give anyone the number yet."

Missy shrugged in response and handed Samantha the black receiver. Samantha was glad the cord stretched all the way to the bathroom. She shut the door and said a curious "hello". Hearing the hoarse, angry response, she began to shake so hard she was afraid she'd drop the receiver.

"So, you finally made it, and you can't call me? I've waited for you to call for three days. You promised me you'd call everyday. Didn't you miss me?" Skyler said angrily.

"I. . ." Samantha took a deep breath in order to calm herself. "How did you get my number? I haven't had time to call anyone."

"I called the campus operator. They list the numbers of all the students in the dorms. You weren't going to give me your number, were you?" Skyler asked sternly, in his finest cross-examination voice.

"Yes, of course I was . . ." Samantha said meekly, hoping her new roommate was not listening at the door.

"Don't lie to me! You didn't miss me either. Maybe I should come up there and remind you of just how close we really are," he said, obviously agitated.

"No. I'm sorry! You caught me off guard. I did miss you. And, really, I haven't had time to call anyone. I got in late last night and I got up really early and had breakfast and then I fell asleep again. I just got up. I—"

"Save it. They are all lies. Every word, a lie. Who is with you in your room?"

"I'm not lying!" Samantha whispered, then quickly added, "Just my roommate; she was the person who answered the phone."

"And who else?"

"No one." When she spoke, her voice was void of all emotion. Everything she had felt earlier was gone, stolen from her. She felt as if he had already tainted her happiness, her place, her new beginning.

"No cute men?"

"No." Samantha said, as an uncontrollable stream of tears rolled down her cheeks.

"You'd better not be lying to me. So where are you off to?"

"We are just going to the cafeteria. I have to spend tonight unpacking the rest of my things and help Missy unpack her car; I promised her I would."

"You'd better be telling me the truth. I have ways I can check up on you, I'll know if you lie to me. I'll call you later. Make sure you answer the phone." Skyler said, hanging up to emphasize his message to her.

She straightened her hair and makeup. What would she say to Missy? Surely, she would ask. Opening the door, she acted cheerful and anxious to get to the cafeteria. To Samantha's surprise, Melissa didn't ask about the phone call, and she didn't offer. As they walked through the hallway, saying hello to all of the bright, anxious faces, Samantha felt that same nagging feeling of helplessness she thought she'd run away from. She remained quiet, nodding occasionally, as she listened to Melissa's chatter.

Finally, as they set their filled trays on the laminated cafeteria table and sat down, Melissa paused briefly and stared at Samantha.

"Why are you so distracted? Are you looking for someone?"

"No. I was looking around to see who was making that

insidious laughing sound. It is really loud."

"Where is it coming from?" Missy said perplexed, looking around the large room. "I don't hear anyone in particular. You must have really good hearing."

"You don't hear that? It's so loud, how can you not hear it? It sounds like it's at our table." Samantha said, turning around to be sure no one was standing behind her. Turning back to a perplexed Missy, Samantha decided not to pursue the issue. She picked up a carrot from her salad plate and she bit into it, hard, hoping the crunching noise would drown out the laughing. It didn't. Samantha's eyes were wide, her ears alert, all her senses on ease, as if she were a cat ready to pounce. Cautiously, she looked around again. No one was there.

And then the laughing disappeared, as if it had never been there at all. Was she going crazy? Samantha looked around again. Missy sat eating contently, smiling at everyone who passed by their table.

Samantha wasn't hungry. She picked at her food, wishing Missy would hurry. Would it be rude to return to their room without her?

"So, are you unpacked?" a deep voice said.

"Hi!" Samantha looked up to see John grinning with a full tray in his hands. Glad for the reprieve from her thoughts, Samantha responded in kind to his friendly grin. "No, actually I fell asleep."

"Can I join you?" John asked, looking as far into Samantha's blue eyes as he could see.

"Sure," Samantha said, suddenly aware he had chosen the chair close to hers. Feeling her heartbeat reacting to his nearness, Samantha looked away casually.

"Hi, I'm John," he said, putting his hand out to Missy.

"Nice to meet you. I'm Missy, Samantha's roommate."

"I'm sorry, I should have introduced you! You caught me off guard," Samantha said, her smile now focused on John, unknowingly sending Missy the clear message he was hers.

John's presence distracted the girls from learning more about each other and focused them on questions related to the dorm and the campus. John held their attention with stories and introduced them to students who passed by their table to say hello to him. By the time they decided to get their room in order, the tables were being cleared and set for breakfast.

Samantha looked at her watch and gasped. "Oh, my God! It can't be almost nine!"

"What's the hurry? Classes don't start till Monday. You've got lots of time." John said casually, silently wondering what her panic was. Surprised at Samantha's overreaction, John raised an eyebrow at Missy, watching her reaction, curious to see if she knew what Samantha was worried about.

"No, it's not that. I promised I'd call my parents. They must be frantic. I haven't called them since I arrived. By now they've probably called the state police!"

"Oh, don't worry. Just go and call them and explain. You said you have brothers in school, I'll bet your parents know what it's like to settle into a dorm and meet new people. You'll see, they'll understand," John said, trying to calm her down.

"I've got to go. See you later," Samantha said barely listening to his response or noticing Missy following her rapid gait.

# # #

Skyler patiently sat at his desk. It had been almost three hours since he had talked with Samantha. Where was she, he wondered, agitated, as his anxious fingers pounded her number again. Listening to the continuous dead ringing, his eyes focused on the corner of the outline of the closing argument he had worked on for hours. The web of counting lines stood out on the white paper. Slamming the phone into its cradle, he added another line and counted them again. Eight lines. One line for every fifteen minutes. Two hours past the one hour it would take her to eat dinner. What could she be doing out of her room for three hours? He would see to it she didn't do it again. She owed him and he owned her. She would take him seriously. He would see to that.

As he rubbed his hand along his cheek, he could feel the day's stubble, rough like sandpaper against his fingers. The rasping sound made him smile. It was a dark smile, a sinister smile; one he saved for his private pleasure. The power Skyler felt in that villainous smile gave him satisfaction. What would her punishment be this time? He pondered, rubbing his stubble more fiercely. Then, looking again at his gold and silver Rolex watch, he pursed his lips. Time to dial again.

# # #

Samantha grabbed her key from her back pocket and began to fit it into the lock. Her body tensed as, through the door, she heard the phone ringing. She knew who was at the other end of the line. Her chest felt heavy. Her heart was beating fiercely and she began to perspire. Clumsily, her key dropped to the floor. Samantha watched as Missy quickly bent down and picked it up. Missy began to hand the key back to Samantha and was about to tease her when she saw how pale Samantha was.

"Are you all right? You look like you're about to faint. Sit down with your head between your knees," she commanded. "I'll open the door."

In an instant both girls were in the room. Samantha plopped her body onto her bed. Fearing she would faint, she let Missy answer the phone.

"Samantha, it's for you. It's your mother," Missy said, walking the receiver over to the bed.

"Samantha, how are you, dear? We were so glad to hear you called and left your number. How do you like it there?"

"It's great, Mom. I've been so busy trying to unpack and meet people. How did you get my number?"

"Why, Skyler, of course. He said you called and left the number with him earlier and you were fine. I'm sorry we weren't home when you called. It was such a beautiful day, your father finished early and we spent the afternoon golfing."

"Oh," Samantha said. Damn him. She listened to her mother's chatter and mumbled an occasional bubbly response; why can't he leave me alone? He had no right to call them.

"Your mom sounds nice," Missy said, studying Samantha as she got up from her bed and hung up the phone. "You look like you're feeling better. I'm going down to my car to get my stuff."

"I'll come down with you and help."

"The way you look? No way. But you can move some of your things so I can get mine in here."

Samantha was glad for a few moments to herself. She needed to collect her thoughts and find a way to not jump every time the phone rang. She took a deep breath and decided to change into her sweats and unpack. That would keep her mind occupied for a while.

The boxes felt heavier than when she and John loaded them into the room. As she began organizing the large chest of drawers, the ring from the phone caused her to jump and broke her concentration. Picking up the receiver, she anticipated she would hear her mother's voice again.

"Hi, Mom. Wha'd you forget to tell me?" Samantha said immediately, dangling the phone between her ear and shoulder as she unzipped the black bulky suitcase.

"Wha'd you forget to tell me?" The deep voice responded.

"Oh. Sorry. I thought it was my mother again," Samantha said, taking a deep breath, closing her eyes and wishing she hadn't answered the phone.

"No, it's just me. Remember me?" Skyler said intensely.

"Of course I—"

"So, where were you for the past three hours?" He grilled her sternly.

"I told you we went to the cafeteria for dinner."

"Who is we?"

"Missy and. . ."

"Who else was there?" Skyler said, intentionally cutting her off, not wanting to give her any time to think, to lie, to deceive. He needed to keep control, and he would, he pledged, as he heard her voice getting softer and more uncertain as she spoke. Surely she was too important to him; he would make sure she never felt his trust. It would keep her honest. He'd keep her on the defensive. It would keep her in line. It would keep her his.

"No one else. We got talking and didn't realize it had gotten so late."

"You mean to tell me no one else sat at your table? No one said hello? You didn't meet anyone else in the whole dorm?"

"Yes. That's right. There aren't many people here yet. Classes don't start until Monday and most of the people are expected on Saturday."

"And how do you know if you didn't talk to anyone else but Missy?"

"At the desk, when I got my room key, I asked."

"Was he cute? Did he ask you out?"

"Who?"

"Don't be coy with me. You know who, the guy at the desk."

"It wasn't a guy, it was a girl."

"And who were you on the phone with all evening?"

"I wasn't on the phone at all, except with you and my mother. She said you gave her my number and I had called you with it. Why did you do that?"

"First of all, I don't answer to you. Second, your parents were worried about you. Instead of questioning me, you should be thanking me for relieving their worry. Now say it. Say thank you Skyler, thank you for taking care of me," Skyler said, directly, forcefully, ending his words with a heightened, playful, intonation.

"Thank you," Samantha said begrudgingly, immediately feeling the bitter taste of those words.

"Aren't you going to tell me who else called? Someone else must have called. There's someone you haven't told me about," Skyler said, as if he were her girlfriend, as if she should need to confide a deep secret to him.

"No one else. I told you already. Would you like me to make someone up?" Samantha asked sarcastically, feeling the need to fight back, to retaliate, to guard herself from Skyler thinking he could elicit the same kind of confidences she and Emily shared. No way. Not any more. She forced herself to talk with him. At least he was miles and miles away. He couldn't touch her. He couldn't hurt her. Relax, relax, she told herself as she listened to him.

"So what else?" Skyler said, softly coaxing, flirting again.

"What do you mean?" Samantha asked as Missy bounded through the door, breathless, dropping the large bulky load she had carried. "Hi, Missy."

"Very good, Samantha. You are learning. I take it your roommate came back from the car."

"Uh-huh."

"So tell me, what else is going on? What are your plans? What's on the agenda?"

"Nothing. Just school. You know unpacking, getting my schedule together, drops and adds, buying my books. The campus is so large, I'm going to carry a map around with me; and I think I might buy a bike." Samantha tried to sound as if she could be talking to anyone, she hoped Missy wasn't paying attention.

"If you do, make sure you buy a good lock. You'd better be careful walking around there, especially alone at night."

"I know. That's one thing you don't have to remind me of," Samantha said bitterly, biting her lip, remembering things she'd blocked out. She felt as if he'd intentionally punched her in the stomach with all of his force. Consciously, she rubbed her stomach, trying to soothe herself. But she could not. The pain, the blood, the memories would flutter inside of her forever . . .

"Well, I'll let you go. I'll check in with you in the morning. Pleasant dreams baby. I'll see you in them," Skyler said in a soft sensual voice.

"Bye," Samantha said casually, holding in both her breath and her anger as the silver cradle cut the umbilical cord between them.

"Geez, you get a lot of calls. Was that your boyfriend?" Missy asked, as she briskly unpacked school supplies into her desk.

"No, just a friend. I feel much better. Would you like me to help you with the next load?" Samantha asked, quickly changing the subject.

"No. You look like you got a good start on filling the chest. Keep going. I can carry my stuff up," Missy said, as she headed out for the next load.

Samantha quickly shut the door behind her and locked it before heading to the bathroom and kneeling over the white porcelain stool. She felt sick. She felt empty and hollow. As warm perspiration beaded between her small breasts, she felt her temperature rise and her breath become irregular and shallow. Her hands hard against the stool, she gurgled as she felt a sudden inner surge. Samantha watched as her clenching stomach let go of its inner knotting and turmoil and rose up forcefully, flowing over the large painful lump in her throat and then down into the cold, hard, wet bowel of the stool. And then again and again. As her shaking, weak, hand reached up and flushed the evidence down, she watched, mesmerized by the swirl of the water that quickly disappeared and returned clear again. She wished everything were that simple.

She steadied herself by reaching onto the counter. Missy

would be back any minute. Quickly, she unlocked the door, moved around a few boxes to make space for Missy's belongings and then grabbed her nightshirt and bag of toiletries. Like lightening she was in the shower. Closing the shower door, she opened her own familiar world and felt safe again. Briskly toweling off and wrapping up in her fluffy pink bathrobe, she felt comforted and revitalized enough to face her roommate. The room was filled with Missy's things when Samantha left the bathroom. But Missy was not there. Surely she couldn't still be unloading her car?

As Samantha moved about the small room, she heard voices and laughter behind the doorway. It sounded like there was a small party in the hallway. The strong smell of pizza seeped in. It was not a pleasant smell to her. Missy must be out there. Good for her, she must have made some friends; Samantha hoped so. Suddenly, she missed her own room; her privacy. She had a lot of adjustments to make, she thought sadly, but tomorrow was another day and she would try again for a new beginning.

As she crawled into her still wrinkled sheets, Samantha thought about how different everything was. So many changes. Change, she thought; and she was then comforted by Nana's voice saying, "something good always comes of it." Samantha placed her hands on her taut flat stomach and crossed her fingers as hard as she could, wishing, hoping, it held true for her. In this way she drifted away into her other "reality" of dreams.

Chapter 21

Lost in the maze of vine-covered brick buildings, Samantha lifted the heavy backpack off her shoulder and set it down onto the soft leaf littered grass, giving her back a rest. She looked down at the campus map she had torn from the college class catalog. The building she was looking for must be near. She looked around. Herds of students walked in every direction. She could ask for directions. No, she intended to do this on her own. After all, she smiled, she had graduated with top honors from high school; she could read and follow a map without any assistance. She had exactly followed the route she had carefully highlighted in yellow marker, and yet she still didn't see the building. She walked a few feet farther and saw a sign by the front entrance, "Bessy Hall." There it was; right in front of her. She smiled proudly, as she entered the hall leading to the first class in her college career.

Climbing the wide mouth of the stairs, Samantha could feel the presence of the millions of students that had climbed the same steps. What happened to all those people? What would be her fate? She mused.

The building smelled freshly waxed and swept, yet old and austere. Looking to the black numbers outside the classroom doors, Samantha easily found room 121. She was early. A few students sat stretched, relaxed in the aged school chairs facing the clean graphite board. They read *The State News*. They were uninterested in her sudden presence. Samantha decided reading the school newspaper must be a ritual followed by students and teachers alike; one her father would approve of. Reading her copy could wait; she was too nervous to concentrate on local news as she took a seat in the second row. Samantha pulled out her textbook and began flipping through the chapters. She was anxious for class to begin. She glanced up at the stark clock. The seats were filling up. The room was small, the faces new and unfamiliar. Samantha was comfortable with that. No one could know anything about her. It was perfect; a perfect way to hide from the rest of the world.

Samantha looked over at the doorway as she heard the loud flicker of the lights being turned on. John? John. What was John doing here? She watched as he placed a tattered brown, overstuffed leather briefcase on the teacher's desk and grabbed a long white piece of chalk from its front pouch. He turned, without yet acknowledging her or anyone else, toward the chalkboard and wrote a list of words. Before finishing, he added his name, his office hours and the due date of the first assignment.

As the clock showed exactly ten, John began class by reading the role. Samantha stared at him. He still had not acknowledged he knew her. She was puzzled. He was a student. Why was he teaching? Why didn't he say anything to her? Carefully, she took notes as he lectured; and, before she knew it, she was consumed in his lecture and class discussion. Samantha was in awe of the examples John presented of various writing techniques. She listened carefully as he read a story about what he did last summer. That was their first assignment; to be read in front of the class, five hundred words.

She frowned and took a deep breath. It wasn't going to be easy to stay anonymous. Worse yet, she had nothing to write about, certainly nothing she wanted to share in public!

When the class ended, Professor Scott put down the chalk, spanked his hands free from the dust and watched the students gather their books before they collectively filed out of the room. He smiled at Samantha, waiting for her to return the smile. Samantha did return the smile. The response was as natural as if she had done it every day for a very long time.

"I can't believe you are my professor. You never mentioned you taught! I thought you were just a student getting your Master's degree," Samantha said, as she walked toward him through the now-emptied classroom.

"You never asked. I'm working on a Master's in English. I'm not really a professor; I'm a T.A.; teacher's assistant. Teaching helps me pay my tuition and bills; being an R.A. lets me live in the dorm for free. I've been accepted to law school. I can begin in two years, but I'm on the waiting list to get in sooner. I need to save my money, and as long as I'm still enrolled in school, I don't have to pay back my student loans. English has always been my first love and law my first interest, so right now I have the best of all worlds."

"I guess I'll have to call you Professor from now on," Samantha said, fidgeting with her backpack, unsure of what to say next. She was impressed with John. She liked him more and more with each new facet he revealed. He was so together—not like anyone else she'd ever met, not like anyone her own age. John laughed and Samantha saw his pronounced dimples. A woman would kill for dimples like that. I can't believe he's my professor, she sighed.

"John will be fine. Professor is too formal. Each time a student refers to me as professor, I want to turn around and look to see who it is they're talking to." He watched as Samantha smiled and shook her head. She didn't have to respond; her warm gestures were sufficiently telling. "Can I walk back to the dorm with you?" he asked, his brown eyes smiling approvingly, hoping he read her right.

"I have another class. Natural Science, I think. Astronomy," Samantha replied, her eyes focused on her schedule and map.

"Okay. See you later?" John asked, as smoothly as if he'd asked her to pass the milk.

"Sure," Samantha responded with a shy smile, as she headed for the door.

"How about dinner?" he called after her.

"Dinner?" she asked, turning her head back toward him, as if she'd never heard of it.

"Yes, dinner. We both have to eat. I'll pick you up from your room, and we can eat at the cafeteria or we can eat at one of the restaurants on Grand River. Whatever you want to do."

"No, I can't. I mean, I have to study. Cafeteria food is fine," Samantha said, her blue eyes absorbed into his brown ones. Samantha felt the seconds that passed between them electrically. Her anxious heartbeat seemed loud to her. Had she just made a date, or was he just being friendly?

"Great, I'll come by your room about 5:30. Okay?"

"That'll be fine," she responded softly with her slow southern drawl, before quickly leaving to find her way to her next class.

John erased his writing from the chalkboard and placed the papers and books in his battered satchel. He had never met anyone so timid, yet so vibrant. Smart, witty, funny, clever, bold and bashful. He could make lists and lists of all the things he saw in her, underneath the beautiful exterior that had absorbed and captivated his every waking thought since the night they met. He'd never met another woman like her. He loved the way she spoke; the soft southern accent that made everything she said tantalizing and important and, sometimes, he smiled, even poetic. He wondered if Samantha said yes to dinner because she would worry about her grade in his class. He would have to advise her of the schools policy against professors dating their students. Next term would come quick enough; he wouldn't be her professor then, he rationalized. Turning out of the room, his arm trailed next to the wall and flipped off the lights. He began to whistle a light tune that matched his long strides and easy gait as he made his way to the library to prepare for the week.

Samantha looked down at her map. She didn't have far to walk. Thank goodness. There were only twenty minutes between classes, and she only had ten to find her way. Racing down the stairs into the freedom of the brisk sunny day, she felt happy. Samantha loved college, even if it was only her first day.

First days at high school had been difficult and tense until she figured out how many friends she had in each class and which teachers she liked and hated. College was so different. It was all up to her, and her happiness was dependent upon herself, not on who was in her class or how well she fit in. No one even noticed what she wore. She took a deep breath; she had arrived at the Natural Science building. Everything falling into place was a good sign, Samantha thought, as she cut through the courtyard inside the mouth of the building and found her way to her classroom.

Samantha felt great as she made her way back to her room after class. The campus was beautiful and she was learning her way around. She would have lunch, buy the rest of her books, and study until John picked her up. As she pulled her books out of her backpack and lined them up on her desk, she heard the sound she had learned to hate; the phone.

"Hello?" She said, momentarily distracted by the mess Missy had left on her desk. She must have come in, dropped her books, and left again in a hurry.

"Where have you been?" Skyler's accusing voice asked.

"Class. Where else?" Samantha said, sarcastically rolling her eyes and pursing her lips.

"I don't know. You tell me."

"I had English and Nat Sci. I came right back to the dorm. I'm going to eat and then I've got a few more books to buy. I've already got lots of homework."

"So, who'd you meet?"

"No one. I don't have much time to meet anyone. It takes almost all the time I have in between classes to make it to the buildings. This campus is huge! This weekend I'm definitely going to buy a bike."

Samantha tried to make sure her words sprinted out of her mouth so it sounded as though she gave no thought to them. She knew if she hesitated in her speaking, Skyler would accuse her of making up whatever she was telling him; of lying. She hated his calls. She hated his voice. She hated him.

"Do you miss me?" Skyler said, in his playful sexy voice.

It made Samantha wince. She visualized him winking at her. It gave her chills. Her eyes grew big and she swallowed hard before responding, "Of course." She made a face as if she'd just swallowed a bitter pill.

"Are you going to give me your final schedule? I don't want to call when you're not in. I don't think your roommate likes me."

"She just doesn't like answering the phone; she doesn't get many calls."

"Give me her schedule, too. That way I'll try to call when she's in class. Would that be better?"

"Yes."

"I've got to get back to court. I'll call you tonight."

Samantha knew she'd better be there when he called. What was she thinking when she agreed to eat with John? How would she explain she'd have to rush off because a man she hated might call? How could she explain he would question her, threaten her and belittle her—that she was afraid?

Samantha hurried to the cafeteria. She had so many things to do, but she couldn't miss lunch even though she wasn't hungry. She had to try to eat lunch; she had promised her mother she'd send the punched meal card at the end of the month, when she got her new one, to prove she'd been eating.

So she had to get it punched, regardless of what she ate. Between Skyler and her parents, she felt claustrophobic. Her breathing quickened; she hated being tied to the dorm, and she hadn't even been there a week! The only good thing was John lived in the dorm. She didn't have to go far to see him. Having him as a friend was a comfort to her. She just had to find a way to hide John from Skyler and Skyler from John.

Samantha spent the rest of the afternoon as she had planned. Looking up at Minnie—she found when she packed she couldn't bear to leave behind her old clock—had she gotten the time wrong? John was late. Maybe he wasn't coming. Samantha took another look at the time and then let go of a loud sigh just as Missy came in.

"Hi, Samantha. Are you going down to eat?"

"In a little while. Are you going?"

"Yeah. Why don't you come with me? I've got a night class, so I've got to eat early."

"No. I'm not really hungry. I'll see you after your class."

Samantha was grateful Missy would not be in the room when John picked her up. She didn't want anyone to know. She couldn't have anyone know. What if Skyler asked Missy questions? She shuddered; she felt cornered. Relax, relax, she chanted, taking deep breaths, reassuring herself everything would be all right, she would find a way.

Just as Samantha closed her eyes to say a prayer, she simultaneously heard a knock on her door and the ringing of the phone. Oh God, her mind screamed, what do I do? Instinctively, she answered the door and put her fingers to her lips, indicating to John he needed to be silent.

"I'll just be a minute," she whispered, as John pulled out and sat on the chair that had been neatly tucked in under her desk.

"Hi. I was just going to leave the office and thought I'd check in with you. What's up?

Skyler's voice was casual, but hearing it caused her heart to pound. She clutched the springy cord nervously. She tried to be nonchalant, but she could feel John watching her, listening to the conversation.

"Oh, I was just going to go down to the cafeteria to eat."

"Is Missy going with you?"

"No. She ate earlier. She has a night class." She mentally

kicked herself for not lying, for not leading him to believe Missy was waiting for her in the cafeteria.

"So, you'll be alone all night? Who's coming to visit you while she's gone? Surely you've had offers?"

"No. No one. I've got to study. I've already got tons of homework. You should see the syllabus I have from just two classes."

"Well, good; that'll keep you out of trouble. So you still haven't told me.

"What? Haven't told you what?" Samantha asked. She forgotten what to defend herself against.

"C'mon, Samantha, you're playing games with me. You're just stalling for time."

"No. Really, I don't remember not answering anything. Can't you just ask me again?" Samantha pleaded, as she felt droplets of nervous sweat drip down into her bra. She was glad she had chosen her new Spartan sweatshirt to wear; it was absorbent and the wetness would go undetected. She wished she could take a shower. She closed her eyes and visualized a shower, her private hideaway. It helped, but only for a second, as she heard Skyler's vexatious voice scream into the receiver.

"Who are you eating with?" Skyler's temper was flaring. He lost his patience. He dug his pen point into the pad of paper on his desk as hard as he could, squeezing the shaft of the pen in his fist. He couldn't help it, she was playing games with him! One minute she wanted him and was nice to him, the next she was cool and aloof. Did she think him stupid?

"No one. I haven't met anyone to eat with, except my roommate."

"I'll know if you're lying. I'm going to ask Missy."

"That's fine. She'll tell you the same thing."

"Did she tell you I called earlier?"

"No."

"You said you saw her. How is it she didn't tell you?"

"I don't know, but she didn't." Samantha tried to keep her voice casual and light despite the immense anger she held in check. She felt as if she was suffocating, drowning in the murk of Skyler's questions and accusations. Would it ever end? She hoped John didn't pick up on how she really felt. She looked at him watching her. She smiled. She loved the way he looked in his tight worn Levis and green jersey. She loved his outstretched long legs folded over each other and his neatly tied Nike running shoes. She craved the warmth of him as much as she feared his touch—any man's touch. His chest was broad and, out from the top of the unbuttoned jersey, she could see the curls of dark hair. He was what she would have wanted in a man before, before . . . She couldn't think about it; she had to get off the phone.

"You ask her about it when she comes in. Tell her to give you your messages from now on. I've got to go; my other line is ringing. If I don't talk to you, sweet dreams, baby."

"Bye."

Samantha looked at John staring at her. She smiled at him as if she were on top of the world; as if her only focus was to have dinner with him.

"You don't like whomever your caller was very much, do you?" John asked gently, looking at her directly.

"Why do you say that?" Samantha asked. Dropping her room key into the back pocket of her jeans, she motioned him out of her room so they could begin the walk to the cafeteria. She didn't want to risk any more phone calls in front of him.

"Because you were fidgeting with the cord the whole time you were talking; you looked nervous. You had an expression on your face as if you were in pain," John said, hoping he hadn't overstepped his bounds. Keeping up with her quick pace down the steep stairs and long halls, John tried to get a full glimpse of Samantha's face. He needed to read her telltale eyes to be sure she would tell him the truth. As much as John trusted Samantha, in the few days he'd known her, he felt there was something odd about this beauty he just couldn't put his finger on. He was willing to take the time to figure it out, and in the meantime he'd give her the benefit of the doubt.

"What do you mean? I smiled at you while I was on the phone. I always walk around the room when I'm anxious to get off the phone because I have something else I want to do. It's just me. I—"

"You were a nervous wreck, and I'd bet all the money I've saved for law school on that," John said, cutting her off, suddenly frowning. "Do you have a boyfriend at home you haven't told me about?"

"No. That was just a family friend. He works for my

father and feels compelled to check up on how I'm doing." Samantha paused, almost breathless from her own pace. "My parents go away a lot, and I think he got it into his head he'd impress the boss through his daughter."

"As long as that's all it is. Although, I think I'm glad he's *your* friend and not mine, based on the expression on your face while you were talking to him." John said gently, smiling at her, immersed in her beauty as he watched her dainty hands and long fingers take the dark orange tray from his hands. He was glad the cafeteria line wasn't long. He couldn't wait to sit and listen to her talk. He wanted to learn as much about her as he could.

# # #

As Skyler left the office, he couldn't help but picture Samantha with another man. He felt angered, dejected, cheated. He wanted to make her pay; but he'd have to wait. He had to be sure. His time would come. He would learn the truth and have his pleasure. They were bound together, whether she knew it or not. She was his to do with as he pleased. He had saved her and now she owed him. A life for a life. He grinned. She would learn that. His twisted face smiled back at him in his rearview mirror. He couldn't resist checking out his reflection while he waited at long red lights.

Hearing an engine racing beside him, Skyler looked curiously at the car stopped next to him. A pretty blonde combed her short bobbed hair with her fingers. As he gazed and winked at her, she flashed her strong perfect teeth at him, coyly admiring not just the car, but the driver. Skyler thunderously revved his engine in agreement, as if to say "ditto, take me on now." He was in the mood for a race. He'd win. His green Jag against her red Camaro. He had the greater horsepower, the greater control; and the greatest motivation.

Winning. It was all about winning. And he was a winner, he thought, revving his engine, letting it loose as the light turned green.

Chapter 22

Samantha awoke to what were becoming familiar sounds between the old dorms thin walls. The slow awakening of her floor mate led to slamming doors, loud whispering voices and alarms that dragged on for what seemed hours before their owners killed them. She hated her early morning classes, even though she only had the eight o'clock classes on Tuesdays and Thursdays. The morning dormitory noises comforted her as much as they annoyed her. At least she wasn't back home, near Skyler. His midnight calls were so distracting she felt tired all the time. Today was no exception. She had better come home for a nap after lunch, she decided, as she dragged herself from her warm, soft sheets.

As she stretched her sluggish body, she looked up at the top bunk and noticed the unrumpled bed. Missy must have spent the night in her boyfriend's dorm room again. She hated having to tell Missy he could not sleep with her in their room. It gave her the creeps to even think about it. Samantha explained there would be no place for her to go since she really didn't know anyone, and she wouldn't feel right not giving them complete privacy. Missy hadn't been happy, but had accepted it, packed a duffle bag of toiletries, and went off into the night. But first she tacked her boyfriend's phone number next to the phone with explicit orders to call her immediately if her parents phoned and lie to them in the interim.

Samantha was sorry she couldn't accommodate Missy, but Missy's absence from their room calmed Samantha's fears of being questioned by her. Samantha felt as comfortable in her dorm room as she did in her own room at home. She loved looking out the large window in the tiny room, seeing the vibrant blush of the maples and oaks erupting as they soaked up the last days of warmth, pressing the sun exquisitely into each perfect leaf. The trees at home wouldn't change this soon. She was delighted Michigan was so different. She looked forward to the cold and snow. She craved as much change as possible. She craved the unusual, the exciting, the new. She hoped, like the trees, she too would shed her problems and by spring, be a whole new person.

Just as she threw her wool blazer over her shoulders and unlocked the door, she heard the phone. Oh God—Skyler. Can't he leave me alone?

Samantha almost decided to ignore the ring. She started through the door, but then she froze, paled. She had to answer it. He wouldn't like it if she wasn't there. He'd accuse her of not having spent the night in her bed, even though he had called at midnight. Reluctantly, she turned back and answered the phone.

"Hi, Sam. I'm glad I caught you before you went down to breakfast. Did you sleep well?"

Skyler's chipper voice caught her off guard. His voice was very different from the angry, accusatory one she heard last night.

"Yes. Fine. I was just going to grab a cup of coffee and go to class." Samantha said trying to sound rushed so he wouldn't keep her on the phone.

"I know. That's why I'm calling. What are you doing this weekend?"

"This weekend?"

"Tom just called and said he had extra tickets to the Michigan-Michigan State game. He wants me to come up and go with him. I thought you might join us."

"Football?"

"Of course. Haven't you been following the football games?"

"Not really. I'm not into sports; you know that. Besides I have had too much homework, so I've stayed in and studied."

"So you don't want to go?" Skyler said sternly.

"I've got too much homework. I didn't think I'd have this—"

"Look, get it done, if you have to stay up all night! I will arrive late Friday night. I'm staying with Tom, and we will pick you up for breakfast. Be on your best behavior," Skyler said, as if he were a teacher giving instructions to a delinquent student.

"Fine," Samantha said meekly, exhaling her frustration with a long deep breath.

"By the way, your parents are thrilled I'm going to see you, and they expect a great report. We wouldn't want to disappoint them, would we?" Skyler said laughingly, before hanging up.

As Samantha again gathered her things to leave, she felt a headache growing in the back of her head. She moved her fingers inside the small zipped pocket in her backpack checking on the presence of her pill case. It was in there. Maybe she just needed to have a piece of toast. She hadn't eaten much lately; she must need to eat. She convinced herself a little food and a few pills were all she needed.

Briskly walking into the cafeteria, she grabbed a tray and quickly filled it. Samantha looked around. Her ears were ringing, buzzing. A soft lull of noise. Her head began to throb louder and louder. As she swallowed her pills, she looked around. It was the laughter. It was the loud, shrill, irritating laughter she'd heard before. Where was it coming from? Who could make such a sound? She looked around as she swallowed a piece of dry toast and a bite of scrambled egg. She had to leave. Her head pounded from the noise. The laughter suddenly scared her. It was so close to her, yet there wasn't anyone following her; there wasn't anyone there at all. She wanted to go to class, to run all the way, to fill herself with knowledge and diversion. And yet, her legs carried her back to her room, back to the safety, the solitude and the quiet of her room.

Tossing her backpack on her desk, vehemently throwing off her clothes, Samantha felt sweat pouring out from every inch of her body. She craved another shower, yet she didn't feel stable enough to stand. The laughter faded as she quickly opened the window for fresh air. After rechecking the lock on the door to her room, she climbed hastily into the sanctuary of her bed. Closing her eyes tightly, she let the pills work and allowed her mind to float instantaneously into the darkness.

Samantha looked out into the sea of blackness. She wanted to find a friendly face, she wanted to find John. But he wasn't there. She followed the music and the sharp laughter. It was back. But she couldn't find it; nor could she run away from it. The faces were around her, hiding, still in various pieces. She wished she could capture the pieces and lay each carefully, side by side, like a puzzle, fitting them into a picture that looked real, that made sense. But she couldn't. She knew if she did match all the faces, there were still pieces missing. The ears, where were they? She looked, spinning around and around. She saw the shadow. It looked familiar. It reached out to grab her shoulder. She felt the cold clamminess of the strong fingers. But she knew it was warm outside. She ran and ran, but she didn't move. It caught her, grabbing her hair first. She couldn't get away. She was frozen; her body, her voice. She couldn't scream. She couldn't breathe. She began to shake as she felt it press against her.

Samantha awoke in terror, her body warm and moist, her throat parched. She craved a drink, but she was too disorientated to get up. Her wide eyes moved around the room, slowly orienting herself to reality. Samantha understood the fine line between reality and fantasy. More and more often, she felt she existed on that line. But sometimes, she wasn't sure which way she teetered; both seemed scary and unnatural.

As she climbed quietly away from her sheets, she stepped over to the white miniature refrigerator and grabbed a diet cola. Popping it open, she guzzled the cold liquid, barely stopping to breathe. It felt good. Taking a deep cleansing breath, she wiped the sticky drips from the corners of her mouth. It was almost noon. She had time to shower and go to her next class. Missing one class was already missing more than she wanted to. Vowing not to miss any more classes, no matter what, Samantha again heard the phone beckon. Fearfully, she answered it.

"Yes?"

"Why aren't you in class?"

"I had a headache. I took a nap. I'm getting ready to go to my next class."

"Who is there with you?"

"No one."

"C'mon. You can tell me."

Samantha knew he was angry. She didn't know how to make him stop. She answered his questions, one by one, each time with more determination, until he let up. She knew he'd never believe her and she had no choice but to answer him.

"I told you, I wasn't feeling well. I'm alone. I'm going to get something to eat and then go to class."

"Who are you walking with?"

"No one. I'm riding my new bike."

"Well, good. I've got to get back to the office. Mr. Castriano is turning over all of his legal business to the firm. I won the case! I was able to get him off. That should get me some real respect around the office."

"That's good." Samantha said, not caring one way or the other.

"You are just like your father. You really don't care, do you?" Skyler growled into the phone.

"I do; he does, too. Dad always says how smart you are. I don't understand what you're saying," Samantha said, confused.

"No, you don't, do you? But you will. Gotta go. I'll call you later."

Samantha plopped the receiver onto the silver wall holder as if it were poison. She couldn't get upset. She simply chanted relax, relax, as she took deep breaths and entered into the cloistered warm spray of the shower.

Samantha sat through class watching slides of art and listening to the professor explain the differences in periods of art. The white rectangle of screen flashed Renoir and VanGogh and countless other artists. She was sure she'd get confused. She couldn't focus, but she tried. She wrote down every word the professor said. Later she would condense her notes into the computer. The computer kept her organized. It was the only friend she had, except for John. But she was afraid of John. He was a good friend. She liked to talk with him and be with him; but each time he touched her hand or her shoulder or simply sat too close, she cringed. She couldn't help it. She wished things could be different.

The class bell rang, and the stream of students poured out of the building, like a heartbeat in sync with the nature of the student body. Samantha liked the predictability of her classes and the people on campus. Everyone was so focused on themselves, no one cared about her. No one questioned her. But, she thought as she climbed on to her bike, it was time she found someone she could question about the law. Maybe she should talk to a counselor about taking some pre-law courses. Maybe she should declare her major as pre-law. It might just make everything easier.

Just as Samantha nodded in agreement with herself, her

body was forced forward and mangled into an unconventional position. Simultaneously, her ears filled with the hollow sound of scraping metal. And then there was blackness.

"Are you alright?" the concerned voice asked, as Samantha's eyes fluttered open.

"What?" Samantha asked, confused.

"Are you alright?" the voice repeated.

"I . . ." Samantha paused and looked around. Her new emerald green bike was laying on the ground, tangled in the bars of an unfamiliar blue bike.

"I'm sorry about your bike. I think they'll both be okay though. Let's see if you can walk. Grab my arm."

Samantha put out her hand and straightened her legs before shifting her weight on to them. She felt bruised, but she was stable. "I'm fine," Samantha said as the auburn-haired student with the long ponytail held her bike out for her and handed her the tipped backpack.

"You should go over to Olin Health Center and get checked. You may get a few bruises, and you're scraped. Can I follow you there, to make sure you are alright?"

"No," Samantha said, with apparent alarm. "I'm fine. Really, thanks."

"I feel bad. I should have been paying more attention."

"No, it was my fault. It was me; I wasn't paying attention," Samantha said, with as much composure as she could find.

"Let's just call it even," the man said, his voice still filled with concern. He watched as Samantha put her feet on her pedals and began to sail away, shouting a "thank you" in the breeze she left behind.

Samantha carefully locked her bike and headed for her room. She took off her blood-and-grass-stained clothes and threw them across the room into the already overflowing clothes basket. Grabbing a few cotton balls from a glass jar and a small brown plastic bottle of hydrogen peroxide, she carefully washed over the scratches on her face and arms with the soaked cotton balls. They stung briefly, but it felt good. It made her feel alive, glad nothing worse had happened. It was too early to see any bruises, but from the aches and stiffness she already felt, she knew she'd be black and blue by morning. Oh well, on with the homework. The computer kept

Samantha occupied for hours. She typed in her notes, compiled information, sent e-mail to her parents, drafted a story, and completed a chart for science. It was getting late. She had promised to meet John in the cafeteria.

"I'd better get washed before it gets too late," Samantha said out loud, slamming her book closed with a loud thud in the too-silent room. It felt good to accomplish something constructive, to feel her mind grow with knowledge—to distract herself—she reflected, as she stepped into the bathroom.

Through the splashing of the sink water, Samantha heard a loud pounding on the door. Carefully, she turned off the faucet, panicked that Skyler had come into town a night early. Unlatching the door, she looked up into the beaming face of John.

"I've been waiting for twenty minutes. I'm hungry! Did you decide not to eat?"

"No. I just got caught up with my homework and lost track of the time. I'll be ready in a minute."

"Is something wrong? Why are you limping?" John said, his eyes now carefully inspecting Samantha.

"I just sat too long at my desk. And, well, I had a little bike accident."

"Are you okay? What happened?"

"Nothing really. I was riding on the bike path and crashed into some guy. To tell you the truth, I never saw him coming—I'm not even sure who was at fault. But neither one of us were hurt, just bruised."

"Did you go over to Olin?"

"No. I'm fine."

"You should get checked. You may have a hairline fracture. That leg seems too sore to just be bruised."

"Look, I don't have time. I promise, if I feel worse or if it swells, I'll go in the morning."

John examined Samantha closely as he listened to her. Her face was scratched and her left temple was red and showed signs of swelling. He put his hand on Samantha's shoulder as he began to speak and felt her entire body stiffen. Quickly, he removed his hand. "Don't worry. I just want you to sit down so I can take a look at your leg. Okay?" John looked at her seriously, putting his fingers softly under her chin, forcing her eyes to his.

"No. I'm fine, really." Samantha's voice went dead as she heard the phone. Surely it couldn't be Skyler again? It would be his third call. He wasn't due to call until midnight. It must be her parents or her brothers, she hoped, as she said hello.

"Hi. How was your bike ride to class?"

"Fine. Class was fine. I was just on my way to eat dinner."

"Have you finished your homework? I'm counting on you to be with me at the game."

"I got a lot done today. So I should be fine."

"So have you met anyone interesting?"

"No. I haven't had time, and Missy spends most of her time at her boyfriend's dorm, so I don't even see her."

"Well that's good. You'll have more time to study. What's on the agenda tomorrow?"

"I have classes; and I had a small bike accident after class today, so I might go to the student health center and get my leg x-rayed."

"Are you hurt?"

"No. Not really, just some bruises and scrapes, and my leg is a little stiff."

"Oh, so you just want to see those young physician residents. Isn't that true?"

"No. I never even thought about that. It didn't even enter my mind."

Skyler cut her off, his voice showing his agitation as he ran his words stiffly together. "How could you have had a bike accident? Were you flirting with the guy that hit you? Is that why you had the accident? You just had to flirt, didn't you!"

"No. I didn't even see him."

"So, it was a guy. I can't believe you hid this from me."

"I didn't, I—"

Did you give him your phone number?"

"No! It happened so fast! It wasn't like that."

"Then why didn't you tell me about it right away? Why did I have to pry it from you?"

"You didn't; I just didn't think that—"

Skyler shouted into the phone in a crazed, ruthless voice, "You are lying! You are a liar!"

"If you would quit cutting me off, I could explain—"

As Samantha heard the click, she felt real fear. Now what would happen to her? He would be there in a day and a half. What if he was still angry? At least they'd be with Tom and his girlfriend. Suddenly she realized John stared at her in quiet disbelief.

"Who was that?" he asked softly, not sure he wanted to hear the answer.

"It was Skyler again. I'm sorry about the interruption. Let's go eat. I'm hungry," Samantha said lightly, trying to dismiss the phone call and any relevance he might think it had to her.

"Why don't you tell him to stop calling? He calls you every day. It's eerie. Every time we are leaving the room, he calls. Something is just not right about him."

"It's okay. I told you, he is just a family friend." Samantha tried to make her words sound care free and casual. She distanced herself from connecting to how she really felt. But she wished she could run into the bathroom and never come out.

"Friend? My God! I could hear him screaming from across the room. Did he accuse you of causing the accident?"

"Well, he had warned me about riding a bike on campus. He was just worried. I guess the thought of me being hurt, without family here, made him upset."

"Samantha, that is not a friendly guy. I don't know what's going on, but I don't like it," John stated emphatically, his thick brows knitting in concern. Pausing before opening the door to let them out, he turned toward Samantha, lightly touching her shoulder, "You would tell me if you were in trouble, wouldn't you?"

"You know I'd tell you if anything was wrong. But everything's fine," Samantha said, avoiding John's eyes as she followed him, promising him she would tell him if things ever got out of hand. But could she? As his eyes swallowed hers, she pondered the strength of his commitment of friendship to her.

Chapter 23

Samantha dressed slowly. She didn't want to believe Skyler could be at her door any minute. He was invading her privacy, her safe space. She didn't want to think about him touching anything in her room, touching her. She felt chills racing through her body, chasing the burning heat she'd felt moments before. She closed her eyes and concentrated, breathing deeply, evenly. Just as she began to feel some relief, the door flung open and her heart jumped.

"Hi. You're up early! Don't worry about being half-dressed. Jack is waiting for me in the cafeteria. Want to join us? I just came in to get some clothes for the game. Jack got great tickets."

"Oh, Missy, you scared me! Sorry, I can't join you. I'm having breakfast with some friends. I haven't seen you for days. How are you?"

"Fine. But you don't look so fine. Who won the fight?" Missy asked jokingly.

"I got into a biking accident. I'm fine. Just bruised and scraped."

"I'm sorry I wasn't here to help you. I've been back to get clothes and things, but you're usually at class. By the way, that guy who calls you at all hours called a few times. I hope you got the messages. He never leaves his name, he just says, 'she knows' and then hangs up without so much as a goodbye. I left them all on the bulletin board."

"Yeah, I saw them. Thanks."

"Who *is* that guy? His voice gives me the creeps! It's so deep and he talks in phrases, almost riddles, instead of sentences."

"I know; he's just a guy who has decided to impress my dad by trying to give me advice about college. I don't like talking to him either."

"The way he talks actually reminds me of a sort of southern Barnabas Collins. Did you ever watch that show? My mother copied them all when the reruns came out. She loves watching it over and over. Dark Shadows. Ever seen it?"

"No. Doesn't sound like my kind of show," Samantha said, forgetting her own problems as she listened to the effervescence of Missy, whose sentences wove and rambled from one subject to the next. It was hard not to like her. Samantha wished she could see more of her.

"So, is he your boyfriend?"

"No. Just a family friend."

"Mmmm. Does he still call every night?"

"Yeah, he's just overly protective."

"Sounds strange to me. I don't know how you can get any sleep. He's nosy, too. He asks me all sorts of questions about you. I don't answer them though, I just keep telling him I haven't seen you. That is what I should say, isn't it?"

"What kinds of questions does he ask?" Samantha asked tentatively.

"Just stuff like, do I know where you are; are you seeing anyone; has anyone else called for you. You know, your basic parental interrogation. It's like the inquisition my mom always gave me when I spent the weekend with my older sister when she was in college. Believe me, if I could get past my mother's questions, I can do it with . . . what's his name?"

Samantha stared at her as she spoke. She had known Skyler had talked to Missy a few times, it sounded as though he'd talked to Missy more than she had.

"Skyler. Skyler Marks."

"Weird name. What kind of name is Skyler, anyway?"

"I don't know. I've never thought about it."

"So how do I look?" Missy asked, grabbing her bag.

"Great. You look great. Jack's probably wondering what's taking so long. I'm sorry if I held you up."

"Don't be silly. What are roommates for? See you later—probably Sunday night, as usual. If my parents call before I get back—"

"Tell them you're at the library," Samantha chimed in, finishing her sentence.

Laughing in unison, the young women said good-bye and Samantha closed the door once again. She had to finish getting ready. She pulled on her green Michigan State sweatshirt over the white turtleneck and decided to wear the matching sweatpants instead of jeans. At home, she never would have thought about dressing so casually. Everyone in East Lansing dressed casually for the games as well as in restaurants and shopping malls. Samantha hoped Skyler would see she was trying hard to fit in. The last thing she wanted was to have to change her clothes while he waited.

The bold knocking told her Skyler had arrived. Taking a deep breath, she opened the door with purse and jacket in hand so she wouldn't have to let him inside.

"Oh, John! You didn't call. I was just on my way out," Samantha said stiffly, stunned that John had shown up. She studied his face, afraid he could hear the escalated pounding of her heart.

"Just wondered if you wanted to go down and eat breakfast with me? I'm surprised you're up. I just thought about breakfast at the last minute and was half way here before I thought about calling. I'm sorry. But you will go with me anyway, won't you? Pleeeze . . ." John said playfully, smiling at her curiously.

Samantha took a deep sigh, "I'm sorry. I can't. I've got plans for breakfast." Samantha watched John's face drop. She'd embarrassed him and upset him. She had to explain. "Look, I'm sorry. I really would like to go to breakfast with you but; but . . ." she faltered, gazing directly into John's strong brown eyes. She wanted to be soaked up into them. More than anything she wanted to ask him to protect her, to wipe the slate clean. She took a deep breath as she felt the pounding of her heart migrate directly to her head, triggering instant distress. The pain was deep and sharp and piercing.

"Sam, it's me. We're friends, remember? I'm not going to be upset. You can tell me anything."

"Okay, but then you've got to leave. Promise?"

"Promise," John said. He had to promise. Samantha was obviously panicked and desperate. It was more than that; she was forlorn and helpless. He wanted to take her into his arms and cradle her until she felt comfortable and secure, until he could clear the distress from behind her clouded blue eyes.

"It's Skyler. He called. He's in town. He and his brother Tom are picking me up for breakfast and some tailgate parties and the game. I don't want to go, but I have to."

"That doesn't make any sense. Just don't go. Tell him

you have too much homework or something. You can't be forced to go."

"I can. I told you, he works for my dad. He'll tell my parents everything; and if I don't go, who knows what he'll say!"

"But that's not right. Just call your parents and tell them why you aren't going."

Samantha knew she had to get rid of John before Skyler arrived or she would be in horrible trouble. Rudely, she cut him off, fearing her own safety at the moment more than his hurt feelings.

"Look, I can't explain any more than that. I have to go and you have to leave. You promised."

"Fine. But if you need me, call. I'll be in my room most of the day," John said stiffly. "Later, when you can talk, I expect you to explain it to me; I want to help."

"Fine," Samantha retorted, reflecting the same stiff voice, as she opened her door and ushered him through it.

Samantha watched John's stiffened body as he exited her room, relieved he was gone. Immediately, she diminished her responsibility for hurting him. Why couldn't he just have left when she told him she couldn't go to breakfast with him? Why couldn't he just take no for an answer? Why did he have to care? Why did he need to know more if he were really her friend? She would be better off if he stayed mad at her. Alone and anonymous was what she wanted.

She pulled open her desk drawer and looked at her worn paper with the legal words. She barely had to read the words. Her eyes skimmed the definitions. She had memorized them, almost verbatim. She would find a way to end this, she vowed, closing the drawer. She strode to the medicine cabinet for her headache pills and swallowed a few with water. Tucking extra capsules into her almost empty pill case, she stuffed the case into her purse. Just as she zipped it, she heard someone try the locked knob before knocking. Biting her cheek and taking a deep breath, she opened the door.

"Hey, Babe! Great to see you," Skyler said, entering the room, kicking the door shut with his freshly oiled brown Dexters, taking Samantha into his arms. "Put down your purse and jacket and give me a real hug. Aren't you glad to see me?"

"Of course I am. I just don't want to be late. Where's Tom?" Samantha asked, trying to distract Skyler with conversation as she set her things on the desk.

"Downstairs waiting with Stacey."

"Who's that?"

"Stacey? You know Stacey, Tom's girlfriend. Remember when they came to visit?"

"Oh. Oh, yeah." Samantha said, puzzled she didn't remember Tom's girlfriend or ever having met her. She did remember he had a girlfriend. Who had told her? Her mother, that must be right; but when had she met her? Oh well, I can't remember everything, she rationalized, shrugging it off.

"So, where's my hug?"

Reluctantly, Samantha put her arms around Skyler lightly, as if he were a stranger. Skyler grabbed her, tightly kissing her. His tongue pried open her mouth, penetrating her deeply.

"Go into the bathroom and take the lipstick off, Sam. You know I don't like it," Skyler ordered. "And get me a cloth as well. You'd better not have gotten any on me."

Quietly, Samantha followed his orders and returned with a facecloth.

"Great. Let's go. There'll be lots of time for us later. Tom thinks I'm leaving tonight, but I'm leaving tomorrow," Skyler said, winking, before putting his arm around Samantha's now jacketed shoulder.

"We'll have a wonderful night together, I promise," Skyler whispered sensually in her ear as they left the room and headed for the car.

As they saw Tom's car, Samantha felt her headache getting worse, not better. Thankful she'd brought more pills, she decided she'd take another tablet at the restaurant.

"Hi, Samantha! It's great seeing you again," Tom said, smiling, as she climbed into the back seat with Skyler.

"Hi. Thanks for inviting me. I know the game tickets were hard to get."

"You remember Stacey, don't you?" Tom said, as he put his arm around his girlfriend and pulled out into the road.

"Of course," Samantha said, gazing at the familiar girl she didn't really remember. Perplexed, she tried to think of a question she could ask that would jog her memory as to when they'd met. Listening to their fun-loving conversation and easy laughter, she stared mindlessly at Stacey. How could she have forgotten her? She couldn't remember meeting her before, although Stacey had immediately recognized her. If they had met, when had they met? Tom and Stacey talked and giggled as if they were part of each other's flesh. Samantha had fleeting memories, glimpses of their kindred spirit from the summer. Somehow that made sense; but not completely remembering someone as vibrant as Stacey, didn't make sense.

Samantha focused on Tom and Stacey, trying to listen to every word they said. The blaring radio interfered with some of their conversation but she picked up enough to know they were planning the rest of their weekend together. Samantha concentrated so intensely on the couple she failed to see Skyler move closer to her, finally grabbing her hand. Weaving his fingers with hers, he used his thumb to caress her. She held her breath and tried not to wince. Skyler moved his free hand in between her thighs, slowly moving it up and down her sweatpants.

Samantha stiffened with fright. She sat rigid with a thin, artificial smile on her face. She couldn't make a sound; she was fearful Tom could see them in the rearview mirror. But Tom never checked the mirror. Tom was so focused on Stacey it was a wonder he found his way to the restaurant, she thought, dismayed his presence was not a deterrent to Skyler's behavior. Samantha was relieved as they pulled up into the steep driveway leading to the parking lot for the Evergreen Grill. Skyler finally removed his hands from her.

Before they were seated, Samantha excused herself and headed for the rest room. With a smile at Tom, Stacey followed her. Closing their respective stall doors, Samantha reached into her purse for her pill case and grabbed a white one with a number three on it. She hoped it worked faster than the others she had swallowed earlier. Quickly, she flushed, opened the stall door and went to the sink, popping the tablet into her mouth.

"Have a headache?" Stacey asked, genuinely concerned.

"Yes. It just started. I didn't sleep well last night. I'd better take an aspirin before it gets worse and ruins the game for me," Samantha said, meticulously washing her hands.

"Hope you feel better. Breakfast will help. They have great food here. I'm really glad you were able to join us."

"It was nice of you to think of inviting me."

"Skyler is really fond of you. He asked Tom to try to get four tickets for the game when we were there over the fourth."

Samantha watched Stacey speak and listened to her carefully, but she felt as if she could see right through her, as if she wasn't really there, wasn't even real.

"That was nice of Tom to go to all that trouble and expense," Samantha said, trying to smile appreciatively.

"Oh, it was a treat for us! Skyler paid for the tickets and sent us a gift certificate for a really expensive dinner. He's a great guy."

"My parents think so too," Samantha said, matter-of-factly, trying to impress upon Stacey there wasn't anything but friendship between them.

"He really likes you. I know there is an age difference; but I don't think age is important, do you?"

"Well, I uh, I never really thought about it. Skyler is like an uncle to me. I haven't ever thought of him as anything else."

"Oh. I'm sure I just misread things. That must be it. He does treat you like family," Stacey added, trying to put Samantha at ease again.

Samantha nodded in agreement. There was nothing else for her to say or do without breaking into tears.

"It's going to be a wonderful day," Stacey exclaimed happily. "I can feel it!"

"I hope you're right," Samantha said, as they moved to find the now-seated men.

Breakfast was almost fun but for the presence of Skyler. Tom was so very different from him. Samantha remembered why she liked him when they first met during the summer. She couldn't remember what she'd thought of Stacey, but she liked her—although she found herself having jealous feelings toward her. It didn't make sense. As she watched Tom touch Stacey, she wanted to slap her. Samantha loved the way Tom smiled at her while she spoke and listened to her as if what she had to say was important. She was surprised at her feelings toward Tom, since she was uncomfortable with most men. Maybe it was because he didn't want anything from her. He was just a nice person.

As they moved on to the governor's tailgate party, they

all had to endure Skyler's bragging about how Mr. Castriano had finagled an invitation to the party for them and it would be an opportunity to meet Michigan's governor. Samantha suspected the invitation had nothing to do with Mr. Castriano and everything to do with her parents and their Washington connections. They'd attended the governor's conference and ball. She also remembered her mother telling her they had made it a point to meet Michigan's governor and first lady, since Samantha would be living in the capitol. She remembered them telling her that even though he was a Republican, they'd liked him; and her father had commented that both the governor and first lady were lawyers. She'd been bored as her father related the long conversation about property tax relief, the deficit and the upcoming elections. Her father had talked about it not just once, but with everyone who entered the house for the next week. Surely her father had passed the invitation on to Skyler, not anyone else!

Samantha rolled her eyes contemptuously at Skyler's bragging. Too bad Emily wasn't here to pick up on it; they'd have had a good laugh. Samantha made a mental note to tell Emily about Skyler when she called. Skyler was fraudulent in everything he said and did! It was more and more obvious to her. Why couldn't anyone else see?

Samantha had never been to a tailgate party. She wasn't even sure what it was, but once she got there, she enjoyed it. Looking out into the crowd, she could see a slow-moving sea of green and white. It was like being at a high school pep rally. Watching and listening to the crowds, she began to feel the excitement of the upcoming game. There were all types of people dressed comfortably, laughing, drinking and eating. Hot dogs and chips never tasted so good! She couldn't believe she ate two and kept them down—at least for the moment. Her headache for the most part was gone. Except for the slight ringing in her ears, she felt pretty good.

Samantha felt safe in the crowd, even though Skyler watched her every move. She tried not to talk to any men, but there were so many people saying hello and introducing themselves. She didn't want to be rude. Each male who said a word to her or glanced in her direction sparked anger in Skyler. She tried to smile and brush off any attention, but it made his anger worse. Samantha didn't know what to do. Finally, she resorted to a trick she and Emily had used at the garden parties their parents used to give. She tried to get lost in the flock. Like a curious young child, she wandered around, weaving in and out of the mass of people, in awe at the crowd of happy faces. She was relieved to realize even people like her, who were new to the group, were graciously welcomed and could meld into the crowd. Suddenly, she bristled, feeling a sharp squeeze of her hand. She thought her tiny bones would tear from the joints of her knuckles and rip through her skin. She looked up through the unwanted tears brought on by instant pain and heard the rough hostile voice she'd grown to hate so much. As she smelled his warm beer and onion breath, she bit the inside of her cheek so hard she tasted blood. The pain she inflicted upon herself was better than the pain he inflicted. Samantha bit her other cheek as she felt the pain move from her hand to her elbow and shoulder. At least her own pain gave her some control of her body and mind.

"Going somewhere?" Skyler asked, with cruel admonishment.

"No. I was just looking around. There are so many people! I didn't know where you were," Samantha whispered through the pain, lying to cover her real motivation.

"From now on, you stay by my side. You are not to be away from me for even a minute. Is that clear?"

Samantha nodded her head and he released her fingers. Putting her hands together, she straightened her fingers and rubbed the pain away gently. As she followed Skyler around the crowd, she kept her hands hidden in her pockets. It was the safest place for them. Skyler, for the moment, was content to grab her by the arm and lead her around. Finally, they caught up with Tom and Stacey. It was time for the game.

The town was so crowded it took them almost an hour to get onto campus and through the stadium gate to their seats. Skyler's announcement about having the best seats in the stadium was the most accurate thing Samantha had ever heard him say. They took their seats on the fifty-yard line.

The game was more exciting than Samantha had anticipated and, by the end of it, they were hoarse from shouting and cheering. Michigan State won the game, to everyone's delight but Skyler's. Unknown to Samantha and Stacey, the brothers had made a bet and Skyler was to stay another day if Michigan lost and would have to buy the foursome dinner at Beggar's Banquet. Tom had made the reservation a month ago. Samantha smiled and sighed in relief at Tom's gleeful announcement of the bet. Dinner with Tom and Stacey delayed her being alone with Skyler and didn't give them any time alone—she hoped.

Once at the restaurant, Samantha marveled at its atmosphere; it was like something Hemingway would have loved to write about. He could have sat for hours watching people and describing the eclectic decor. It was wonderful! She wished she were there with John, not Skyler. She'd have to invite him to lunch or dinner and bring him here to make up for having been so mean to him earlier. Samantha frowned, suddenly uncomfortable again.

"Is something wrong with your drink Samantha?" Tom asked. "I can order a different bottle of champagne. I'm sure Skyler would love me to add it to his tab." Tom winked at Skyler, playfully jabbing his arm.

"Rub it in, why don't you, little brother," Skyler said laughingly, pretending to spar with Tom as Stacey rolled her eyes at the two of them.

"It's fine. It's just been a long day. All that fresh air has made me tired, that's all," Samantha said politely to Tom. She loved the way he looked at her. She hated the way Stacey looked at him when he looked at her. Stacey seemed to like her, yet there was something she'd begun to notice; was Stacey jealous of her? Why did she have all of these growing negative feelings about Stacey? Samantha felt out of place again.

Samantha tried to fit into the conversation. She could feel Skyler's eyes penetrating her. As dinner was served and the conversation dwindled, Samantha excused herself and went to the rest room. She went into the one-stalled brightly painted room and proceeded to vomit. She tried to stop, but it kept coming up. Her stomach empty, she dragged a weak hand to the lever and flushed. Hypnotized by the absolute relief she felt, she watched what had been part of her diminish into nothing. Taking a deep, cleansing breath, she went to the sink to wash her face and brush her teeth.

"Samantha, are you all right? The guys wanted me to make sure you hadn't fallen asleep in here," Stacey said, stepping into the small room.

"I'm fine. I just felt a bit warm in there and wanted to brush my teeth and put cool water on my face."

"Oh. That's just the champagne. You don't drink much, do you?"

"No. It's never really agreed with me."

"You'll get used to it. You'll figure out what you like to drink and what you can tolerate. Believe me, you'll have plenty of opportunity."

"What do you mean?"

"Well, aren't you going to the bars with the friends you've made?"

"The drinking age is twenty-one."

"Yes, but you got served with us. I'm sure you can get served in the bars. We always did."

Samantha looked at Stacey. As much as she liked her clothes and free spirit, she felt disgust for her values. They were so different from her own.

"We'd better get back. I'm sorry I took so long."

"No problem. It was time for me to get up anyway."

Samantha was glad she had thrown up her food. It gave her room for the dessert Skyler had ordered for her. As she painstakingly ate it, she watched him take pleasure in every spoonful of chocolate mousse she swallowed. While her headache had dulled, she still felt its lingering lull in her temples.

"Well, thanks, you two. It's such a great night, I'm going to walk Samantha back to her dorm. I'll take a taxi back to your place."

"Why don't you let me drive you?" Tom asked.

"It looks like Samantha could use some fresh air and, after all I ate, I could use the walk." Skyler said oddly, as if it were an order instead of an explanation. "You two stay here and spend some time alone. I'll tell them to put anything else you want on my tab." Skyler said jovially, but with enough additional force Tom knew he wasn't to argue any further.

"Thanks, it was great seeing you again. I had fun." Samantha said to Tom and Stacey, as she slowly put on her jacket and grabbed her purse.

Not listening to their good-byes, absorbed in her own thoughts, Samantha wished she could think of something to delay them, but nothing came. She'd walk slowly to the dorm.

She'd complain of pain in her leg from the bike accident. That was it; that was the start of a good plan, she reassured herself. They stepped out onto the well-lit street. Samantha crossed her arms in front of her body as she walked. She did not want Skyler to grab her hand or touch her in any way. She could not give him the opportunity to touch her or allow him to think it was acceptable for her to be touched by him. Samantha concentrated on the sidewalk as if she would lose her footing any moment.

Skyler whistled as he walked, casually, with his hands hooked into his pant pockets by his thumbs. He wished he could be in college again and stroll down the street with his girl beside him whenever he chose. But his harmonious picture faded as he pictured Samantha with someone else. His anger swelled and rose from deep within him. She would never have the opportunity to be with another man. He knew how to control her, and tonight was the perfect opportunity to reinforce her previous lessons.

Samantha began to worry as the night walk silenced Skyler. His whistling had been annoying, but his silence was terrifying. Yet she was afraid to speak.

"What are you thinking about?" Skyler asked, curiously studying Samantha.

"Nothing really. I was just replaying the day. We really did a lot of things. I hadn't been to a college game since I went with my dad and brothers, and it really is different when you're rooting for your own school in such a huge stadium."

"It was a great game," Skyler agreed. "But you just like those guys in their tight pants."

Samantha remained silent. She knew what he was leading to, and she didn't feel like playing his word game. She'd only lose. Her mind raced for a topic she could quickly divert him with.

"Does Tom live far from here?"

"No. Why? Do you plan on going to visit him?"

"No. I just wondered."

"I saw you staring at him. You like him, don't you? You'd like to try him out to see if he's better than me, wouldn't you?"

"No! I didn't mean it that way. I may have stared at him because he looks so much like you. Have you always looked alike?"

"We're brothers, of course we look alike; but we've grown more alike as we've gotten older. You didn't answer my question. You'd like to be with him, wouldn't you?"

"No! I don't want to be with anyone," Samantha said defiantly. That included him.

"Except me, of course. Isn't that right, Samantha?"

Samantha sighed and echoed his words. "Yes, that's right."

"Good. Just so we understand each other. I wouldn't want anyone else to have you—or even think about having you."

"Well, here's my dorm. Thanks for the walk," Samantha said, dismissing him.

"No, no. You don't understand. We have a lot of work to do. We have to baptize that little bed of yours," Skyler said, pulling her toward him, pressing her hips to his. "And I've got just the thing to do that with."

Like a stunned deer, Samantha felt his hardness. She couldn't move. She was locked into him. His face was so close to hers she stopped breathing in hope of dismissing his scent from her senses. Kissing her gently, he pulled back from her and winked as he squeezed her hand and rubbed his finger up and down the inside of her palm.

"Men aren't allowed on our floor after midnight," She said, averting her eyes.

"Come on, Samantha. It's been a while since I've been to school, but things haven't changed that much. There were always as many women as there were men on my floor and the same went for the girls' floor."

"But what if Missy is there?"

"She won't be. She told me she spent the weekends with her boyfriend. Has that changed?"

"No. But what if she stops by for clothes or something?"

"Then we'll deal with that. Don't worry, sweetie. I'll take care of you."

Samantha's headache grew as they stood outside the dorm entrance. She felt as if she might vomit, but she vowed she would not; she'd find another way to stall him. "Can I show you around the dorm?"

"I'm not interested in the dorm, just you."

Samantha began to breathe deeply. She kept telling herself to relax. Her headache became impossible to bear. She began to weave down the hallway and, as they began to climb the stairs, she clasped onto the railing with all her strength. She couldn't think of any way to stall for more time. With each step she felt as if she were climbing to the cliff of doom.

"Would you like me to carry you up the stairs?" Skyler laughed as he hugged an arm tightly around Samantha's tiny waist. "I don't know why we didn't take the elevator. You really should learn how to hold your liquor."

Samantha could no longer hear his voice. She was inside her head telling herself to relax; visualize the safety of her room. She pushed out all thoughts of Skyler, trying not to acknowledge the nearness of him and his impending invasion of her space.

Samantha knew time was running out, as the hammering of her headache struck out each second that passed. In the few moments that remained, before they entered her private domain, Samantha tried her hardest to push away the panic, to picture herself alone and safe. She began to believe he had disappeared from her sight. Was it the alcohol that made her believe it? She felt a calm rush over her. Had Skyler gone?

She looked around, she saw her room, her bed. Sleep. She needed sleep. "What are you talking about, Tom?" Stacey said wearily.

"Very funny. You'll pay for that," Skyler said. Why was Samantha being so belligerent to him when she knew it would not be in her best interests? His eyes focused on her face. She was more tipsy than he'd anticipated. So, it must be the alcohol talking; everyone knows alcohol is a truth serum—at least that's what his mother always said. That fleeting reflection angered him from deep within. After their conversation about Tom, the mention of him when they were so near her bed sent Skyler's blood racing, pulsing with anger. So Samantha did want Tom. He'd cure her of that, he mused, infuriated with her behavior. "Where are your keys?" Skyler asked, reaching into Samantha's jacket pocket. "Never mind, I've got them."

Skyler opened the door, lifting Samantha immediately onto her bed. Watching her close her eyes, he retired to the bathroom. He rummaged through her toiletries, annoyed there was nothing he could use against her: no evidence of another man. He threw her hairbrush into the sink, but not before removing a few strands of hair, carefully placing and sealing them into the small, clear plastic bag he retrieved from his pocket. Quietly, he removed his clothes, hanging them on the back of the door. Stepping softly toward Samantha, he gazed at her. There she is, he whispered, Sleeping Beauty; *my* Sleeping Beauty.

Slowly, he removed her clothing, kissing her, caressing her, playing with every inch of her body. Alcohol or not, his affection would wake her. As he poured his hot breath over her, a relaxed Stacey put her arms around his neck, returning his kisses. As his fingers pried into her most private, sensual crevices, they insulated themselves one by one into the warmth of her soft delicate cavity.

Stacey remained mute. She looked at Tom. He was handsome. Even in the darkness, the moonlight seeping through the open windows cast shadows on his strong athletic features, accentuating his intense robust face and the immense muscular bulges of his torso. Stacey saw the look of rapture in Tom's eyes. She held his gaze, immediately laying back, allowing his body to be one with hers.

Gently he began. Moving slowly, carefully in and out, rubbing himself deeply inside her. He did not notice her inability to move with his weight fully on her. He did not notice his hands and arms had firmly pinned hers down. He only noticed his body moved more fiercely inside her than it had moved with any other woman. The more he took, the more he wanted. Soon he began to whisper, "You're mine. All mine. Tell me you love it. Tell me you love it, right now!"

Stacey heard the words echoing in her head. She didn't comprehend them. She was not used to Tom treating her like this. She felt uncomfortable; she didn't like it. She remained silent.

"Bitch," Skyler said, pausing his movement in her. "You like it don't you?"

Stacey looked at him. There was something different about him, but she wasn't sure what. Suddenly, she felt pain as his hands fiercely pinned down her shoulders and put his lips to her, kissing her deeply. Then, almost growling, he took her bottom lip between his clenched teeth and gruffly said, "Didn't you hear me?"

In pain, Stacey looked up and said "Mmmm," trying to answer him with her lip still locked in his teeth.

Understanding she had given in, Skyler let go of her lip and listened to the meek response.

"Yes. You know that."

"I know what? C'mon baby, tell me."

"You're great. You're the best. No one could do what you do to me. After all this time, you just get better and better." Stacey said, looking up at Tom in the darkness, still wondering why he was being so rough with her.

Empowered with Samantha's answer, Skyler moved inside of her until his body felt full and fluid and ripe. As his eruption rushed forward, filling her, his knuckles clasped the mattress, eyes closed tightly; and a low, self-satisfied moan echoed in the silence.

Now, resting on her nakedness, he waited for his body to rejuvenate. Suddenly, as if he had been tapped on the shoulder, he looked up, startled by the luminescent arms in the clock on Minnie Mouse's dress. He had time for another taste of her, he thought smiling, as he again caressed her dozing body.

Minnie Mouse. He stared at the simple pristine caricature with the big eyes and innocent face. He pictured Samantha looking at her every day. He thought of the parallels between them, as he stroked her supple skin and ran his thumb along her slim waist and curved hips. She is such a child, such a naive creature; and she is all mine. With that thought, he felt a strong urge to take her again, to feel her youth, her innocence surrounding him. She stirred as he entered her; and, as he rose and fell, pulsed and thrusted, groped and grabbed, again confident he was king and he was meant to be served.

# # #

Quietly, stepping under the warm spray of the shower, Skyler stretched before lathering himself. Physically he was refreshed, yet emotionally he was disappointed the alcohol knocked Samantha out so quickly. Maybe he shouldn't have pushed the walk. From now on, he just wouldn't let her drink. That would solve the problem, he thought, staring in the fogged mirror as he brushed his wet hair back and towel-dried himself. After all, he decided with a raised eyebrow, he wanted her to remember their sex together, not see it or remember it in a blur.

He could have lasted all night, if he had wanted to—over and over and over again. He laughed out loud at that thought. Too bad he had to go to Tom's, he contemplated, as he imagined how many times he could take Samantha in one full night. He'd have his chance, he was sure of that. Things would be very different next time, he vowed, as he straightened his clothes, tucked the sheets and comforter around his sleeping beauty, and quietly left her room.

Skyler looked at his watch as he walked onto Grand River Avenue. It was almost one. Still time to catch last call before taking a taxi. As he walked down the brightly lit street, he remembered a little bar near, but below, the restaurant they'd had dinner in. While he didn't remember its exact location, he could find it. He watched as crowds of students, still celebrating Michigan State's win, walked the streets. Skyler admired the scene. Young female coeds everywhere, walking, laughing. They were young, vibrant, alive, full of energy.

Skyler hastened his gait, stepping onto the dimly lit side street in anxious anticipation of finding his young prey in the bar below the street.

Chapter 24

Samantha awoke, startled at the dryness in her throat, the nausea in her stomach and the dull throbbing in her head. The familiar effects of too much alcohol caused her to close her eyes again. Her breathing slowed to shallow puffs. She wished she could dissipate like vapor into thin air, and she was grateful for the serene silence in her room. She heard no movement beyond her door and, except for the calming chirp of an occasional bird outside her window, even nature in its sunlit glory remained peacefully at rest; it was Sunday morning.

Snuggled beneath the warmth of her tangled sheets, still in the fetal position, she decided to rest until Minnie set off her alarm. She felt stiff and more bruised than after the bike accident. Blinking, she tried to focus as she lay still. Something beckoned her in the far recesses of her mind, as she replayed the previous day with Skyler and Tom; breakfast, the tailgate, the game, dinner. What happened after dinner? They took a walk. He walked her to the door. The stairs. She remembered not feeling well. Skyler grabbed her to steady her and then . . . Then, what? She couldn't remember. Had she blacked out? Samantha was frightened. So many things had happened to her she couldn't remember.

As her stomach began to cramp, she quickly leapt from the bed. She felt as if her body had been invaded. Samantha ran for the bathroom; she had no control. Instantly, she heaved yesterday's remnants into the clear stool. The pungent smell of soured alcohol made Samantha grab her toothbrush and toothpaste, turn on the faucet and climb into the shower. Brushing her teeth as hard and fast as she could, Samantha let the pulsating of the scalding water cleanse her. She brushed her teeth again and again, uncontrollably; then she scrubbed her skin raw with a fully lathered washcloth. Her gums were bleeding; the sweet blood tasted good.

Stepping out of the shower into her comfortable, familiar,

pink fluffy robe, she felt soothed, except for a nagging in her mind she couldn't shrug off. Grabbing panties and a comfortable sweat suit, Samantha decided to get dressed and go to the cafeteria for coffee. She could really use some fresh black coffee. She re-dried her shoulder from her dripping hair.

What's this? Samantha squinted her eyes to focus them, as she saw the dark spots on her shoulder. Moving toward the mirror, averting her eyes directly from her full reflection, she examined her shoulder. Bruises. Small bruises. Where had they come from? Not the bike accident, she would have noticed. She pondered the bruises, then counted them. There were five sets of oval bruises, some small, some larger. Five fingerprints, bite marks. Oh God! Samantha wanted to scream. She froze. She couldn't scream; there was no one to hear her. Even if they could hear, her mind raced, she couldn't let them hear.

Carefully, not wanting to know the answer, but needing it, she pulled her other shoulder toward the mirror. It was the same, five sets of oval bruises. Hurriedly, without further inspection, she pulled her green and white striped sweatshirt over her head, not caring her hair left trails of wetness inside, not caring she was too sore to wear a bra. As she brushed her hair and pulled on the rest of her clothing, she felt a rush of panic. The reasons for the bruises escaped her. But, she knew they had something to do with Skyler. She knew she must have blocked out how he had given them to her. He had talked to her about needing her, wanting her, showing her a good time. Over and over again, he'd told her in detail what he wanted to do to her. How he would touch her, how she would like it, how she would beg for more. Her hands rushing to her head, holding them over her ears tightly, she began to rock back and forth.

Moments passed. She stopped. She began to remember something. It was . . . it was . . . She concentrated. What was she seeing in her mind? It wasn't something she was remembering; it was a low sound. A real sound. What was it? Closing her eyes, she heard it. The familiar laughter. Its sound intruded on every thought, tainting her emotions with rising fear. Where was it coming from? There was no one in the room.

Samantha sat on her bed, paralyzed, pulling up the comforter closely around her. She shook uncontrollably. The laughter got louder. Her head pounded fiercely. More fearful of the raw pounding pain than of the laughter or the forgetfulness, Samantha rose from her comfortable nest and reached into her cabinet of pills. Without inspecting the labels, she threw four into her mouth, swallowing them hard with gulps of lukewarm water, unable to bear to wait for the water to turn cold. Crawling back into bed, she lay still, listening to the laughter, thinking it was in the room with her, it was someone playing a trick on her. Maybe Skyler? She contemplated that possibility, then dismissed it. By now, he would be safely at the airport away from her; at least, she hoped so.

Firmly pressing a pillow over her head, clutching its ends over her ears, she tried to block out the laughter. She couldn't. Slowly, as the moments passed, the sound blurred more and more. Before long she floated into an anesthetized, lifeless slumber, where her terrifying thoughts became, for a time, extinguished.

# # #

Skyler checked in at the airport and searched out a phone. He had to hear Samantha's voice again before he departed. How was she doing with what had to be a miserable hangover? How well would she remember their night together? Too bad he had to go back to Tom's, he thought, smiling at his vision of what could have been. As he listened to the unanswered ringing, he hung up. She had to be there. He dialed again. He was tired; he hadn't had much sleep, and he'd had an early breakfast with Tom. He must have dialed wrong. Counting the rings, his annoyance grew with each. Ten, eleven, twelve . . . He felt his anxious stomach tighten, his hands trembled with nervous anger. Fingers shaking, he grabbed a handkerchief from his pocket and wiped his sweating brow. Where was she? Where could she have gone? Had she faked her drunken state last night? There was no way she would be out this early; it wasn't possible! Hearing his plane being called, he slammed the phone into its cradle, picked up his briefcase and boarded.

# # #

Sundays were relaxed in the dorm. After ten, breakfast became a brunch that was served until two; dinner was not served at all. John and Samantha had a ritual of eating brunch together at eleven. It was an unspoken date. A casual meeting for two friends to catch up on their weekends and their studies. John looked forward to his Sunday brunches with Samantha. It was the highlight of his week, because it was usually when she was the most relaxed. He had never met anyone like her; and he had an unquenchable thirst to be with her, even if it was just as friends. He made it clear he might want more. She made it clear she wasn't ready and couldn't handle more. Their mutually agreed upon pact was to take it a day at a time, no pressure, just good friends.

John looked at his watch, tapping on the crystal to make sure it was still working. She was late. He was hungry. Could she have forgotten? Maybe she decided not to eat; he knew she didn't eat very much. Suddenly, it occurred to him, although he'd promised not to interfere with Skyler's visit, maybe she wasn't all right. Maybe she was still with Skyler. Leaving his books open on the round cafeteria table, John decided to check on her. Walking at a rapid pace to her room, without hesitation he knocked. He knocked again, harder. No answer. She must have forgotten. Disappointed, he wrote her a note on the laminated Garfield board tacked to her door.

Returning to his books, he decided to have a quiet study brunch. As he ate he barely tasted his food. He couldn't concentrate on his literature; thoughts of Samantha crept in. Maybe he should have persisted in his questions about Skyler and his request to meet him. He'd promised Samantha he wouldn't push, but his intuition told him something was not right.

# # #

Missy walked into the darkened room. Was Samantha sick? It was almost six and she looked as if she'd been sleeping all day. She quietly threw her clothes into her laundry bag and refilled her backpack with clean ones. Should she wake Samantha? Maybe she was sick. She looked so peaceful, it was a shame to wake her. But, maybe she was *too* peaceful.

Grabbing a small mirror she placed it under Samantha's nose to make sure she was breathing. Finally, she decided Samantha was just in a deep sleep. She looked carefully around the room. A stack of open books sat on Samantha's desk. Missy decided it was in Samantha's best interest to wake her up.

"Samantha? Samantha? Wake up. Don't you have to get up and finish your assignments for Monday? Samantha?" Missy said, shaking her shoulder, her voice getting louder.

Samantha stirred. She inhaled deeply and then exhaled loudly. Yawning, she opened her eyes to see Missy, shaking her.

"What? What's wrong?" Her groggy voice said, blinking the heavy sleep from her eyes, trying to focus them on Missy.

"You tell me! I thought you were dead or something. I've never seen anyone sleep so soundly. You sick or something?"

"No, not really. I had too much to drink between the tailgate, the game and dinner. I just have to learn I can't even have one drink. My body and alcohol just don't agree."

"Yeah. I can't drink much either. Jack gets some really great weed. We both smoke a little before we go out. It's great. No hangover, no smell, just a great buzz. You ought to try it. I can get you some, if you want."

"No. I don't smoke. I've tried cigarettes and they don't agree with me," Samantha said, looking curiously at Missy.

"Grass is different. You've never tried it?"

"No. I've never really had any interest. I've been thinking I might want to go to law school, and I just can't get caught with any illegal drugs. It would spoil my chances of getting in. Besides, you know my dad's a lawyer. He'd kill me."

"Bull. Grass has been used by everyone, including the president and half the judges you can name. It's not like it used to be. Besides, you won't get caught," Missy said casually, as she finished packing her things and exchanging her books. "Jack and I will come over one night and we'll share a joint. You'll see. It's really great."

Samantha watched Missy as she considered her words. She was curious about smoking marijuana, but she'd never really thought about actually trying it. She wondered what other things Missy did she'd never done, she'd never even thought about doing. Missy was a curious girl indeed. Samantha admired her confidence and free spirit. She wished she could behave irresponsibly and feel good about it the way Missy did, but she couldn't. She sighed. Looking at the clock, she jumped from her bed.

"Oh, my God! I can't believe I slept so late! John is going to kill me," Samantha said, running to the bathroom to freshen up before calling him.

"Why would he do that?" Missy curiously inquired. "Are you dating him?"

"No, nothing like that. I promised to meet him for brunch. He said he'd help me with an assignment I was having trouble with."

"Well, that explains the note on the door."

"What note?"

"Look," Missy said, opening the door, reading it out loud. "Sam, call me when you get in. Dinner? J."

"I'd better call him," Samantha said, grabbing the receiver.

"I gotta go. See you tomorrow," Missy said. "Remember, if my parents call—"

"You're at the library."

# # #

Samantha looked around the cafeteria for John. He hadn't sounded very happy with her over the phone. What would she say? How could she explain why she had missed brunch and what had happened yesterday with Skyler?

"Hi, Samantha. You look great," John remarked, relieved to see she looked okay. Her phone call hadn't convinced him "everything was fine" and "absolutely nothing was wrong," as she had said repeatedly to him. He needed to look into her eyes; he needed to see reality in them. It was impossible for those pure blue eyes to lie to him. They both knew that.

"Hi. I'm really hungry; let's go over to Jersey Giant and share a sub. Then we can come back here and study, unless you want to go to the library," Samantha said nonchalantly, smiling as if nothing had happened in the last thirty-six hours that needed discussing. She couldn't decide what to say to John; how much to explain. He didn't deserve her lies, yet he didn't deserve the truth either. She wished she could turn off her mother's stilted voice as it rang in her ears "men don't like bruised fruit." She wasn't just bruised; she was a little mangled, too. Would that matter to John? Would the truth affect their friendship, or would lies affect it more? So much to ponder, only moments before she was confronted with it all. Samantha took a deep breath and told herself to relax. Looking up at John, she smiled lightheartedly, trying to make them both believe it.

John wasn't sure if he should be comforted by her attitude or warned by it. He'd thought he'd be able to read her in an instant. Now, looking at her confidently guiding him to Jersey Giant, he was torn with conflicting emotions. Part of his inability to decipher her was his insipid inhibition, his fear of offending her, or scaring her into silence; most of all he feared losing her friendship. He would take it very slowly. He had no alternative, he decided reluctantly.

As they ordered the Jersey Giant sandwich, they silently watched it being made, cut and placed onto the burnt orange trays with their drinks and chips. It was easier to be engrossed in the preparation of their meal than to talk. Silently, they emptied the contents of their trays onto the table. The small talk they finally made was obviously designed to fill the growing uncomfortable silence between them.

Samantha sipped her milk quietly as John slowly stirred his coffee and looked into her eyes. The scent of his freshly soaped and cologned skin comforted her as much as it scared her at that moment.

"So," John said, "how was the game?"

"We won," Samantha answered.

"No kidding. I meant with Skyler. He did come in, didn't he?"

"Yes, he did. He picked me up for breakfast with his brother Tom and Tom's girlfriend, Stacey. Then we went to the governor's tailgate party and the game and dinner. It was okay"

"Nothing else?"

"Like what?" Samantha said, looking up at him with raised eyebrows.

"You know. Geez, Samantha, why are you playing games about this? I've been upset, worried about you, ever since you told me he was coming. I just want to know if everything was . . ." John stopped. He stared at Samantha, who was intently pulling pieces of bread off the sub, to make it thinner. She knew what he wanted her to tell him. He knew she knew. He also now knew there was much more to the story or she would have talked openly about her day, with lots of detail.

Samantha felt him staring. She couldn't look at him; she couldn't face him. He knew she was avoiding the truth. That was the way it was between them. Finally, after several minutes of silent fidgeting with their food, Samantha put her sub down and placed her hand over his, biting her lip as she felt his warm flesh. It wasn't comfortable for her to touch or be touched by a man, any man; but with John it felt different. There was a morsel of trust that had developed between them, enough trust for Samantha to break down some of the barriers she'd built.

John stopped and looked at her, waiting for her to speak.

"Look, you're right. There is more. I want to—no, I need to talk to you about it. I promise I will. But please, not tonight."

"When? You know I care. You know I will help you," John said, trying to be calm when what he wanted was to shake the truth out of her.

"I just . . ." Samantha stopped and looked into John's serious face and caring eyes. "I have two papers due, remember? One is for your class, Professor; and I have two midterms." Samantha paused, taking a second to look squarely at John. "What about Saturday?" She asked meekly, testing his receptivity to her proposal.

"Saturday? You can wait that long?" John asked quizzically studying Samantha with thick knitted brows. "Usually when people have problems, they don't schedule the discussion of them a week later. I'm sorry. I'm trying to be patient, to understand—to be your friend. But it just doesn't make any sense to me."

"I know. I know it's unfair of me, but I just can't let my problems interfere with school. It's a promise I made to myself a long time ago and I just can't break it. Believe me, it will be the only commitment I've made to myself I've kept in a long time," Samantha paused briefly, taking a slow, deep deliberate breath. "Please don't hate me. I just have to do this my way." Samantha looked at her plate as she spoke, knowing he was scrutinizing her, examining every word, every movement.

"Fine. But you promise if you need me, for anything, you'll ask. You know I'll help you any way I can," John said, putting his hand over hers, squeezing it comfortingly before releasing it. Clearly, he could not push her; he knew without any explanation she had been pushed too many times, in the wrong direction, by the wrong person. He wanted more than anything to help her so he could move her in the right direction and someday be more than just friends. For now, he had no choice but to agree with what she wanted and to be who she needed him to be.

"I know. I promise," Samantha responded, with a soft, gracious smile.

"A large cookie for dessert?" John asked with levity. He stood up, bowed toward her, imitating a prince wanting to escort his princess to her throne. Samantha responded in kind with her slow southern drawl, as she reached her hand up for him to lead the way. "Why thank you, kind sir."

Chapter 25

"Hey Samantha, who was that cute guy you were with Saturday night?" Jennifer asked, as she set her full laundry basket on the empty washing machine.

"What?" Samantha asked, surprised.

"You know, the cute guy who was all over you? I walked David out and saw him unlock your room with your keys. You looked a little out of it, so I'm not surprised you don't remember seeing us. We said hello."

"Oh, yeah. I forgot. We went to the game. I had too much to drink and he brought me home," Samantha said casually, pulling her wet clothes from the washer.

"No kidding," Jennifer said, with playful sarcasm. "So, who is he?"

"Just a friend who flew in from home for the game."

"Must be a good friend to fly in just for the game. You're lucky Missy is always at her boyfriend's so you never have to worry about kicking her out when you have a guy over."

"I didn't have a guy over, at least not like that; he left to stay at his brother's apartment a few minutes after he dropped me off," Samantha said, trying to convince herself as well as her floor mate.

"Right," Jennifer said, rolling her eyes. "Look, I was just curious where you found him. He is so gorgeous! I don't care who you sleep with, so don't worry so much! No one cares."

"Okay, but for the record, I didn't sleep with him. We're just friends; and, trust me, his looks are deceiving. I'd rather sleep with an ugly man than him," Samantha said, trying to close the subject once and for all. "So, who else was around?"

"No one. Don't worry, I won't say anything. If you ever think of it, and if you're still just friends, can you introduce me next time?"

Samantha turned on the dryer, rolled her eyes, shook her head and scoffed. "Sure. Whatever you want. But I guarantee, you'll be disappointed."

"No way!" Jennifer yelled, as Samantha turned and left.

Just as Samantha entered her room, she heard the phone ring. She looked up at Minnie. Eight o'clock. She sighed as she picked up the receiver. "Hello?"

"Well, it's about time. Where have you been?"

"Mostly in my room being sick. Most recently, in the basement doing laundry."

"Not true! I called you from the airport! I called you when I arrived! I called you before I had dinner! Shall I go on? Or, would you like to tell me the truth?" Skyler shouted, pounding the receiver on his kitchen counter in between each statement.

"Stop it! Stop it!" Samantha said, as moisture beaded on her body and her breath quickened.

"Then stop lying to me!"

"I'm not! If you would just listen to me and stop slamming the phone—"

"Listen to what? You haven't said anything!"

Nervously, Samantha sat on the floor of her room and began again. "I woke up really early and I got sick. I shouldn't have had any alcohol. You know it always makes me sick."

"Yeah, yeah. You still haven't said anything."

"I threw up a few times and I got the dry heaves. Then I was going to go down and get coffee, but I had a really bad headache so I took Tylenol; but what I really swallowed was Tylenol with codeine. It knocked me out for most of the day. When I got up, I realized what I'd done, so I went to the cafeteria and had something to eat."

Skyler cut her off. "I'm still waiting. Who was with you?"

"No one. I was alone all day."

"You're lying. Didn't you eat with anyone?"

"No, I —"

"You're lying. That's it, you're just a liar. I worried about you all day. I didn't hear from you, and you didn't answer the phone. How'm I supposed to react when I don't hear from you? And just how many times do you think I am going to call you? I fell asleep worrying. Today I was in trial all day and couldn't call until now. I really have enough pressure! I don't need your lies!"

"I told you the truth. I must have slept through the phone calls. I have been ill. I've had terrible migraine headaches. If you don't believe me, you can ask Missy. She woke me up; she told me I looked dead. She's checked on me every day. And you're the one who told me not to call you!"

"Oh, I'll be asking Missy all right. I told you not to call me at the *office*. But you could call me at home, or on the car phone. Doesn't that conversation ring a bell, or have you conveniently forgotten it, like everything else I say these days?"

"Okay. Okay. Next time I'll call," Samantha said, solemnly twisting her hair around her forefinger.

"There better not *be* a next time. Call me when you leave your room if you're going to be away, other than for class. Charge the calls to me, then no one has to know; it will be between us. Then we won't have any problems; if nothing is going on, then you won't have any problem doing that, will you?"

"Fine. I'll call. Where?"

"Leave me a message on my cell phone or my home phone. No one else has access to those answering machines, and I can get my messages any time."

Samantha remained on her floor for several minutes, weeping with self-pity. She wanted him out of her life. She didn't want people to associate him with her. She wanted the lies to stop, no—she *needed* the lies to stop!

Saturday. She began to look forward to it instead of dreading it. It was time to get help, time to tell the truth, regardless of the consequences. She needed John; confiding in him was her only hope.

Looking at her empty laundry basket, she took a deep breath. Time to get her jeans from the dryer and finish her homework. She had to do well on the rest of her midterms. Four more days. Her school work was the only thing keeping her sane at the moment. Well, she thought, turning the knob, that and John.

Chapter 26

The Red Cedar River ran crisply over the jutting rocks, caressing the leafy banks with its rapid course. It didn't know the coming season's northern chill would soon restrict it. The warmth of the bright fall day gave no hint of autumn's impending surrender to winter.

Samantha and John strolled along the banks, jumping on and off each large rock and in and out of every pile of fallen leaves. Like small children, avoiding the traveled paths, they explored and created their own. They knew, in time, they would find their chosen spot and, calling it their own, begin their personal journey.

Seeing a cul-de-sac of trees occupied only by a few lost ducks, they stopped, untied their jackets from around their waists, and laid them on the cold ground. Quietly, they sat facing the beauty of the river. It was their private nature center. Samantha took deep breaths of the brisk air, slowly releasing them from her lungs, as she picked at a few blades of dormant grass. John watched her running the long blades through her lips, as much in awe of her beauty as in the fact she was with him and she wanted to be with him. Her dark curls, piled in swirling layers, framed Samantha's thin face, capturing in her subtle expression a radiance that beamed only for its current beholder. Had there been viewers, they would have been embarrassed to be part of such a private, intimate moment. John understood it. He felt it. He took pride and joy in it. And he reciprocated it.

"You can see under my skin," Samantha said suddenly looking up at John. She could see into his enormous eyes. Every subdued gold speckle in the soft brown pools reflected a different private thought or part of her. Somehow they were together because they'd been together in another time; and now it was time to catch up, to yield to a stronger, more powerful energy and unite as one force.

"Yes, I can see inside of you. And the fact you know

proves you should trust me; that you *can* trust me. Whatever the problem, I will help you. I promise, I will find a way," John said, with such earnestness only the raw truthfulness of his words could emanate, putting to rest any doubt or hesitation.

Samantha felt the sincerity in his voice; she saw the honesty in his face, in his strong brown eyes. But she had trusted once before. He couldn't know the pain she felt. Pain had taught her it was better to fly solo. How could she explain, telling him everything would make what she preferred to think of as a bad dream become real—no longer a nightmare she could float in and out of. But she must try. Samantha prefaced her confession with a deep exhalation, as if to release an obstruction. Slowly she began. Her words were honest in their deliberation, but carefully chosen. Her voice was soft, quivering with a hint of uncertainty.

"You may hate me after what I tell you, and I won't blame you. I hate myself."

"I could never hate you," John interrupted, not understanding the gravity of what he was about to hear. "No matter what."

Samantha heard his words but could not look at him. She continued speaking, hoping he would not interrupt her again. Didn't he know how hard this was? She forced out the difficult words. "Last spring I was studying late at the library. I didn't take my car; I walked. It was nice outside, and the library isn't far from my house. I lost track of time and, by the time I left, it was late and dark outside. My parents travel a lot, so when they're gone, they call to make sure everything is all right. I was afraid I would miss their call and they would worry. So I took the shortcut home." Samantha's voice quivered, and with each word, her vocal tone began to get lower and lower.

John stared at her. He saw the sudden change, the sheepish look, the pink growing in her pale cheeks. He frowned with concern. As if he were watching a beautiful fawn, he remained still, not wanting to scare her. The sound and meaning of her next words caused his throat to clam up, clutching in a tight mass. Trying to form a compassionate response, he found he was incapable of speech. His anger rose, with each uncomfortable word he heard, to a height he had never known.

He continued to watch in silence, as a tear trickled from the weighted, watery edge of Samantha's eye.

"I wasn't supposed to cut through the alley. I . . . He came out of nowhere. I didn't see him until it was too late," Samantha stopped. She composed herself, ignoring the tears washing over her face. "He raped me. I couldn't fight him off," she gulped hard, her arms tightly hugging her knees as her body began to rock back and forth, as if she were sitting on a rocking chair. "I tried, I really tried, but I couldn't breathe. I couldn't move or . . ." Samantha's voice trailed off and she paused briefly, staring into the horror of a memory she had avoided for so long. "I may have passed out for a minute or two. I don't remember. I wondered if I was alive. Then I saw blood. My blood, everywhere. My hands, my broken nails, torn clothes. I didn't feel any pain. I couldn't stop shaking. I remember running home. I felt like I had wings on; like I was in someone else's body. Like I was watching a movie." Samantha paused to wipe her face. "I don't remember telling myself to run, but I did. I ran as fast as I could, letting the wind wash over me, hoping it would blow his monstrous fingerprints off of me. My skin still crawled with his touch, even though he was gone. I couldn't shake him off. No one was home when I got there. Cook, the maids, everyone gone. I didn't know what to do; I could feel his hands, his body all over me. I took a shower. I threw away my clothes. I don't remember sleeping. In the morning, the doorbell rang. I didn't even think about anything; I was numb. I went downstairs and answered the door. It was Skyler. He helped me, at first," Samantha stopped and looked at John, waiting for a reaction. She saw his compassion, his concern, his growing fright for her. He did not need to respond, she felt his caring. "I trusted him. He helped me through everything. Then, just when I thought everything was over, he told me he would tell everyone, everything, if I didn't have sex with him. At first I thought he was joking, I misunderstood, because I'd had a few drinks the night he told me. Finally, I believed him," Samantha said forlorn, pausing to take a deep breath and sniff her running nose. John handed her his handkerchief and she again wiped her face and tried to compose herself. Samantha looked up at his strong compassionate face, bit her lip and continued. "He'd made a tape of our conversation of me telling him everything that morning. I don't know how he did it. He gave me a copy. I listened to it. It's every word we said. He says he has other things, too. My parents wouldn't understand; they wouldn't believe me; they wouldn't like being in the newspapers."

John nodded slowly, encouraging her. He wanted her to know she was not at fault, he would help her. What happened didn't matter to him. But right now, he had to know more. He wanted her to fill in the details. He had so many questions; so much didn't make sense. He touched her arm lightly, reassuringly. She needed time to regain her composure and strength before he asked any questions. He needed time to formulate unintimidating questions to fill in the missing pieces. He had to be careful with Samantha's fragile state of mind.

They both needed a break, so he reached into the black-strapped bag he had brought along. Unlatching the velcro closure, he pulled out a large wide-mouthed thermos of cafe au lait and poured them each a steamy cup. Silently, they sipped the hot brew, letting its warmth coat their insides, reminding them they were alive and well, despite the awful truth she had verbalized, intruding like a dark cloud on their sunny day.

Samantha appreciated John's sensitivity. She'd never felt as secure with anyone as she felt now with him. Somehow he would help make her whole again and put the past behind her forever. She looked gratefully into his face and felt immediately reassured by his tender smile and his strong arm around her shoulder. Samantha took a long sip of her coffee. Reaching into her pocket she pulled out the familiar worn paper. Without unfolding it, she handed it to John.

"What's this?" he asked gently. Slowly, he opened the tattered paper. Samantha blinked at him in silence. Her rocking subsided as she watched him read the careworn words. "I don't understand."

"They're words, legal words. I need you to help me understand what they mean."

"What will that do?"

"It will help me get away from Skyler. He told me the law is on his side and he isn't doing anything wrong; that blackmail for sex is legal, that there's no law against it. And. And,"

Samantha couldn't say the words. Her mind raced, her heart pounded. Rocking again, she blurted out the words she feared the most. "And an illegal abortion is murder and I can go to jail."

Silence drew a line between them. John absorbed her words and reread the definitions on the thin, frayed sheet. He understood her behavior, her fear, her desperation. He was thankful she had finally trusted him. He had to pace his reaction; he was aware his anger and empathy were mingled. Frustrated, he dismissed his faith in his abilities to separate out his feelings for Samantha. He didn't have the competence to independently help her. They would need to seek outside help. But how long would it take to convince her of that?

As they depleted the contents of the thermos, Samantha meticulously answered John's questions, feeling as if she'd stripped herself naked and was now allowing him to look at her through a magnifying glass. John asked her carefully constructed questions, fusing as many of her answers as he could together. The rest would come in time. He was careful to keep Samantha's downcast eyes in constant check, worried rehashing everything would put her in emotional jeopardy.

Finally, satisfied in their deeper commitment of friendship and trust, John and Samantha sat mesmerized by one another; he in her raw need of him; her in his absolute acceptance of her, despite what he'd just learned.

Breaking the silence reluctantly, John put the cups and thermos back in the bag and threw it onto his shoulder. He got up from the hard ground and offered her his hand. "Let's go," he said, still taking in Samantha's quiet beauty.

"Yeah, I guess we'd better. Besides, you-know-who will be calling. I told him I'd be at the library for a few hours," Samantha said matter of factly, sighing, feeling freed from at least part of the nightmare, relieved she could now discuss it all with someone she trusted completely, without any hesitation. "I'm sure he's already called ten times, trying to pinpoint my exact time of arrival."

"Samantha," John said, turning toward her, grabbing firmly onto her shoulders. "You cannot take his threats lightly. Remember what I told you. Blackmail for anything is illegal. There are laws against what he's doing. He knows that. He is very dangerous. Don't underestimate him! Make sure you act as naturally as you can. I don't want you to tip him off in any way till we can figure out how to handle this. Promise me."

Samantha looked forthrightly into his sincere face. She understood his compelling plea and the gravity of his words. Nodding, she inhaled deeply and then loudly exhaled. "I promise."

"Pinky swear," John said, smiling, offering her his curved pinky finger.

"Pinky swear," Samantha said, giving him her pinky to twist around his.

The pair paused, united; uniquely bonded. Slowly, they walked back to the dormitory, each lost in thought, but comforted they were together.

"I'll walk you to your room," John said politely.

"No. I'm fine. I'll see you in an hour for dinner," Samantha said. "Really, I'm fine. I want to take a shower and get the leaves out of my hair and put some clean clothes on."

"Okay. An hour. How about a movie after dinner?" John said. "I think we both need a diversion. It'll be great to get out."

"How will I explain it?"

"Don't. After you talk to him, leave your phone off the hook. Tomorrow, tell him you hung it up wrong."

"Okay. I haven't tried that before. I hope it works." Samantha's blue eyes were clearer than he'd seen them all day, her aura stronger.

# # #

True to her expectation, as soon as Samantha returned to her room and prepared for her shower, the phone rang.

"Hello?"

"Well, well. What have you been doing? You sound in too good a mood to have been at the library all afternoon," Skyler said with glib curiosity.

"I am in a good mood. I got more done at the library than I expected. After I eat dinner, I'm going to put all my notes on the computer and do the first draft of my paper. I feel pretty good about it. I thought it would be a lot harder than it was."

"Well, good. I'm glad you are adjusting well. Now tell me who else was there?"

"Lots of people were at the library. I didn't know anyone, though."

"Then why were you there for so long?"

"I told you, research. You know how long it takes to do research."

"Yeah, but I also know you were looking at all those muscle-bound college men. It's all right, you can tell me."

"I wasn't; I didn't," Samantha said, unsure, trying to remember John's words, his comforting support of her. Her stomach cramped into her throat and she felt weak.

"You'd better be a good little girl and save it all for me. You know that, don't you?"

"Yes," Samantha said, meekly, feeling the back of her head pounding.

"Tell me you love me. Tell me there's no one else. You know I love you, don't you?"

Samantha felt her body heaving as she slumped down the length of the wall and sat cramped up on the floor. "Yes."

"Yes, what?"

"Yes, I love you."

"Good. Now, go eat, and I'll call you after dinner."

Samantha ran to the toilet, leaving the receiver on the floor as the dark acidic afternoon's coffee spewed into the bowl, vehemently, over and over again. Wiping her mouth and her watery eyes with the nearest towel, she grabbed her toothbrush and stepped into the shower, avoiding the mirror. Her mind didn't even have to tell her body what to do anymore. I respond and act on instinct; like an animal, I've been conditioned. She tried to absorb and analyze her reactions, hoping for a moment of relief.

The water revitalized her, the soap and toothpaste cleaned her. She hated Skyler, now more than ever. The urgency of having to confide in John made her realize, as she heard her own haunting words out loud, she'd been responsible, in part, for believing his lies. Samantha closed her eyes as hot water pounded her body, clearing soapy mounds from her scrubbed wet flesh into the drain. Hopefully, soon, her problems would go down the drain too. John would help her make up for some of the mistakes she'd made; but could he really? She stepped into her robe. And was she putting him in any danger?

# # #

John felt the change in her demeanor as he stepped into her room. He watched her carefully as she grabbed her coat and purse. He wanted to ensure she was really all right after her painfully candid revelations. He loved looking at her eyes. They lit up her face and were a clear mirror into her heart; her pure soul. Unlike earlier, her eyes had a sparkle, a gleam of happiness he had never seen in such marked brilliance.

"You look wonderful," John announced. "Are you ready?"

"Yes. Just let me grab my key."

"Hey, nice job on the phone!" John exclaimed teasingly. It was tangled in the cord, on the floor next to the dresser, as they shut the door behind them.

"Thanks. See, I do know how to follow instructions," Samantha said, before relaying Skyler's most recent call as they walked to dinner.

"Tomorrow. Tomorrow and every day after we'll find a way to get you out of this, to help you. Tonight we forget about everything. You've been through too much today. We're going to eat and go for a walk; and then we'll see that movie I promised." John looked at her across the table. He lifted his milk glass to her. "Okay?"

"Okay," Samantha said, clinking her milk glass with his, drinking it down in sync with him.

# # #

The phone was still quietly sleeping on the carpet when Samantha switched on the light and threw her purse on top of the dresser. She kicked the receiver against the wall instead of replacing it on the cradle. She felt more normal than she had in months. She finally believed it would soon be over. Samantha smiled at the relaxed fun she'd had with John at dinner, the movie, and dancing. It had been a long time since she'd done any of those things. Trusting John had been the right thing to do. She felt so much better, free, healthy.

Preparing for bed, Samantha felt a slight pounding in her head as she contemplated the freedom she would have once she never had to speak to Skyler again. Swallowing a sleeping pill and something for her headache, she climbed beneath her soft comforting sheets and relinquished herself to her dreams.

# # #

When John fell into his bed, he was both emotionally relieved and emotionally exhausted. He hadn't expected to hear Samantha's words. He'd known she was hiding some secrets; it wasn't hard to tell from her odd behavior and excuses, her sometimes darkened eyes. But he had not anticipated her story; those pain-driven words were unexpected. He was still absorbing them as he closed his eyes and pounded his fist, hard, against the cold wall next to his bed.

John wasn't sure if he had ever believed in a particular God, but he knew there was a stronger force that kept the world evolving. He believed now was the time, if ever there was one, to ask God to show himself—by guiding him, by helping him to help Samantha and protect her from further harm. In the dark quiet, he pictured her innocent face and the cruel, immoral journey she'd traveled alone. Vowing to help her, he pounded the wall, again and again, gladly feeling the warm dull pain throbbing in his hand instead of his bursting heart. Angry tears painfully burned down his face.

Chapter 27

Samantha gave John a sidelong glance as he finished his breakfast. Sipping her coffee, she wondered when he would raise the issue of Skyler. It had been a week since she'd confessed everything to him, yet he hadn't approached the subject of what they would do. John continued to ask Samantha about every conversation she had with Skyler. With each dialogue she conveyed to him, his face grew frustrated with anger. He couldn't hide his depth of emotion from her. John would eventually give her a plan, but when?

"Samantha, I know what I'm about to ask you will be difficult, but I believe it's important," John said gently. He gazed into Samantha's eyes as he continued. "I've been doing research. I found out it is illegal to tap a phone, except under certain circumstances, like when the police are involved. But you can record conversations on your own phone, as long as it is not for illegal purposes; the tapes can be used in court, and they can be given to the police for proof of a crime." John paused, watching her freeze at the mention of police, then nod her head, encouraging him to continue. "So, I want you to begin a diary of all of your conversations with Skyler. If you can't do it word for word, verbatim, do it as close to it as possible. Can you do it?"

"Sure, if you think it will help. I type faster than I write; couldn't I keep it on my computer?"

"Yes, but keep a backup disk. Don't tell anyone what you're doing."

Samantha cut him off. "Think about it, who would I tell?"

"Okay. I'm just trying to tell you we have to be careful. Do you have a password on your computer, or can anyone log on?"

"I don't have a password. Should I?"

"Yes. Buy one right away. Use it. You should also buy a computer disk case with a secure lock for the backup disks,"

John said seriously. "Promise. Do it today. I'm going to look for a small answering machine you can hide so you can tape your conversations with Skyler. I'm fearful Missy will find the machine, unless we can hide it well, or Skyler will see it if he returns. You can't afford to let him know you're documenting anything. So let's just see if I am able to find what I want. In the meantime, you know what you have to do, right?"

"Yes. Whatever you say. I promise. I've got to get to class. So do you, Professor," Samantha said playfully, trying to lighten the mood between them.

Looking at his watch, John immediately got up from the table. "See you later. Dinner? I'll pick you up at six."

"Sure," Samantha quickly responded, watching his brisk gait out of the cafeteria, as she put on her jacket.

"Hey, Sam! I thought I might find you here," Missy called from across the room.

"Hi, Missy. What brings you here so early?"

"What else? Clothes and books. And Jack's roommates are making me crazy. They're slobs! Are you on your way to class?"

"Yeah."

"I'll walk out with you. Oh, that guy, your weird friend Skyler, called again. Actually, he's the one who suggested to me you were eating breakfast before class."

"Oh? What'd he want?" Samantha asked, as casually as she could.

"He wondered who you were dating these days and who your friends were, how often I saw you, who else slept in our room. Honestly, the questions are worse than those of any parents I know, including my mother! Are you sure he's not interested in you? There is just something really strange about him, eerie. Why don't you tell him to stop calling? Or tell your parents to ask him to stop calling. He gives me the creeps." Missy said, staring as Samantha's face drained of all color.

"Are you all right?" Missy asked, concerned Samantha might faint.

"Yes. I've just got another headache. And you're right about Skyler; he is weird. He's really not a threat, though; he's too far away. He's just lonely. I wouldn't want my parents to worry, so please don't say anything to anyone and please make sure you don't give him any information about me. Okay?" Samantha said, staring at a concerned Missy.

"Fine. I won't say another word about him, and you know I never give him any information and I never will. But you have to promise me something. You have to promise you'll go to Olin for those headaches. You have to find out what causes them. I'll go with you if you want," Missy said, showing genuine concern for her roommate, feeling as if she had to do something for her.

"I've got class in a few minutes. That's not enough time to go now, but I promise I'll go later."

"I'll meet you back here and go over to Olin with you. Okay?"

Samantha couldn't think how to avoid it gracefully, without offending Missy. Exasperated, she gave in. "Fine. I get out at eleven fifty. I'll be here around noon. How about we eat and then go?"

"See you then," Missy said, turning to walk back up the dorm stairs, returning to their room to study until Samantha returned.

Samantha took her time walking to class. It was really cold outside, and the potent gales of wind brought with them tiny white flakes of snow. The flakes felt good against her exposed face and hands. She was glad she hadn't taken her bike. It would have been too cold to ride in the wind, and she needed to walk off her anxiety and, hopefully, her headache. Missy's words about Skyler rambled around in her head. She felt pressure, nausea. She walked faster, her heart and breathing in quick tandem. Sweat poured down her chest. Her face perspired. Her hearing became deaf to the sounds around her, except the laughter. It was back. It got louder with each step.

Samantha ran pell-mell into the building. She found the bathroom instantly. Dropping her backpack onto the scuffed, cold, marble floor, she turned on the faucet, cupped her hands under the cold water and splashed the healing wetness onto her face. Then taking a deep breath, she reached into the small unzipped pocket of her backpack for the pill bottle. Popping off the white lid, she slid two red capsules into her palm along with a white and green one. They had to work, she prayed.

Quickly, she popped the pills into her mouth, again cupping her hands under the still-gushing faucet. As she gulped the water from her hands, she felt the pills stiffly tumbling down her esophagus. Grateful for the long old couch in the rest room, she sat, leaning her head against the overstuffed back pillow. The fabric smelled old and worn—musty—her senses became keenly aware of her surroundings. She listened, suddenly remembering. The laughter hadn't followed her into the building. It must have been the wind, she concluded, trying to convince herself, as she glanced at her watch. Class began in twenty-five minutes. That should be enough time for the pills to work. She replaced the pill bottle in her case. One thing was for sure, she decided with resolve as she closed her eyes, she had to see a doctor; she needed more pills. How could she survive without them?

# # #

Olin was lined with students. Missy knew her way around, so Samantha followed her.

"Get your student I.D. out and stand in line. I'm going to get in the one next to you. I need a refill on my pills," Missy said, pointing to the counters and falling into line. "Don't worry, they have good doctors here. You'll like them."

Samantha nodded and listened as Missy rambled on. She was glad she didn't have to talk, just respond to Missy's occasional questions and observations. After checking in, they waited for almost an hour on hard faux leather couches, reading magazines.

"Samantha, that's you. Didn't you hear them call you? Follow the red line. Wait for me by the checkout if you get done before me," Missy said, staring at Samantha's dazed look. "Samantha, did you hear me? Are you Okay?"

"Oh, yes. I'm fine," Samantha said, wishing she could shrink away through the seams of blue carpet tiles in the waiting area. She heard her own footsteps loudly pound onto the white tiles, and felt apprehensive. The young nurse, who led her into a room, helped her feel more at ease. Telling herself to relax, she took deep breaths and tried to smile at the crisply dressed woman.

"Are you feeling faint, dear?" The nurse asked.

"A little."

"Do you need to lie down?"

"No, I don't think so."

"Is that why you are here?"

"Sort of. I've been having a lot of headaches – migraines. I need something for them. They get so bad I faint and get nauseous. I hear things, too."

"You mean like ringing?"

"Yes, that's it," Samantha said, deciding not to mention the laughter or the forgetfulness.

"Anything else?"

"No."

"Are you on any medication?"

"No. I mean, I take aspirin, Tylenol, Excedrin for Migraines; but I think I need something stronger, because they just don't work anymore. And. I'm . . ." She took a deep sigh. "I'm taking birth control pills. I need a prescription for a refill."

"Did you know those can be the cause of your headaches?"

"No."

"Well, I'll note it in your chart. The doctor may have to change your prescription or method of birth control. That could be one cause of your headaches. Anything else?"

A blank-faced Samantha answered "no" and watched the nurse dismiss herself. Samantha sat in the stark room, chewing the nail polish off her nails. She'd never before been a nail biter, but she didn't know what else to do. Watching the flakes of polish fall onto her sweater and jeans, her heart pounded compulsively, louder and louder, her anxiety growing with each beat.

"Hi there," said the white-jacketed man. "I hear you've been suffering from headaches." He handed the chart to the nurse who shadowed him, as he pulled out a small flashlight and looked into Samantha's eyes.

Samantha gulped and nodded. She wished she had demanded a female doctor. She hated answering his questions, mostly because he was a man. Patiently, she listened to his lecture about how underweight she was; she instantly dismissed it.

"I know you want something for your headaches. I believe you're suffering from migraine headaches. I'm giving you a diet to follow and some pills you should take every day. They have been proven to relieve migraines in some sufferers. Also, we'll give you a series of pills and a shot you can administer if the headaches get too bad. I want a phone call after you use the shot. I want to know how it works for you. I'm only giving you six shots. You shouldn't need them all; but if you do, you have them."

Samantha nodded as she listened to his instructions. She felt she should take notes as he handed her four prescriptions, and the nurse jotted down every word he said in her chart.

"About birth control—are you sexually active?"

"Well, not really. No."

"You either are or you aren't. Have you been checked for sexually transmitted diseases, and have you had a pap smear this year?"

"Yes, my family doctor at home; but he wanted me to be checked by a doctor here and make sure the pills were the right dosage for me," Samantha said, lying. She didn't want him to touch her like that. Not a man. Not ever. She began to perspire profusely.

The gray haired doctor stared at her with a raised eyebrow. "Samantha? Are you feeling okay? Can you hear me?"

Samantha heard a loud ringing in her ears; she couldn't hear the words the doctor was saying. Suddenly, everything went black.

"Samantha? Samantha?" She heard her name over and over again as she smelled the ammonia sharply infiltrating her nostrils. Fluttering her eyes open, she saw the doctor standing over her and felt the nurse checking her pulse.

"You fainted. You're okay. We're going to keep you here for a little while. Did you come here with someone? When was the last time you ate?"

So many questions. Samantha just wanted to leave. She wanted her prescriptions and she wanted her room, her bed. She nodded, she answered the questions. She smiled, hoping her cooperation would be the key to her release. Samantha watched the nurse stare at her as she drank the carton of milk and the vending machine sandwich that had been brought in.

"Are you feeling better, dear?"

"Yes. Can I go? My roommate must be worried."

"She's waiting in the hall. I'll bring her in."

"No. Wait! Please don't. I mean not until after I see the doctor again and he releases me."

The nurse shrugged and nodded. A few minutes later, the serious faced doctor returned.

"I feel fine. Really. Can I go?" Samantha asked, trying to act chipper and alert.

"What happened here concerns me. I know students forget to eat; I see dozens every week, like you. But you need to know your body is giving you a warning, a message you need to treat it better. Do you understand?"

Samantha nodded in agreement with everything he said. She had no choice.

Finally he released her, after scheduling several tests, a follow-up appointment, and the lowest dose of birth controls pill he felt she could handle, even though he advised her "another method, in your case, would be better." Samantha didn't care what he said. She had her prescriptions in hand and had met her goals.

Missy listened as Samantha explained she'd fainted and that's what had taken so long.

"I can't believe they didn't admit you!" Missy exclaimed.

"He told me I'm just a bit underweight, and I need to eat more and gain a few pounds. I have to follow a special diet for my headaches. He gave me some pain medication, too."

"See. Now aren't you glad I made you go?"

"Yes. You were right."

"How about if I stay and we go to dinner together? I can meet Jack later; we're going to a movie and then to Harrison Road House's. You could join us, if you feel up to it. I really don't want to leave you alone."

"I'm meeting John for dinner, and I really want to go to bed early," Samantha said, immediately regretting she'd let John's name slip out.

"John? You're seeing John, as in dating? Why haven't you told me? I thought you two were just friends."

"We are just friends. We get along really well." Samantha stopped Missy and touched her arm. "Please, don't tell anyone."

"You mean Skyler," Missy stated, looking squarely at an anxious Samantha. "Your secret is safe with me. Really. Don't worry. I haven't told him anything so far; besides, I owe you for covering for me with my parents." She paused. "If you feel like it, why don't you and John meet us at Harrison Road House's?"

"Maybe. I'm not sure what he has planned. Let's just play it by ear, and if we decide to go, we'll find you there. Okay?"

"Great."

# # #

By the time John picked up Samantha for dinner, she had showered, rested, and had avoided a call from Skyler by having Missy tell him she was in the shower and then on her way to bed because she was ill and had fainted.

"How was your day?" John asked.

"Interesting."

"What does that mean?"

"Well, after you left, I ran into Missy, and we spent the day together, sort of. It's a long story." As Samantha explained her day, John watched, concerned. Skyler called more frequently and asked more detailed questions.

"So you didn't buy the password program, like you promised?"

"No, I didn't have time; I was sick. I swear I'll get it tomorrow."

"Forget it," John said. "I had a feeling you'd forget. I stopped in between classes."

"Thank you," Samantha said, putting her glass of milk down, reaching for the disk. "And I am sorry. I should have followed your instructions. I've just felt so much better having someone on my side."

"Well, we have lots to talk about. Where would you like to talk?"

"My room?"

"As long as we won't be disturbed."

"We won't. Missy left; in fact, if you want to, she asked if we'd like to meet her and Jack later."

John loved her newly found enthusiasm, but he had serious things to discuss with her. He didn't want to commit to doing anything but the task at hand. He wanted her nightmare to end so they could see if there was any other future for them. "Some other time that would be great. Are you ready for dessert?"

"I think so, but not soft serve. I think I'll try some apple pie," Samantha said, pushing her spaghetti around her plate as if she'd eaten quite a bit. "You sit here; I'll get some for both of us."

John watched Samantha protectively. Even though he knew there was nothing to fear in the cafeteria, his gaze on her did not waver.

Samantha returned with the pie and two fresh glasses of milk. John's brown eyes looked deeply recessed, dark circles revealing his sleepless nights. She'd been so self-absorbed she hadn't noticed the toll on him. She felt an immediate ache in her throat. How could she be so blind to think this wasn't as hard for him as it was for her? He was now carrying her burden. "I'm sorry to have involved you."

"Samantha, don't you know how I feel about you? I care a great deal for you, maybe more than I should." John looked at her as she played with her pie, putting only morsels on her fork at a time. "I'm glad you were able to confide in me. I *want* to be involved. Thank you for trusting me enough to let me help you."

"Still, I shouldn't have involved anyone—even you. I'm sorry," Samantha said putting her hands over her face, embarrassed by her own words, by her earlier confession, by her ultimate and absolute need of him.

"Let's go," John said gently, pushing away the rest of his pie.

Samantha followed him to her room. She opened two small bottles of sparkling water and handed one to John. His face had become serious and sullen.

"Sit down, Samantha. We've got to talk," John said, pulling her down beside him on the carpeted floor, their backs leaning against the bed. "I've done some research. And, I've talked to some people."

Samantha gasped. "You promised! Oh my God, what have you done!"

"Samantha, you have to trust me. No one knows it's you. I didn't use your name," John said, pausing to let her absorb his words before he continued. "I mentioned a hypothetical situation and posed some questions to a law professor in the

College of Criminal Justice and a professor who teaches criminal law at the Detroit College of Law."

Samantha bit her lip. "What did they say?"

"Blackmail for sex is illegal. Just like I told you. Rape is a felony and an illegal abortion won't put you in jail, but it could put the doctor who performed it in jail, along with anyone else who participated in it. If it was a licensed doctor who performed it on a minor, he could lose his license to practice medicine, if he had one to begin with." John closed his eyes a minute before focusing on Samantha's anxious face as she took in his words. "There is so much to tell you I just don't know where to begin, so I guess first things first."

"What do you mean?" Samantha asked, looking into John's benevolent face, hearing the tiredness in his voice.

"How far are you willing to go?"

"Go?" Samantha's radiant blue eyes grew wide, and she began to panic.

"You want to be rid of Skyler and of being blackmailed and the rape, the whole mess, right?"

"Right."

"The only way I can see all those things happening, or even any one of those things being taken care of, is for you to prosecute, to call Skyler's bluff. Catch him in the act. Facing it is the only way all those things will stop," he added, turning to her, his face more serious than she'd ever seen it. "It's the only way you can free yourself and move forward with control of your life."

"But my parents—"

"They'll understand. For God's sake, your father is a lawyer! I'm sure he'll be the first to agree you need to get these guys."

"You don't know them," Samantha said frowning, her eyes staring blandly into his, her bottom lip quivering uncontrollably.

"I know you. They couldn't have raised you as you are without a strong degree of self-confidence. You are, hidden under all this, a fighter. They gave that to you. They can handle this. Trust me. Anything else doesn't make sense."

"But the family name . . ."

"Are you telling me your family name is more important than you taking your life back? Because if you are, then I can't help you, nobody can."

"No, that's not what I'm saying."

"Then you are willing to go the distance?"

Samantha took a deep breath. Her eyes unwillingly filled with tears, her hands again hid her face. "I need this to be over. I will. I will do whatever it takes. You're right. You're right," She said, sobbing.

"Good. Now, we have to talk to the police. I have the name of a detective. He'll probably have to get the FBI involved because there are two jurisdictions, Arkansas and Michigan; and we'll need to set up a sort of sting operation to trap Skyler. We have to get enough unimpeachable evidence to make it stick."

"Unimpeachable—what's that?" Samantha asked, taking a tissue from John's strong hand. That small gesture gave her strength. She wasn't sure why, but it made her feel closer to John than she already felt. He really understands, feels my pain, really cares. She dried her face, staring at him as he answered.

"Evidence they can't challenge or throw out. Right now we're starting from scratch. One thing we have going for you is that Michigan has passed strong anti-stalking laws. That's what Skyler is doing to you, essentially; he stalks you through the phone. That's illegal."

Samantha's eyes grew wide. That thought hadn't even occurred to her. "You're saying, even though I don't have any evidence, we could use the phone to get some?"

"Exactly."

"But you said wiretapping is really illegal."

"Yes. But the police, the FBI—they can use wiretapping in some cases. They get a court order that allows the wiretapping. The attorney I talked to said your case, the hypothetical case I asked about, would be one of those."

"Attorney? You said you talked to professors."

"Yes. The professors at DCL are also lawyers. He gave me the name of a good criminal attorney we can talk to, a contact in the prosecutor's office and the FBI. Don't worry, I told him I was doing research. He doesn't think I was talking about a real person or a real situation."

"When do we start?" Samantha said, as the phone began to ring.

Grabbing her computer, she quickly switched it on.

"Hello?"

"Hi, sweetheart. I heard you weren't feeling well. What are you doing?"

"Oh, I'm fine. I think I just have a twenty-four hour bug. I was just reading in bed."

"Alone?"

"Of course."

"No, really, who is in bed with you?"

"No one. Just my book."

"What book are you reading? Something that'll turn you on?"

"No. Just something dry for school. I hoped it would put me to sleep."

"Well then, I have perfect timing, once again. You can dream of me. Dream of me inside you, touching every part of you. You need me, we have something special together . . ."

John grimaced as he read the screen. Samantha carefully continued to type in the words. His anger rose with each word. Sheer force of will kept him outwardly calm, despite his luminous eyes filling as much with rage against Skyler as with fear for Samantha.

With the phone secured in its cradle, Samantha focused her eyes on John who sat, staring, in trancelike thought. Taking a deep breath, she found her voice, steadied it and spoke to him. "Still want to save me?" she asked meekly, again biting her lip.

John took a big mouthful of the bottled water. He gulped from the bottle, trying to wash back utter disgust and nausea. Staring for a time at the now dimmed computer screen, he finally felt composed enough to respond to Samantha without scaring her with his gut-wrenching fury.

"I can't believe this guy. I can't believe you've put up with that kind of garbage every day. We have to move quickly. We'll need to contact a criminal psychologist. I want to make sure we handle this right, for your protection."

"Okay. Whatever you say, I trust your judgment. Did I do alright?"

"You did great. I see you've also learned to lie. I must say, you had me convinced. That's good. He at least believes what you tell him. We can use that in our favor."

"Yeah, I've told a lot of lies. But not to you. I hope you believe me. If it weren't for you—" Samantha couldn't say any more; she bit her lip. She felt weak, scared. She wanted a shower. She wanted her bed. She needed to be alone. She needed to take some pills and rid herself of the growing throb in her head.

"Don't worry. I'll see you through this," John said, lightly touching her arm, knowing she wouldn't be ready for more than that for a very long time. Feeling Samantha's body recoil from his touch, John wanted to hold her, to tell her he would make it better; but knew he couldn't. He wondered again, as he had so many times before, if she could ever respond to him as he desired her to.

"I'm really, really tired. Tomorrow's Saturday; I don't have much homework," Samantha said, feeling as if her dinner were in her throat. "Maybe then we can go over your plan, and we can install the program you bought me? Okay?"

"Sure. I'll go back to my room and do a few hours of work so I can give you the whole day. We really do have a lot to do."

Samantha saved the document of her transcribed conversation with Skyler after John left. Meticulously, she shut down her computer and put it away. She couldn't read what she had written. It wasn't real if she didn't read it; another day she'd face it, but not tonight. She was too depleted to think about anything. She needed to relax.

After swallowing a few of the new prescription pills, she poured several capfuls of bubbles in the tiny tub and climbed into the sweltering suds. Resting her head on the small, clam-shaped, plastic pillow suctioned on the back of the tub, she closed her eyes. Her big toe slid in and out of the still pouring faucet flow. Her thoughts drifted as the water continued to rise; she couldn't dismiss John's face from her imagination. His haunted stare at her as she talked with Skyler. Much as she wanted his help, she wished she could insulate him and hide herself. "Mmm. I've been through enough for both of us," Samantha said, thinking out loud. She shut the faucet off. Under the nearly overflowing water, the mounded bubbles towered over her. She felt as if she were floating in clouds. Samantha wanted to stay in the water forever. Feeling her wrinkled extremities, all she could think of was life was about to get really tough; she wasn't sure she could handle it, even with John's help.

Crawling into her sheets, relaxed but emotionally spent, Samantha retreated into her dark haven, drifting heavily as the pain pills dulled any sense of reality.

# # #

Stirring, Samantha felt as if she were being summoned. But it was dark. Who was there? Where was she? She tried to focus; she couldn't. Carefully she moved her fingers, her arm. She sprang up from her pillow, wide-eyed. She wasn't dreaming; she was awake. The phone. Samantha sighed loudly, crawling out from underneath her barely creased sheets.

"Hello?" Samantha said, grabbing her computer, turning it on in the darkness.

"Hi, baby. I just had to hear your voice before I went to sleep. I've been working all night. I need you here with me in these cold sheets. We'd warm them up, wouldn't we? You know you have a great body, don't you? Such soft, sexy skin; it really turns me on. But you know that, don't you?"

"I'm really tired. What time is it?" Samantha said sleepily, looking up at Minnie.

"Two-fifteen."

"My clock says three-fifteen."

"Daylight savings. Turn your clock back. You lucky girl, see, you get to sleep in an extra hour. Do you know what I'd do with you in that extra hour? Do you?"

"I really have to get some sleep. Can we talk tomorrow?"

"No, damn it. Who is there with you?"

"No one."

"Well, then, tell me something nice. Tell me how you like my mouth all over you. Tell me how I feel inside you. Tell me how I'm the best lover you ever had. You know I am, don't you?" Skyler's voice was direct and sensual, clear and driven.

As Samantha heard him speak, she was sure his words had the underpinnings of pure evil; the devil's voice. Samantha stared at the keyboard as she listened to Skyler's words. She heard him breathe more heavily, his words pulsating with his body. Her skin began to crawl, her head pounded. As his rapid, breathy words instructed her, she felt herself drifting as if she were floating in and out of sleep.

"Take off your panties."

"I can't," Samantha whispered, her heart pulsing loudly in her throat and head. She shook with small rigid tremors.

"Are they off? Now, Samantha. I want them off."

Samantha began to perspire. She tried to concentrate on her typing. She felt faint. Putting her head between her knees, she closed her eyes and pictured herself in her bed, relaxed, sleeping. Laughter. In the darkness she heard the laughter. Louder and louder. Her head pounding, she stopped typing and pushed hard on her temples. Sleep, she needed sleep . . . Relax, relax . . .

"Now, take your hand . . ."

Excited to hear Tom's voice, Stacey moved onto the bed, almost tripping over the computer. Stretching the cord, she laid in the darkness and followed Tom's instructions.

As they finished, Skyler smiled, pleased with his captivating performance and her complete submissiveness. She had finally learned. He smiled in the darkness as he retied his silk pajama pants and threw the now sticky washcloth toward the hamper in his closet. Falling into a deep comfortable sleep, he pictured Samantha serenely in his arms where she would soon be when she came home for Thanksgiving break.

Stacey lazily dropped the phone and fell quickly into a deep black sleep, where she pictured herself comfortably in the safe crook of Tom's broad shoulder.

Chapter 28

The wiry young man entered the stark room. He fit there perfectly with his pale blue eyes, freckled skin and fiery hair. His worn, overstuffed soft leather briefcase was not indicative of his age but was, rather, reminiscent of his character. As his white knuckles released his tight clasp on the worn handles, the sound of its weight intruded on Samantha's preoccupation with John's impenetrable expression. From across the room, she gazed, disconcerted, at the man's stiff, frigid manner. She hadn't expected it. Pushing her long dark curls from her apprehensive face, she meekly grasped the nearly albino hand, mechanically shaking it. He quickly sat in his threadbare chair, bent forward over his desk and asked them to sit down.

Clasping his hands over his white legal pad, he looked at the pair of questioning eyes studying him. After a decade of prosecuting criminals, he instantly was able to differentiate between the deviants and the victims. Clearly, one or both of these carefully veiled faces belonged to victims with a dark truth from which they craved to be purged. "So, how is it I can help you?" The powerful voice emerged into the stillness of the room.

"I—we have a problem we hope you can help with," John said, looking back and forth between the prosecutor and Samantha.

"Mr. Kincaid, it's really complicated, and I guess really it's my problem. John came with me for moral support. Can I ask . . . well, is everything I tell you confidential?"

"Absolutely. I will take notes, and I may wish to tape our conversation later on, if that is acceptable to you. But, for now, why don't you tell me what is on your mind."

Samantha looked at the corner of his desk and studied the stack of files intently, as if interested in them for some other purpose. She knew her eyes couldn't face him directly. She didn't want to see his face, his response.

Candidly, she began. Almost at once, she heard the graphite of his pencil scratching notes on the once-bare pad and then, eventually, the flipping of page after filled page. John remained silent, not interjecting until she reached the point in time when they had met. Samantha almost recoiled at the abruptness of John's voice. He explained the phone conversations he'd witnessed, the words on the computer he'd read, and the fear he watched growing on Samantha every day. Samantha heard John's words with her heart more than with her mind, emotionally flinching as she absorbed them, as if a bullet had pierced her body. She had been blind to the obviously raw caring and concern John had for her. It was now plainly conspicuous.

Mr. Kincaid stopped occasionally to ask questions; but until the pair concluded their stories, he painstakingly took down their words, noting questions in the margins, without any hint of emotion or surprise. Lost in their own thoughts, each having expected an empathic reaction, Samantha and John now stared at the expressionless red-haired prosecutor. Wanting to scream in the pregnant silence, Samantha bit her lip and held herself mute, her eyes tracing the plain nameplate on the desk. Kyle Kincaid, Assistant Prosecutor. It looked so formal on the informal desk, but Samantha had learned to accept the incongruous as normal. And, she decided, on this desk it fit.

"Without real proof, I can't help you," the voice boomed into the silence. Kincaid's beady metallic blue irises, it seemed to Samantha, immediately turned colorless, absorbed by the whites in his eyes. "But," he continued, "I know people who can. And I will help you build a case, assuming there is one."

Samantha sighed deeply. It wasn't much, but it was a beginning. This long journey couldn't be stopped until it was over, regardless of the outcome. She had shown her cards, and they would be played out, one by one. She had no choice; she had boxed herself in and reality was about to take over.

John stood up with carefully outlined notes of their instructions in one hand. He shook hands with Mr. Kincaid with the other. Samantha murmured grateful remarks and stared bleakly at the two men. How could they know how she felt, what she had been through? How could they understand she didn't want to prove her innocence and Skyler's guilt? She didn't want to prove anything; she just wanted it to all go away.

Mr. Kincaid smiled a tight, confident smile as they left the room. He hadn't yet tried a stalking case of this nature that included rape and blackmail. But this could be the one case that made him, that helped him get elected to chief prosecutor, maybe judge. Kyle pondered his ambitions. His curiosity may have overwhelmed his judgment. It was up to them now. If they returned with evidence and a lawyer who believed in their case; if he were able to convince a judge to allow the wiretapping of her phone; and the FBI agreed to become involved; if he were able to prove other criminal activity and convict . . . So many ifs, he thought, closing his door behind him as he strode to meet his wife for lunch. But, so much possibility . . . .

Chapter 29

Rebecca Smalley was anything but small, Samantha thought, as she entered the intimidating office. Walking slowly on the thickly woven paisley carpet, she studied the large boned woman with the high white-collared shirt and loose auburn bun pulled atop her head. Her fair skin and rosy cheeks suited her and completed the setting of the austere Victorian office.

Prosecutor Kincaid's intense regard for Rebecca Smalley rang in Samantha's ears as she tried to act as if she were at ease. He had recommended her highly and distinguished her qualifications from other attorneys who handled cases dealing with family and criminal matters. He'd said she was highly trained in her ability to put together minuscule details. She often worked with the police department and the prosecutor's office on a variety of sensitive and complex high-profile cases. Most of all, Prosecutor Kincaid had suggested Samantha have a woman to talk to that would be involved with her case. Samantha knew the inference in his suggestion; she had many times listened to her father discussing, in general, the delicacy of gender issues between lawyer and client. Samantha pictured her father and how distraught he would be if he knew; how disappointed he would be she hadn't confided in him, that she didn't ask for his legal expertise to help her. But how could she ask him without evidence? How could she tell him about Greg and Skyler? How could she risk the disapproval in her parents' eyes or put her parents needlessly in the public eye? How could she explain the foolishness she felt every time she heard herself explain her situation?

Samantha looked around the room carefully. It reminded her of home, yet that was no comfort to her. The heavy leather-bound books were as ominous and looming as those in her father's office. She stood apprehensively before the tremendous cherry wood desk with its brass claw feet.

"What can I do for you?" The attorney asked. Samantha

tried not to stare at her cranberry red mouth. Too much lipstick, Samantha's mind ticked off unconsciously.

"My name is Samantha Armstrong. Assistant Prosecutor Kincaid recommended you. I am filing a complaint and he thought it best I talk to outside counsel. I thought, well, that I could hire you to help in my case—help in putting together the evidence, so I have a case."

Rebecca briefly studied the attractive, fragile-looking young woman, curious at what could have brought her.

"Well then, please sit down and tell me what I can help you with."

Samantha stared at the large woman's face, the blank legal pad and the tape recorder. How many times would she have to tell her story? How many people would have to be involved?

As she began, she heard her voice, as though it were a stranger's, reciting the saga of her life for the past nine months. She wished it could all come to term and end. She wished John were with her, but she knew he couldn't always be. She was glad she finally had a woman to talk to, even if it was one she didn't know very well.

Rebecca listened diligently as Samantha's words cut deeply. She had been molested as a child, and she relived it every time she listened to a client talk of forced intercourse. Rebecca wasn't always as understanding of rape as she felt she should be, because, even after years of counseling, she fell back into feeling as if her victimization was her fault. Helping clients, though, always brought her back to reality and kept her grounded in the fact that victims remained victims by choice, and fighting back was their only real weapon.

Studying the young coed, she knew Samantha did not lack financial resources, unlike many of her clients. Her sweater, skirt and heels were designer label. Her pearl earrings and matching necklace looked real. And the long, wool, London Fog coat hanging over the back of the chair next to her was a superior quality and limited cut.

"Did Prosecutor Kincaid tell you I don't come cheaply?"

"Yes. As I explained to him, money doesn't matter. I mean it does. You see, my father is a lawyer. We have money. I have money I put in a bank account for emergency use and well, I guess this is an emergency." Samantha's eyes filled with the image of her prospective attorney studying her as if she were under glass. "But . . ."

"But what? If I'm going to represent you, I need to know everything, without hesitation. Is that clear?" Rebecca studied a still wide-eyed Samantha before continuing. "One lie means I relieve myself from representing you. That is not negotiable. Do you understand?"

"Yes. I was going to say—well you see, my father doesn't know any of this; no one does, except Missy, and she doesn't even know everything, just bits and pieces. And, John, my friend from the dorm, I told you about; he knows everything."

Samantha's tone got lower, desperate in her plea. "I don't want anyone else to know, at least not yet—not until we have enough proof against Skyler and Greg—"

Rebecca watched Samantha closely as she explained how she wanted everything to work and who should know and who shouldn't. Finally she interrupted her. "Once we get under way, I will proceed with the case as I see fit. Much as I'll try to protect you and your family, these things have a way of getting out. If there is a trial, it will be impossible to keep the details shrouded, given the nature of the crimes involved. Are you prepared for that?"

Samantha blinked and pursed her lips before carefully responding, "Does that mean you'll help me, you'll represent me, Ms. Smalley?"

"Yes, provided you let me handle the case as I see fit. Call me Rebecca. We'll work closely with Prosecutor Kincaid and will look at both criminal matters and civil claims. I'll draft a contract, which we will both sign. You will pay me a large retainer. I will give you an accounting of your retainer every month."

Listening diligently, Samantha felt comfortable this woman was now on her side. She would be worth the money. Samantha wrote her a five thousand dollar check from her special account. A gleam of understanding flashed through the attorney's eyes as Samantha told her story. It was so unlike telling a man. It made everything not just real, but like it really mattered to someone, other than John. It mattered to an independent person, a woman who did not dismiss another woman's feelings.

Samantha made notes of everything she had to bring to

their next meeting, and advised Rebecca that Mr. Kincaid had set up a tentative meeting with an FBI agent at the end of the week. Rebecca nodded and wrote it in her book. Her secretary buzzed in, advising her of the arrival of her next appointment.

Leaving the historic downtown office building, Samantha drew her black wool coat closely around her as the heavy wind lifted her long, wool, pleated skirt. White winter flakes whirled around her, seemingly born from the sheer movement of the wind. Letting the flakes fall freely over her face, she felt newly alive, reborn.

As she got into her car, her body felt unfamiliar pangs of hunger. She drove out onto Capital Avenue and headed back to meet John for lunch, eager to tell him about Rebecca, despite the oncoming headache she felt stemming from the base of her neck.

Never had she felt so optimistic about her dilemma. She carefully drove through growing clusters of snowflakes. Samantha had not seen so much snow, outside of a glass Christmas snowball, and she began to be hopeful for the coming new year. For the first time in months, a future seemed possible.

Chapter 30

Samantha stared at the man who entered Rebecca's office and closed the door behind him. She was no longer nervous. His intense mystical aura captured her immediately. His confidence radiated and transcended success or accomplishment. If such a man was on her side, Samantha knew she had nothing to fear. His charisma was stronger than any she'd known; her father's, Skyler's. They didn't have the raw charm this silver haired government advocate broadcast by his mere presence—and the investigation hadn't even begun.

"I've reviewed your file. I've met with the assistant prosecutor, Mr. Kincaid. I've read the transcripts of the phone calls you've recorded on your computer. I want to help you. We want to get this guy as much as you do. But I will need to know everything. I'll also need the tape he gave you when he began blackmailing you," said the man they had referred to as Agent Everett Lloyd. He pulled out a small leather-bound notepad. "I don't want you to touch it. I'd like to come to your room and take it from wherever you've hidden it. We'd like to see if there are any fingerprints that can be identified, besides your own. We'll need you to go to the police station and have a full set of fingerprints taken, as well. That is, if your attorney agrees."

"That will be acceptable, Agent Lloyd," Rebecca answered, not waiting for Samantha's response.

Carefully studying the agent, Samantha wondered if she could get him to look at her directly, eye to eye, despite his training that required him to avoid direct eye contact. It would be fun to try, Samantha mused.

"Just remember, it's not my client that is or will be on trial," Rebecca cautioned.

"At this point, without sufficient evidence, no one is on trial," Agent Lloyd responded dryly. "We all need to work together, Ms. Smalley. Prosecutor Kincaid said you were hired by Ms. Armstrong to assist us. I hope we can count on you."

"Of course," Rebecca answered swiftly. "One other thing. Do you suppose I could get the tape for you? I know how to avoid fingerprinting it any further, and my client and I have discussed its necessary use in her case. I'll use your evidence bag and follow any instructions you give me. I want to save my client from questions anyone in the dormitory may ask about you or your men entering her room. It's in all of our interests we keep this thing as low-key—if not invisible—as we can at this point."

Samantha looked from Rebecca to Agent Lloyd, watching them volley comments and questions back and forth as swiftly as if they were playing a game. They were more interested in one-upping each other than in her; maybe they'd forgotten she was in the room. At least they were on her side, not against her.

"You understand we need access to her room in order to do the wiretap once we get the court order?"

"Yes. But you could do that at an hour few people would be awake, maybe disguised as the telephone repairman or whatever disguises you guys use these days."

"Yes ma'am. We can do that. We are more than adequately trained in this sort of thing," Agent Lloyd said, as if it were common practice to be second-guessed in everything he said.

Samantha respected his manner, his way of behaving. As elusive as it was, it tantalized all those who surrounded him. Samantha had never known anyone like him. She watched as the pair sparred with their words and never-ending questions.

She felt secure in the agent's confidence; assured by his easy ability to shrug off attacks and insolent behavior. His charisma radiated through his dry manner; his command was illustrated even by the behavior of her attorney. The two complemented each other and were a remarkable team, Samantha thought, smiling, as they turned toward one another, lists in hand.

"I believe Judge Claude will sign the order to allow the wiretapping if we go together and explain the circumstances. I've prepared the order for signature," Rebecca said, handing Agent Lloyd a file. "My secretary is setting up an appointment for sometime this afternoon. Can you make it?"

"I'll be there. Samantha, we need you to join us in case the judge wants to ask you any questions. Can you get away again from your classes?" Agent Lloyd asked, He looked into Samantha's face; his watchful gaze guarded the periphery around her.

"Of course. I've tried to stay ahead in my classes. I've had lots of time alone. Skipping my afternoon classes won't be a problem," Samantha said, looking from Rebecca to Agent Lloyd.

"Fine. Let's meet after lunch, say one-thirty. We'll review the facts before we walk over to City Hall," Rebecca said. She grabbed the note from her secretary, who walked in unobtrusively at that moment.

Upon reading the brief note, Rebecca announced an emergency hearing inside the judge's chambers had been set for three o'clock.

"May I bring John with me?" Samantha asked, before turning to leave.

"He can't come inside with us since he has no real knowledge, other than hearing your end of the conversations with Skyler. If you need him there for moral support, that's fine, but we'll be there to help you; we're talking about a long, complex legal process. John will have plenty of time to get involved," Rebecca said, as if she were an older sister to Samantha instead of her lawyer.

Solemnly, Samantha nodded her head in understanding and sighed. It had begun.

Chapter 31

Feeling infinitely weary of answering questions and constantly explaining what was happening, Samantha leaned closely toward John, whispering softly the day's events as they ate dinner at a somewhat isolated table in the corner of the cafeteria.

"The judge granted the order allowing the wiretap. The bug will be installed immediately. We can't tell anyone, not even Missy. Actually, they never really said I could tell you," Samantha whispered. John bent his head down to hear her soft voice more clearly.

"How long will it be in?"

"They didn't say. I guess until they get enough evidence and they believe me."

"Did they tell you they don't believe you?" John asked with a raised eyebrow.

"Well . . ."

John put his silverware down and looked squarely at Samantha. "Answer the question. I think it's a very important consideration," John said anxiously, pausing before adding, "And I need to know. Did they say they don't believe you?"

"Rebecca says she believes me, but she talked to me about the evidence problem. Agent Lloyd hasn't said one way or the other. He just says he's there to help, to get to the truth. As much as I like him, I'm not sure what he thinks at any given moment. But he's impressive, don't you think?"

"From the brief time I saw him. I haven't had a chance to talk with him or hear him talk to you. But you have to understand the way FBI agents are trained, they're not supposed to let on how they feel or what they know. I bet by now they've looked up Skyler and Greg—and you, and your whole family, for that matter. They probably have files on each of you."

"Really?"

"Yeah. Haven't you noticed how formal he is, how he

doesn't look anyone directly in the eyes, how he takes notes on everything?"

"Yes, but how did you know if you haven't really seen him?"

"They're all the same. FBI, CIA. All agents go through very specific training. What about Kincaid?"

"He seems disinterested. I don't know. Maybe he doesn't believe me; maybe he does. He still seems as skeptical as the first day we walked in. Still, he did recommend Rebecca and I really like her." Samantha let her thoughts trail into silence as she became aware of John's easy smile, his kind expression and the warmth emanating from his body. The realization she had nothing to give him for all his help and support saddened her. As tears began welling in her eyes, she held her gaze on her barely eaten salad, hoping she could shove the watery film back into the pain-filled recesses from which they came.

"Did I say something to upset you?" John ventured, seeing her sullen face.

"No. I just wish it were over. I wish I hadn't involved you but, I'm also glad I did."

"Look, if things were reversed and I needed help, you would be there for me, right?" John asked. Samantha silently nodded. "I want this to be over as much as you do. I told you I'd go the distance with you, and I mean it. Has Skyler been calling as usual?"

"Yes, and," Samantha bit her lip, pausing momentarily, trying to deflect the discomfort she felt. "He wants me to come home for Thanksgiving break next week. I told him I wanted to stay here and study, but he had a fit."

"Are you still transcribing the conversations?"

"Yes."

"I would think you should keep doing that even once they tap in. That way, if they ever question your computer diary of the conversations, you could compare the accuracy of what you've written with what they have on tape."

Samantha looked at John admiringly. "I love the way you think. You're always thinking ahead. My father would admire that in you. You'll make a great attorney some day."

"Thanks," John said, his expression brightening with her favorable notice of his protection of her interests. "Would it bother you if I read what you've typed?"

"Well . . ." Samantha shifted in her chair uncomfortably.

"Don't say anything. I understand. But I'd like to hear, or read, what he had in mind for Thanksgiving; I think you should tell Rebecca about it, if you haven't already."

John noticed Samantha's growing look of utter detachment as they continued to discuss the details of what was happening. He tried to soothe her, deflecting the discomfort he felt hearing her answers. One thing was certain, she was in good hands. If there was a way to resolve her dilemma, she was with the right people, whether they believed her or not. He knew she was telling the truth. He had watched her terror in progress. What he knew, the others would soon see and feel.

Finished with their dinner, John walked Samantha to her room. They both knew without saying a word, it was time for her usual phone call. Wondering if there had been sufficient time for the wiretapping to have occurred, they silently entered the room, both pairs of eyes on the phone.

"Oh, I forgot to tell you, Rebecca came to the dorm to get the tape Skyler gave me. She was with another woman. I don't know her name. She looked really young and I got the idea she was an FBI Agent. They didn't say and I didn't ask. It was really cool the way Rebecca handled herself. It was like watching a female Colombo. She took the tape from the bottom of my underwear drawer with tweezers. She put it in a labeled evidence bag. She and the other woman were going to make a copy for Rebecca and then give it to Agent Lloyd."

"Have you ever listened to the tape?"

"Not really."

"He blackmails you with a tape, and you don't listen to it?"

"Yes. No. You see, I listened to the first few words and then I remembered. I couldn't listen to it any further once I began hearing my own sobbing words. I tried. It made me sick, gave me a headache. Every time I thought about listening to the rest of it, well, I just couldn't," Samantha said, her eyes downcast, the disappointment in herself clinging to every word she said.

"I'm sorry." John pulled her toward him, ignoring the stiffening of her body at his touch. As he hugged her, he heard her pounding heartbeat, as if she were a scared animal about to bolt. Stroking her soft long curls, he took in a deep breath of her scent. He'd hoped she'd relax in his bear hug, but she didn't. He wanted to keep her close, protect her, tell her it would soon be over and she'd survive. But he chose, instead, to say nothing. He didn't want to make any false promises, knowing the worst was ahead of her—ahead of them.

As they heard the ominous ring, John released Samantha. She grabbed her portable computer and the phone simultaneously.

"Hello."

"Hi, honey. Your mother and I wondered how you were doing. Every time we call, you're out."

"Hi, Dad," Samantha said, relieved. "Where's Mom?"

"Right here, dear. We decided we'd each grab a phone. How are you, dear? Are you eating?"

"I'm fine, and yes. Yes, I'm eating more than I should. Didn't you get the meal ticket I sent you? I made most of my meals, even breakfast."

"Listen, dear, Skyler said he called you a few days ago to see how you were doing and he said you weren't coming home for Thanksgiving. Is that right?" Anne asked her daughter earnestly.

"Well, I just thought since our break isn't even a full week and I have so much homework, I'd stay here. It's too long a drive and too expensive to fly for just a few days, even if I could get a ticket at this late date. "

"You'll do no such thing! I want all my children home with me. We'll send you a plane ticket, and be at the airport to pick you up. There's no homework you can't do at home. We have libraries, too."

"Fine, Dad," Samantha said, taking her orders with pursed lips and squinting eyes.

John watched, confused, as Samantha talked to her parents. Samantha's voice turned childlike, her sentences diminishing into short responses. Single-handedly, they had the ability to turn her into Jello. Why? Were they truly as self-involved and self-centered as she had said?

"Parents," Samantha said, hanging up and shaking her head. "They never let you grow up." Just as she cradled the receiver, it rang again.

"Who were you on the phone with?" Skyler demanded as she put the receiver again to her ear.

"My parents."

"No, really, I want to know, right now. What man were you talking to?"

"My father."

"I can check. I will check," Skyler said stiffly, clenching his teeth tightly.

"Fine," Samantha responded, her eyes focused on the gray computer keys.

"Well, what did they want?"

"Me to come home at Thanksgiving."

"I told you you're coming home, so what's the question? You know you need to see me. You know you want my hands in those moist thighs of yours. I bet you're wet right now, aren't you, baby?"

Samantha bit her lip so hard she drew blood. She felt the gnawing pain at the base of her neck stemmed up through her head, toward her temples, in hard heavy throbs. Nausea gripped her stomach as she continued to type.

John watched Samantha carefully, as he read the words flashing on the lighted screen. Her face turned from pale pink to white to ashen. He understood her reaction and wished he could relieve her from her task. But he couldn't. No one could.

Watching, mute, as Samantha hung up the phone and retreated instantly to the bathroom, John turned off the computer, after saving her document. He carefully returned it to her desk. He didn't know what he should do. He stared at the bathroom door for what seemed hours. He listened to the radio. There was little he could do until Samantha emerged. He didn't want to leave until he was sure she'd moved past her pain. Just as he turned toward her desk to find a notepad, he heard the running water stop and the door open, slowly revealing a dripping Samantha, a fluffy pink terry robe tied tightly around her. She didn't acknowledge his presence as she sat on her bed, staring at the wall and brushing her hair aimlessly.

"Samantha, are you all right? Can I do anything for you?"

Samantha shook her head slowly, back and forth, a dismal, bleak expression on her face. She looked right past him.

He scrutinized her. Her eyes were glassy, her movements slow and somehow uncoordinated. John had never seen her this way, this upset; out of control. He shouldn't have pushed so hard this afternoon with all his questions. He should have let up. Worried, he began speaking slowly and softly to Samantha. She laid the brush down on her lap, eyes staring vacantly down at it.

"Samantha," John whispered, as he turned on the small lamp on her dresser and switched off the ceiling light. "You've got to get some rest. I'm sorry I pushed you. I'm sorry about everything. You need to get some sleep." Touching her shoulder lightly, seeing her pupils immediately dilate, he removed his hand as if it had been burnt. "Samantha, I won't touch you. I promise. But you need to get in your bed. You need some rest. You need to sleep. Please." He removed the brush from her hands and laid it on the chest.

Samantha followed what she heard of his instructions, crawling under her comforter. The drugs had begun to take hold. As soon as her head rested on the pillow, she realized just how heavy it had become and how difficult it had been to hold up. She wasn't sure when John left, because to her he was no longer there the instant her ear touched the pillow. She was now comfortable, safe in her own world . . .

Chapter 32

Samantha wiped her blackened fingers on the stiff paper towel Prosecutor Kincaid handed her, while a police officer took the finger-inked card downstairs to the laboratory to match with the prints found on the tape.

"Now what?" Samantha asked, frowning at the prosecutor's studious look.

"We wait. It won't be long before the prints are matched. Detective Spaulding has been assigned to work with Agent Lloyd. They'll be in contact with you or Ms. Smalley as soon as they know anything."

"Exactly what are they doing?"

"Your prints will be matched with any found on the tape. The computers will be checked for matches on any other print found. Arkansas has been contacted and should fax us Skyler Marks' fingerprints."

"Do they have them?" Samantha interrupted.

"All attorneys are fingerprinted before they are licensed. They'll be on file."

"Will they tell him? Will he know?" Samantha asked fearfully.

"No, don't worry about that. No one will know," Prosecutor Kincaid said warmly, emanating assurance to the young crime victim.

Samantha nodded, timidly.

"One other thing you ought to know. They're transcribing the tape. Your attorney will have a copy of the transcript as soon as we do. We'll go over the tape together with you. We may need you to answer more questions." Prosecutor Kincaid stopped, seeing the sudden paleness in Samantha's face. On the verge of asking her if she felt sick, he found himself instead grabbing her as she fell, unconscious, to the floor.

Blue uniforms moved into action. One called for an ambulance, another checked for a pulse, two others straightened the awkwardly twisted bodies of Kyle and Samantha. Within minutes, Samantha's eyes fluttered and opened, unsure where she was. Why did several pairs of eyes stare at her? Was she dreaming? A knife-like pain stabbed through her. Her head hurt so much she had to close her eyes again. What had happened to her? Had she been in an accident? She tried to move, but was restrained.

"Samantha, lie still. We have an ambulance coming. Relax, you're in good hands," Kyle whispered. He pushed her hair from her face as an officer covered her with a gray wool blanket.

"I'm fine, really," Samantha said, trying to sit up. She felt too weak to stand on her own.

"They're here, Samantha. They'll take you to Sparrow Hospital. It's just down the street a few blocks. I'll follow you in my car to make sure you're all right. Is there anyone I can call? John? Your parents?"

"No!" Samantha protested fiercely. "Call anyone and I won't go. Swear!" she said, with all the hysteria and defiance her weakened condition allowed.

"Okay, okay. No calls, I swear," Kyle said, trying to calm Samantha down.

Kyle hoped there wasn't anything wrong. Frowning, he grabbed his keys from his jacket pocket, threw on his overcoat, and followed the stretcher out of the police station.

# # #

When the nurse called Kyle into the curtained examination room, he saw a serious black-haired doctor with whom he quickly exchanged introductions.

"How is she?"

"Severely underweight. I'd like to keep her here for observation tonight, but she doesn't want to cooperate," Doctor Walker said sternly, his eyebrow raised at Kyle.

Before Kyle had a chance to say anything, Samantha responded. "It's not that I don't want to, I can't. I've missed too much school already and . . ."

"I'll be happy to contact the school, your professors, whomever. But you need to stay the night, maybe a few days. There are some tests I'd like to run before you leave, just to make sure there's nothing else going on."

Samantha didn't want to explain. She didn't want to fight. She just wanted out. Exasperated, she finally agreed. "Fine. I'll stay, but no one is to be called. I'm eighteen; I have my health insurance card in my purse, and I can sign the paperwork, can't I?"

"Yes, but don't you think you should talk with your parents?" Dr. Walker asked with professional concern.

"No. They'll just worry. I don't want them alarmed for no reason. Promise?"

"Promise," the men said in unison with reluctance.

As the doctor excused himself to write Samantha's orders for the nurses and the lab, Samantha motioned to Kyle to come closer to her.

"What about Skyler?"

"What about him?" Kyle asked, not understanding the question.

"What do I tell him when he calls and I'm not there? What will I tell him tomorrow? I can't tell him this. He won't believe me. He'll tell my parents," Samantha said, with closed eyes and a severely dry mouth. Her head still pounded even as her body began to relax from the shot the doctor had given her for her migraine headache.

"I'll call Agent Lloyd. We'll put a recording on your phone, saying the phone has been temporarily disconnected; I'm sure he can fix it with the phone company, in case they are called, to say a phone line is down. Would that make you feel better?"

Samantha sighed deeply, nodding her head thankfully. "John . . .?"

"I'll call and explain. I'll tell him you're sleeping and you'll call tomorrow. Will that work?"

Samantha tried to open her eyes, but she couldn't. Instead, she nodded slowly and waved as if she were satisfied and wanted him to leave.

"I'll stop by in the morning. Feel better," Kyle said. The attendants lifted the sleeping Samantha onto a bed with wheels. After covering her and placing her purse in her arms under the thin white blanket, Kyle followed Samantha down the hall, watching silently as they entered the elevator. Once the door closed, he returned to his car and headed back to the station. He had a lot of work to do; they all did. He wondered what the real story was behind the beautiful southern girl with the biggest, bluest, saddest eyes he'd ever encountered.

Chapter 33

The bottom of the crisp white coat floated behind the lab technician as she set the file in front of Dr. Walker.

"Thanks, Mindy, for bringing it here. Join me in a cup of coffee?"

"Sure. Sit, doctor; I think, while I'm up, I'll get you another cup. You look like you were up all night."

Dr. Walker nodded gratefully as he opened the chart marked "Armstrong, Samantha Anne." Puzzled, he read the workup on his patient a second time. Surely there had to be a mistake.

"Something wrong, doctor?"

"No," he said, keeping his observations to himself. Smiling at her, he picked up the steaming coffee she placed in front of him and added in a serious tone, "I just wonder about these college kids. They have everything, and still it isn't good enough. They have to be thinner, happier, higher, richer, have better clothes and faster cars."

# # #

Dr. Walker strode swiftly down the long white corridor to Samantha's room. She wasn't yet awake, but with the rattle of breakfast trays just minutes down the hallway, she soon would be. Placing her chart on the bed table and replacing his pen in his outer breast jacket pocket, his warm hands gently lifted Samantha's left wrist. Silently he counted the pulses. Shaking his head, he wrote down the number in his notes.

Samantha stirred and looked sleepily at the solemn face. She had a desert-dry mouth and her head pounded with a dull thud, different than the pain she had yesterday; but now she also felt nauseous. She thought she'd have gotten used to the pain, instead she had become almost afraid of it. She wished she were in her own room so she could take some medication. She felt increasingly nauseated and her bladder was full. Samantha didn't want to talk with this doctor again; she didn't want to ask for his help to get out of bed. She wanted to be released. She had to get up, she thought desperately.

"How are we this morning, Samantha?"

We? She wanted to scream. We are not anything. I am not really fine, but I'll never tell you that. Her mind shouted its silent reprimands, but her voice responded as politely as she could make it. "Fine, I guess. I have a bit of a headache, but I'm better. Can I go home? Is that why you're here, to discharge me?"

"No. I'm here to discuss your health," he responded somberly.

Samantha did not respond. She waited for him to continue, not wanting to show any response, feeling her full bladder knocking at her to get out of bed.

"Can you tell me—"

"Could I . . . I know you're busy, but could I use the rest room?"

"Oh, I'm sorry. I'll get a nurse to help you, and I'll return in just a minute."

Samantha returned to bed with an emptied bladder, brushed hair and teeth, and a washed face. She hoped if she looked better, the doctor would see she was fine and wouldn't be so serious. The nurse straightened her sheets and grabbed the breakfast tray from the heavy white-capped aide. Samantha ignored the food and waited. She stared at silent television, waiting for the dismal-faced doctor to return. Several moments later, he did return, looking more stern than before.

"Not eating?"

"I'm not hungry. I feel a bit nauseous and I have a dull headache pounding away; but I feel so much better than I did yesterday."

"How often do you have headaches?"

"I don't always sleep well, studying and everything; it's my first time away from home. I have headaches every few days, I guess, depending." Samantha looked down at the baby blue printed hospital gown she was wearing, consciously avoiding his eyes.

"Do you take anything for your headaches?"

"Yes. I went to Olin Health Center on campus. The doctor prescribed something called Pamelor. I'm supposed to take it every night, but sometimes I forget."

"What else?"

"Midrin and Fiorinal number three. He gave me a prescription for a shot, but," she paused, feeling as if she would get yelled at. "I didn't get that filled. I was afraid of using it. I don't like shots."

"Anything else?"

"No . . ."

The doctor sighed. His expression softened. He knew she was lying, but he knew being harsh with her wouldn't help. After asking a few more questions about her headaches and writing down several notes, he closed the chart and stared at his patient.

"What else are you taking?" He got no answer. "I've had a lot of schooling. I deal with hundreds of people every day. I deal with thousands of college students every year. I know how tough it can be. I know instead of seeing a doctor, it's easier to take an old prescription or something from a friend. I got the results of the tests we ran on you yesterday. The tests show you have taken other drugs. A lot of other drugs—they have made your body toxic. I can only help you get healthy if you tell me exactly what it is you've been putting in your body."

Samantha felt like crying. Her head hurt. She'd been kindly admonished, but admonished just the same. Her lip quivered as he continued.

"Do you ever look at yourself? I mean *really* look at yourself?"

She blinked as tears stained her face. She bit her lip to control it, to stop it from quivering. It didn't work; it didn't stop.

He continued. "You are severely underweight. Unless you eat better, you will die. I'm not saying that to scare you. I'm simply stating facts. I'm going to put you on a diet. You will eat several times a day. You may need to talk to someone who can help you figure out why you don't eat." He let his patient absorb his words, before continuing. "When you came in, your eyes were constricted, your blood pressure was extremely low, you were lethargic. You were suffering from respiratory depression, which explains, in part, why you fainted.

You have the same symptoms this morning, although to a lesser degree. You say you have a dull headache? That's common. It's rebounding, something that happens when you get addicted to a drug, take too many drugs, or the wrong combination of drugs. That's what's happening to you."

Samantha didn't want to hear any more. She took the glass of orange juice he handed her and drank it down as he studied her. She found the courage to look at him. He looked sad; she had that effect on people. She sighed as his voice broke the silence.

"I want to help you. But you have to want to help yourself." He stared at her hoping for a response.

"I . . ." Samantha sighed, bit her lip and wiped the flowing tears, trying to calm herself before she continued. "I began to get headaches several months ago. My parents worry too much, so I just went into their cabinet and took some of my mother's migraine medicine. She gets them—migraines, I mean—a lot. She has so much medicine I just took some labeled for headache. I guess I shouldn't have."

"Do you know the names of the drugs?"

"Tylenol 3, Percoset, Valium. Sometimes I take sleeping pills. I also take birth control pills." Samantha said, almost whispering. "The doctor at Olin told me they can cause headaches."

"Well, that pretty much matches the toxicology drug screen report. We checked your urine and blood for alcohol and narcotics. The combination of drugs you described accounts for your elevated liver function test. The drugs you've mixed are very dangerous together. Samantha, I need you to know they're not just dangerous, but deadly. You're playing with your life by playing doctor. The result is worse if you mix alcohol with any of the drugs you've taken; there may not be a second chance."

Samantha heard the doctor's words and frowned. Nervously she twirled her hair around her forefinger, listening to his concern, his advice, his orders. She was ashamed, frightened; she did not want to die. She hadn't known what she was doing to her body. How would she survive the headaches, the sleepless nights, Skyler?

###

Kyle Kincaid entered his office with his usual red-and-white-striped wax bag containing two extra frosted raspberry jelly donuts. Today he did not open the bag. Setting it on his desk, he prepared for his day, sipping coffee and sucking jelly off of his fingers from the donut he'd already finished. Grabbing his messages and stuffing them into the pocket of his wool jacket, he told his secretary he'd return within the hour.

Before entering Samantha's hospital room, he paused. He heard voices through the door. Peeking in, he saw the drawn curtain. She must be in with the doctor; great timing. Standing at the nurses' station, watching the hustle of the morning medication delivery and the removal of breakfast trays, he was glad he was not the patient. He hated the way hospitals smelled, although he loved the mashed potatoes they served, drowned in golden gravy.

"Doctor? Doctor Walker? Hi, I'm Kyle Kincaid. I don't know if you remember, I'm the person who brought Miss Armstrong in. How is she?"

"How well do you know her?" Dr. Walker asked, studying Kyle's face.

"Not well. We're working on a project together."

"Well, she's very sick. She needs a lot of help; a lot of support. Since you're not family, I can't discuss her case with you beyond that without her permission. But I'm sure she'll be glad to see you."

"Thanks for everything," Kyle said, shaking the doctor's hand before turning into Samantha's room.

"Hi. How are you? Lookin' good!" Kyle said, lightheartedly waving the Quality Dairy bag in front of her.

"What's that?" Samantha asked curiously.

"The best donuts in Michigan," Kyle answered, setting down the styrofoam coffee cups and the waxed bag. "I thought you might like real food, even though you haven't been in that long. When are you getting out?"

"After lunch, I hope. Can you take me to my car?" Samantha asked sheepishly. "I'm sorry I've been so much trouble."

"Don't worry about it." He paused and bit into one of the donuts. "So, can I ask what's wrong?"

"The doctor wants me to gain some weight—you know,

eat better—and, I've been getting migraine headaches like my mother so they'll do a C.A.T. scan before I go. The doctor made me promise to take only the medicine he gives me."

"That doesn't sound too bad. I'm glad you're all right," Kyle said, licking his sticky fingers and washing his donut down with coffee. Her version didn't sound as ominous as what the doctor had implied. He raised his brows so high his forehead wrinkled.

"What?" Samantha asked, noticing his strange expression.

"Nothing. As soon as I finish my coffee, I've got to head back. I'll be back about one, then I've got a hearing at two-thirty. Okay?"

She didn't seem sick, Kyle thought, inconspicuously studying her as they made small talk. A few minutes later, puzzled, Kyle made his way out of the hospital and into the courthouse to begin his busy day.

Chapter 34

Rebecca Smalley wore a gray wool pin-striped pantsuit with a high-necked white silken blouse. She wore her hair, as usual, in a bun atop her head. Leaning against her desk with her arms folded, she blended in like wallpaper with Agent Lloyd, Prosecutor Kincaid, and Detective Spaulding.

Samantha sat on the needle-pointed carved rosewood Victorian couch, several feet from where they stood in a circle reviewing Detective Spaulding's case and then a larger one brought by Agent Lloyd. She tried to listen to their comments, but missed some of their hidden whispers. She wished they would fill in the empty chairs around the coffee table and tell her what they had discovered. She felt butterflies in her stomach; her breathing became uneven and droplets of sweat dripped from beneath her arms and between her breasts. She poured herself a glass of orange juice from the tray of donuts, bagels and coffee sitting on the coffee table. She quickly drank it down, fearing another fainting spell; she wished they would hurry.

Hearing Samantha sigh, Rebecca smiled at her. "I'm sorry, hon. We'll be with you in a minute. Help yourself to a bagel and some cream cheese. You look a bit pale."

Samantha nodded and chose a swirled rye and white bagel. Slowly opening it, she spread the cream cheese and butter inside, feeling as if she were being scrutinized. She wondered what and how much they knew. What had Kyle told them? What had the doctor said? Swallowing hard, she felt the usual lump in her throat that was there whenever she ate. She had tried to follow the doctor's orders and eat better, but it was difficult. She envisioned his concerned face, heard his serious voice at every meal. She did not want to die. She would prove him wrong—she hoped.

"Samantha," Rebecca said as the group moved toward her and began pouring coffee and grabbing bagels and donuts from the tray. "We have several things to discuss with you."

Samantha looked at the group, now sitting around her in a gray-and black-wool collage. She knew these serious faces were on her side, but she felt as if she were somehow being negatively scrutinized. She kept telling herself to relax, as she felt the rampant beating of her heart. Unconsciously, she clutched her bagel so hard she left crackles in the crust and finger indentations that forced the cream cheese to ooze out of the sides. Realizing she was being watched as cream cheese trickled out onto her thumb, she released the bagel onto a small plate and wiped her fingers with a napkin. Looking questioningly into her attorney's eyes, she was glad Rebecca was sitting next to her.

Detective Spaulding began matter-of-factly. "We were not able to get good fingerprints of anyone else on the tape, except yours. The conversation clearly tells your side of what happened to you; but it does not implicate Skyler Marks in any way, except that he had knowledge of a crime, which he failed to report. He could use the argument of attorney-client privilege to get out of that, because he works for your father's firm and, under these circumstances, a logical argument could be made. And, it could be confirmed by your requests to him to not tell anyone."

"Skyler was very good on the tape. He is an excellent trial attorney, and he certainly used those skills on the tape," Agent Lloyd added.

Samantha listened carefully, feeling her anxiety rise instead of diminish with their words.

"But," Detective Spaulding continued, "we do have quite a file on Mr. Marks, thanks to Agent Lloyd."

Samantha looked puzzled. Nervously she picked apart her bagel, focusing her anxiety on over chewing morsels of the fresh bread.

"We have been watching Mr. Marks already because of a client he has been representing," Agent Lloyd said plainly, now looking down at the name and photo in his file.

Samantha looked at the black-and-white photo he put in front of her, puzzled at what the shriveled man in the picture could have to do with her. Within seconds, she recognized him from the newspapers back home. Looking up at their collective faces, they realized she recognized him too. She hadn't been able to hide her recognition or her surprise. So what did he have to do with her?

"You know who he is, don't you?"

Samantha looked from Agent Lloyd to Rebecca, who nodded at her to answer. "Yes. I believe his name is Castriano. I don't remember his first name. I've never met him. I've seen his picture in the newspaper at home."

"Did you know your father's firm—specifically, Skyler Marks—is representing him?"

"Yes. Skyler brags to me about him sometimes. He represented him in a trial he worked on most of the summer; and then, this fall, he told me he'd get him off on some technicality; and then he did it. My father is always saying Skyler has a knack for finding technicalities," Samantha said, picking apart her bagel again. "What does any of that have to do with me? I don't know Mr. Castriano, except from the newspaper and what Skyler told me."

"We believe you can help us, if you're willing," Agent Lloyd said, seriously.

Samantha felt as if she were part of a play and she had either lost her script or was on the wrong stage. She fell silent, focusing her questioning eyes on Rebecca. Rebecca immediately understood those eyes. Everyone in the room understood them. It was difficult for such frail innocence to hide behind any self-created or imposed mask, at least to those with trained eyes.

"Gentlemen, I'd like to go into the conference room with my client while you help yourself to more coffee. If you need anything, please don't hesitate to ask my secretary. She beckoned to Samantha, who put her plate down and followed the large-boned attorney.

Safe behind the closed door of the conference room, Rebecca motioned to Samantha to sit down facing her.

"I don't understand. Does this mean they are, or are not, going to help me?"

"It means they believe you. It means if we aren't able to get Greg Maston on rape and Skyler Marks on stalking, blackmail, and whatever else we can think of, there's a chance we can at least put Mr. Marks behind bars."

Samantha understood, as she listened to her attorney outline the rationale; but she couldn't help but instinctively, fearfully, interrupt her. "My father, what about? I mean, he didn't have anything to do with Mr. Castriano. I know, because Skyler told me several times he was upset my father didn't want him to take him on as a client."

Rebecca suddenly understood. "Oh dear, no. They are not after your father, at least not as far as I know—not from anything I've seen in the file." Not seeing her client's face relax, Rebecca gave it another try. "Look. You are my client. Your interests are what I'm concerned with. Say the word, and I will call off any further talk of this Castriano person."

"No, I want to help. But I want you to make them promise to keep my family out of it. Please, that's the only way! I can't handle anything else." Samantha's voice began strong and definite, but ended in a tearful screech.

Rebecca paused for a few minutes, as she watched Samantha recompose herself.

"There is one other thing you need to know, before we go back in there," Rebecca said softly, placing her hand on Samantha's forearm. "You will not be able to tell *anyone* about this. Not even your friend John. Can you do that?"

Samantha frowned. Alone again she took a deep breath but nodded with pursed lips. What choice did she have?

"It's for everyone's safety. I will be here for whatever you need. Do you understand?" Rebecca asked, watching her client closely. "Do you have any questions before we go back?"

"No," Samantha responded meekly, following Rebecca back to their anxiously waiting audience, making a pact with herself to keep silent about all of the tapes she had privately made of her conversations with Skyler. She didn't need or want to deal with anything else; even if the tapes would help her. Samantha feared new information. She couldn't fear it if she didn't remember it existed, she rationalized.

# # #

It was almost noon by the time Samantha arrived back in her room. She didn't feel the need for lunch; she had managed to eat her whole bagel under the watchful eye of Kyle and the remembered voice of her doctor. She hated that now she also had Dr. Walker's voice roaming inside her head, infiltrating her own thoughts, with all of the other things she had to deal with. It was just another thing she did not have control of, she decided helplessly.

Grabbing the phone as it rang, she hoped she remembered all of the instructions she had been given over the course of the morning.

"So, how was your morning class?" Skyler asked into the phone.

"Fine. We got out a bit early because the professor was leaving for Thanksgiving break and figured we all were too. I was surprised."

"So when are you coming home? I'd like to pick you up from the airport."

"My parents are picking me up. They couldn't get me on a flight before tomorrow, so I'm leaving tomorrow morning—around ten, I think."

"What are you doing tonight? Any hot plans?"

"No. I'm packing."

"What else?"

"Nothing. The dorm is really quiet. I think most everyone has gone home already."

Skyler sensed a different Samantha. He wasn't sure why, or what was different, but his instinct told him something was amiss. "What else is going on, Sam?"

"Nothing. I'm just happy to be going home. It'll be nice to see everyone. Emily wrote and said she and her family might be joining us for a pre-Thanksgiving dinner."

As Skyler listened to Samantha running on, he became more confused and more convinced something was wrong. She never offered information in such detail. She was too casual, too talkative, too . . . nice? He pondered her behavior, as she talked on. Intuitively, he knew it was a sign something was wrong; but what?

Samantha mindlessly answered Skyler's questions as she concentrated on typing her usual script. It had become more than just a habit. It had become a security blanket, a way of dealing with what was happening. She learned she could tuck Skyler away, tune him out, shut him off and lock him out of her mind, as long as she concentrated on typing, as if it were a job.

Samantha was amazed at how clear the phone line was, despite the wiretap. So far, it had remained undetected by everyone. She was astonished at how at ease she felt talking into the phone, despite her knowledge she was being recorded. She tried to remember the information she was supposed to solicit from Skyler. She tried to stay one step ahead of him in order to fit the questions naturally into the conversation.

"Am I invited to the pre-Thanksgiving dinner?"

"I don't know. Ask my parents."

"No, I think that's your department."

"I'll try."

"No; you'll succeed."

"Are you still busy with your trial?"

"Which one?"

"The . . . the Castriano case."

"Don't you listen to anything I say? I told you a few weeks ago about that trial. Remember me telling you, as I had predicted, I got him off on a technicality?"

"Oh, yeah. Sorry. I don't remember how you did it, though. What happened?"

"I convinced the judge the evidence was tainted and I had it thrown out. Winning my motion meant the prosecutor had no case."

"Was he happy? Mr. Castriano, I mean?"

"Of course."

Did he . . . I mean you said he was going to give you a bonus. Did you get what you wanted?"

"Mr. Castriano never goes back on his word. Why all the questions?" Skyler asked sternly. "You've never been concerned or interested before."

"Oh. Well, I guess it's because college is opening my eyes, and I'm just more curious about what lawyers really do. I mean, you know my father doesn't talk much about details of what he does. I thought you'd be pleased. You're always saying that I don't listen to you or that I don't care about what you do . . ."

That was it, Skyler thought, as he listened to her rambling. He had dealt with too many criminals to not sense a scam, to not sense danger. Something was definitely wrong. Had she told someone? Was she seeing someone else? What was she hiding?

"I've got to grab a quick sandwich and then run over to court. I'll call you later, and I'll definitely see you tomorrow."

Hearing the sudden click was not unusual to Samantha. She had grown accustomed to his erratic behavior. Samantha began packing her bag, hoping to finish before John stopped by. It looked as though Missy had been in their room earlier and had dropped off all of her books, leaving them piled high on her desk. She must have gone home, Samantha concluded, as she checked Missy's closet. Not dealing with Missy would be a relief, Samantha decided, as she finished packing and pulled out her traveling clothes for the morning.

"Hi, Samantha," John said, as she opened her door to his knock. "Looks like you are packed already. Can I take you to the airport tomorrow?"

"No, I'm just going to take a cab and leave my car in the student parking lot. When are you going home?"

"In the morning, I guess. It only takes me an hour and a half to get home to Saginaw, or less, depending on traffic. I thought maybe we could go out; leave your phone off the hook again, just for a few hours?"

"Okay, but, we've got to talk." Samantha sat on her desk chair, pulling Missy's chair out for John and motioning him to sit down. "I met with Rebecca this morning. Actually, everyone was there. I guess we are on to the next stage of my case, and they've asked me to not discuss it with anyone." Samantha paused and looked cautiously into John's wide eyes. "Including you."

"I don't understand. I'd like to help," John protested curiously, studying Samantha's expression and crystal blue eyes for clues.

"I know. They know that too. They just don't want any more people than need to be involved. I'm sorry," Samantha said, with downcast eyes.

"You have nothing to be sorry for. The professionals have to do it their way. I just want what's best for you."

"I know. I appreciate your help. You know I do!" Samantha tried to reassure him with him her soft smile. Purposefully she batted her dark lashes, revealing flashes of sincerity from her baby blue eyes.

John couldn't help but to agree not to pressure her for information she had been told not to give; although he didn't quite understand why they wouldn't want him involved. After all, wasn't he the one who initially brought her to them? Finally, he returned her smile and, shaking his head at her said, "I don't understand, but it's fine. It's your case. But if you need me for anything at all, you promise you'll ask?"

"Yes. I swear," Samantha said letting her southern drawl drag just enough to make him feel like the hero who had rescued her and brought her to safety.

# # #

Skyler looked at the fluorescent clock on his nightstand. Eleven-thirty. Time to call Samantha. As he heard the busy signal over and over again, he continued to redial. Agitated, he called the operator, who informed him it was off the hook. Skyler slowly replaced his receiver, puzzled once again. She had left the phone off the hook. Where was she? How many times could she hang up the phone wrong? What was going on? Was she with someone else? He shoved his phone off the nightstand purposefully. Hearing it crash brought him back to the present and triggered more anger. She had to be stopped! Whatever she was doing to him, she had to be stopped. He would teach her to lie, to cheat, to tease. He would have absolute control of her. He would have her or no one would, he vowed as he slipped on his jeans, shirt and blazer. Tossing his keys into the air and catching them again, Skyler confidently began to whistle "Ain't no mountain high enough . . . to keep me away from you, babe . . ." Then, getting into his Jaguar he headed to his favorite bar for another "lucky night."

Chapter 35

Samantha boarded the plane with nervous anticipation. Her anxious stomach and pounding head had become so normal she'd automatically begun her day with medications, trying not to mix the wrong ones. She popped them into her mouth, and hoped she'd understood what the doctor said she could take and what she should stay away from. She wasn't sure. What she was sure of was taking the pills felt better then not taking them, even if she didn't take them exactly as the doctor said. She'd deal with everything later.

She made a conscious effort to eat, which should count for something, she decided. The doctor had explained she had to take Pamelor with food because if she took it on an empty stomach she might experience pain and nausea. She had to admit she felt better taking her medication with food, except when she had a migraine headache. Grabbing a blanket and pillow before taking her seat next to the window, all she wanted to do was relax. She put her purse under her seat and the pillow against the window, hoping she'd be able to sleep a few hours before having to deal with her parents and Skyler. Clutching the lightweight blanket as the plane departed from the gate, she closed her eyes and rested. Drifting into sleep, she heard a hushed evil laughter, as if it were coming from the person next to her, or behind her . . . She looked around. Everyone was quiet. No one was visibly laughing.

"Tom's mine," a voice now whispered. "Keep your hands off him, he's mine!"

From the dormant recesses of her mind, Samantha felt a twinge of familiarity in the voice; in the laughter. She didn't recognize anyone on the plane. The voice whispered fiercely, relentlessly laughing at her discomfort.

She looked around again. Maybe it was the drugs. The ringing in her ears. Her headache. Maybe the pain was getting to her. Maybe she took the wrong mixture of drugs.

Samantha had to shut it all out; she didn't want to think

about it. The laughter continued. She pressed her head against the pillow as hard as she could, covering her other ear with her hand. She couldn't rid herself of the voice, of the laughter.

Pushing the call button anxiously, Samantha asked the answering steward for a glass of milk. As he returned with a cold carton and a plastic cup, Samantha nodded her thanks and popped another pill in her mouth. It would help her sleep. It would rid her of the voices. It would make everything more tolerable; she didn't care what the doctor said.

"Miss? Miss?" The concerned stewardess shook Samantha's shoulder. "You need to deplane. We've arrived. Do you need assistance?" the flustered woman finally asked, seeing Samantha's unsteady, lethargic, movements.

"Oh. No, I'm fine. I just fell asleep."

"You look a bit pale; can I help you up?"

"No, thank you. I'm sure my parents are here."

Teetering out of the plane under the watchful eye of the captain and crew, Samantha made it down to baggage claim to the waving arms of her mother.

"It's so good to see you! How was your flight?" Anne Armstrong asked as they walked toward the baggage area. Travis echoed her hello with a light kiss on her cheek.

"Fine, Mom. The noise on the plane gave me a headache and, just as I fell asleep, we landed," Samantha said groggily, hoping her mother wouldn't scrutinize her closely.

"Travis, why don't you bring the car around while we get her suitcase? I think we need to get Samantha home so she can take a real nap before dinner."

Samantha was relieved as her father pulled the car into the driveway and ordered her bags taken upstairs. Entering her room, she felt immediately guarded—exposed rather than relieved as she expected to feel. Why? She tore off her clothes without thinking, and entered the safety of her shower, before climbing between her familiar sheets.

# # #

"Samantha?" her mother called into the darkened room. "Your father and I are getting ready for dinner. Cook's made a special meal, we're having guests. Get up," she happily prodded, turning the light on before she pulled the door closed.

Samantha slipped out from the warmth of her bed. She'd had the dream again; she'd seen parts of people's faces. None of the faces were whole. She'd heard the laughter and the voices and the music box. She'd watched it all parade by her. She tried to cry out, but she'd lost her voice. What did it all mean? She sighed and took a deep cleansing breath as she began to get dressed. The pills. All this was happening because of the pills. She must have taken the wrong ones. Opening her purse, she pulled out two red ones. These would help her get through dinner and her still-pounding headache. When would she get relief from her dreams, from her headaches? She imagined a life without problems or migraines. She gulped down the capsules.

In the second it took to turn out her bedroom light before descending the staircase, she saw the phone. It looked as if it was in the same exact spot she'd left it in, as if it hadn't been touched since she left. But had it? She looked inquisitively at it wishing she had x-ray vision. By now, surely Agent Lloyd had ordered her phone bugged, probably her parents' phones too. Would the investigators tell her? She entered the dining room.

"Well, well, well. The college coed returns to us," Skyler said, bemused with her startled expression. Surely she had expected to see him? Another game?

Thanks to you, Samantha snarled inwardly. She wished she could scream those words at him. Instead, she smiled with as much sweetness as she could force from the depleted reserves within her.

"The twins won't arrive until late Tuesday evening. They couldn't miss any classes. I'm really proud of those boys," Travis boasted loudly, into the lull, nodding at Hyrum to pour the wine. He motioned everyone to be seated.

Samantha couldn't listen to any of the dinner conversation. She couldn't concentrate. She felt as if she were in the room under remote control; someone pushed a button and she responded; and in the interim, she lay dormant.

"May I be excused?" she asked her parents politely, avoiding Skyler's narrow piercing eyes.

"No dessert, dear?" Anne asked, looking skeptically at her daughter's pale face and fidgety movements.

"I'm really so tired I'm not sure I have the strength to eat it. Save me some?"

"All right, dear," Anne said. She put her cheek in the air deliberately, waiting for a kiss.

Samantha complied with her mother's silent request, kissing her, and then her father, good night.

"Nice seeing you, Mr. Marks. Good night," Samantha said, as if he were a slightly known family acquaintance.

"I'm glad you're doing so well in school, Samantha! It was a pleasure seeing you again. I hope I'll see you again before you leave," Skyler responded forcefully.

Samantha knew Skyler was upset with her. Her body went cold and rigid the instant she heard the familiar tone in his voice, the slur in his words. She wished she could scream for the others to wake up. But they did not.

Once in her room, Samantha spent a lazy hour on the phone, catching up with Emily. She wasn't able to discuss Skyler with her in detail. When Emily inquired as to any developments, she shrugged it off as if school and distance had taken care of his interest in her. After hanging up, she drifted into a deep comfortable sleep.

# # #

Samantha awoke, immediately frightened, startled by the strong hand over her mouth. In seconds, her eyes focused on the face close to hers.

"It's me, Samantha. Don't scream. It's just me."

Samantha tried to relax, but he scared her. He wasn't supposed to be there, in her room. Skyler had now invaded her most private place; there was no place left to turn, to hide.

He removed his hand slowly, intimating with his sharp, deliberate movements that if she spoke up, gave him away, she would pay. She remained silent. She had no voice with which to respond; and no voice could respond kindly to him, she nodded as if in agreement with his terms.

"You are so beautiful, Samantha," Skyler whispered. He filled his lungs deeply with her warm fresh scent. He ran his hand through her hair, and clasped his fingers tightly around the thick clump of curls. "Next time you will stay in the room—whatever room we're in—as long as I am there. You are to be with me; do you understand?"

Samantha's eyes grew wide. She clenched her hands tightly on the edges of her comforter as he she heard him slip off his loafers, unbuckle his belt, and unzip his pants. Samantha focused on the ceiling. She couldn't watch; she knew what was coming.

Skyler slipped silently between her sheets. Samantha slipped into a deep, peaceful sleep, where there was no danger, no threat or violation. Stacey entertained Skyler exactly as he instructed.

Chapter 36

Wednesday evening, Greg Maston sat quietly in the conference room of the firm's office, pouring over the firm's accounting books, preparing the year-end report. He knew his numbers were accurate. Travis Armstrong would be by shortly to have the first look at the figures before they reviewed the final numbers with the partners early Monday morning, after the busy holiday.

Greg was glad the firm was closed for the long holiday weekend. He didn't have family to spend Thanksgiving with. It gave him time to concentrate. He got up from his calculator to stretch his legs a few minutes in nervous anticipation of Travis' arrival. The stiffness in his back and legs made walking around the long conference table and placing a year-end report at each chair a welcome task. He didn't like working after hours and on weekends, but using the firm's office had benefits his office didn't. As he walked through the connecting door to Travis Armstrong's office, he went to the bar behind the movable panel.

Attorneys know how to live, Greg thought, making a small toasting gesture before he swallowed a double shot of Irish whiskey and poured another. His thirst satisfied, he closed the panel and turned the key to lock it again. The alcohol calmed his nerves. In the past few years, he had enjoyed such drinks daily. He worked better if he was relaxed; he got more accomplished, or so it seemed to him.

The stillness of the office matched the lull in the nightly traffic noises. Greg hastened to finish his last notes and pack up his briefcase. He wanted to be prepared for Travis' review so he could leave for the evening. He had a standing date at The Bishop's Pub and was anxious to take his seat by the television at the bar.

Bending over the extra copies of the report, he aligned them, deciding not to take them with him. Just as he began to straighten his back, he felt a sharp pain, as if he'd been punctured by an enormous razor. Confused and in pain, he turned to see what had happened. Had he run into something broken? His mind raced. He stepped back to take hold of the knife as the black gloved intruder struck again. His shirt was wet. Looking down, alarmed, he saw the sudden red appearing on his shirt, on the floor, the spattering of blood on the table.

His blood. It had to be. Yet, he felt no pain, only alarm and adrenaline. What had happened? He wasn't aware of his breathing, of any movement. Time stood still. His body moved in slow motion, his mind raced, questioning. His heart pounded with imminent fear, sensing the intruder's animal instinct to hunt him down like prey, to finish the job. But he was strong, he rationalized. He could fight this attacker; he could survive.

He faced the darkly clad figure, trying to avoid a long lash across his stomach. Awkwardly, his leg caught the chair adjacent to him. He lost his balance, reached up, just missed the table, and hit his head hard against its corner.

Then, there wasn't any pain. Yet he knew instinctively the gurgling noises must be coming from him. The intruder jabbed repeatedly at his flesh. He peered through blood at his attacker. Then, his energy depleted, he felt his body release.

The office returned to silence. The lights clicked off.

# # #

It was just before eight. The building had emptied, except for the plump, dark woman, who talked to herself as she unlocked the heavy glass doors. She retied the scarf that held her unruly hair hidden and off her face while she did her routine cleaning. She prided herself on her organized efficiency and on having the most successful single-person cleaning service in town. She'd done very well for herself, keeping this account, when many of the large firms had hired cleaning companies. She looked first around the waiting room and cleared the coffee tables of the disarray of magazines.

Walking to the cleaning closet, which held her supplies, she opened each office door and flicked on each light switch she passed. Hearing the sound of keys, she turned and smiled in acknowledgment as Mr. Armstrong greeted her.

"Good evening, Frieda. Getting an early start, I see. How are you?"

"Fine, sir. I'm doin' good these days. Gotta start early and work late so's I can fit all my customers in," Frieda smiled broadly at the handsome man and admired his fine threads. "You workin' late for a Wednesday! I thought you'd be home, with your chil'ren home for the holidays."

"I just came to do a little paperwork; then, you're right, I'm going home to see Samantha. The twins arrive late tonight."

"Sure do miss see'n those fine young ones of yours! They sure growed up fine."

"Thank you; we're proud of them. Have you seen Greg—Mr. Maston—anywhere? He's supposed to meet me here."

"No, sir. Maybe he's runnin' late. You all just run, run, run. I don' know how you do it."

Frieda continued on toward the end room and opened the conference room door. Turning to unlock the supply cabinet in the adjacent bathroom, she grabbed the gray supply caddie, and walked into the conference room. Suddenly she saw him. Blood everywhere. She screamed over and over again, trembling as her hands clutched at her heart. She began to pray.

Travis heard the scream and thought Frieda had hurt herself. He darted from behind his desk toward the direction of the shrieks, instinctively looked at her kneeling form to see where she was hurt, then followed her gaze to the bloodied body of his friend. The stench of violence and coagulating blood on the arms of the chairs and edges of the tables made him pale. It was everywhere. He released Frieda's shoulder, ran to his friend and reached for the wrist to find a pulse. There was none.

# # #

Minutes passed like hours after Travis' trembling 911 call brought ambulance, detectives, police, and a medical examiner to the crime scene. Then hours did pass before all the samples were collected, photos were taken, and questions were asked. Police sealed the crime scene and the entire office. Now motionless, he sat in his car, unable to drive. What the hell had happened? His mind exploded with emotion, with questions. How would he tell his family?

"Mr. Armstrong?" Detective Winston asked, as he tapped on the window. "Mr. Armstrong?"

"Oh. I'm sorry. Did you need something else?" Travis asked. He rolled down the window.

"Are you all right? Can I drive you home?"

"No. I . . . Thank you, but it's not far. I'll be fine."

"There's one other thing we'll need as soon as you can arrange it. We need a set of fingerprints of all of your employees and family who have been in the office this week. Also a list of clients, anyone who's been in the office or has access to the office. The entry was not forced. More than likely the person who did this knew the victim.

"Prints from everyone? That'll take some time. I'll help any way I can; we all will."

"The investigation will be much smoother with everyone's cooperation. Hopefully, we'll find one good print from the assailant. Can you arrange a time for us to meet with you and your staff individually?"

"Sure. Of course, is tomorrow soon enough? I can't think about it tonight."

"That'll be fine. If you're sure you don't need a ride, I'll get back to the station. I really am sorry about your loss."

Travis nodded, no longer listening. He played the crime scene over and over in his mind. He couldn't bear to think the words, let alone say the words he needed to. There was no way to explain such a brutal crime.

"I'll call you in the morning," Travis said to the detective, dismissing him, as the window slowly slid up and barricaded any response there may have been.

When he got home, Travis called his wife and daughter into his study; but first he poured a tall martini, drank it down, and then poured and drank another. Upon seeing Anne's questioning gaze, he poured one for her, refilled his glass, and then asked them to sit. Behind closed doors, they sat as a family, and Travis told them the evening's events. He finished, not waiting for their questions. It was ten. Time for the news. It was the lead story.

"Well respected accountant Greg Maston, found brutally

murdered in the law offices of . . ."

The trio watched the screen in silence. Seconds later, the phone rang.

Within minutes, people were at the door; partners, police, detectives. The media positioned themselves on their front lawn. Travis said he would make a brief statement.

Samantha couldn't watch. She couldn't listen. She had wished Greg dead and now he was. She was glad he was dead. And she felt guilty for feeling glad.

With an odd sense of calm, she struggled with a nagging suspicion she couldn't have been this lucky. Willing people dead was nothing more than wishful thinking, she rationalized; she wished it would happen to Greg, to Skyler. There, she had said it—maybe not out loud, but to herself; no crime in wishing . . .

"Samantha, you and your mother will need to join us," her father said gravely, intimating there was to be no question or discussion.

Following his orders, Samantha got her mother from the kitchen, where she was quietly talking with Cook. The pair walked in silence through the long halls to the living room full of people. Seeing his family present, Travis summarized the night's events.

"I met earlier with Detective Winston. An investigation is under way, but they've asked for our cooperation. I have assured them we will cooperate. The first item they asked for is a complete set of fingerprints from everyone with access to the building and law offices, so any prints that don't match can be isolated more easily. Second, they need a list of persons who have been in the conference room, law offices and building for the past week. Third, interviews with everyone who knows Greg well or has had contact with him in the past few weeks."

Samantha listened as her father coldly barked out orders, directing the lives of everyone in the room and beyond. She couldn't believe he wanted her and her mother fingerprinted; by the way he rested his eyes on them, she knew they were included in everything the firm was cooperating in. She wished she hadn't gone to the office to visit her father yesterday. She wished she hadn't waited for him in the conference room while he was with his last client. What if her prints were in the wrong place? What if they thought she did it? Mistakes happen. She heard her father talk about cases where the wrong person was arrested and put in jail. She had a motive, a reason to kill him. But no one knew that. She could never tell anyone about the rape. She could never let Skyler tell.

Samantha felt trapped. She pictured them finding her fingerprints all over the room. Her head pounded. Her breathing became uneven. Suddenly her father's voice began to fade; she heard ringing in its place. She listened harder to his words; she tried to focus on the faces in the room. But she couldn't. Her flesh became moist and her heart beat loudly in her ears. Her mother gasped as Samantha fell to the plush white carpet. Her mind was blank, her body limp. Travis and Skyler moved toward her, carefully picked her up and moved her to the couch. Anne found a blanket in the hall closet and placed it over her daughter. She leaned over her, stroking her cheeks, whispering, "Samantha, dear, it's your mother. Can you hear me?"

Samantha felt as if a ton of bricks were on top of her. Her eyes fluttered open, she felt aghast as she saw Skyler in the crowd leaning over her; there with her mother's worried face and her father's stern one. My God, where am I? What happened?

"How are you feeling, dear?" Anne asked. "You fainted. We should have thought this might bother you. Should I call a doctor?"

Samantha's eyes grew wide and her mind raced at the word doctor.

She shook her head. "I'm fine, really. I just pictured him . . . and the blood," she lied, pausing long enough, her eyes downcast. "I'm sorry." She looked into her mother's eyes, then her father's, then at the crowd.

"Samantha, you have nothing to be sorry about. You get yourself upstairs and into bed. I'll send Cook up with a glass of warm milk."

Samantha nodded, declining her father's offer of help. She planted her feet firmly on the carpet, then bid everyone a polite good night. With determination, she made her way to her room, relieved to be alone.

Feeling more sadness than relief, Samantha slipped into

her sheets after swallowing a handful of colorful pills. She wanted to relieve herself of her nagging migraine and sleep deeply. She didn't want to dream tonight. The pills would be her insurance.

By the time Cook brought her the large mug of warm milk, Samantha felt very relaxed. She barely had the strength to raise her head from the pillow. She drank the milk, as Cook's soft face watched her with compassion. Trying to cheer Samantha up, she told her the twins had arrived and they'd been instructed not to disturb her, but they wished her a good night. Samantha nodded as if she heard every word. Handing the empty mug to Cook, Samantha smiled, replacing her heavy head on the pillow. Already in her desired, deserted blackness, she did not remember Cook turning off her lamp or leaving her room.

Chapter 37

It had been less than twenty-four hours since the murder. Each available employee of the firm had been ordered to be fingerprinted and questioned. No one wanted to talk about it, yet everyone was curious about any leads that may have been found. The first forty-eight hours in any case were the most critical. They all knew that, yet no one wanted to be the first to ask about progress.

Thanksgiving dinner was subdued. Family and friends gathered. While cutting turkey, scooping mashed potatoes, piercing stuffing and salad, each utensil rang loudly in their ears. Each morsel of food they placed in their mouths and swallowed, reminded them of their friend, lying in wait of a proper burial on a cold slab in the morgue. Silent, each prayed the forensic tests would give the police enough evidence to apprehend the murderer.

Everyone except Samantha. She tried to show sorrow; but she was gleeful, thankful God had used another's hand to strike her assailant dead. She looked at Skyler across the table, and couldn't help but wish it had been he in the office working late when the attacker entered. She hated the way he looked at her, as if she were being served on his plate. Winking. She hated his winking. It made her flesh crawl; it made her throat close; it made her wish, as hard as she had ever wished for anything, he was dead.

Anne hated long periods of silence, but had already asked her children every question she could think of to make small talk without being obvious. She looked around the holiday table, saddened and frustrated. Surely she couldn't have exhausted all of the safe topics of discussion? She worried, flipping through her mind's rolodex. We will not talk of tragedy at my holiday table when it's the first time in three months my family has been together. With desperate eyes, Anne looked at Travis with a stare that announced loudly to him he needed to pick up his end of the entertaining.

Travis prided himself on being an exceptional host; but today he didn't feel like eating, entertaining, or celebrating. A man who had been like a brother to him and one of his oldest friends had been brutally murdered in his office. He felt responsible; he felt cheated.

"I'd like everyone to stop eating for just a minute. I have something I'd like to say," Travis announced, after whispering a few words to Hyrum. Everyone immediately looked at Travis, as Hyrum refilled their champagne glasses. "Yesterday we lost a very good friend who was as much a part of this family as anyone sitting here today. I think it important we remember who he *was*, not how he left us. I think, more importantly, Greg would want us to remember him fondly and enjoy this time together, as if he were here. Because he is here. To Greg."

In unison, glasses were raised and clinked and emptied. Everyone joined in, except Samantha, who silently declined her champagne and crept to the bathroom to release her dinner into the cold basin. Her tears flowed freely as she rinsed out her mouth. Her stomach felt painfully empty and her head throbbed, but she had to make herself presentable. She found her purse and grabbed one white tablet and one red capsule and swallowed them. Then she silently slipped back into the room.

"Samantha, are you feeling ill?" Anne asked her daughter, puzzled, as she returned to the table. When had she left?

"Fine. I just needed to get up and walk for a few minutes. Champagne gives me headaches. Could you please pass me more mashed potatoes and gravy?" Samantha asked, knowing her request for food would temporarily distract her mother from asking any more questions.

Samantha slid small spoonfuls of the potatoes down her throat, making sure her mouth was full each time someone might talk to her. It was hard work. She didn't want to eat, but she had no choice. What she wanted was more important than her desire to eat or not to eat. She wanted to be left alone. As much as she'd missed her room, she now felt more at home in her dorm room. She didn't understand her feelings. She didn't have time to explore them. There was an underlying dread, a silent cancer growing inside her; she could feel it; she was sure of it.

By the time dessert was served, laughter and conversation were in full flow. Anne beamed at Travis, and he returned a knowing smile to her. Her family was together, intact. Those were the things that really mattered. She made a mental note to plan time for more family gatherings. Life is too short. She lifted a forkful of pecan pie to her lips and listened to her children discuss classes.

No one paid attention to the doorbell until Hyrum entered and whispered to Travis. Travis followed him out to the foyer.

"Detective Winston. Happy Thanksgiving. Have you come with some news?" Travis asked, surprised Winston had two police officers accompanying him.

"In a way, yes. I need to talk with your daughter, Samantha." He paused. "I'm sorry sir. This is a formal visit. We need her downtown, and you'll need to bring her attorney."

Travis looked stunned. He didn't believe what he was hearing. There had to be a mistake.

"Surely, you can't believe Samantha had anything to do with the murder?"

"We do, sir. You're welcome to come downtown with us. But I insist she come with us now."

"Not only have you made a mistake, but you've interrupted Thanksgiving dinner." Travis tried to keep the anger out of his voice.

"I know that, sir. I'm sorry. " He handed Travis a folded document, "I have a search warrant for your house."

Travis read the paper, alarmed. "We have guests. Could you at least be quiet and avoid the dining room? I'd like this as private as possible."

"Yes, sir. We can do that. We will be careful not to disturb you or your guests."

Shock and anger vying for primacy, Travis shook his head. He didn't understand it, but he would get to the bottom of it. Walking into the dining room, he whispered into his wife's ear and then Samantha's. He didn't want anyone to know. Samantha followed him out of the room.

Anne watched the pair leave. "Sorry for the interruption. Samantha hasn't been feeling well. A specialist who's only in town for the day can see her now. They'll be back soon."

Samantha grabbed a sweater and her purse and met Travis in the foyer. She was apprehensive the moment she saw Detective Winston and the officers. As Detective Winston approached her, Travis put his hand up, motioning the group outside.

"Samantha," Travis spoke softly, putting his hand on her shoulder. "These gentlemen want to ask you a few more questions. They've asked us to go to the station with them. I'll follow in my car." Travis spoke sternly. "I don't have to remind you she has counsel. He requested that no questions be asked outside of his presence."

"Are you representing her?" Detective Winston asked.

"That's right. Now let's get on with this charade, so I can return to Thanksgiving Dinner with my family."

Detective Winston raised an eyebrow at the officers and directed them to leave.

Samantha sat quietly in the back seat of the police car, heart pounding, mind racing, and watched the three-car procession. As the cars parked, Samantha looked at the solemn faces. She was surprised they hadn't handcuffed her. She studied her father's face. It was graver than when he told them about Greg. Surely they weren't arresting her on her fingerprints? Questions pounded through her mind. Her fear grew deeper. Over and over, she asked herself why they were at the station house? More importantly, why was she there with them?

# # #

Hours passed. Samantha felt familiar with each gray line in the cold, dark room. Where had everyone gone? Why wasn't anyone questioning her, if that's what they were there for? She crumpled the emptied paper coffee cup and tossed it into the scratched and dented metal garbage can. The noise of the cup echoed, a loud solitary thump, like the last beat of a heart. Her eyes darted toward the door as it creaked open.

"Samantha, I know you didn't do anything. There's been some terrible mistake; but you're a suspect in Greg's murder," Travis said. He studied his daughter's reaction.

"I didn't do it. I haven't seen him since . . .since my birthday party. I couldn't kill anyone." She wilted, her body trembling, her face pale with fright.

"I know. I'll get you the best attorney I can. Skyler. Would you like that?"

"No! No. Not him. Promise me," Samantha said desperately, her voice dry, her eyes wide and unblinking.

"But why in hell not? He has the highest criminal defense record in the county. You need the best."

"Not him. I won't talk to either of you if you force me. I . . . I'd rather go to jail."

Travis frowned at his daughter in frustrated puzzlement. Skyler had been a friend to her. He would do a good job for her. What could her objection possibly be?

"Promise, Dad. Promise me!" Samantha said with a voice as forceful and desperate as she'd ever used.

"Fine, Samantha. I promise. I don't understand, but I'll promise. Maybe he can consult—"

"No! Not a word to him. Not one word! You promised. I want my attorney," she blurted.

Travis stared at her, alarmed. "Your attorney? Have you called someone while you were waiting?"

"No. I met an attorney at school. I want her."

"Met her? Who?"

"Rebecca Smalley. She's a criminal lawyer in Michigan."

"Look, Samantha, first of all, I don't know her or anything about her. Second, she's a Michigan attorney and, unless she's licensed in this state, she can't practice here without special permission. Third, understand you are in serious trouble, and I want the best for you."

"I won't talk to anyone unless Rebecca is with me. I don't care how much trouble I'm in. I just don't care anymore . . ."

Travis put his arms around his sobbing daughter. He felt as if he was in a Fellini film. Nothing was real. It was all in slow motion; it wasn't happening. "Fine, fine. You can have this Rebecca Smalley, but she'll have to work with an Arkansas attorney. We'll find you one together."

Samantha nodded and made her final request. "I want Rebecca to help us. I want someone she likes."

"Whatever you say," Travis said, exasperated with her. He'd deal with it later. He'd find someone, but who?

"Can we go home?" Samantha asked in a quavering voice, looking at her saddened father.

"No. They're holding you for questioning. They have evidence that places you in the room. They want to read you your rights and talk to you. I'll tell you what we do, let them read your rights, then tell them you want another lawyer. That will buy you some time. I believe they will release you to me. Do you understand?"

Samantha nodded.

Travis got up, opened the door, and let Detective Winston in. Winston turned on the tape recorder he had set on the table, and read Samantha her Miranda rights. On cue, Samantha timidly asked if they could wait until her attorney arrived before she answered any questions.

"I thought your father was acting as your attorney," Detective Winston said.

"I changed my mind. I don't want any attorney with my father's firm. That includes my father. I'm sorry," Samantha said nervously, hoping she wasn't saying anything she shouldn't or anything to insult or hurt her father.

"I understand. That's your prerogative. When you have an attorney, we'll continue with questions."

"Can I go?" Samantha asked anxiously.

"No. I'm sorry," he sighed. "As I stated when I read you your rights, you are a suspect in the murder of Greg Maston. We have the right to detain you for twenty-four hours while we make a determination on charges."

"You know she isn't going anywhere. Will you release her into my custody? I will be responsible."

"On the condition we know where she is at all times and you have an attorney within forty-eight hours. We do not want any unnecessary delay."

"Understood," Travis said, standing up simultaneously with Samantha.

Once outside, the silence between father and daughter was deafening. Neither had the energy or inclination to speak. Neither expected the other to understand their perspective or comprehend the reality of the impending disaster that was about to befall the family. And neither had the courage to acknowledge the truth.

Chapter 38

Rebecca Smalley arrived at the Armstrong house as afternoon tea was served. She now knew why Samantha wasn't hesitant about being able to pay her fee. What had happened that made Samantha call her frantically and request her urgent arrival at any expense?

Samantha stood on the landing of the staircase as her parents introduced themselves. Pleasantries were exchanged. Samantha held her breath. She hoped Rebecca wouldn't tell her parents anything; she sighed in relief as her father asked, "Would you like to talk privately with Samantha before meeting us for tea?"

Rebecca nodded. Samantha led her to her father's study. Once behind closed doors, Samantha nervously stared at Rebecca, not knowing where to begin.

"Samantha, I need you to tell me everything that's happened since you came home. I brought my dictaphone and I'll tape you. The tape will be used for my reference, nothing else."

A long, still pause fell between them. Samantha tried to gather her thoughts. As she studied her, Rebecca hoped, in time, she could rekindle the beauty that now seemed stiff and drawn on the young girl's pale, almost lifeless, face.

"I haven't told my parents anything about Greg or Skyler. I'm afraid to. I wanted to talk to you first. I don't know what to do. The police think I killed Greg."

Rebecca stared at Samantha, telepathically asking if she did it.

"I didn't, I swear."

Rebecca frowned. Had she killed the man who raped her? She watched Samantha's eyes as Samantha gave her as much detail as she could remember about what she'd done the day Greg was murdered.

"Are you sure you were taking a nap when Greg was murdered?" Rebecca asked when she finished.

"Yes! I remember talking to Skyler; he called after dinner. I wasn't feeling well. I went upstairs, took something for my headache and lay on my bed. Just as I lay down, the phone rang; and it was him."

"Do you remember the conversation?" Rebecca asked. She knew the FBI had recorded the conversation and she had access to the tapes; she needed to hear Samantha's recollection to hear, firsthand, how accurate her memory was, how acute her senses were, after taking the obviously strong medicine she took for her headaches.

As Samantha recited the conversation, she faltered. She didn't recall how the conversation ended. "I must have fallen asleep while we were talking . . . I don't remember saying good-bye," Samantha said haltingly.

"That's fine, Samantha. They should have it on tape. You haven't discussed any of this with anyone else, have you?"

"No."

"Not even Emily?"

"No. I've kept everything to myself; I asked John not to call me at home so he stays out of it. I really don't want him involved. He's already done so much for me."

"I understand," Rebecca said. "I'll need to get those tapes, or a transcript. They might help you, although we'll have to talk with the prosecutor and fill him in. Are you willing to do that?"

Samantha took a deep, slow breath. "I'll do what I have to. I just want to make sure my family isn't hurt. You should've seen my father's face," Samantha whispered, her voice cracking as tears splashed through her lower lashes onto her cheeks.

"I'll contact Agent Lloyd. You bring in your father. I understand he's discussed your case briefly with the prosecutor and I'll be working with co-counsel. I'll try to get waived in, just for this matter. We will need to talk with your father. Are you ready to be honest with him? I'll be with you to help you through it."

Samantha nodded. She had to be ready to tell the truth; there was no other choice. She was cornered. She couldn't let them send her to jail forever. She knew she didn't do it, but why couldn't she remember what happened after the phone call?

Samantha asked Hyrum to bring her father to join them.

When he entered, he had a file in his hand with her name on it.

"Here are copies of the documents from the police file," Travis said bleakly to Rebecca. "I was owed a few favors. I thought you could use them."

"I appreciate that. Next time don't interfere. You and I both know, as Samantha's attorney, they'd have to show me the file," Rebecca said dryly. She took the file. "Whom have you chosen to represent Samantha? I understand she does not want anyone from your firm. Under the circumstances, that's wise."

Travis took in a deep breath, focusing on Rebecca as she turned the pages of the police report. If she was as good as his daughter thought, she'd pick up on the discrepancies in the report and the circumstantial evidence that could convict his daughter.

Samantha also watched Rebecca read the file. She watched her father watch Rebecca. She was thankful no one watched her and her mother was not in the room with them.

Rebecca made a list of questions and made notes in the margins of her notepad. Finally, she looked up and closed the file.

"Samantha, are you aware of how Greg was murdered?" Rebecca inquired.

"Yes, Dad told me he was stabbed; that was also mentioned on the news."

"Do you know with what?"

"A knife, I guess. I don't know. Is that a trick question?" Samantha asked, puzzled.

"Do you know how your fingerprints got on the murder weapon?"

"My prints . . . on the weapon!"

"Yes. How did they get on the weapon? There were only two sets of prints, yours and Greg's."

"But I didn't do it! How could there be prints? I swear, I wasn't there!"

"Okay, I believe you. We'll get to the bottom of this. I just need to ask you a few questions."

Samantha nodded, avoiding her father's eyes, amazed he wasn't participating in any of the questioning.

"You said the last time you saw Greg was at your birthday party. Do you remember what he wore?"

Samantha paused, puzzled at the question, not understanding the relationship between her birthday and the murder. "No. It was warm outside. I really don't remember. Maybe a polo shirt and some khaki pants. I'm not really sure."

"Is it possible he was wearing a white shirt, the kind he might wear to work?"

"I guess so. Why?"

"The police matched a hair sample from you with ones found on Greg's body. There were a few hairs around a shirt button. They were stretched, as if they were pulled out in a struggle."

"A hair sample from me? I didn't give them any of my hair."

"Maybe not, but when you went in for questioning, they knew about the fingerprints matching and, as with most women with long hair, you shed a few hairs. They tested and it was a match. They also took a sample from your hairbrush when they searched your room. The curious thing is there were several strands of hair; one appears to be from a third person."

Samantha stopped twisting her hair around her thumb and forefinger.

"I swear, I wasn't there. I didn't do it."

"Samantha, just a few more questions and then we'll discuss and analyze what we're working with—working against, rather. Assuming he had the same shirt on as when he was at your birthday party, how close were you standing to Greg?"

"Not close. I—well, you know, I wouldn't stand close to him. I *couldn't*." Samantha said slowly and emphatically. She focused on her shoes so hard she could imagine her toes beneath the leather. She wished she could hide behind a curtain of leather as she answered Rebecca's questions in front of her father. "I don't even recall speaking to him. He was with Skyler. I think I spoke to Skyler just for a few seconds."

Up to this point, Travis had remained silent and expressionless, trying to piece together the questions and answers to play out possible defenses and put holes in the evidence. His unwavering lawyer's mind was curious about some of the questions Rebecca asked, but he remained silent. At

Samantha's unexpected comment on Greg, he repositioned his body on the love seat and focused his eyes on Samantha. Her expression was the saddest he'd ever seen her wear, her voice the most timid he'd ever heard; it was more timid than when she was a child, Travis reflected, conjuring up a vision of Samantha as a youngster.

"We could ask Skyler what he remembers," Travis piped in, curious as to why Rebecca hadn't raised that point.

Rebecca looked directly at Travis and to Samantha's relief said, "Mr. Armstrong, I know you're concerned about your daughter and her welfare. However, she has asked me to represent her. I am qualified to do so and it is up to me to ask the questions. Please do not interrupt again. You will, for the moment, have to trust both me and your daughter. There are things you're not yet aware of."

Travis stared in disbelief at the two women in front of him. What the hell was going on here? He didn't like the situation they'd placed him in, nor did he appreciate being talked down to in his own home in an area of law he considered himself an expert in. He stood rigid, his mind baffled but on the alert. But he remained silent, begrudgingly.

Rebecca handed Samantha a photocopy of a black-and-white photograph of an earring. "Is this familiar to you?"

Samantha stared at the picture. "It looks like an earring I lost several months ago. It was one of my favorites—until I lost it, I mean. The one in the picture can't be mine."

"Do you have the mate to the one you lost?"

"I don't know."

"Think. What did you do with it? It's important. We may be able to prove the earring they found is not yours."

Samantha wished she could remember. "I'll check in my room."

"Do that this evening. If you find it, I want it. Don't give it to anyone else. I suspect they'd have found it in the search if it was in your room. Is it possible it's at school?"

"I don't know; it's 14-karat gold, I wouldn't have thrown it out after I lost the other one. I'll check my room here and then my room at school when I go back."

"Samantha, you're probably not going back to school, this term at least, unless we can settle this in the next few days. I'll contact my partner and we'll find whatever box or drawer you think it might be in, and she'll look through it. Will that be okay?"

"I don't have a choice. I'll call my roommate, she'll get my stuff for you. Can you tell me where the earring was?"

"Under the body. I assume the police believe the earring was lost in the struggle."

"Then it can't be mine. I wasn't there. I swear! Besides, there must be thousands of earrings like the one in that picture," Samantha said, trying to reassure them and herself, as warm, fresh tears streamed down her face.

Rebecca and Travis stared at her, silently nodding. They knew it was bad, all three of them. No one said it out loud.

"Mr. Armstrong, I know you want to be involved in your daughter's case. I'll keep you apprised, with her approval. But it's imperative you do not discuss any—not even the smallest detail—with anyone in your firm or anyone else.

"Also," Rebecca said, putting the photocopy back in the file, "I will take this file. There can be no copies of any part of your daughter's case in your firm's files."

"What is going on, Ms. Smalley?"

"First we agree, then we fill you in."

"Agreed."

"Samantha?" Rebecca looked toward Samantha with questioning eyes.

Samantha bit her lip. She felt sick. She wanted to slip into a crack, never to be heard from again. She tried to find her voice and a place to begin. The lump in her throat returned, larger than it had ever been before. Never had she felt so insecure, so worthless, so dirty. Her voice quavered, barely audible. Finding the words was strenuous. The visualization in her mind was painful and exhausting as the labored words passed from secrecy to exposure. Samantha filled in as much of the detail as she could, taking long breathy pauses. Rebecca prodded her with questions until finally the next disclosure appeared. The inevitable unmasking of the naked reality of her ordeal rendered Samantha unable to speak coherently, unable to tell her father every detail.

Travis sat still as his daughter broke down. His shoulders hunched at a stiff awkward angle, his face a mask for his crumbling inner core. He heard her riveting voice but he barely recognized it as the words cut him deeper and deeper. Dividing his interest between that of his profession and that of a father confused his comprehension; he couldn't absorb it at once. He remained motionless, suspended, as if he were hearing and watching someone else, not his innocent daughter. No wonder she'd been so troubled these past months! How could he have been so blind, so insensitive it took the prodding and understanding of a stranger to bring the truth to him? How would they tell Anne?

"Let's give your daughter a break. I'm sure your wife wonders what's going on, maybe you'd like to speak to her. We need to tell her what's happening, but not every detail. We need as few people informed of the facts in the case as possible and that includes your wife. We can't afford to have any information leak. Do you agree?"

Travis breathed a heavy sigh, shaking off his emotional paralysis a little. He met Rebecca's eyes and nodded. Stepping out into the hall, he motioned Hyrum to him. "Hyrum, could you take Samantha to her room and ask Cook to bring her a tray?"

Hyrum obediently entered the study and escorted Samantha up the long staircase. Rebecca followed Travis into the sitting room. He poured himself a martini. Rebecca declined his invitation to join him, instead taking a soda with a lime twist. She was awed by the beauty and serenity of the lavish home. It was like an immense museum with few signs of habitation, she thought, wondering which rooms they really lived in.

"Travis, Miss Smalley, have you finished talking with Samantha?" Anne asked. The twins followed silently behind her. She looked at the solemn faces purposefully, but thought it best not to push for information.

"Please, call me Rebecca. Your daughter needs a break. She is resting."

"Travis?" Anne asked, turning her body toward him, knowing he would understand she expected to be kept informed—whether or not she was included in any closed-door meetings and whether or not she actually asked.

Travis began hesitantly, but regained his customary authority as he went on. "There are some things we need to discuss as a family. I want you boys to listen, but I don't want this to interfere with your school. Come Sunday, you'll both be on the plane. Understood?"

The twins frowned silently, raised eyebrows at one another and reluctantly nodded at their father. That was how it had been their whole lives. They'd been born as part of their father's shadow, mirroring him, following his orders. It had been said, for generations, the umbilical cord flowing through the Armstrong male blood bestowed a special link, an intuitive knowledge strengthened by mother's milk; the unspoken Armstrong male bonding. Anne gave no argument to it. She had learned to like it, to even appreciate it and take comfort in it.

Now Anne sank into a stiff winged chair next to her boys, instinctively knowing she was about to hear something she did not want to hear.

Chapter 39

Agent Lloyd listened to the taped conversations, meticulously writing on the paper in front of him. He stared at the box of labeled tapes of Samantha Armstrong's phone conversations both at school and at home. He flipped through the corresponding transcript of each conversation as he listened to the graphic voices. At least the conversations kept his interest. He stared at his notes.

Something wasn't right. Samantha's moods on the phone swung like a pendulum. Was she trying to set Skyler up? He pondered. She seemed, at times, to enjoy Skyler's illicit suggestions, even to follow along. Then there were other times she seemed annoyed or too timid to cross any of Skyler's aggressive behavior or negative comments. He sighed. Her behavior was increasingly disjointed, disoriented and dysfunctional; yet sometimes it was clear, convincing and colorful. He knew Skyler was not what he seemed, and he was relieved they had gotten this break on the Castriano case and Skyler Marks. But there were too many unanswered questions. He dialed Rebecca Smalley's hotel room.

"Ms. Smalley?" Agent Lloyd said into the receiver, as a tired voice answered.

"Yes?"

"I need to meet with you as soon as possible."

"Agent Lloyd?"

"Yes, ma'am. I'm in Arkansas. I arrived a few days earlier than I planned. I'd really appreciate meeting with you as soon as possible."

"Do you realize it is almost midnight? Can't this wait until morning?"

"No, I don't think it can. I've been listening to the tapes we have on your client. They don't add up. You might be able to enlighten me."

Rebecca climbed out of sheets she'd barely warmed. What could Agent Lloyd be talking about? Surely Samantha hadn't done anything in the last few hours since she'd seen her? The urgency in his voice and her own instinct told her whatever he'd uncovered, it was imperative she meet him, the sooner the better.

# # #

The police station was quiet for a Friday night. She found Agent Lloyd in an interrogation room behind stacks of papers, boxes of tapes, cold coffee cups and half-emptied diet cola bottles. She placed a fresh cup of coffee and a custard donut in front of each of them, then rifled through her massive briefcase for a notepad.

"Thanks, just what I need, some sugar to go along with my overdose of caffeine."

Rebecca nodded. "From the looks of things, I should have brought you a sandwich. How long have you been at this?"

"Most of the day. I didn't want to stop. I compiled a list of inconsistencies," Agent Lloyd explained, pushing his notepad in front of Rebecca before lifting the plastic lid off the coffee. He sipped slowly and Rebecca compared his notes with the transcript.

Rebecca remained silent for a long time. Looking finally at Agent Lloyd, she watched as he took out another notebook, computer paper and a disk.

"Do you remember the boyfriend, John?" Agent Lloyd asked.

"Of course. What does he have to do with the wiretapping?"

"I'm not sure; probably nothing. But my notes of Samantha's story jogged my memory. I decided to look at her transcripts, the one the boyfriend asked her to make. I hadn't before, because I knew they may not hold up in court, and she wasn't concerned with the contents. I remember her saying there wasn't much in them, just more of the same of what we now have."

"Yeah, I remember, and I have a copy of the disk as well. What's your point?"

"I'm not sure," Agent Lloyd paused. "Let's look at what we have. At John's suggestion, she makes her own transcripts of every conversation as each conversation takes place. She follows his advice."

"You're not telling me anything new. What's your point?"

"Well, I'm assuming they are still together."

Rebecca nodded. "Yes, I believe they are still friends."

"I assume he never read the transcript he asked her to make; he respected her privacy. Read it. Then tell me what you think."

Rebecca flipped through the pages, scanning one after the other. Finally she removed her glasses, sighed deeply and shook her head.

"I guess I'd better have a talk with my client. Something's wrong."

"Want to shed some light on what you are thinking, counselor?"

"No. Speculation is a waste of time. But you are right. We need to clear these discrepancies up."

"Want to know how I see it?"

"Sure."

"She was raped. It was brutal and traumatic. Skyler Marks comes along and helps her. Like a night in shining armor; he takes care of everything. She feels better, maybe decides she can forget what happened, her life is back to normal. He took care of everything, like the servants she had been used to all of her life. Then she dismisses him, relieves him of his duty to help her. He doesn't like to be dismissed after all he's done, so he blackmails her for sex. We know he's not the saint he pretends to be. Maybe initially she doesn't like it or him or both. But there is a part of her that grows dependent, even addicted to him. She has conflict within herself; but the one thing she knows is that she now has a boyfriend, John, who Skyler is interfering with," Agent Lloyd stopped, waiting for any response.

"And?"

"We're dealing with an emotionally disturbed girl. I'm not saying she doesn't have reason to have emotional problems; but, nonetheless, they are severe enough even if we are able to get Skyler Marks, nothing she says may be credible."

Rebecca raised her eyebrows and sighed. "I hear what you're saying. After reading the transcripts, I understand your concerns. I brought them with me, but I hadn't taken the time to read them. Everything happened so fast. But I'm convinced, now, more than ever, there is more to all of this. There has to be. I believe her. I believe her disgust for Skyler Marks. I believe she's innocent of murdering Greg Maston. But I also believe your version could be bought by a jury; in that case, she'll be charged, tried and convicted of a murder I know she is not capable of."

"I hope you're right. We all have our work cut out for us on this one."

"We? So you aren't buying the scenario you recited to me?"

"What I believe is there is much more to this whole story. The rape, the blackmail, the murder—all of it. We haven't even scratched the surface."

Rebecca nodded. "Now, I have a question for you, Agent Lloyd. Why have you shown me every transcript, except the one from the day of the murder?"

"You are as good as they say, Ms. Smalley. I saved the best for last." Agent Lloyd pulled from the seat of the metal chair next to him a final transcript and handed it to Rebecca.

The room stood in dismal silence as she read the transcript. He studied her. How would she feel about her client after reading the transcript?

"Have the police read these? Has Detective Winston added this information to his file?" Rebecca asked.

"No. I wanted you to have first crack at it. Once they read it, once they hear the tape, your client will be arrested and formally charged. They will have no choice."

"So you wanted to give me a head start? I thought you FBI guys always went by the book. Why are you helping us?"

"Like I told you, there's more to this case than meets the eye. And if they put your client behind bars, we may lose Skyler Marks and blow the Castriano case, a case we've worked on for three years. I've balanced the interest of justice and, in this case, your client's interests weigh heavily in her favor, regardless of whether or not she murdered Greg Maston."

"Judge and jury. I'm impressed, Agent Lloyd. You've made the right decision."

Rebecca got up from her chair and extended her hand to Agent Lloyd in thanks. When she reached the heavy metal door, he said, "By the way, get your client psychologically analyzed as soon as possible. I'd like to see any reports."

"Good night." Rebecca said, noncommittally, before she disappeared.

Rebecca left the windows open on the drive back to her hotel, letting the cool wind hit her cheeks, reminding her body of just how tired she was and how wound up her mind was. Sleep. A few hours of sleep and then join Samantha and the young Arkansas attorney she'd chosen for them to work with. They were scheduled to meet after lunch. She'd call and ask Samantha to get together for lunch before the meeting. They had to talk. There was no choice.

Chapter 40

Saturday morning arrived too early for Rebecca, who had only had a few hours of restless sleep after her meeting with Agent Lloyd. So many pieces to this puzzle! Too many questions. The biggest one right now was the question of her client's mental health and stability.

The pieces didn't fit; questions continued to compound. The largest one haunted her. Why would Samantha allow her phones to be tapped if she planned a murder, if she was infatuated with Skyler? *Was* she emotionally disturbed?

Assured the servants had retired to their duties and they were eating their lunch in solitude, Rebecca said, "I need to review a few details before Philip Reeves arrives."

"What made you decide on this Philip Reeves?" Samantha asked. "I hoped you would choose a woman to work with us."

"I chose the person I felt would be most aggressive in your defense. Mr. Reeves worked in the prosecutor's office five years before going into private practice. He has a very good reputation and is hungry for a big case to boost his practice."

"Are you sure he's the right one to help me?"

"Yes, I am. I want you to be comfortable enough to talk about everything with him. If you can't talk with him, and disclose intimate details, he can't do his job."

"If you think he's good, I'll try," Samantha said meekly, trusting Rebecca.

"He has contacts in the prosecutor's office and police department. Those will benefit you. He'll work hard for you and, since he's still hungry, he has a strong drive to win. His background as assistant prosecutor gives him the strong criminal background we need, along with the desire to find the truth. He hasn't practiced long enough to become tainted. Mr. Reeves believes, as I do, there's more going on here than meets the eye," Rebecca paused, staring at Samantha. She hadn't yet eaten anything from her plate. "Do you understand?"

"Yes. I think so."

"If you don't like him, for any reason, I'll find someone else. Now, I need to ask you some questions, but I want you to feel free to eat as we talk. You'll need all your strength this afternoon."

Samantha nodded as she stirred the casserole around under the watchful eye of her attorney. At least she didn't feel the massive lump in her throat when she was with Rebecca. She swallowed the warm casserole and sweet-and-sour dressed lettuce leaves.

"Think, Samantha. I need every detail on the day Greg Maston was murdered. I know you were sleeping. I want to know each detail of the day, regardless of how small and insignificant you think it is. I even want to know what you dreamt about, if you can remember. Do you understand?" Rebecca placed a small dictaphone tape recorder next to her pallid client.

"I've tried to remember everything. I've told the events so many times, I can't be certain about anything."

"That's okay. Let's start with something you haven't talked about," Rebecca said gently, trying to soothe Samantha's nerves with her softened voice. "Dreams. Dreams tell a lot. Let's see if you can remember yours."

Samantha closed her eyes and took a deep breath, releasing slowly. "I don't remember. What if I did it? What if I killed him?" Samantha sobbed angrily at herself, at her attorney.

Rebecca looked at the tear stained face of her client. She felt her fear, her terror. What if she *had* done it? What then? What if Agent Lloyd's fears were right and she had done it? Trauma. Could it have been so traumatic she'd blanked it out? Could it be the rape and the past months had been too much, and she simply snapped? Is that really what was going on? Could she really be that troubled? Questions compounded as her client withered into a needy, uncertain child. Rebecca spoke to her in a strong, confident tone, hoping to retrieve Samantha's maturity. "We'll worry about it if we have to. But we need to start from the premise, there is something else going on. I don't believe you are capable of murder. Do you?"

Samantha shook her head, shutting her eyes tightly, trying to remember.

"Picture yourself in your room. You were in bed and the phone rang. You picked up the phone. It was Skyler. Try to remember the conversation. Are you there?"

"I can see myself in the room talking on the phone. I pick it up and it's Skyler. I don't want to talk to him, but I have to. I had a headache, so I took some medicine for it and climbed into bed. I feel really sleepy; and I remember trying to make my voice sound like I'd been sleeping, so he wouldn't keep me on the phone long. He asked what I had done all day. Who did I talk to? Why didn't I answer my phone, if I'd been home? The usual questions he always asked."

Rebecca pulled out a file and laid it next to the half-emptied, flowered china plate in front of her. She followed the typed pages, making notes in the margins as she spoke.

"I remember he talked about my skin, how soft it was. And my hair, how he loved the way the curls fell around us when we . . ." Samantha stopped. She saw blackness. She didn't remember any further conversation. Her mind went blank.

"Keep going, Samantha. You're doing great," Rebecca said encouragingly.

"I can't. All I see is blackness. I don't remember anything else. I must have fallen asleep," Samantha said. How could she fall asleep at that point in the conversation? Suddenly she heard laughter. She opened her eyes and looked up. Rebecca was not laughing. Rebecca's expression was serious, and her eyes wandered between Samantha's face and the paper in front of her. The laughter continued. Samantha looked behind her. She looked around her. There wasn't anyone else in the room. It must be her imagination, her fears taking control of her. She couldn't tell Rebecca about the laughter; she tried to concentrate on Rebecca's questions, tried not to feel the sudden throbbing of her head.

"Samantha, do you feel all right?" Rebecca asked.

Samantha nodded, a small, forced smile crossing her face.

"Just tell me when to stop, and we will take a break. I want to read you the transcript of the wiretap of your conversation with Skyler. You have a good recollection of the conversation until the point where you believe you fell asleep. I'll read you what they have on tape. You tell me if it refreshes your memory."

Samantha nodded. Rebecca read the typed pages in front of her. She tried to take a few more bites of food, hoping the nourishment would relieve her headache. Suddenly Samantha shuddered and her body trembled. "No! No! I swear I didn't say those things! I couldn't. Something is wrong. Someone got to the tapes! Someone is setting me up. I hate Skyler! I never would have said those things!" Samantha cried out, passionately. Her quaking hands hovered over her face. Her head shook from side to side.

Rebecca placed her hand over Samantha's, gently squeezing it in support. "That's fine, Samantha. That's what I wanted to know, what I wanted to hear from you. Please calm down. Let's take a break and have dessert. Change the subject for a few minutes. It's almost one-thirty. Mr. Reeves will be here at two. Let's just relax. Okay?"

Samantha nodded as she watched the plates being cleared. Custard and fresh coffee were served.

"There's just one other thing, Samantha, I will need you to talk to a psychiatrist and to take a polygraph test. Are you willing to do that?"

"I'll do anything you want me to do, but why do I need a shrink and a polygraph? Do you think I am crazy? Don't you believe me?"

"I don't think you are crazy. Yes, I believe you. First, your state of mind will come out at the trial, if there is one, so we need to be prepared. Second, if you pass the polygraph test, we will offer they give you one; it will support your innocence. If you fail the polygraph test, we bury it and don't agree to take one. The test is not admissible anyway. Do you understand?"

Samantha nodded, confused, as she slid small spoonfuls of custard into her mouth. Things were slipping around her. She tried to ignore the laughter sliding in and out of her consciousness. She wished someone else could hear it. Why her? Why did she hear the laughter again and again? *Was* she crazy? Would she pass the lie detector test, or would she be too nervous and fail it?

"Can you think of any questions you want to ask me before Mr. Reeves arrives?"

"No, not really. "

The luncheon dishes were cleared. Samantha and

Rebecca moved into Mr. Armstrong's study and awaited the arrival of Mr. Reeves. Samantha thought it peculiar her parents had kept their word and had not interfered. She and her parents had decided it was in her best interests they stay removed from the case for the time being. They and the twins had agreed to visit friends and spend the day Christmas shopping.

Apprehensively, Samantha looked at Rebecca as the doorbell chimed the announcement of Mr. Reeves. Hyrum showed the young, dark-haired attorney into the study, and Rebecca introduced him to their client.

Samantha studied the tall man in the deep olive double-breasted suit. Her eyes moved from the top of his head to the bottom of his Italian shoes. Rebecca wondered what Samantha was factoring in, as she noted Samantha's silence in between his questions and her timid answers. They reviewed the cases together, first the rape and blackmail and then the murder, as well as the FBI's interest in Castriano. Rebecca could see Samantha felt more at ease with Mr. Reeves. She was certain of her comfort level once she heard Samantha refer to him as Philip. Clearly, the three of them *could* function as a team and work together with Agent Lloyd, Detective Winston, the FBI and the rest of the police department.

They were about to take a much needed break, when the doorbell chimed. A moment later, Hyrum ushered Detective Winston and two female police officers into the study.

"Samantha Armstrong?" Detective Winston asked.

Rebecca answered, annoyed at his formality. "You know who she is, and you know Mr. Reeves and I are representing her. What is this about?"

"First, let me introduce Prosecutor Hiller. Jim Hiller . . ."

Samantha watched silently, witnessing the ceremony, wondering why they'd chosen to collect themselves in her home.

"Samantha Armstrong, you are under arrest for the murder of Greg Maston," Detective Winston said, turning his attention toward Samantha. "You have the right to remain silent . . ."

As he read the Miranda rights, she turned pale. She nodded that she understood her rights. The burly female officer to the right of the detective moved Samantha's arms in back of her and placed cold silver cuffs on her slim wrists while the other female officer patted her down.

"Is this really necessary?" Rebecca asked. "She's not armed or dangerous."

"She's accused of murder. It's necessary and it's the law. You know that, Ms. Smalley."

Clearing his throat, Philip Reeves interrupted. "There's no need for this, I assure you. Why don't you do your job, and we'll do ours. We'll meet you downtown."

"Agreed." Detective Winston said. The officers moved Samantha out of the study into the foyer.

"Just one thing," Philip said. "Why arrest her now? What other evidence have you found?"

"Very good," Detective Winston said sarcastically, conspicuously looking into Philip Reeves' pale blue eyes as if to measure a reaction. "A witness places Samantha outside the crime scene in a car owned by her father at about the time of the murder. We'd love to hear your client's explanation of that, in light of the previous evidence you've both had an opportunity to review."

"Just remember, no questions till we get there," Philip said in reply, as if Detective Winston hadn't said a word. Watching the foursome leave the house, Philip reminded Samantha she needed to remain silent and assured her he and Rebecca would follow them to the station.

"That's why I came along," Prosecutor Hiller said. "I wanted to insure each procedure was followed to the letter of the law. Over the years, I've worked with Mr. Armstrong; and I want to insure, for everyone's sake, procedure is followed and due process is afforded."

"I'm sure that will be a comfort to him when he discovers you agreed to the arrest of his daughter," Rebecca said sarcastically. Prosecutor Hiller tipped his hat and followed the men out the door.

"Hyrum, please ask Mr. and Mrs. Armstrong to call us at the police station," Rebecca said, handing him her card with a note and additional numbers on it. "Also, could we see Mr. Armstrong's car; the one Samantha usually drives?"

"Yes ma'am. It's in the garage, but it ain't just Ms. Samantha's car. It's an extra car the chil'ren use when they be home. I believe the twins have their own car at school."

"Yes, Hyrum. I don't remember Samantha having a car at school. She didn't drive home?"

"No, ma'am. She took the plane home. They sent her a ticket an' ordered her home."

"She wasn't planning on coming home?" Philip asked curiously.

"No. I overhear them talkin' on the phone and then arguin' about it later. Mr. Armstrong called his office and ordered his secretary to send a ticket overnight mail to Ms. Samantha. I believe everyone in the house heard him yellin' the instructions in the phone. He was upset she didn't wanna come."

Rebecca and Philip looked at each other as they followed Hyrum into the garage.

"Hyrum," Rebecca began, "when the police searched the house on Thanksgiving, do you remember if they checked the cars?"

"Yes ma'am, they did. I don't know if they find anythin'. I was just told to show them anywhere they wants."

"Which car do the children drive?" Philip asked.

"This one. I just polished it," Hyrum said proudly pointing to the crimson Saab.

"It's a beauty," Rebecca said, looking at the car and taking notes on the license plate number, the color, the ivory leather interior. Satisfied she had every detail written down, she thanked Hyrum and followed Philip to their respective cars.

At the police station they found Samantha dressed in a gray jumpsuit with big black letters on the back announcing she was now part of the county jail. She looked forlorn, as the pair were escorted into her temporary cell.

"We've contacted a bondsman and the judge. We have asked for an immediate hearing, but it looks like you'll be held until at least Monday morning. It's the holiday weekend and that's the quickest anything can be arranged," Philip said, looking sympathetically at the despondent girl in front of him.

Samantha stared at the handsome man with caring blue eyes and wanted to apologize for being such a burden. She wished his lined face, soft eyes and strong features could hide his concern for her; but they didn't, and it frightened her into complete silence, despite her growing trust in his abilities to help her.

Rebecca outlined what would happen the next two days and at the hearing on Monday. She assured Samantha her parents would be allowed in to see her and she and Philip would be with her as much as possible, reviewing her case, whether they had to or not so she wouldn't be alone in her cell for too many hours at a time. Despite Samantha's quaking exterior, she understood them; and Rebecca tried her hardest to seem optimistic as they stood to leave the cell.

On request, the guard unlocked the door. The awful sound of the heavy metal doors reverberated mournfully and cut through each of them. Rebecca and Philip walked out, then heard a dull thud behind them. Samantha lay on the cold cement floor. Rebecca screamed, "Open the cell! Philip, get a doctor."

The group moved quickly. Rebecca grabbed a gray blanket from the soiled mattress and covered Samantha. Raising Samantha's limp wrist, Rebecca was relieved to find a faint pulse.

Hours later, the medical team arrived and carried Samantha into the ambulance. Rebecca and Philip followed the police-escorted ambulance to St. Mary's Hospital emergency room.

After speaking to her doctor, Rebecca was allowed to see Samantha.

"Hi. How are you feeling? You gave us quite a scare," Rebecca said, as her eyes studied the grim expression of her young client. Noticing the dark circles underneath Samantha's naturally vibrant eyes, she hesitated before pressing her with any questions. Hearing no response from Samantha, Rebecca watched her hands tightly clasp the white sheet and blankets covering her. As she stroked her long curls, she spoke softly. "The doctor says you fainted and you'll be fine. They want to keep you here a few days and make sure you eat properly. They're concerned because you're underweight. They want you to get your strength back before they release you. In the meantime, there will be a guard posted outside your door. Monday we'll go to court and explain you are in the hospital and we'll get you released—I promise. I've left a message with Hyrum, and he is trying to locate your parents. Philip and I will stay until they arrive. Do you understand?"

Samantha nodded and tried to smile at Rebecca through a veil of unwanted tears. She tried not to be scared, but she couldn't help it. Closing her eyes as they wheeled her into an elevator and through long corridors, she held tightly to Rebecca's hand, remembering her safe place with Nana. Her memories shielded her from this insane reality. She drifted into the solitude and serenity of her Nana's room.

Samantha's tight grip relaxed within minutes of the orderly transferring her onto the starched sheets of the newly made bed. Samantha looked more peaceful. She dozed in a relaxed sleep, obviously a result of medication dripping into her tiny veins through the I.V. The doctor had said she'd sleep for at least a few hours. Hopefully, her parents would be found by the time she woke up. Then she and Philip would have time to review the newly obtained evidence. Rebecca left the room and found Philip, who was still waiting.

"They didn't waste any time getting a guard for her room," Philip said, as Rebecca came within earshot of him. "Hyrum said her parents have been reached and they are on their way to the hospital. Shall we wait for them?"

"No. I want to review the new evidence. Then we can come back. There's nothing else we can do here."

"Agreed," Philip said. "Let's take my car."

Rebecca nodded as they quietly exited the hospital, each lost in their own thoughts.

Chapter 41

"As scheduled! I knew you two would land in my office eventually. I trust this is what you are looking for?" Detective Winston said. He handed Rebecca the investigation file and moved toward his office door. "You two may want to go down to the evidence room, if you haven't been there already. I've got some other cases to attend to. Feel free to use my office. Just lock the door on your way out. I never saw you here with this file."

Rebecca placed the file between herself and Philip, and the pair read each detail in unison. Neither spoke as they carefully perused each page.

"Here it is," Philip said. "The statement of the witness."

Rebecca sighed as she reviewed the sworn statement. "This doesn't make any sense."

"Samantha said she was sleeping, yet the witness I.D's her at the approximate time of the murder," Philip said, turning toward Rebecca. "Look at what you don't see."

Rebecca paused. She reread the statement.

"It places Samantha, or someone who looks like her, in a car that may or may not be hers, with a license plate that is seen, or in this small town is just known, to be part of the Armstrong fleet. Let's assume for the moment it was Samantha in her car. Let's assume she drove herself to the office and waited for Greg Maston."

"I'm following; keep going with your line of thought." Rebecca said, picturing his images as he painted them.

"She parks the car and waits in front of the building so she can make a quick exit. She waits just long enough so Greg becomes totally absorbed in whatever he's doing and won't see her enter the office. She arrives after the firm's employees are gone and before the cleaning staff arrives, so she can't be seen."

"But," Rebecca chimed in, "she can't possibly know for sure everyone in the office is actually gone; it's after eight

Wednesday night, so she'd have no way of calling to ask who was in the office. Remember, too, on week nights, the cleaning person could clean anytime after closing and before opening the next day. And on holidays and weekends, according to Mr. Armstrong, she had her choice to clean the offices anytime."

"Right. Not only is it unlikely Samantha would know with certainty when the offices would be cleaned, she wouldn't have had time to watch as each person entered and exited the building, because she'd been home most of the day. She wouldn't have any way of knowing who was in the office working and who wasn't."

"Agreed," Rebecca said. "And she would not put her car in front of the building so either she or the car or both could be recognized, even at night."

"Yes," Philip said. Rebecca's cheeks grew red with excitement. He hoped this would be the beginning, the moment of truth, where she understood his value to her in this case. "Now, the most critical point: she's seen in the passenger's seat. Not the driver's seat. Why does someone driving a Saab slide into the passenger seat?"

"They don't," Rebecca said emphatically. "So we've got to find a way to discredit this witness."

"We've got to find the truth," Philip said plainly. "There are too many missing pieces and, unfortunately, they're missing on our side."

"I can't believe they think she did it. You've worked closely with these guys; will they stop looking for the real murderer, now that they have Samantha in custody?"

"That's the usual practice; but given who her father is, I doubt they'll leave any stone unturned. If it helps, Detective Winston rarely leaves anyone alone in his office with a file. It's not his style."

"And that's a good sign?"

"I take it as his way of wishing us luck and letting us know he doesn't believe she did it, despite the file."

Rebecca raised her eyebrows and sighed hopefully as the pair continued to review the remaining pages of the file. They locked the office door, notes in hand, and headed for the evidence room. The uniformed officer placed the bagged and labeled items on the wooden table. They organized each item in a row for careful inspection.

"The murder weapon," Rebecca said quietly, carefully picking up the bagged knife. "A knife is an odd weapon for a woman to use, especially one as frail as Samantha," she added, turning it over.

"But, to play devil's advocate, it's a simple weapon to obtain. This knife actually looks familiar to me," Philip said. He turned it over and looked at the fine sculptured edges of the blade and its bulky black and silver handle. "I'm quite sure it's a steak knife from a local restaurant. I'll run a check on where this kind of knife can be obtained in this area."

"So anyone could have access to such a knife," Rebecca responded.

"True, but the only fingerprints found on the weapon were Samantha's."

"Look at this earring," Rebecca said. "Do you have a quarter?"

Philip reached into his pocket and pulled out a handful of loose change. Plucking a shiny quarter from the pile, he quizzically handed it to Rebecca.

"Look." She placed the quarter on top of the bag, where it nested inside the gold hoop earring.

"It's a quarter in an earring. I don't get it."

"The shape. If it was pulled out of an ear during a struggle, why is it still perfectly round? A delicately looped earring such as this, even of a fine quality, more than likely would have been bent out of shape. That happens even just with regular use. But to be torn from an ear . . ."

"Got you! So if we can get Samantha to locate the one she lost, we can compare the shape of them and, if it is shaped the same—"

"Then, even if it is hers it may not have been pulled out during the struggle. She could have lost it earlier in the summer, as she said. After all, she and her father both said she had been in and out of the office several times during the summer."

"And, if it appears to be the same earring and the shapes don't match?" Philip inquired.

"I don't think we'll have to worry about that," Rebecca said confidently.

"Officer?" Philip called. "What about the hair, nail, and

tissue samples? Any idea if the lab has completed the reports?"

"No, sir. We send out anything that requires DNA studies. I don't know how backed up they are. Check with the lab guys on Monday; that's your best bet."

"They don't work weekends?" Rebecca asked surprised.

"Anything sent out is dependent on the mail, and this *is* Thanksgiving weekend; but we could check the computer system and ask the lab to fax any report." Philip remarked, as the onlooking officer nodded. "Are you finished with the evidence?"

"Yes," Philip said. He nodded at Rebecca. "We'll follow you to sign it in."

# # #

Samantha opened her eyes from her heavy sleep to a full bladder and a nauseous stomach. The I.V. in her arm was taped too tightly to her flesh. Her fingers reached for the call button hanging on the silver rail. How long had she been asleep? A nurse appeared in the doorway.

"How are you feeling?" the nurse asked. She lifted Samantha's wrist with soft, cold fingers.

Samantha watched as the nurse took charge of her and charted every bodily function. "Fine, I guess. Actually, I have to go to the bathroom and I feel sick to my stomach."

"That's from the medication they gave you. You'll feel better after you've had something to eat. As for the bathroom, I'll help you there, but you'll need to fill a bedpan."

Samantha half-listened to the nurse's instructions and explanations of hospital procedure and doctor's expectations for her to eat.

"Is there . . . has anyone come to see me? I mean, while I was sleeping? Is there anyone waiting outside for me?"

"I just came on shift, but I don't recall anyone saying you had a visitor. There is a guard at the door, and you won't be able to receive or make any outside phone calls. I'm not sure if you're allowed visitors; I don't think so."

"What?" Samantha demanded.

"I'm not sure why. I think the doctors just want you to rest," the nurse said sweetly, cheerfully, trying to calm

Samantha down.

"I have to make a phone call. Can you make it for me?"

"I'm sorry, I can't. I will, however, tell your doctor you are awake. Maybe he can help you."

"When? When will he be here?" Samantha insisted.

"I don't know, but I'm sure it won't be long. In the meantime, here's the remote control to the television. Someone will be in with your dinner soon. You must eat everything on the tray. They've ordered you a high-protein meal. You should enjoy it."

Samantha watched the too-cheerful nurse exit as quietly and as quickly as she had come in. She saw, as the door opened, the blue-clad officer standing at attention at her door. Closing her eyes, she tried to remember the events of the past few days. How had things gotten so far out of hand? Where were her parents? Skyler? Why suddenly had he virtually disappeared from her? Clenching her sheets tightly between her fingers, she pictured her room. She pretended she was there, alone in her room. Safe in her room. No. Her room was no longer safe. Why wasn't it safe? She tried to remember. She couldn't. Nana. Nana's room was safe. She could picture herself there, sitting with Nana, holding her yarn, listening to her stories, smelling the lilac-water scent she always wore.

Samantha drifted, as her thoughts calmed her immediate fears. She was safe in the arms of Nana; protected in their private cocoon. She relaxed; she felt as if she were floating, calmly and peacefully. Suddenly, she was in the dark. Nana, her room, her safety, all disappeared. She was there in the darkness, standing, turning slowly around. Looking at the familiar pieces of faces, listening to the evil laughter and the music box. The music was soft, low and familiar. The eyes. The mouths and noses were now together. Could she see whom they belonged to? Did they fit together? The ears. They were there too! She had to concentrate. She put her hands over her ears, trying to shield herself from the laughter, the music. She tossed and turned. The doctor, who had entered unnoticed, took notes, listening to her mumbling. How could such a beautiful and privileged young girl have turned her whole life into a nightmare? She was disturbed, even in sleep. The valium he had ordered in her I.V. had not served its purpose. Placing his hands on her shoulders and gently grasping them, he called her name. "Samantha. Samantha! You're fine. Everything is alright. You are safe. It's okay to wake up. Samantha? Samantha?"

Startled, Samantha opened her eyes with inner urgency. It took seconds to realize she was not dreaming. The face before her was old and kind and whole. Not like the ones passing before her just seconds before. She gasped.

"You're fine. Just a nightmare," the white haired man allowed her to focus. "I'm Dr. Evans. I hope the rest of your stay here is less frightening than your dream. Do you remember it?"

"No. No, I don't," Samantha said, color rising in her cheeks.

As the doctor read her chart and conducted his examination, Samantha did as she was told and answered each question with as much composure as she could find. Finally, she posed the question she'd been waiting to ask.

"Doctor, could you ask them to hook up my phone? I'd like to call my parents."

"Your phone? Oh, I see," he responded. He closed the chart and took a seat on the edge of her bed.

"I'm sorry; it's not up to me. The police detective said no visitors other than your family and attorneys; he said you could not have any outside phone calls. You'll have to take that up with your attorneys, I suppose," Dr. Evans said sympathetically. "But I'll tell them about your need to have a phone to reach your parents, if you make a promise to me you'll eat your complete tray of food. I can hear it coming down the hall now. You need to gain a few pounds before I release you."

Samantha tuned the doctor out as soon as he denied her request for a phone. She'd find a way out of this mess; she had to, she cried silently. She felt increasingly like a hollow shell. Hearing a loud clamor of trays and smelling the familiar aroma of mashed potatoes and gravy, she looked up, expecting the door to reveal another starched white nurse with a tray of food. Samantha was pleasantly surprised to see her attorneys had found their way back to her side.

"Look what we brought just for you," Philip said. Rebecca placed the tray on the swiveled desk next to Samantha's bed.

"Actually, we'd have made it ourselves, but you've kept us too busy to spend any time in the kitchen," Rebecca joked, trying to keep the mood light so her client could eat her dinner with as little stress as possible.

Samantha smiled. The doctor introduced himself before leaving. Philip followed him outside the door.

Rebecca lifted the cover from the plate and made small talk with Samantha as if she were just casually visiting a friend in the hospital. Samantha twirled her fork in the potatoes and cut her steak into minuscule pieces. It was more like a dissection than a meal. Rebecca tried unobtrusively to study Samantha.

"Why can't I have a phone?" Samantha asked stubbornly, pressing Rebecca for a satisfactory answer, yet not waiting for one. "Have you talked with my parents? My brothers? Have you asked the judge to set me free?"

"We'll talk when Philip gets back in here. I promise we'll answer all your questions. Your job right now is to eat. I may be able to get you out of jail, but only you can get yourself out of the hospital," Rebecca responded, mirroring exactly Samantha's stubborn tone.

Samantha painstakingly ate her meal, one tiny morsel at a time, as Rebecca watched her swallow, with some difficulty, each forkful. Eventually Philip joined them, bringing in two styrofoam cups of coffee. "Sorry it took so long. Long lines in the cafeteria." Rebecca caught his raised eyebrow, while Samantha concentrated on pushing her food around her plate and into her mouth. Rebecca knew Philip needed to discuss something with her, but she could think of no way to leave their client in her present state of mind without first answering her questions and calming her fears.

"Samantha," Rebecca said, "We spoke to your family earlier, first in the morning and then a few times this afternoon. They know everything that's happened, and I assure you they care about you."

Samantha looked from one to the other, trying to read the bottom line. Her confused look prompted Philip to intervene.

"Samantha, we have people working around the clock on your case. Agent Lloyd has been consulted every step of the way, and he's working on aspects of your case that involve Skyler in more than you or the murder of Greg. He's assured us they're making progress, and that in the interest of the safety of both you and your family, he won't tell us everything."

"We went through the evidence this afternoon while you rested. We discovered some things we may be able to use in your defense. We also need you to contact your roommate, as we discussed; and we've made a list of items we need. My secretary will pick up the items and overnight them to us," Rebecca said, watching Samantha's expression. "Agent Lloyd still monitors your phones, and he may want to search your room at school. I didn't see a problem with that, but I've instructed my secretary to be there and take notes of everything."

"But, why? Don't you believe me? Don't they believe me?"

"Everyone believes you, Samantha," Philip said softly. "But there's much more going on here than anyone knows, and you somehow are in the center of it."

"My family. When can I see them?"

Rebecca's eyes met Philip's. "Agent Lloyd asked them to go about everything as a family and act as if this weren't happening. Your brothers will not assist on the case, although they requested. They'll be in classes Monday morning, as planned. Believe us, they fought us every step of the way! They'll call you; we'll arrange that. Your parents will be here as soon as possible."

"But you still haven't told me why they—"

Philip interrupted forcefully as Samantha's voice began to whine and crack.

"Your parents have been asked to keep Skyler occupied and out of town—too busy to read newspapers or make calls, too interested to want to return to Arkansas. They're all in Washington. He eagerly accepted an invitation from your father to join them. Under the guise of merging law firms and your brothers' clerking positions, your parents have introduced him to people he's wanted to meet."

"Skyler? What does he have to do with my being charged with Greg's murder?" Samantha asked, confused.

"We're not sure. What we do know is that he was the last person you talked to before the murder and the first person you spoke with after the murder. Agent Lloyd and Detective Winston are working on this with Assistant Prosecutor Kincaid." Rebecca spoke in an upbeat, positive voice. She wanted to be optimistic; they had a long way to go. "We communicate with them every day. They are working hard on this case. Believe me, Samantha, we're following every possible lead and looking at every angle."

Samantha let out a deep sigh. She had a terrible headache and wished she could have something for it. She was afraid to ask, hearing the voice of the last doctor she'd seen in Michigan. If they had taken blood samples of her, surely they'd see she had pills in her system—lots of pills. Surely they'd have found the pills in her purse; in her medicine cabinet, everywhere. What could she do? She rubbed her temples slowly.

"Samantha, you look like you need to rest. I'll call the nurse," Philip said, vanishing into the hallway before Samantha could protest.

"Samantha," Rebecca said, moving the table away from her and seating herself next to Samantha on the bed, "I know you're upset. Believe me, we are making progress. I need you to agree to do something for me."

Looking at the seriousness of her attorney's face, she stiffened. "The transcripts of the tapes. We've read them. We read the transcripts you and John made on your computer. The conversations are curious, but consistent. Do you understand?"

Samantha shook her head and remained silent trying to concentrate, trying to understand Rebecca's words and what they were leading to.

"What you've told us, what you remember," Rebecca paused, looking squarely into Samantha's crystal blue eyes, "doesn't make sense with the contents of the transcripts. That's why we need you to talk with a psychiatrist, maybe agree to hypnosis, if you are comfortable with that."

"You think I'm crazy?" Samantha asked, biting her lip, almost forgetting the pounding headache and the flaring nausea.

"No. But we need to explore every aspect of the case; and, after all you've been through, the prosecutor may try to make that assertion. In fact, they may have you see a psychiatrist of *their* choosing, in addition to the doctor we've chosen. Understand?"

Samantha did not respond. Her eyes focused on Philip, who had returned, followed by a brisk nurse, who measured and weighed the now-cold food and liquids on her forgotten tray.

"How do you feel?" the nurse asked. She motioned the visitors out of the room.

"Feel better, Samantha!" Philip said, as Rebecca murmured they would return soon.

"Not well," Samantha responded, as she watched the room empty. "I have a headache and I feel nauseous. Can I have something for pain?"

"Your doctors haven't written anything for you in the chart; they are waiting for the toxicology report from the lab. Are you allergic to anything?"

"No," Samantha said, taking the icy metal kidney-shaped pan from the nurse.

"I'll call the doctor. In the meantime, relax and get some sleep. We'll bring you another tray of food in a few hours. Maybe you can try to do better next time," the nurse said, adjusting the drip of the newly changed I.V. bag, before drawing the curtains and turning off the lights. She faded from the room as quietly as she had materialized.

Chapter 42

On Monday morning a conference was held in Judge Bingham's chambers with Rebecca and Philip, Agent Lloyd, Detective Winston, Prosecutor Hiller and, on the speaker phone, Assistant Prosecutor Kyle Kincaid from Michigan.

"I've reviewed the files, various motions and the accompanying briefs that have been presented, along with the police report; and I am prepared to hear arguments on whether or not the woman in custody, Miss Samantha Armstrong, should be held with or without bond," the middle-aged Recorder's Court judge said. "I'd also like to remind you my review of the evidence, as well as anything additional either side may present, is no indication as to whether the evidence will or will not be admissible in trial. Is that understood?" Judge Bingham looked at each person in the group individually, watching as they nodded in agreement. "I understand Mr. Kincaid is part of this meeting, by consent of all parties, because of another matter defendant is involved in that may or may not be related to the case at hand. Is that your understanding, Mr. Kincaid?"

"Yes, your honor," the voice from the speaker said.

"I'd like to hear from the prosecutor's office first," Judge Bingham said, folding his hands on his substantial dark oak desk.

"Thank you, your honor. What you have in front of you is evidence of a brutally murdered man. The police report indicates evidence from the crime scene points to the defendant, Samantha Armstrong. Fingerprints taken at the crime scene match those of the defendant, to include those on the furniture and the murder weapon. Hair matching the defendant's was found tangled on a button of the victim's shirt, pulled as if in a struggle. Nail and tissue samples haven't returned yet from the lab where they were sent, but we believe they will conclusively place the defendant at the crime scene. An earring found under the victim belongs to the defendant;

we have a witness who identified the defendant in her car, in front of the building where the victim was found, at or near the approximate time of the murder." Flipping a page of his legal pad, Prosecutor Hiller continued. "Additionally, the victim worked for the defendant's father, as an accountant to defendant's father's law firm. It has come to light since the murder, the victim allegedly raped defendant last spring. I should mention that defendant failed to report the alleged rape. It is our contention defendant wanted revenge and she got her revenge, by carefully planning and subsequently taking the life of the victim," Prosecutor Hiller said, scanning his notes briefly before completing his summary. "I believe Samantha Armstrong is a severely disturbed young woman, that she murdered Greg Maston in cold blood, and that she should remain behind bars until such time as she has a jury trial and that jury decides her fate."

Judge Bingham raised his eyebrows, jotted a few notes on the pad in front of him, and then asked the defense to speak.

"Your honor," Philip Reeves said, pausing to clear his throat, "What Mr. Hiller says is only one interpretation. Ms. Smalley and I have found many pieces of this case that don't match the crime and the defendant. We believe, despite the evidence against Samantha Armstrong, that she did not commit, nor is she capable of committing, the crime of murder, for which she is charged. Samantha met Ms. Smalley and Mr. Kincaid in Michigan where she approached them for assistance in resolving a problem she was having with a man who had been blackmailing and stalking her. At that time, she chose not to take the law into her own hands, but rather use the law to her advantage. The FBI was called in and—"

"I know we are not on the record, but I have to object. Counsel is testifying to matters not in evidence, and I fail to see where this is going, your Honor. There is no evidence in the file regarding blackmail or stalking, and I do not believe your authority extends to crimes that may or may not have occurred in Michigan," Prosecutor Hiller stated confidently.

"Mr. Reeves?" Judge Bingham said, waiting for his response to the challenge.

"It is relevant, in that it shows the defendant's state of mind; there is, your Honor, evidence in the file. There are transcripts of the defendant talking with the blackmailer; the tapes, authorized by federal warrants obtained by the FBI, place defendant in her bedroom at or near the time of the murder, despite the witness's identification of defendant outside the building of the crime scene." Philip spoke with equal confidence.

"Mr. Hiller, as you are well aware, nothing is in evidence, and this meeting is to determine whether or not defendant will be allowed bond. Mr. Reeves, I'll allow your comments up to this point, but I advise you to keep your comments limited to the issue at hand. Please proceed."

"Thank you, your Honor. We—I mean, Ms. Smalley, Prosecutor Kincaid, Agent Lloyd, Detective Winston, and others have kept close tabs on the defendant, both in Michigan and in Arkansas. She knew she was being watched carefully, by her own request, to allow the police and FBI to obtain evidence against the man who was allegedly blackmailing and stalking her. It is our belief, even if she wanted to commit such a crime, she would have feared being caught by one of us. She knew her phones were tapped. Furthermore, as to any hair on the button, the victim was at the defendant's birthday party last August. That's the last time she claims to have seen him. It's possible the day he was murdered he wore the same shirt he wore the day of the birthday party. As to the earring, there is no real proof it belongs to defendant, other than her statement she had a similar pair from which she lost at least one last summer. The tissue samples are not sufficient. They have not yet been matched to defendant. The fact defendant knew the victim and may have been raped by him are not sufficient evidence for a murder charge to stick. Additionally, the Armstrong family is well known in town and Samantha Armstrong has no history of criminal activity; indeed she never even received a traffic citation. She graduated at the top of her high school class and had she been given the opportunity to finish her first term at Michigan State University, I'm sure she'd have received acceptable grades. Her family and teachers say she'd adjusted well to college life and being away for the first time. We, therefore, ask you set a reasonable bond for Samantha Armstrong and release her into her father's custody."

"What is your response to the signed statement of the witness who claims to have seen defendant outside the office building?" The emotionless Judge asked.

"We've scheduled a deposition of the witness. From her statement, it is not clear she saw the license plate of the car or any identifying mark on it. Furthermore, she described a woman who looked like the defendant, but she has not yet identified her in a lineup. Additionally, even if she saw Samantha Armstrong, she committed no crime by sitting in her car outside the office. The witness doesn't state she ever saw Samantha Armstrong leave the car, enter or exit the building."

"Mr. Hiller?" The white streaks in the judge's dark hair reflected the florescent lighting as he turned his head.

"Your Honor, all the evidence so far, points at the defendant. The witness places her at or near the crime scene; and defendant, in her statement to police, states she was asleep, home all evening when, in fact, she was out. It may not be a crime to sit in her car outside a building, but it is a crime to lie under oath. We have a sworn statement from her, which her attorneys, who were there, are well aware of."

"I believe I've heard enough. Does anyone else have anything to add before we go on the record?"

The group declined to argue further. The judge dismissed them so he could review the file and prepare to go on the record, knowing each would place their arguments on the record.

"All rise. Here, here! Court is in session, the Honorable William Samuel Bingham presiding." The officer's voice boomed into the courtroom. A crowd filled the long rows of wooden benches, rose, and then sat as the judge, clad in his robes, entered and sat in his perch. The courtroom, filled with curious onlookers, most of whom appeared to be reporters, hushed at his presence. The attorneys made their motions and arguments, answered the judge's questions, and took their chairs again.

"I have carefully reviewed this matter and the extenuating circumstances of this case. The defendant is adequately represented by counsel and co-counsel and is unable to be here due to health reasons. I understand from defendant's counsel she is aware she faces a charge of murder in the first degree and she is, or will be, competent to stand trial. I understand she is the daughter of a well-respected attorney and she has no previous offenses. I therefore, after reviewing the evidence, the statutes, the preceding case law and arguments on both sides, in addition to considering the fragile health of the defendant, set bail in the amount of two-hundred fifty thousand dollars. Upon posting of any bond, I request defendant be advised by counsel she is not to leave the state and she be released to the custody of her father. I understand he has agreed to take responsibility for her. Is that correct, Mr. Armstrong?"

"Yes, it is, your Honor, thank you," Travis said, approaching the microphone at the attorney's podium.

"Furthermore, I order psychiatric evaluations of defendant to be completed before pretrial by a psychiatrist counsel on both sides agree to, that name to be submitted to me in three days. If an agreement cannot be made, I will choose one. If you do not have access to a list, my office can provide you with one. Pretrial is set for Tuesday, January 4th, without hearing any objection."

The gavel went down and the judge's clerk handed him the next file of the day. Reporters descended on the attorneys and Travis Armstrong, flocking around as they left the courtroom, waiting to flash cameras until they were through the doors and had stepped onto the black-and-white marble floors of the wide hallway. Both sides declined to speak to the press, seeking the safety of the parking lot and their vehicles.

Travis Armstrong drove to the bail bondsman and posted bail for his daughter. He took care of the paperwork, his mind was preoccupied, wondering what had transpired in the judge's chambers. He felt uneasy knowing that both people he knew, as well as complete strangers, had access to information about the Armstrong family, the law firm, and his daughter's future he had been denied access to. The more he tried to understand the reasons for his limited access, the more he didn't understand. So far, despite objections, Samantha's attorneys handled her case properly. He wished that were enough to ease his nagging mind.

Grimly, Travis dialed his home, wishing, the moment he heard Anne's sad voice, he could hang up and remain silent. But he knew he couldn't. Carefully, calmly, he explained the judge's orders and gave her instructions for the household. Only as many servants as absolutely necessary were to work.

Cook and Hyrum were the only servants who would deal with Samantha once she was home from the hospital; they were to keep their eyes on her and report everything to him and Anne. No one was to talk of the pending trial or the charges; any servant caught talking to anyone outside the house was to be dismissed immediately. Media was to be kept outside the property boundaries. The twins were to be kept informed, but were to remain in school . . .

Anne Armstrong slowly hung up the receiver. She had dark circles under her eyes and could not hide the fear she felt for her only daughter—her beautiful, delicate daughter. She wished she could protect her; she wished she'd recognized the cry for help. Hindsight was always twenty-twenty vision, she thought dismally, hoping their blindness towards their daughter's crisis could be remedied—even if she was guilty. After all, Anne rationalized, Samantha had reason to murder the man who raped her, a man she'd trusted since birth, a man they had all trusted . . .

# # #

Skyler paced on the burgundy, cream, and blue floral Persian carpet in Travis' office. He was angry at his inability to reach Samantha. The Armstrong family refused to discuss what Samantha was going through. How could they spend the weekend with him in Washington without any discussion of their daughter? How could they have left her alone in custody? Was it possible they hadn't known? He wondered anxiously, awaiting the arrival of Travis.

Travis was drained as he grabbed messages from his secretary. Flipping through them, he said, "Hold all calls. Buzz me when Ms. Smalley and Mr. Reeves arrive." He did not give her any chance to say Skyler awaited his arrival in his office.

Opening the door, Travis spotted Skyler at the bar pouring himself a double shot of whiskey. "A little early to be drinking, don't you think?" Travis asked blandly, tucking his emotions deep inside, holding his promise to his daughter and her attorneys. Looking at Skyler, Travis felt more helpless than ever. He took a deep breath and watched Skyler as he emptied the crystal glass, turning the bar back into a bookcase.

"I'm sorry for everything you and your family are going through. I wish there were something I could do. Maybe I could go over her file with you and assist in her defense," Skyler said. His voice was compassionate. Travis reminded himself he had damaged his little girl and had possibly put her so far over the edge she had committed murder. He reminded himself he needed to protect her, act normally, not let on anyone suspected Skyler of harming Samantha.

"Thank you. It's all been quite a shock. I, Anne and I, decided in the interest of the family and the firm, to put Samantha's defense in the hands of someone not affiliated with us. Otherwise, the media will have a field day, and Samantha could suffer more than she already has," Travis said, looking into Skyler's eyes, numbly trying to read his reaction, waiting for a response.

Skyler rubbed his jaw with his fingers, thoughtfully absorbing Travis' words. What was really going on? Had she said anything to them? "I think that's a wise move. If there's anything I can do, please let me know. Anything at all. Can I visit Samantha? I'd like to reassure her, let her know I support her and believe in her. I think we should get several of her friends to do the same."

"The doctors have advised me she'll need a lot of rest and we need to make sure she eats around the clock. She's anorexic, and won't be released from the hospital until she's stronger. Only family is allowed. It has to stay that way, at home too, for a while. I'll let you know when they say she can have visitors."

"That'd be great. I'll just call her and give her my regards—"

Travis cut him off, sharply. Skyler instantly sensed his anxiety. "She's not allowed any phone calls, newspapers, or news programs. She'll be in a restricted environment for the next few weeks. Please do not try to contact her; she needs complete rest and seclusion."

"Surely she'll want to talk to me! Surely you can make an exception," Skyler pressed on politely. "I've grown fond of her, of your whole family. She's become like the little sister I never had."

"I appreciate that and I'm sorry. You know my daughter—my children—mean the world to me. I can't go against doctor's orders. I want Samantha back to her old self as soon as possible; surely you can understand that," Travis said, so softly Skyler had to strain to hear his words. He studied Travis. The shadows from lack of sleep showed. He'd never seen him like this, so worn, so meek, so . . . what was the word he was looking for? Timid.

Skyler sighed. "Sure. I just want you all to know I'm there, for whatever you need. I guess I'll get back to my office."

"Yes, thank you. Oh, I understand congratulations are in order. You picked up several promising clients. The firm is proud of you," Travis forced a smile as if he were truly grateful.

"I'm trying, sir. I hope someday to make partner, as you know. I want to make you proud," Skyler said with a grin. Second only to the devil, Travis thought as he looked at Skyler. How could he be so two-faced, so evil? Travis could barely keep hold of his emotions, he felt such loathing. He wished Skyler were dead, too.

Turning toward the door, as if he were about to exit, Skyler hesitated before casting one more line for information. "One other thing. I saw the midday news report. They said the bail hearing for Samantha was virtually behind closed doors, in judges' chambers. Why weren't arguments heard on the record?"

Travis paused, caught off guard by the question. "Arguments were made on the record, enough to preserve the record for appeal. There was discussion, however, that was in chambers solely to protect Samantha's mental health and safety. Since she's barely an adult and she's in the hospital, the judge agreed any additional strain on her might prove harmful. He agreed to keep her case sealed and confidential, for the time being, until her health improves. He agreed evidence shouldn't be carried in the news. The evidence, as you know, would be raised in the question of setting any bail."

"That makes sense. But what's this about her safety? Why is that suddenly an issue?" Skyler pressed.

"The real murderer is still out there. He, or she, might try to harm her," Travis said, distracted. The words spilled from between stiff lips. "In fact, I've hired a private guard for her room now that she is no longer in custody. I felt safer when she had the officer outside her door, despite the fact she was under arrest."

"Travis, aren't you taking this a bit too far? I mean, surely Samantha didn't commit the murder; and whoever did wouldn't want to see her harmed, just convicted." Skyler said. The color rose on his boss' neck.

"No," Travis stated emphatically. "Whoever the real murderer is, it would be cleaner if the suspect were dead and the investigation dropped. I won't take the risk the real murderer might hurt Samantha," Travis forcefully continued. "Samantha will be protected from any harm as long as there is a breath left in my body."

"You're wise. If she were my daughter, I'd do the same to protect her," Skyler said, with apparent empathy. "Remember, call me if there is anything I can do." He walked out and closed the door quietly behind him.

What didn't he know about his daughter's case? Travis numbly stared out the window. What did Skyler know about it? He thought about the questions Skyler had asked. Why had Skyler so desperately wanted to see Samantha? Surely he would want to stay clear of her. Impulsively, Travis turned toward his desk, grabbed a notepad, and wrote down their conversation exactly as he remembered it. Rebecca Smalley would be interested. He tore his scribblings from the pad and sealed it in an envelope, printing her name on it.

# # #

Skyler flipped through his Rolodex in the privacy of his office until he found the name he was looking for. Dialing the number, he counted the rings. One, two, three, f—"Hello?" said the meek voice.

"Hi there," Skyler said in his most playful voice. "How are you? It's been so long since you called—"

"Skyler? Is that you?"

"Yeah, babe. Did you miss me?"

"You know I did; but as I recall, it was you that was supposed to call."

"Now, now. You know what a busy caseload I have. Listen, I was thinking about dinner tonight?"

"I have to work. I'm just on my way to the hospital right

now. I'll be off duty around eight."

"Great. Say a late dinner. I'll pick you up around nine?"

"Fine. I'll see you then."

"Margaret? Wait a minute. Since you're going to the hospital, could you find out the room a friend of mine is in and whether or not she's allowed to have flowers?"

"One of your other girlfriends?"

"No, of course not. It's the daughter of my boss, Samantha Armstrong. I'd ask the family for the room number, but they've asked we don't send anything. I'd like to anyway. She's a good kid; suffering from anorexia, and I just want to show we are all rooting for her."

"Sure, no problem. I've really got to run."

"Thanks, sweet thing. I owe you," Skyler said softly, before quietly hanging up.

# # #

Travis was relieved when he saw Rebecca and Philip enter his office. After coffee was poured and polite conversation dwindled, they immediately turned to Samantha's defense.

"I have spoken with Samantha's doctors," Travis said. "She is really quite ill. They advised me she has anorexia, probably brought on by the trauma of the rape and murder. She is also anemic, and her blood has a high amount of morphine in it, which indicates she's been taking drugs; not illegal ones, I hope. They think she's taken a dangerous mixture. She refuses to cooperate with the doctors. She also suffers from migraine headaches, which I don't find surprising. Her mother gets them, too. They are bringing someone in, a teen counselor, to talk with her. The doctors don't want me, or any of us, interfering at this point. They said they need a few days where she isn't pressured by the trial. They're afraid she could go into herself. They also said she has severe nightmares. I thought you should know right away."

"Thank you for sharing that information with us," Rebecca said compassionately. "We've grown fond of your daughter. I know how difficult this must be for you. We have no trouble spending a few days researching her case and limiting our visits. We can discuss other things with her. I'd just like to check in so she doesn't worry, if that's all right with you?"

Philip nodded in agreement. "We need Samantha to be as strong as possible, in case we go to trial. At this point, it looks like we are going. We've spent some time going over every tiny detail of the murder; and we've found some questionable areas, but not, at this point, enough to definitely point to another murderer."

"Can I help? Are you able to share any more of the details with me than you have? For God's sake, I am her father!" Travis stated emphatically, almost tearfully.

"I'm sure there will come a time when you can become more directly involved, but for now you must just focus on supporting your daughter and being a good father. She needs her family, now more than ever," Rebecca responded.

"I've placed a private security guard at her door. He'll keep a log of everyone who visits or inquires about Samantha. He reports to me daily and will pass those reports on to you," Travis said.

"That's fine, Mr. Armstrong. That's a start," Philip responded. Then he asked more formally, "Do you remember the day they first took Samantha in for questioning and conducted the search of your home and the surrounding premises?"

"Of course. You don't forget an intrusion like that. I'd never realized what my clients have been through, until the moment I saw my own possessions being touched and viewed by perfect strangers."

"Do you remember the search of the garage?" Rebecca asked.

"Yes. I believe they searched the entire garage and each of my vehicles. Why?"

"There is a witness who places your daughter in a red Saab you own, outside your office building, at the approximate time of the murder," Philip said. "Was she there with you perhaps? Did she drive you to the office in the Saab?"

"No. I wasn't scheduled to go in until later to meet Greg, when we were to go over the year-end report for Monday's meeting. We had company, and I was at home all day until I found Greg, later that evening. Samantha was in her room. No one saw her leave the house, and I don't remember seeing the Saab at all that day."

"We read the police report, and the witness signed an affidavit that identifies the Saab as yours; and she positively identified a picture of Samantha as the one seated in the passenger side of the car," Rebecca said.

"The passenger side?" Travis looked at the pair confused. "Then she would have been there with someone, if it was really her. Samantha loved to drive the Saab. If she had taken it, she would have driven."

"We don't want to keep you, Mr. Armstrong. Would it be possible for us to stop by after dinner? We would like to take a look at the car," Rebecca asked.

"Of course. I'd be disappointed if you didn't want to see the car. I'll advise Hyrum, he'll let you in." Remembering his wife's hollow voice and feeling his own tiredness, Travis added as an afterthought, "Although, it has been a long day; could you possibly wait until the morning to come out to the house?"

"Sure. We have plenty to keep us occupied until then. I would like to ask anyone who has access to the car be advised it is to remain untouched. That includes you, sir. You must leave the car as it was left by the police," Philip said in a dry manner, as if to drive his point home. "*Has* anyone driven it since the search?"

"I'm not sure. But I don't think it's been touched at all. The children like the Saab. Anne and I have our own cars to choose from; neither of us prefer the Saab. Hyrum would know. He has the task of maintaining the cars and the keys to them." Travis responded, intrigued by their questions.

The trio spent the next hour engaged in what Travis felt to be endless questions and answers, many of which he'd already gone over with the police. He was relieved when he was finally left alone. Pouring himself an iceless drink, he stood at the window, watching the winter sun quickly drop. Through the glass, he looked at the busy streets, feeling quite alone and empty inside. How could this have happened to his family? How could he have let it happen? His inner voice rang, as a lone silent tear escaped its mute captivity.

# # #

Samantha disliked the I.V. flowing into her veins. She did not like the shots the brisk nurses injected into it with each bag of fluid they changed. She did not like them pressuring her to eat. She hated measuring each morsel she ate and each she failed to eat. Most of all, she did not like anyone touching her body, peering at her flesh.

She stared at her phone. Finally, it had been connected. Her father had been her only caller; her mother her only visitor. At least she had a phone. Maybe Emily could visit? Had anyone told Emily she was in the hospital? It wasn't like Emily to stay away. Surely Emily would stop by if she knew. And John! She missed him. Did he miss her? It was strange to have relied on him so heavily over the past few months and then not to speak to him at all. Samantha wished she and John hadn't agreed to keep contact minimal, but she feared Skyler finding out about him. She sighed deeply. What was the real harm of contacting John? Should she risk it? She knew there was a tap on the phone. She didn't care. She had nothing to hide, despite the fact she was being charged for murder. A murder she did not commit. A murder she was glad about. "Turnabout is fair play," she said out loud in the silent room. He murdered me inside; he deserved to be murdered. She shuddered, pushing her memories back, not letting any spill forward into the present. She had enough to deal with.

The silence of the phone haunted her. As much as it comforted her to have access to the outside world, it distressed her. Would Skyler call? She lay stiffly between the white sheets and blankets. Would he visit her in the hospital? Would he whisper his sick, twisted, controlling words to her? Would he touch her when no one was looking? Samantha felt nauseous; her head pounded and the familiar pain crawled forward from the base of her neck. She pressed the buzzer, and a nurse with a painted smile and a stethoscope hanging around her neck appeared almost instantly.

"How are we feeling today?"

We? Samantha shouted silently in her head. Why do people always ask how "we" are feeling when they don't have a clue or even really care how *I* am feeling? Closing her eyes in silent exasperation, she replied in a low voice. "I have a terrible headache and I'm nauseous. Could you give me something for the pain?"

Looking at the chart, the nurse smiled, muttered something about calling the doctor, and left. Minutes later she returned and put another needle into the I.V. bag, increasing the drip. "You should feel better soon. I'll turn the lights off so you can rest."

Within moments, Samantha nodded off into a deep, silent sleep. The clear medicated drips froze out any thoughts or worries or mental wanderings. Hours passed. The noise of clattering food trays in the hall woke her. She reached behind her, turned the knob of the bed lamp, blinking out the sleep from her eyes, breathing in the familiar bland aroma of hospital food. As she sat up and turned toward her bed tray, she saw a beautifully wrapped bouquet of flowers, a sealed envelope taped to it. Reaching up curiously, she freed the small white envelope. Carefully opening it, she read the typed words twice before letting the card fall to her lap.

"Silence is golden."

Looking up at the tissue-covered vase, she grabbed at it, tearing at the paper covering it.

Then she gasped, almost dropping the vase. A dozen perfectly shaped gold roses surrounded one black rose.

Her heart quickened. It became difficult to catch her breath. Paralyzed, she stared at the ominous black center. She knew. Her body sweated profusely and then shook. It had to be from Skyler. The message was clear. Someone must have told him she had told! He knew! What would she do? What could she do? Samantha stopped shaking almost as quickly as she had begun. She heard the trays moving closer to her room. Quickly, she moved out of bed, stepping onto the cold floor, being careful not to pull or tangle her I.V. line. Grabbing the vase, she placed it in the back of the colorful array of flowers, plants, and balloons that had collected on the shelf facing her bed. Confident it could not be easily seen, she tucked the card inside one of the novels her mother had dropped off earlier. She slipped back into bed and carefully smoothed the sheets around her, trying to calm herself. She had to talk to her attorneys. They had to get him. They had to make him stop. Surely they had heard enough on the phone? Surely they could put him away . . .?

Chapter 43

Philip and Rebecca arrived at the Armstrong home just as breakfast was served. Hyrum, not understanding they wanted to work, showed them into the breakfast room, where a solemn Anne and Travis Armstrong sat silently reading different sections of the *New York Times.* Neither had expected to be joined for breakfast, so their eyes did not waver from the paper as Hyrum entered.

"Sir. Madam. Shall I have two more places set for breakfast?"

Looking up at the pair that had followed Hyrum into the room, Anne spoke first. "Yes, Hyrum. Please have Cook bring two more place settings." Travis politely got up from his chair and pulled out a chair for Rebecca. He shook Philip's hand.

Philip and Rebecca tried to object, not wanting to waste time or be questioned by the Armstrongs. Politely, they each took a china coffee cup and fresh lemon muffins.

"We really didn't mean to intrude," Rebecca said. "We spent the evening making a chart of the evidence and the positive and negative aspects of the case. Just to ease your mind, we do believe things are falling into place."

"Then you'll be able to tell us more about our daughter's case?" Travis asked.

"Not yet. You must trust us. It's difficult for you both, I'm sure, but it is necessary. There are too many pieces to your daughter's case that must remain confidential until we know more," Philip said.

"Can you at least tell us what you're looking for?" Anne asked loudly, placing her empty coffee cup in its saucer.

"No. We are afraid if it leaked out that you knew the facts, not only would you be stormed by the media, but you might be in danger—"

"Danger?" Travis questioned, immediately seizing on the word.

"Danger may be too strong a word," Rebecca ventured,

when she saw the raw emotion on the faces of Samantha's parents. "But it is a correct summary if we look at the worst-case scenario. Being an attorney, you know we have to be concerned about that. We have to be concerned with the safety of everyone involved."

Philip began to feel uncomfortable with their defensiveness. Politely, he stood up; Rebecca followed him. "We must excuse ourselves. Could Hyrum show us to the garage?"

"Of course," Travis said. Anne stared at the trio as they left the room.

Once in the garage, Hyrum took the cover off the shiny red Saab.

"Hyrum, has this car been touched since the police searched it?"

"No, sir. I covered it after they left."

"Has anyone driven it since then?"

"No, sir. Not that I am aware of."

"Do you keep track of the mileage? Is there any sort of log?"

"No, Ma'am. Only for the checkups. Not for regular driving."

"Did Samantha drive the Saab at all when she came home for Thanksgiving vacation?"

"Yes, sir."

"Did she drive it the day Greg Maston was murdered?"

"No, sir."

"How can you be so sure?"

"The car spent most of that day getting its winter tune up."

"Where did it spend the rest of the day?" Rebecca asked, opening the glove compartment.

"In the garage."

"And to the best of your knowledge, no one, including Samantha, took the Saab out of the garage, not even for a spin around the block."

"That's correct, sir. Will there be anything else?"

"No. We'll let you know when we've finished," Philip said, climbing into the driver's seat beside Rebecca.

"Find anything interesting?" He asked her.

"No. Nothing. The car is spotless. It even smells brand new," Rebecca said sighing. "I've brought the camera. How about we take a few pictures before we leave? I'd like to get out of here before the Armstrongs decide to come and watch us work."

Rebecca and Philip dropped off the rolls of film, and headed to the hospital. There they found Samantha sound asleep. But as they turned back toward the door, they heard her voice and simultaneously looked back.

"Samantha?" Rebecca asked, waiting for a response.

Philip put up his hand, signaling Rebecca not to awaken Samantha. "Listen," he whispered, motioning her to move with him closer to the bed rails.

Rebecca pulled from her briefcase a small dictaphone and placed it as close to Samantha's mouth as possible without touching her. Several minutes later, Samantha rolled over and began to wake up. Rebecca carefully placed the dictaphone in her briefcase just as Samantha opened her eyes.

"Hi. How long have you guys been here?" Samantha asked groggily.

"Just a few minutes. We were about to leave. You look like you need your sleep," Rebecca said, smiling kindly as she noticed Samantha's bloodshot eyes.

"All I do is sleep and eat. They keep giving me some drug that makes me tired. They told me I would be going through withdrawal from all of the medicine I took for my headaches. So far I just sleep. Please stay a while," Samantha said. "Tell me what you've found out."

"First, tell me what you were dreaming about. Do you remember?" Rebecca asked.

"Not really. I saw faces and heard music. I tried to put the faces together and run away from the music. Then it went black, and I woke up and saw you two. I've had the same dream before. I don't know what to make of it, but it's mild compared to reality."

"I know this is hard on you. But you need to pay attention to your dreams. They may help you remember something that could help us. I'll leave a writing pad with you and I want you to write down your dreams, no matter how silly or insignificant. Can you do that for us?" Philip asked.

"I guess."

"Samantha," Rebecca added, "who is Stacey?"

"I don't think I know a Stacey."

"Are you sure? You called out her name in your dream," Rebecca asked, hoping the name would trigger a memory for Samantha.

"I can't think of anyone by that name I would dream about," Samantha replied. "Can you tell me if you've found out anything that would help me?"

"We've found some problem areas. We are still searching for evidence to prove you couldn't have been at the murder scene and the car the witness saw was not yours. Is there anything you can remember about that day? Anything at all you haven't told us?" Rebecca asked empathetically.

"No. But I . . ." Samantha paused, looking around the room. "I got this," she said, pulling out the card from her pillowcase, handing it to Rebecca.

Philip and Rebecca read the card. "The flowers arrived when I was sleeping. I don't know who delivered them. I didn't dare ask anyone. They might ask why I want to know."

Philip examined the roses. Rebecca watched carefully, making conversation with Samantha, while Philip checked the roses as well as the rest of her flowers for eavesdropping devices. Once he was confident there weren't any, he asked, "What do you think the note means?"

With downcast eyes, Samantha bit her lip. "It's Skyler. I know it is. He always told me if I told anyone anything he would hurt me and my family. I know it's a warning I'd better be quiet."

"Is it possible it is from anyone else?" Philip asked.

"No. Who else would send such a note?" Samantha asked, wide-eyed.

"I don't know, but we need to find out. Do you mind if we keep the note and flowers?"

"No. I want them out of this room, away from me. I almost threw them away myself, but I knew you'd want to see them," Samantha said in a childlike voice.

"Hey, Sam," Emily briskly walked toward Samantha's bed and placed a stack of magazines on her bedside table. "I got special permission to see you. Your father told the guard it would be okay for me to come!"

"Emily! It's so good to see you!" Samantha said. She received a comforting hug from her friend and began introductions.

Philip and Rebecca excused themselves and went to retrieve the film they'd dropped off earlier. Rebecca pulled the photographs out of the package, as Philip paid for the development.

"Anything interesting?" he asked as they walked out of the shop.

"I don't know. Looks like nice pictures of someone else's car. Here."

Philip flipped through the packet of pictures as they headed back to their car.

"Let's get some coffee and check in to see if the reports came back from the lab. They're due in sometime today," Philip said. He put the key in the ignition. They drove to a nearby restaurant for badly needed coffee. It was time to get serious about the looming evidence against their client. Everything pointed to her. It was too easy, they agreed, as their waitress poured their coffee and took their order.

"Let's lay out the photos of the car and make comments on each one – sort of free association. Are you game?" Rebecca asked Philip rolling back her pages of notes to place an empty page from the yellow pad in front of her.

"Great idea," Philip smiled approvingly at the robust woman in front of him.

Carefully dating the paper, she laid out the pictures on the starched white tablecloth. Philip stared at the first picture, a full color shot of the Saab, then the second, a similar view, except it was black-and-white photography.

"Taking a roll of color and then a roll of black-and-white, really was a great idea," Rebecca said, finding the black-and-white photo distracted her less than the color.

"Yeah," Philip responded, trying to focus his thoughts on the pictures, "Something I learned in the prosecutor's office. I'm always amazed at the reaction of juries to color photographs. I learned early on to take both. Just by chance, I began to see, depending on the type of case I was handling, either one or the other would prove useful in making my eyes sensitized to the real story in the picture. It's a lesson you learn in practice, not in law school."

"Let's hope it helps us with this one," Rebecca said, writing brief statements on her paper.

As the pair studied the two rolls of film crowding the

length of their table, they became disheartened. They barely noticed the waitress who kept their coffee cups flowing until she placed their pasta platters in front of them. Suddenly the pair looked up, feeling pangs of hunger as the steam filled their nostrils.

"You two buying a new car?" She asked, as she cleared away their salad plates.

"No," Rebecca said, disinterested in any conversation other than the one she was having with Philip. She put her notepad on the empty part of the booth seat.

"Oh," the waitress rambled on. "I've been renting different cars—you know, get the feel of the kind of car I want and how it handles. I haven't found one I like and can afford. I'd love to have a beautiful red Saab like the one in your pictures. Maybe I'll rent one for fun." Sighing wistfully before she departed, the tiny waitress who had gone unnoticed suddenly sparked Rebecca's interest.

"That's it!" She said, moving away her spaghetti plate.

"What's it?"

"Look at the pictures," Rebecca said. "We've been looking for something that's not in the pictures."

"Not in the . . .?"

"Look at the windows. Look at the rear and front bumpers."

"Yeah . . .. So?"

"What if it wasn't the Armstrongs' Saab? What if the witness saw a rental car? Rental cars always have some kind of sign the car is rented. Remember, that was the big thing in Florida when tourists were getting murdered. Then the auto leasing and rental agencies took off their identifiers."

"So, you're saying the pictures are missing a rental sign, a sticker, whatever. So whatever we are looking for isn't there, because the car we have pictures of and the police checked for evidence wasn't the one used the night of the murder."

"Right," Rebecca said, twirling long threads of angel hair pasta cleanly onto her fork before plopping it joyously into her mouth.

"Okay. I'll buy that, but, you've forgotten the license plate the witness remembers is exactly the one on the Armstrongs' Saab, and Samantha was identified as sitting in it."

"Okay, it's not perfect," Rebecca conceded, noting their

latest thoughts on her notepad. "But there's something we just aren't seeing. Let's eat and then try again."

"Yes, boss," Philip said jokingly, breaking apart his garlic bread.

Chapter 44

Agent Lloyd's instincts sharpened as he turned the corner several car-lengths behind the green Jaguar. He was not worried as it disappeared into the night; it was too easily found. He passed by the dark alleyway and saw it. Smiling to himself, he turned off his lights and parked his car. After jotting down a few notes, he radioed in the lighted license plate number of the black limousine. Satisfied with the verification, the name Castriano was absorbed into his consciousness and his notepad, he kept his eyes carefully focused on the cars. Fifteen minutes passed before Skyler returned to his adjacent car, shoved a thick white envelope into his breast pocket and climbed into the low bucket seat. He reversed his car into the street. The limousine followed quietly, turning out of the alley in the opposite direction, leaving its lights off until it was halfway down the block. "Interesting," Agent Lloyd said out loud, as he watched the lights of the limousine flicker on in his rear view mirror.

###

Skyler grinned as he drove into the night. He felt good. He felt on top of the world. He wanted to celebrate. Too bad Samantha was off limits for the time being. Too bad she had to go and mess things up. Well, whatever the outcome, she was still under his thumb, and she knew it.

Dialing his car phone, he reached a meek voice that was filled with confusion.

"Hey babe, want to come out and play?"

"What? Huh? Skyler . . .?"

"Margie, baby, I thought you'd miss me! You don't seem happy to hear from me."

"I am . . . I'm just surprised. I didn't get home till midnight, and we had a lot of emergencies. What time is it?" she asked, turning the her alarm clock to face her.

"Not too late for fun, baby. You and me. I'll be there in about fifteen minutes. Be ready," Skyler said, still playful, not noticing the forcefulness in his own voice.

"It's almost three. How about in the morning—"

Skyler cut her off, irritated at her resistance. "Something wrong? You've got another man there, don't you?" he said sternly.

"No, you know I don't." She sighed. "I want you to come over. You just caught me by surprise. I'll put some coffee on."

"Great, but we'll need something better than coffee. See you there," Skyler said, smiling. He always won and he loved it. Victor, he thought grinning to himself. I should have been named after the thing I love. "Victory!" he said out loud, raising his right hand triumphantly as he spoke.

# # #

Agent Lloyd parked his car in the lot facing the nurse's window. He'd long suspected it had been a nurse who'd placed the flowers in Samantha's room, and Margaret Parks had been the only nurse on the guard's list who didn't have a direct purpose for being in Samantha's room. When she'd been questioned with the rest of the hospital staff, she had claimed to have placed an extra blanket on Samantha's bed, saying she had a request for another blanket and must have confused the rooms.

Agent Lloyd asked her why she assisted a patient who was not on her floor. She explained she had stopped upstairs to see a friend and found the nurses' desk unattended. She decided to answer the room that was buzzing for assistance. She was sure no one else had seen her. Her prints, she explained, had been found on the vase of the flowers because she'd watered the flowers when she was in the room. That was all she knew, so she claimed. Agent Lloyd reflected on her statement. Did she know what she was really doing? The lights turned on and then off in her small apartment. Making notes, he turned on the radio and grabbed the silver thermos he had belted into the passenger seat next to the small cooler. He had been on too many cases to sit out the night on an empty stomach. That was for rookies. He bit into the smaller half of his hearty submarine sandwich. He didn't mind waiting.

# # #

"Hey babe, you look great. Come here and take off that robe," Skyler said, with a husky lust in his voice.

Margaret did as she was told. She knew better than to resist. The bruises had faded, but the pain lingered. She knew better than to refuse him again. She'd learned her lesson when she refused to deliver a second present to his friend. Her fear of him only recently disappeared; she did not want it to resurface. She took a deep breath, pushing back her thoughts. She didn't want to remember their fight. It had been her fault. She shouldn't have upset such a vibrant, caring man. She'd helped him once; of course he'd expect her to do it again. But she just couldn't after the FBI agent had questioned her. She was told not to tell anyone she or anyone else had been questioned. She hadn't told Skyler. She was scared to. She hadn't told the FBI about Skyler either. She was scared to do that, too.

She opened her robe, let it drop to the floor without taking her eyes from his, as if he'd captured her mind, immersing it in his. He moved slowly toward her, and grabbed a handful of hair from the nape of her neck, pulling it toward him, kissing her deeply as if he wanted all of her, as if he were connected to her.

"Oh, so you did miss me," he whispered in her ear, his hot breath hinting of whiskey.

"Mmm," Margaret responded agreeably, pairing her movements with Skylers, trying to remain alert even though she was exhausted and could only think of sleep. She closed her eyes, following his every movement. What was she feeling? Why was she with him? She opened her eyes and looked at him. He was so handsome—almost too attractive. His eyes mesmerized her. She looked away from them. His cologne filled her nostrils, his scent mingling with hers, making her confuse reality . . .

"Can you feel how he missed you?" Skyler said, pressing his hips into hers.

Margaret followed, as his strong arms maneuvered their melding bodies to her unmade bed . . .

# # #

Agent Lloyd sat reviewing his notes again. He condensed them, page by page, into an organized, itemized list. Then he began another list, this one of questions. As minutes faded into hours, he matched the two lists. The car. The witness. Had they found the rental car yet? Did Skyler have anything to do with the murder? If so, what?

Doodling one note after the next, Agent Lloyd remained occupied until he saw Skyler's dark shadow seep from the apartment building into his Jaguar. Seconds after Skyler pulled onto the street, Agent Lloyd followed him.

Chapter 45

"Hey Missy, heard from Samantha lately?" John asked, setting his tray next to hers. "Mind if I join you?"

"Go ahead. You're lucky you got any food; I thought they closed the cafeteria half an hour ago."

"I've got pull. They let us resident assistants raid the kitchen once in a while," John said, scooping up a mouthful of lettuce leaves drenched in French dressing.

"So, have *you* heard from Samantha?" Missy asked curiously.

"A few letters. Sometimes she writes every day and then there are weeks at a time when I don't hear from her. I want to call," John looked into Missy's watchful eyes, "but they told me not to."

"I know; me too. We weren't as close as you two were, but I still worry about her. Her attorney called and asked me to send a box of things to her—weird things—and I haven't heard anything since."

"Weird things? Like what?" John asked curiously.

"The contents of her junk drawer in her dresser and in her desk, hairbrushes, jewelry box and makeup bag." Missy stopped eating. John did not react. "Okay, I guess they weren't so weird . . . I mean Samantha didn't own anything weird. I just thought the collection was strange, and also I miss using her stuff when I leave mine at my boyfriend's place."

"So what do you have of Samantha's left in your room?"

"Nothing, as of last weekend. Her parents sent me a check and asked me to pack up and ship all Samantha's belongings to them. They seemed so cold about it; I mean, I was expecting someone from her family to come pack her things—not just send a letter and a check."

The silence between them was contemplative. John finally broke it.

"So I guess she isn't coming back," he said in a serious and disappointed tone.

"Not till next year, I guess. When I asked, they told me they hoped she'd be able to come back next year." Missy watched as John's face brightened.

"I hope I'll see her again. I didn't know her long, but I feel as if I did. There's just something about her that . . ." John paused. He looked up at Missy. He didn't want to finish his sentence. He knew he didn't have to when he looked at Missy's approving smile. She patted her hand on his shoulder. She got up from her chair. "You wait. Things'll work out. Gotta run. Call me later if you need to talk . . . and I'll let you know if I hear anything."

John nodded, then pulled out Samantha's last letter and reread it.

Dear John,

I wish I were back at State. I wish I could hear your voice. Things are so hard here. The trial is coming up and no one will tell me anything. So I lay day after day in this hospital bed thinking the worst. They keep policemen outside my door. I think they want to send me to jail, though no one really says that. I can read between the lines. The newspapers, television and radio broadcasts must be bad too because I'm not allowed to see or read any. They say it's for my health. I don't believe them. I reread your letters all the time. It helps knowing you believe me. I didn't do it. I couldn't have . . .

Skyler still stalks me. He sent me black roses. I'm not supposed to tell anyone. I'm scared. I can't believe they haven't done anything to him. Maybe they don't believe me? But Mr. Kincaid is here from Michigan and Rebecca is still here. They have a lot of people working my case and for that I have you to thank. I can't think about what would've happened if I hadn't reported Skyler's stalking . . .

But murder. I didn't murder anyone. If I did, doesn't it make sense it would have been Skyler . . .? Of course, I'm not exactly unhappy it was Greg... I guess I shouldn't say that. I'm sorry. No, I'm not sorry. We've always been honest, haven't we? Let's keep it that way. Okay?

Hopefully, they'll figure this mess out and leave me be. I can't wait to be free of this stark white medicinal smelling hospital room. My doctors tell me I can set myself free if only I'd eat. But I do eat. I swear to you I eat. I'm just not as hungry as they want me to be. This hospital food is worse than dorm food.

If you don't want to wait for me or my situation is too depressing, you don't have to write. I'm sorry for everything and I understand if I don't hear from you ever again. Well, I can hear the clanking of the dinner dishes. Gotta go. Maybe they'll have a new set of shows for me to watch with dinner . . .

Fondly,
Samantha

P.S. I read the book you sent me every day. I focus on the phrase you highlighted, "Nothing real can be threatened." I hope I believe it someday. Write, soon.—S.

John lay the letter next to his notepad and jotted words of response as quickly as he could. He missed talking to Samantha. He missed her blue eyes and the long, thick, black curly mane that flowed around her face and down her tiny frame. She was so beautiful. He couldn't get her out of his mind. He was glad she had been reading the *Book of Miracles* he sent to her. He knew she needed one.

He wrote about classes and how he wished this term would go as well as the last two terms had gone—without her it was going very slowly. He wished he could tell her he'd stayed in contact with Rebecca and had answered all her questions. He wished he could tell her he knew the trial was about to begin and he'd try to talk Rebecca into letting him come and support her. He joked with her and told her she should be glad no one let her watch the news. He was thankful she did not know what was being said about her. Even in Michigan she was infamous. He kept the clippings. He also kept ones Rebecca sent him when he threatened to break her rules and visit Samantha. He stayed away only because it was for the best and Rebecca promised she'd fly him in the minute it was safe, the minute it was all over. Whatever that meant. He folded the fervently written five pages into the Hallmark card and placed the bulging paper into the crisp blue envelope addressed to Rebecca. She'd know it was meant for Samantha.

At least Rebecca made sure Samantha got his letters and he got hers. He licked an extra stamp and placed it in the corner. He'd promised himself he'd try every day to send a card, a letter, books—anything he could think of to distract Samantha, now that the trial was about to start. Rebecca promised to keep him posted. He hoped his mail would remind her.

Chapter 46

Samantha stared at the long white plastic bags shrouding clothes on hangers, dangling from her mother's fingers. She didn't care what she wore to the trial. She didn't want to go. She didn't understand why she had to go. She didn't do anything wrong; yet they were going forward with the trial, pulling her right out of a hospital bed and whisking her into a courtroom, as if she were a paper doll!

Even Rebecca didn't understand. Samantha was tired of answering questions, reviewing information, and looking at evidence. Most of all, she was tired of being poked and prodded and force-fed. The hospital walls closed in on her tighter with each passing day. She wanted out of the four bland walls confining her. She had stopped asking when she would be released, because she knew the answer by heart and was sick of hearing the recapitulation of her situation, sick of hearing the hospital was better than a jail cell. At this point, Samantha wasn't sure she saw the difference.

"I thought you'd appreciate a few new suits and dresses. Emily helped me shop. We had a nice day together. She really cares about you; she's always been such a good friend. Whatever you don't like, I'll send back," Anne chirped optimistically to her blank-faced daughter, noticing her folded arms had not opened to receive the clothing. She avoided using the words "court hearing," or "trial." It was difficult. She didn't know what to say. It was tedious trying to be cheerful all of the time. She smiled at Samantha as if everything were all right, as if they were in their own home. She could see Samantha's disdain and made a conscious effort to ignore it.

"Would you like me to help you try them on?"

"No, Mom," Samantha said, pursing her lips, sure now her mother's gifts were just an excuse to look at her body to see for herself if she had gained any weight.

"Okay. I'll just show them to you and hang them up in your closet. You can try them on later."

"Whatever, Mom," Samantha said impatiently. "Have you heard anything about the trial? Will it be delayed, or is it still set to begin on Thursday?"

"I haven't heard anything new. What's Rebecca been saying?"

"That everything will be fine."

"I'm sure it will be, dear," Anne said, straightening the bed covers.

"I didn't do it, Mom."

"I know dear. Don't worry. Everything will be fine."

Samantha didn't hear her mother's words, nor was she comforted by them. She only heard the laughter from within her head. She tried to ignore it. The colors of clotting blood blended before her, as her mother moved around the room in slow motion.

". . . Samantha? Samantha? Are you feeling all right? You look so pale . . ." Anne asked, her thinly lined brows suddenly knit together.

"Fine, Mom," she finally responded, her ears assimilating and separating her mother's voice from the ones in her head. She had long ago placed her mother's questioning voice and her thinly lined and knitted brows into the category of "better give her a response before she lunges through the door and makes a scene."

"Are you sure? You didn't hear a word I said."

"Mom, it's just the trial. I'm distracted. I thought when I heard footsteps, they were Rebecca's. But it was you . . . I mean I'm glad to see you, Mom. I'm just curious to see what other evidence they found. If any."

"I can understand that, dear. Your brothers will be by later. Maybe they've heard something. They've been reviewing your files with your father at home. I mean, not everything, just what Rebecca gives them. They are looking for clues your lawyers might have missed—" Anne stopped short. She'd already said too much. She didn't want to let Samantha know how worried everyone was and how hard they were trying to piece the evidence together. She changed the subject, seeing Samantha's expression change to one of worry. "So, what else can I bring you to make you more comfortable?" Anne asked, as she fluffed Samantha's pillows.

"A cake with a silver file in it," Samantha said sarcastically.

"You must be feeling better. You're getting your sense of humor back," Anne said in disapproval. "I'm only trying to help. Things will get better, and you'll be out of here soon. Think positively. You've come a long way, whether you see it or not."

"I'm sorry, Mom. I'm just tired of being locked up in here."

"You are not locked up. You should be grateful you are not in prison. You wouldn't make such comments if you had spent any real time in prison."

"I know, Mom. I'm sorry. I miss my friends and school. I'm missing so much."

"Well, hasn't Emily been by to see you?"

"Yes, but that's not what I mean."

"I know what you mean; but for now, you just have to make the best of things and follow doctor's orders."

"And attorney's orders and psychiatrists' orders and hospital rules, and, and, and. I could make a list a mile long!"

"Just make the best of it. It'll be over soon. I promise. I've got to run. I'll be back later. Try on your new clothes in the meantime, and let me know," Anne said, brushing a kiss on Samantha's cheek before swiftly vanishing into the white hallway.

Anne took a deep breath as she made her way into the elevator and pushed the button to the second floor. She found her way down the hall. What would she be told by the chief psychiatrist reviewing Samantha's case? She could use some encouraging news. She needed it. She popped two white pills into her mouth before stooping over the cold fountain water.

# # #

"May I help you?" the receptionist asked the woman with the glazed expression.

"Oh, yes. Anne Armstrong to see Dr. Levanstein."

"You may go back to office five. He'll be right with you."

"Anne?" Dr. Levanstein asked the woman he'd grown familiar with over the past few months. "Is something wrong?"

"Just the usual. I'm sorry. I was just daydreaming. So much has happened and seeing Samantha takes so much out of me. How is she, doctor?

"She's improving. She wants to improve, to get better; and that's helped her recovery."

"She's eating better and gaining weight. Is she past the danger zone?"

"Not yet. But there has been a marked improvement, and she's made it past her drug addiction, although her sleep is somewhat irregular. Have you ever known her to have bad dreams, nightmares?"

"Occasionally. Every child gets them, don't they?"

"Yes. But Samantha's are different. Of course, since the rape, they would be different; and the murder has triggered a lot of deep-seated anxiety and emotional upset. Much of which is to be expected, but . . ."

The pause frightened Anne, as he flipped open the thick file he'd brought in with him. She tried to make sense of what she was being told. It didn't sound as if Samantha was making any progress, yet the doctor had told her she was improving.

"How are her nightmares different?"

"Her nightmares don't follow any particular pattern and then, all at once there comes a point she calls out the same words; and, at that point, there is a pattern or similarity. Have you ever heard her talk in her sleep?"

"Nothing I can remember. She usually wakes up when I come into her room at night. She's a light sleeper. She's always been a light sleeper," Anne said. "What kind of words has she been calling out?"

"I cannot discuss those particulars with you. Samantha has asked me not to, and I must follow her wishes."

"But I am her mother. I have a right."

"She is eighteen, and my first responsibility is to her and to the doctor/patient relationship. Surely you understand that?"

Anne drew a deep breath. She knew he was right and she hated it. "Fine. I won't ask; but I'll trust you'll tell me anything I need to know as a parent."

"Of course. Now, can you tell me about your daughter's relationship with the woman she refers to as Nana?"

"Her grandmother? There's not much to tell. She spent a lot of time with Nana when she was a little girl and loved to be alone with her. She loved her more than any other family member I know. I was sometimes jealous of their relationship, but I've always been grateful Samantha had Nana when she was growing up. Is there something in particular you're looking for?"

"Did she sing Samantha a special song, or perhaps play her a particular piece of music," Dr. Levanstein asked. Anne shook her head no at each suggestion. "Or give her a musical instrument or perhaps a music box?"

Anne paused. "Yes, there was a music box. She received it on her fifth birthday. She's always loved it but. . ." Anne paused. She couldn't remember what happened to it. Samantha always had it on her dresser next to her Minnie Mouse lamp. When had she seen it last?

"Does she still have it?"

"I'm not sure. It spent years on her dresser, but I can't think of the last time I saw it."

"Anything else you can remember about Nana and Samantha's relationship that might help me?"

"Not really. Nana was a very private person. She enjoyed her time alone. Samantha inherited that trait from her. But I don't think that's anything unusual. I'm sorry, I just don't remember, and I'm sure it can't be that important with what's happened."

"No problem. I'm sure you're right. We're just trying to look at as much information as possible. How was Samantha when you saw her earlier?"

"Nervous about the trial. She's gaining weight. She's looking more like herself, although she has a long way to go. She's still moody, but she can hardly be blamed for that."

"How would you define moody?"

"You know, the usual teenage mood swings. She's irritable and sulky. Sometimes she just mumbles; and then, other times, she is so aggressive in her speech, it's as if she's transformed into someone else. I try to ignore it; after all she's been through, she's entitled to some outlet. Can she testify at the trial? It's coming up in a few days and I'm not sure she's up to it."

"I believe she will be able to stand trial. At this point, she's eating better and I have no solid proof she is unable to testify."

"Are you sure?" Anne asked, surprised.

"No. I'm not sure; but I believe there is a chance, at the trial, when she is confronted by the prosecutor and questioned about the murder, her reaction may open a window that will allow me to put the pieces together to begin to really heal her."

"So you're using her as a guinea pig? The trial as some kind of experimental treatment? I thought you were the best. I thought you were trying to heal her. You could cause permanent damage if she is not ready to stand trial!"

"She is willing to take that risk. We have discussed the options."

"And I have nothing to say about your approach?"

"I'd hoped you'd trust me to do what you and your daughter have hired me to do, and that is to help her heal herself."

Anne didn't want to listen any more as Dr. Levanstein explained his rationale. She was tired of feeling left out of her daughter's life and out of the worst thing that had ever happened to her and to their family. She needed fresh air. She needed to be out of the small office and the smell of hospitals. Swiftly grabbing her purse, she fled from the office, thinking only of the safety of her home and her own room.

Chapter 47

Anne and Travis Armstrong sat numbly as their daughter moved like a perfectly shaped plastic doll. They listened to her meek childlike voice. Silently they were glad, as bodies shifted along the long table of attorneys, they became hidden from her view for long periods of time. They were thankful she could not see the pain they were unable to hide. They shared it with her. They wished they could take it from her. As she sat in the stiff wooden chair, close to the judge's desk, her eyes closed tightly. Her body swayed back and forth, like a small child on a wooden rocking chair, holding her skirt like a comforting blanket between her fingers. She rubbed the faded blue cotton unconsciously with her thumb.

The Armstrongs held their heads high, sitting as a family with the twins, recently graduated, by their side. They were proud of their children; they were a proud family, and it showed. Their neatly dressed sons sat next to them, their bar review outlines peeking out of the briefcase on the floor in front of them. The July bar exam was just weeks away. Recesses usually found the twins hiding behind their books. People left them alone to study instead of intruding with probing questions.

Occasionally, their eyes looked at the end of the row, at the man sitting angled toward Samantha. As they stared at the back of the lanky man with the thinning hair, they could see the top of his sketch pad. The subdued hues of his gentle markings blended into the sweet sad eyes of their sister. He'd captured her gripping pain permanently on the once-empty sketch pad. For the twins, watching the sketch of their sister take a life of its own, mesmerized them as they listened to her words.

Stillness surrounded Samantha as she remembered. The viewers watching intensely, curiously, as Samantha confronted her memories. Drawing in her limbs, tightly adhering them to her body, she answered each question. They watched as she tried to mask the fear, the pain. But she felt each spectator must be able to see she was trying to keep the laughter, the voice, from harming her and controlling her. She heard the voices, knowing she could not tell anyone about them, knowing only she could tell the rest of the story. The untold truth was her only hope of salvation.

Prosecutor Hiller motioned to his assistant to turn off the recording as the voices went dead and silence filled the tape. "Samantha, you have testified this tape was made by Skyler Marks and then given to you later, is that correct?"

"Yes."

"Can you tell this court why you never reported the rape to the police?"

"Skyler—Mr. Marks—told me I had washed away the evidence and no one would believe me."

"Did he force you or coerce you into not reporting the rape?"

"No."

"Then I ask you again, why didn't you report the rape?"

"Objection," Rebecca called out. "Counsel is badgering the witness. She is not on trial for not reporting a rape."

"Your Honor, I believe the issue of the rape is critical to the case and goes to the Defendant's state of mind."

"Overruled. Please answer the question," Judge Bingham instructed Samantha.

"Thank you, your Honor."

Samantha looked at Rebecca as if she held the answers. She bit her bottom lip, her hands clenched together. Taking in a deep breath, she began. "I was afraid no one would believe me. I took a shower. I don't think anyone was around . . . no one came to help me. I was embarrassed. I thought I'd let my parents down."

"You are a beautiful girl; you must have had a lot of boyfriends in high school. Did you?"

"Objection . . ."

"Overruled."

"Did you have a lot of boyfriends?"

"A few."

"How many is a few? More than five? Less than ten?"

"I . . . I don't know. I guess around ten."

"Around ten boyfriends. Were these steady boyfriends?"

"No, not all of them."

"How many of the ten did you go steady with?"

"About three."

"About three or exactly three?"

"Three."

"Thank you. Now, Miss Armstrong, how many of those boyfriends did you have intercourse with?"

"None."

"Come now, Miss Armstrong. By your own admission, you have had ten boyfriends, three of which have been steady. Do you mean to tell this court you have not had intercourse with any of them?"

"Yes."

"Is that yes you have had or yes you have not?"

"I . . . You are confusing me. I have not had sex with any of my boyfriends."

"Come now, Miss Armstrong I didn't say sex. I said intercourse. Had you had intercourse with any of your high school boyfriends before you were allegedly raped?"

"No."

"But you let them kiss you."

"Yes."

"Touch you?"

"I—"

"Objection." Rebecca sprang up seeing the fear and confusion in her client's pained eyes. "Counsel is badgering the witness."

"I will allow the questioning, but please wrap it up; you are on a fine line. Overruled."

"Thank you. The fact is you have, with at least some of your boyfriends, had sex. . . I mean explored more than just what a kiss felt like."

"I don't understand."

"Have you done anything more than kiss a boyfriend, but done less than actually having sexual intercourse?"

"I . . ." Samantha closed her eyes as she felt herself flush. "Yes, but we only—"

"That is enough, Samantha. 'Yes' is sufficient," Prosecutor Hiller said abruptly, instantly moving on to his next question.

"Were you a virgin, until the time of the alleged rape?"

"Yes."

"But you stated you had some sexual experience?"

"I—"

"Yes or no, you have had some sexual experience?

"Yes."

"Didn't you ever wonder what it would be like to make love, to have actually had sexual intercourse?"

"Yes, but I—"

"Why hadn't you had sexual intercourse if you had thought about it?"

"I was waiting for marriage, for someone I love."

"So having sexual intercourse with someone you love was important to you?"

"Yes."

"Did you love Greg Maston?"

Samantha lowered her eyes. She didn't want to answer; she didn't want to picture him. She had loved him. She also now hated him. She felt a tear slide through her long lashes as she heard her voice answer timidly, "Yes."

"So you did lose your virginity to someone you love?"

"No, I—"

"Didn't you just tell this court you loved Greg Maston?

"Yes, but not—"

"So at the time you had sexual intercourse with Greg Maston, you loved him, yes or no?"

"Yes."

"And you failed to report the act as one of rape, isn't that correct?"

"Yes."

"Could that have been because you enjoyed it, because it was something you had thought about and you had wanted, to have sexual intercourse with someone you love?"

"Objection. Counsel is badgering the witness and is putting words into her mouth," Philip called out, as Rebecca and Agent Lloyd whispered between themselves.

"Sustained. Please keep your questions limited to the case at hand."

"Yes, your Honor," Prosecutor Hiller said, taking a moment to glance at his notes. Flipping the page on the notepad in front of him, he began again. "Now, Samantha, you have told this court you were raped by Greg Maston, and yet you want us to believe you did not murder him. Is that right?"

"Yes."

"And you also want us to believe you had no reason to murder him, to want him dead, even though he allegedly committed a heinous crime against you, against your body. Is that also correct?"

"Yes."

"You never wished he were dead?"

"Objection," Philip called out. "Prosecution is again putting words into the defendant's mouth."

"Sustained. Please rephrase the question," Judge Bingham said, almost disinterestedly, scratching notes on his pad.

"Thank you, your Honor. Did you ever wish Greg Maston had been punished for his alleged crime against you?"

"At first, I— "

"Please, Miss Armstrong, just answer the question, yes or no," Prosecutor Hiller said evenly, trying not to be rude or offensive, as the wide eyed jury watched their interaction.

"Yes."

"Thank you. Now, I'd like to move on to the day of the murder. Do you feel up to answering a few questions about that?" Prosecutor Hiller asked, his voice full of concern, apparent empathy emanating in full force for the jury.

"Yes," Samantha said taking in a deep breath, her frightened sea blue eyes focused on Rebecca's encouraging smile.

"You testified your phones had been tapped by the Federal Bureau of Investigation. And we heard Agent Lloyd testify as to the authenticity of the tapes we have entered into evidence. Is that correct?"

"Yes."

"Your Honor, I would like the tape made on the date of Greg Maston's murder, just prior to the approximate time of his death, played for use in questioning the defendant."

"I am assuming counsel has had time to review the evidence. Without objection?" The serious-faced judge paused, his eyes on Samantha's attorneys. "So ordered. Bailiff, would you begin the tape player."

"Thank you, your Honor," Prosecutor Hiller said. All eyes focused on the gray box as the "play" button was pushed.

Samantha felt uncomfortable under the eyes of the courtroom audience in the pregnant silence. As the conversation on the tape recorder began, she identified the voices; her own and Skyler's, echoing the familiar conversation. Suddenly her ears burned. The voice was hers, but was not familiar. The prosecutor stopped the tape, staring at her. Everyone's eyes burned into her; her cheeks flushed and her head pounded. Pain climbed up from the root of her neck.

"You testified earlier you did not leave your house on the night Greg Maston was murdered. Is that correct?"

"Yes. I went to sleep and I stayed in my bed all evening. I wasn't feeling well."

"But you did in fact leave, didn't you?"

"No! I was sleeping."

The prosecutor turned the tape on again and the audience listened intently as Skyler's voice asked her to meet him down the street; and a soft, sexy, playful voice agreed. The voice sounded like hers, but she didn't remember saying those words—or meaning any of those words, even if she'd said them. She'd never spoken to any man like that.

The voice inside her was laughing loudly. It grew. It swelled into gales of laughter. Her head pounded as she put her hands over her ears. She didn't want to hear any more. It wasn't true. It wasn't true! She screamed inside her head. The pain was now so piercing it numbed her into darkness . . .

And then she spoke, the words falling uncontrollably from her mouth. "I don't understand your problem," the sultry, sophisticated northern voice began loudly. "There is nothing wrong with me going out with my boyfriend. Tom and I have been dating for so long we're practically married."

A gasp filled the room and then immediately hushed as the prosecutor spread his hands out as if silencing a symphony. The crowd understood and listened. The jury, intense, leaned forward in their chairs.

"Who is Tom?"

"My boyfriend."

"What is his full name? Can you give me his first and last name?"

"Thomas Steven Marks. Everyone calls him Tom."

"What is your name?"

"Stacey."

"What is your last name?"

The room watched as Stacey stared at him as if she hadn't heard the question. The prosecutor repeated himself to no avail. Fearful he would lose her, he continued, disregarding her non-responsiveness.

"Stacey, tell me where Samantha has gone."

"Samantha? She's a wimp. She can't handle anything."

"So you handle it for her?"

"Yes, that's right."

"Where is she?"

"Sleeping, I imagine. She's always sleeping."

"Can you wake her up?"

The audience stared. The meek-mannered Samantha had turned into an energetic, vibrant woman. Her carefree mannerisms and outgoing language were unlike Samantha's. She shrugged her shoulders and raised her eyebrows casually as if it were an insignificant request that had been made.

"Please. I need to talk with Samantha. I need to make sure she is okay,"

"Samantha's fine. I take care of her."

"Is that what you did the night Greg Maston was murdered? Did you take care of her by murdering him in cold blood?"

"Me? No, I didn't murder anyone."

"You were there. The night of the murder. You met Tom. You drove Samantha's car and met Tom, and then you murdered Greg. Did Tom help you?"

"I didn't murder Greg. I didn't drive Samantha's car. Tom was parked down the street. I met him. I walked, like I always do. We didn't want to wake anyone up." Stacey said firmly, obviously annoyed.

"Do you remember the color of the car?"

"Red. Fire engine red."

"What kind of car was it?"

"It was a Saab."

"Are you sure?"

"Yes."

"Did you see the license plate?"

"No."

"Are you sure?"

"Yes."

"Do you remember anything else about the car?"

"No, except there was a sticker in the bottom corner of the windshield on my side."

"The passenger side or the driver side?"

"I said my side. I was in the passenger seat."

"What did it say on it?"

"I don't remember. I could see through it, except for where it had a letter and a number on it and some small printing on the bottom. It was dark."

"What else do you remember?"

"Nothing. I didn't murder anyone, especially for the wimp."

"Thank you for answering my questions. Can you bring back Samantha? I really need to speak with her."

Silence fell upon the startled crowd. Moments passed in hushed suspense until the meek voice returned.

"Sleeping. I told you I was sleeping and I didn't leave all night."

"Your Honor," Rebecca interrupted, "May we approach the bench?"

"You may," said the judge with a wrinkled forehead, watching the group intensely. The two members of the defense council and the prosecutor approached him. Agent Lloyd stayed at the defense table fervently scratching down notes.

"We would like to claim surprise at our client's condition. While we'd suspected there was something wrong, none of our psychiatric experts found a multiple personality. We were told the differing voices were due to the drugs and a confused psyche because of the rape—sorry your Honor, alleged rape. We request a recess at this time," Philip said quietly.

"Not a continuance?"

"No, your Honor. I believe we can continue with the rest of the evidence without our client. By then, we can have her properly evaluated and continue with any examination of her the prosecution wishes—pending, of course, approval of her physician."

"Any objection from the prosecutor?"

"No objection."

"While this is highly unusual, I will agree that as long as this matter proceeds and you do not waste this court's time."

nor the time of the court."

As the courtroom emptied until the next morning at ten, reporters and cameras swarmed around the Armstrongs, the attorneys and the FBI agents. Even the prosecutor refused to give a statement. Too much was uncertain. Too much was at stake. Too many lives could be affected. Many unspoken concerns were captive in each party's thoughts as they entered their respective cars and departed, anxious to prepare for the morning hearing.

Chapter 48

"Look, doctor, there's no history of mental illness in either my husband's family or my own. Samantha's problems were brought on by her circumstances, and she will get over it. She simply has to! She has good strong genes."

"I have no doubt Samantha will do well. She has made great progress. What concerns me is her second personality, the one that calls herself Stacey. I need to figure out as much as I can about what triggered her creation of Stacey to help her."

"We *know* what did it. It was the rape. Surely you aren't one of those doctors who blame the parents for everything? Samantha has had the best of everything, including the love of her whole family."

"I'm not doubting that. I'm just trying to ask you for other leads—clues to unlock other reasons for Samantha's dependency on her second personality so I can dislodge her need for it."

"I'm sorry, doctor. I don't have any idea. Samantha has always been a good child. Very independent. Her father and I never worried about her. She followed our rules to the letter, and we always felt comfortable when we left her at home alone with the servants. You see, in recent years, we've spent quite a bit of time in Washington raising money for one candidate or another or for any number of good causes."

"So you really wouldn't have seen any changes in your daughter?"

"Yes, doctor, I would have; and I told you I didn't. Maybe we should find another doctor. I don' like your approach. I'm a good mother; I'm not to blame here—"

Dr. Levanstein stared at Anne, jotting notes as he listened and watched her. Finally, he interrupted her and tried to reassure her.

"I'm sorry. I don't mean to imply anything about your parenting skills. I'm just trying to get as much of Samantha's background as possible to piece together the things that have influenced her or impacted on her, both good and bad. It's part of her treatment and recovery process. I believe we had discussed this early on. I know you didn't approve of putting her on the witness stand, but it has proven useful. Maybe I should review the approach we are taking with Samantha?"

"No. No, you're right. It's just been a long day already, and it's not even half over. Can we continue this later this week? I've got quite a headache, and I need to go home and rest," Anne said, putting on her dark sunglasses. She reached out her hand to the doctor. The meeting was ended regardless of his response.

Chapter 49

The filled courtroom hushed as the jury filed in and the bailiff announced Judge Bingham. Some onlookers in the courtroom noticed the absence of Anne Armstrong. The Prosecution called Melanie Harper to the stand. As she was sworn, the Armstrong men sat at attention, studying the woman who had placed Samantha at the crime scene.

"Miss Harper, may I call you Melanie?" Prosecutor Hiller asked, as if he were asking her for a date. The witness nodded. "Can you tell us where you were on the evening of Wednesday, November 23rd of last year?"

I was walking toward my sister's alterations shop. We were meeting for dinner. When she wasn't at the restaurant, I thought she got delayed at the store—she often worked late before the holidays. So I left my car in the restaurant parking lot and walked to her shop to meet her and walk back with her."

"About what time was that?"

"I believe it was around seven-thirty. I remember because I asked to have our seven-thirty reservations changed to eight. The hostess didn't mind since they weren't busy."

"Are you familiar with the Armstrong law firm?"

"Yes."

"How is that?"

"My sister and I often pass by the Armstrongs' office building when we meet downtown for lunch or dinner; and a few years ago the firm helped us settle our grandparent's estate and set up trusts for me and my siblings."

"Do you know Samantha Armstrong?"

"Yes."

"How is it you know her?"

"Oh well, I think everyone knows the Armstrongs."

"Objection," Philip called out, not looking up from the notepad he was scribbling on. "Witness can't know that."

"Sustained. Please, Miss Harper, confine yourself to answering only those things you know."

"Yes, your Honor. Sorry. I recognize her from pictures in her father's law firm. There are a lot of family pictures. I like to look at pictures. When I was in the waiting room or conference room, I'd always look at the photos. I asked who the people were. I also remember seeing Samantha in the newspaper, her graduation photo. She graduated in the top of her class. The paper said she was going to college in Michigan."

"Mmm, thank you," Prosecutor Hiller interrupted. "Aside from photographs, have you ever seen Samantha Armstrong in person?"

"Yes."

"Tell us when the last time you saw Samantha Armstrong was."

"It was the only time I saw her. It was that night, when my sister and I had dinner. She was sitting in a red car . . . a Saab, I think. The car was running. I remember thinking it must be nice not to have to worry about saving money and being able to run the engine for such a long time."

"What do you mean when you say for such a long time?"

"Well she was parked there in front of the building, with the engine running, for several minutes. There weren't many people on the road, and hers was the only car parked with the engine on."

"Several minutes," Prosecutor Hiller repeated. "You just walked past the car, is that correct?"

"Yes."

"Then how is it you know she was there for several minutes?"

"Because I walked all the way to my sister's shop and then back to the restaurant, and she was still sitting in her car with the engine running."

"So you saw her twice. Once going to meet your sister and once going to the restaurant with your sister."

"Yes."

"Did you ever see her get out of the car?"

"No."

"Could she have gotten out of the car, without you seeing her?"

"Yes."

"Did you see anyone with her?"

"No."

"Did you happen to see the license plate number of the car?"

"Just on the way back to the restaurant. We were walking toward the car and the back faced us. My sister was closest to the car, but we were talking and her head was facing me. The plate was in my view. It was an easy plate to remember."

"How's that?"

"It was sparkling clean, like it was polished and waxed with the rest of the car. And it had a catchy number."

"What was the plate number, exactly as you remember it?"

"A-U-T-O-4," Melanie spelled out carefully, looking confidently and steadily at the jury, just as she'd been instructed.

"I have no further questions at this time, your Honor, but I reserve the right to recall this witness. Additionally, I'd like to offer into evidence the license plate from a red Saab, registered to Travis and Anne Armstrong. The number embossed on the plate A-U-T-O-space-4 has been verified by the Secretary of State."

"Without objection..."

"No objection, your Honor," Rebecca replied confidently.

"The exhibit will be marked. Defense counsel, do you wish to examine this witness?"

"We do, your Honor," Philip said, rising, while taking a sheet of paper from Rebecca and another from Agent Lloyd.

"Miss Harper, how dark was it at about seven-thirty on that November day?"

"Oh, it was very dark; but there were a lot of street lights, so it didn't seem as dark as it was."

"Did the person you saw have a light on in the car?"

"No."

"Was the car parked under a street light?"

"No."

"Was the car parked near a street light?"

"No, but—"

"Just answer the question."

"No."

"And you say, aside from a few pictures, you never saw Samantha Armstrong in person, until that night?"

"Yes."

"And when you saw her, you saw her in a dark car on a dark street on a winter evening. Is that correct?"

"Yes."

"Miss Harper, how is it you can be sure it was Samantha Armstrong you saw that evening? Let me rephrase that. Are you absolutely, without a doubt, certain it was Samantha Armstrong you saw?"

"Yes."

"Come now, Miss Harper. Did you see the woman's eyes?"

"Yes."

"Really? Can you tell me what color they were?"

"No."

"Can you tell me whether or not she was wearing earrings?"

"No."

"Was she wearing makeup?"

"I don't know."

"Then I ask you again, are you absolutely, without a doubt, certain it was Samantha Armstrong you saw?"

"I . . . I . . ." Melanie stuttered, looking helplessly at the prosecutor as if the answer was written plainly on his face.

"Isn't it true you aren't really sure who the woman was you saw and you just assumed it was Samantha Armstrong because of the location of the car in front of the Armstrong offices?"

Melanie Harper's hands clenched the arms of the wooden chair in the witness stand so hard her knuckles turned white. She was angry; she felt like a fool, like her words were not her own. She hated the way the defense attorney molded and twisted her words, but she had to answer the question, and, as he repeated it, she found her voice and uttered "Yes."

"I have no further questions at this time, but I reserve the right to recall this witness."

As Judge Bingham recessed the court for lunch, Travis told his sons to meet him at the hospital where Anne had taken Samantha for her evaluations with several prominent psychologists.

Travis watched as the twins made their way past the reporters. Quietly, he moved beyond the dark oak rail separating the legal minds from the audience. He cautiously moved up to the trio who were nodding their heads together over the afternoon witness list. Rebecca put her hand on his shoulder and gave it a friendly squeeze.

"How's Samantha?" she asked. The group shifted to allow him in.

"We don't know yet. Anne has been staying at the hospital as much as possible. We're meeting for lunch. I'm on my way, but I promised her a complete update—'Rebecca's interpretation, not yours' were her exact words."

Rebecca smiled. "It's going well, regardless of how it may appear—"

Travis cut Rebecca off anxiously. "Look, all I see is you and the prosecutor have successfully placed Samantha in her car outside the scene of the crime. The jury—"

"The jury," Agent Lloyd broke in, "doesn't have all of the facts, and you know as well as I do things aren't always what they seem."

"Why do you keep telling me not to worry? We're in the middle of a trial that will determine the rest of my daughter's life, and you're still piecing together information and looking for new evidence. How is that supposed to comfort me?" Travis said sternly, his eyes a cold steel blue.

"There is much more you don't know and the jury has yet to hear and explore. Keep faith in your daughter. Believe me, with all we know, we are still working around the clock to help her and put the real murderer behind bars." Agent Lloyd answered with confident sternness, as if to slap Travis into reality.

Before Travis could respond, Philip interjected. "We have a few more leads and, believe it or not, things are falling into place. I think we'll be able to piece this thing together; and your daughter will, hopefully, be going home with you to stay. We will all be working together, night and day, until this is over."

Rebecca rubbed Travis's shoulder comfortingly, nodding her head in agreement with the comments made by her co-counsel. They were right. Travis knew that, but he lost his objectivity the day his daughter became involved in the murder investigation. He looked appreciatively at Rebecca and smiled his thanks, but he could not hide the dark lines of worry that showed the world how deeply his pain cut into him. They couldn't guarantee a favorable result. Samantha might be found mentally incompetent to know what she did, if they did find her guilty. How could he and Anne live with their daughter in jail or in a mental institution? It was too hard for him to comprehend. It was so different when it was someone else facing life imprisonment and someone else's family he was dealing with. Sadly, he walked to his car, wondering what the doctors' prognosis would be and silently compiling questions to ask Anne about possible past mental illness in their family tree.

Chapter 50

Skyler wasn't allowed to be a spectator at the trial. All of the witnesses were sequestered. Skyler was called as a witness by both the prosecution and the defense. Moments of initial panic had long since subsided for him once the first newspaper accounts failed to mention his name in connection with the trial. Samantha had played it smart, Skyler decided. She had believed his threats. No one would believe she hadn't *wanted* to have sex with him, even if she decided to tell. No one would believe a murderer, especially one with mental problems and such a strong motive.

Leaning against the bureau in his hotel room, Skyler cracked his knuckles wondering why Samantha had never called him. Each passing day without a phone call from Samantha had stoked his anger. How dare she challenge him after he had been such a good friend to her! How dare she not find some way to get in touch with him!

Diligently, yet unsuccessfully, he'd repeatedly tried to call her before the trial started. It was difficult to reach her with the close surveillance ordered by her doctors, attorneys and family. Sequestered in the hotel, Skyler felt completely isolated from Samantha. Shaking with outrage, he threw his schedule book at the black silent phone. He hadn't yet found a way to make outgoing calls. He knew Samantha's phone had been removed. A guard remained posted outside her door. All this increased his fury. He longed to have Samantha feel his angry breath against her. That would send a stronger message than the note and flowers.

But someday the trial would end and he could at least visit her in prison . . .

Skyler conspired slowly, stroking his chin in wicked thought. An evil grin appeared on his face as cracking knuckles again broke into the silence.

Chapter 51

The only thing Samantha was sure of, as the weeks turned into months, was time was passing. Isolated, she was painfully aware of the changing seasons outside the window. Time's passage could also be marked by the windowsill, now cluttered with months of magazines, stacks of videotaped movies, and boxes of CDs.

A rack filled with books of all kinds kept her mind occupied. John sent books from courses she would have taken had she remained in school. She was happy for the work. John also sent her Michigan State University's policy on receiving college credit by taking an examination. It intrigued and occupied her. It made her feel closer to John each time she picked up one of the books he'd sent or read his letters. It made her feel far away from the murder, Skyler, and the trial.

Samantha glanced at the collage of paraphernalia. She wished her cluttered library included real information on what was happening on the outside. She wished she could read the newspaper and have free access to television and radio. But she couldn't. They were forbidden until the trial was over or until she was released, whichever came first.

Which would come first?

She'd become accustomed to the scheduled noise and movements outside her door. She was a master at anticipating the nurses in their stark uniforms sneaking in and out of her room; the choppy start and stop gait of her doctor; the hollow high heels of her mother; the brisk, heavy walk of her father; Emily's apprehensive, soft, slow-paced footsteps. The twins' energetic voices announced them before she could hear their walk.

As she lay hostage amid the dull solitude of her captivity, she felt tucked away, withdrawn deeply inside herself. Yet she also felt as if she were wholly exposed outside of herself. She could not pull the two feelings together, nor could she eliminate one or the other. She tried to feel normal, but wasn't sure what normal felt like. She wasn't sure how to feel. She wasn't sure what she *should* feel. She wasn't sure she was still able to feel.

Looking up just before the door began to open, she heard the hypnotic voice of her psychiatrist. Samantha sighed. She was tired of the mild-mannered man, and his questions.

"How are you? Haven't you been out of bed this morning?"

"No real reason to get out of bed, I guess," Samantha said, eyes downcast, nervous hands clenching one another.

"Of course there is. I see from your chart you are eating better and you have gained another pound this week. A few more pounds and you may be able to go home. How do you feel about that?" The monotone voice asked, as he closed the silver metal chart and opened his notebook.

"I don't have any choice but to eat. Every time I turn around, someone is bringing me food and standing over me, watching me eat it." Samantha answered, annoyed at his stern face.

"Are you feeling hungry at all?"

"No."

"It's taken a long time, but you are eating and you are looking much healthier. It is a positive step. Learning to want to eat will take time as I've told you before. In time, you will regain an appetite. When you do, you will be very close to going home. Have you thought about going home?"

"Yes. I think about it a lot."

"What do you think about?"

"I think about my room and my clothes and my stuffed animals, my furniture, my wallpaper, my pictures."

"What else do you see?"

"My Minnie Mouse clock. I miss my Minnie Mouse clock. My Nana gave it to me when I was really little. And she left me her music box when she died. We used to listen to it together. I miss touching it; I miss hearing it play. It comforts me when I detail the room in my mind and see my things there."

"Obviously, you like your room. What else can you tell me about it?"

"I like to think about it. It makes me happy to take my mind away from this room. I can take my own little trip there."

"Did you have a phone in your room?"

"Of course; I've only mentioned it to you about a thousand times," Samantha said sarcastically, not hiding her annoyance.

"What about your phone?"

"What about it?"

"You talked on your phone quite a bit, isn't that right?"

"Yes. You know I did."

"But you didn't mention it. A few moments ago you gave me a very detailed description of your room. You mentioned everything. Everything but your phone."

"I thought I did mention it. I have my own line," Samantha said, trying to remember everything she had listed in the conversation previously.

"You didn't mention it. It is important to talk about the reasons why."

Samantha began to feel tired. She didn't want to answer any more questions. She didn't want to talk anymore. She closed her eyes and sighed.

"What are you talking to her for? She always fell asleep on the phone, if you really want to know."

"Stacey?"

"Of course. The wimp is asleep again! When things get tough, she calls on me."

"And she needed to call on you a lot, didn't she?"

"Yes. Sometimes she needed me a lot."

"What times were those?"

"You know; times when *he* wanted her. But it wasn't really her he wanted, it was me. He was *my* boyfriend."

"Who was your boyfriend?"

"Tom."

"Tom who? Do you know his last name?"

"Marks."

"Think. You are confused. Take your time. Picture him, listen to his voice. Hear his voice. Can you do that?"

"Of course."

"Then it isn't Tom Marks you are seeing, is it?"

Suddenly, in sweat-drenched clothes, Samantha awakened. The onset of truth; a parallel vision, clear and true, evoking an almost hypnotic awakening.

"Skyler! I think . . . it was Skyler . . ." Samantha cried;

strong warm tears streamed down her face, dropping into her lap.

"Can you tell me your name?

Samantha paused. Who was she? Whose voice had come out of her? Samantha could feel the psychiatrist waiting for her answer. His piercing eyes made her feel uncomfortable.

"My name? My name is Samantha. Samantha Armstrong."

Moments passed. The quiet startled her. Suddenly, she felt her facial muscles loosen, as confusion turned to understanding.

"I didn't do it. Did I?" Samantha whispered.

"What do you believe?"

"I didn't do it."

"You are sure?"

"Of course."

"What if you just don't remember? What if you blocked it out? Do you think that is possible?"

"I couldn't commit murder. I know the evidence seems to . . . Truthfully, I thought I might have, that maybe I just didn't remember. I forget a lot lately. But now, I don't think I did it. I didn't murder Greg," Samantha paced her words slowly, thinking out loud, feeling a flood of genuine relief.

In the ensuing silence, she watched the doctor's hands quickly scribble notes. Instantly, she became panicked.

"Could I have done it without remembering it, without knowing it?" Samantha paused, taking it all in. "Could *she* . . ."

"You tell me."

Chapter 52

Prosecutor Hiller rose in response to Judge Bingham's order to call his next witness. He wished Samantha were well enough to retake the stand. She wasn't. He agreed to proceed with the trial anyway. There was no reason to wait. He was surprised *her* attorneys had decided to move forward in her absence. He knew early on that they needed more time to pull their case together. Even he saw some gaps; but the evidence, as it stood, clearly pointed to Samantha Armstrong. He wasn't about to let her off without clear proof the evidence was not what it appeared to be.

"The prosecution calls Skyler Marks to the stand."

Skyler grinned boyishly as he was being sworn in. He carried an aura of success. As he confidently took his seat, it was clear he had a high opinion of himself. Sitting coolly in his freshly pressed powder blue Brooks Brother shirt with its white collar neatly tacked in 18-karat gold, he smiled. His tie, silk and conservative, blended perfectly with the tailor-made navy double-breasted suit. His tanned features, bright teeth, and sensually hypnotic voice accentuated his easygoing manner. It was apparent to Prosecutor Hiller that Skyler would have the jury eating out of his hands like hungry deer.

"Could you tell us how you know the defendant, Samantha Armstrong?" Prosecutor Hiller asked from the podium, his body language casual and friendly, his tone congenial. He knew he had to ask questions that would either make his case against Samantha or break his case against her. He was ready for the truth; as prosecutor the truth was his first priority. Justice would follow.

"I've known her and her family for approximately eight years. I'm currently employed by her father and have met Samantha on several occasions, both socially and work-related."

"Is it true Samantha Armstrong told you she had been raped by Greg Maston?"

"Yes, it is."

"Can you tell us how it is she came to confide in you?"

"I stopped by the Armstrong house to check on a matter with Travis Armstrong, and found Samantha alone. I was not aware Samantha's parents had gone to Washington until then. She was home alone."

"What was her condition?"

"She was disheveled—bruised, incoherent. She was rambling."

"What did you do?"

"I asked her if I could help, and I tried to calm her down."

"Were you able to?"

"I think so. I asked very simple questions. Samantha just sort of nodded at first. I could see how upset she was. I was patient. Eventually she calmed down. I asked questions."

"What kinds of questions?"

"Where were her parents? Did she need anything to drink? How was she feeling? Did she need a doctor? Could I bring her anything? Where had she been last night? Who was with her? How did she get home?" Skyler paused before adding, "Things like that."

"Did there come a point when she explained what had happened to her?"

"Yes. After quite a few questions and prodding, Samantha told me she had been raped by a man that looked like Uncle Greg."

"Uncle Greg? Did you ask her what that meant? Who that was?"

"Yes. She told me it was Greg Maston. That he had raped her."

"What happened next?"

"I asked her if she went to the hospital or called the police. We talked for a long time about the need to report the rape. She said no. I repeatedly advised her she should call the police—immediately, not later. I offered to make the call for her and to take her to a hospital."

"What was her response?"

"She told me she had taken a shower and she didn't want anyone to know about it. She really had it quite planned out."

"Could you explain what you mean by that?"

"She had it planned, down to the little details. She explained to me she would get an AIDS test and a pregnancy test in another town."

"Did she tell you why?"

"Yes. She explained she didn't want her parents to know and she didn't want the papers to print anything bad about her or her family."

"What was your response?"

"In her state of mind, I respected her wishes."

"You are aware we have the microcassette tape you made that same morning, are you not?"

"Yes."

"We played that tape for Samantha in this courtroom. She told this court you used the information contained on that tape to blackmail her. Is that true?"

"Absolutely not. I told her I had taped our conversation for the police in the event she decided to report it. It was for her benefit. I gave the tape to her later, when it became apparent she was sticking to her decision not to report the rape."

"Are you aware much of what you have just told us is not on the tape?"

"Of course. I only taped the initial conversation. The tape was a sixty-minute tape. That means there is about thirty minutes on each side. I never turned the tape over to the other side."

"Is it fair to say you did not turn the tape over because you did not want Samantha to know she was being taped?"

"No, it is not."

"Then why didn't you turn the tape over?"

"Actually, I was so concerned about Samantha I forgot I had even turned the recorder on."

"On that day, did you ever make it known to Samantha you were taping her?"

"No. There was no reason to. I did it for her benefit. She wasn't thinking clearly."

"But it is fair to say you believed she was thinking clearly enough to have thought out and actually devised a plan to deal with the alleged rape?"

"Yes. Samantha has a high capacity for self-preservation."

"Is it fair to say that, eventually, you made the tape known to Samantha?"

"Yes."

"Is it fair to also say the first time you made Samantha aware of the tape was when you used it to blackmail her?"

"No. I'm not even sure what you are referring to."

"You are stating here, under oath, you never used that tape to make Samantha succumb to you."

"I'm not sure what you mean."

"Did you ever use that tape or any information on the tape, about the alleged rape, to coerce Samantha into having a sexual relationship with you?"

"No."

"Did you at any time have a sexual relationship with Samantha?"

"I like Samantha. Her family has been good to me."

"Yes or no. Did you at any time have a sexual relationship with Samantha?"

"I want to say no, but she just wouldn't leave me alone. She interpreted my being nice to her as my wanting to have a different kind of relationship with her."

"Did you have a sexual relationship with her?"

"Yes. I tried not to, but I finally gave in."

"When was that?"

"I don't really remember, but I think it was when I visited her in Michigan. We got to be very close."

"I see."

"Prior to that—your visit in Michigan—it is your position you did not have sex with Samantha Armstrong?"

"Objection, as to the relevance of this line of questioning," Rebecca interjected.

"Counsel?" Judge Bingham asked, peering over his bifocals at Prosecutor Hiller.

"Your Honor," Prosecutor Hiller argued, "it is important to understand the relationship of Ms. Armstrong and Mr. Marks as it directly impacts on her state of mind and her motive in the murder of Mr. Maston."

"Overruled. However, the relevance had better come to light soon. I will only let you go so far."

"Thank you, your Honor." Prosecutor Hiller responded.

"Again, prior to your visit in Michigan, it is your position you did not have sex with Samantha Armstrong?"

"That's correct, to the best of my recollection."

"To your knowledge, did Samantha have any other sexual

relationships in Michigan?"

"If you mean did she have a boyfriend, I wouldn't know that for sure."

"But it is fair to say you and Samantha Armstrong had formed a friendship and had gotten close?"

"Yes."

"Did she ever tell you she was seeing anyone else?"

"No."

"Did you believe her?"

"I had no reason not to believe her."

"Over the course of the time you spent with Samantha, could you describe how close you and she had become?"

"Very close. She confided in me. We talked all the time, even though we didn't get much opportunity to see each other, with her in school at Michigan State."

"Did she talk with you about the rape, about Greg Maston?"

"At first; but then as time passed, she talked less and less about it and him. I assumed she was healing. She seemed better."

"What do you mean 'seemed better'?"

"Well, after the rape, she became withdrawn; she hardly ever left her house. When I was invited to her parents' house for dinner, she didn't eat much. We all noticed. It was hard not to." Skyler paused, looking into the jury box. "Then, after a few months, she opened up more. Once in a while, her parents and I coaxed her, convincing her to go out more often. She would either go out with me or with her best friend, Emily. That was a big improvement, so I thought she was getting over it."

"Do you believe you know her well enough to make the assessment she was, as you say, 'getting over it'?"

"Absolutely."

"To your knowledge, she never discussed the alleged rape with anyone else."

"That's correct. That's what she told me, anyway."

"And you believed her?"

"I had no reason not to believe her."

"Did you find it strange she did not discuss the rape with anyone else?"

"No. She discussed it many times with me. I don't think

she felt the need to discuss it with anyone else."

"To your knowledge, did she ever have any kind of professional counseling about the alleged rape?"

"No, she did not. I'm sure she would have told me she was going to counseling."

"Because it is your opinion she told you everything."

"That's correct."

"Did she tell you anything about Greg Maston after the rape? I mean anything beyond the initial conversation, the one you taped?"

"Not really."

"Not really? Mr. Marks, what did she tell you, if anything, about Greg Maston?"

"That she hated him."

"Did she at any time tell you she intended to kill Greg Maston?"

"No."

"Did you ever see any behavior that might indicate to you she was mentally disturbed over the alleged rape?"

"Objection. Not qualified to make that assessment," Rebecca called out.

"Sustained."

"Did Samantha ever talk with you about Greg Maston, beyond statements that she hated him?"

"No. After the first few months, she never mentioned his name and neither did I. I knew it bothered her. I knew he had hurt her. I was trying to help her, trying to protect her."

"And it is fair to say you didn't raise the rape or the name of Greg Maston to Samantha Armstrong after the first few months following the alleged rape?"

"Yes."

"Okay. Can you tell this court if you saw Samantha Armstrong when she came home from college for Thanksgiving?"

"Yes, I did."

"Could you explain the contact you had with Samantha Armstrong during that time?"

"I had dinner at the Armstrongs' the night she came home from college. And we spoke on the phone several times. I remember she came to the office to visit her father. We talked in the conference room, where she was waiting for him. They were going to lunch. I believe he had clients with him in his office. I kept her company for a few minutes. The next time I saw her was at her parents' house for Thanksgiving dinner."

"Let's get back to lunch. When Samantha Armstrong came home for Thanksgiving break, she and her father met for lunch. Is that correct, to the best of your recollection?"

"I believe so."

"Do you know where they went?"

"Samantha told me they went to MacArthur Station. It's a restaurant not far from our offices."

"Have you ever eaten there?"

"Yes, many times."

"I am holding up for you a knife that has been identified and marked into evidence. Prior to today, have you ever seen a knife like this one?"

"Mmm." Skyler began, taking it in his hands, turning it over, he studied it.

"It is a steak knife of some sort. I can't place it, but it looks like a common steak knife. They all look the same to me."

"Do you eat steak, Mr. Marks?"

"Yes. I order it often."

"When you eat at MacArthur Station, do you order steak?"

"Yes, they have the best steaks in town."

"Then could it be you recognize that knife as a steak knife served with the steaks at MacArthur Station ?"

"Yes. That is possible."

"And it is your belief from your conversation with Samantha Armstrong that she had lunch at MacArthur Station shortly before the violent murder of Greg Maston."

"Objection as to the characterization of the murder. I would ask that the statement be stricken from the record," Rebecca chimed in.

"Granted. I would ask the record reflect the description by counsel of the murder be stricken from the record, and I instruct the jury to disregard the description."

"Thank you, your Honor," both attorneys responded in unison.

"Is it your belief Samantha Armstrong had lunch at MacArthur Station just before the murder of Greg Maston?"

"Yes," Skyler said, artfully inclining his head as if he had been forced to say something he didn't want to say.

"Could Samantha Armstrong have taken a knife from MacArthur Station during her lunch with her father?"

"Objection. That is nothing more than subjective speculation. Counsel is out of line and has no proof," Philip stated.

"Sustained. Counsel, please ask your questions more carefully."

"Your Honor," Philip interjected before Prosecutor Hiller continued.

"What is it now, counsel?"

"We would request the prosecutor's last question be stricken from the record and the jury be advised to disregard it."

"So ordered. Jury will be advised to disregard the prosecution's question. Prosecutor will continue. Carefully, I might add."

"Yes, your Honor, thank you," Prosecutor Hiller said. Then, turning back toward Skyler, he began again.

"Now, let's think back to the evening of the murder, did you see Samantha on the evening of the murder?"

"Not that I remember. That was several months ago."

"Did you talk to her that evening?"

"I think so. Yes. We spoke almost every day during that time. I called her to see how school was, and I told her I hoped to get a chance to take her out over her break."

"Did she seem upset to you?"

"No. I believe when I called she was napping, and she sounded a bit groggy. She'd been having a lot of headaches and was always taking one drug or another."

"Drugs? What kind of drugs."

"Not drugs really. I should have said migraine medicine. I'm not sure which medicine exactly. She never really said. Actually, I don't think I ever really asked."

"Did she say anything that day about Greg Maston?"

"No."

"How can you be sure?"

"Because if his name had been mentioned, I'd have remembered."

"Did she seem upset or aggravated?"

"Objection. Witness is not qualified to assess that," Philip called out.

"Overruled. I believe it has been established that there was enough of a relationship that to make a judgment, but I would ask counsel to limit this line of questioning," Judge Bingham said in a flat voice, his eyes peering over his reading glasses to the audience, before again focusing on the notes filling his pad.

"Thank you, your Honor," Prosecutor Hiller replied, then repeated the question.

"No. She was too groggy for me to tell."

"Too groggy to drive a car?"

"I'm not sure."

"It is possible, based on your description of Samantha, she may not have been able to drive. Is that a fair statement?"

"I don't know."

"Then, is it possible, based on your description of Samantha, she would have been able to drive?

"Maybe. I don't know."

"Do you know what kind of car Samantha Armstrong usually drives?"

"Yes. A red Saab."

"Do you know the license plate of that car?"

"Yes."

"Isn't it odd to know someone else's license plate number?"

"No."

"Can you tell us how it is you know Samantha Armstrong's license plate?"

"Yes. All the Armstrong cars have the same license plate, except for the number. They all have A-U-T-O and then the number, depending on the car. Travis Armstrong's limousine is AUTO 1; his Mercedes he drives every day is AUTO 2. Anne Armstrong has AUTO 3; it is a champagne-colored Corvette. And the children have cars, AUTO 4, the red Saab Samantha usually drives; and then the twins have AUTO 5 and AUTO 6, which I believe they took to law school with them."

"What kind of cars do the twins drive?"

"I don't remember. I haven't seen their cars since they went away to school."

"Did Samantha Armstrong take a car to Michigan?"

"I'm not sure."

"But you're sure she drives the red Saab with the license

plate A-U-T-O-4 when she is home."

"Yes."

"And you have seen her drive it?"

"Yes."

"Did you see her drive the red Saab after she arrived home from Michigan, during Thanksgiving break, before Greg Maston was murdered?"

"I don't recall. I must have, though; it is the only car I've ever seen her drive."

"But you really can't say for sure, can you?"

"Yes, I believe I can."

"Your Honor, I have no further questions for this witness at this time, but I reserve the right to recall Mr. Marks," Prosecutor Hiller said, as he flipped through his notes before placing them inside the manila file in his open briefcase.

"Does the defense wish to cross-examine the witness?" Judge Bingham asked.

"Yes, your Honor," Rebecca said, walking toward the witness stand as she unfolded and read the note Agent Lloyd had given her.

I've got an idea. Philip and I are going out to follow it. Stall for time. Ask for a continuance, if you have to. At the very least, if you need to buy us some time, make your motion to recall Skyler. We may be gone an hour or a day or two. We'll be in touch. Page me if you need either one of us.

"Miss Smalley? Are you ready to continue or do you need a recess?" Judge Bingham asked.

"I'm sorry, your Honor. I am ready to proceed at this time." She turned to Skyler. "Mr. Marks, you testified Samantha Armstrong was sure Greg Maston raped her, is that correct?"

"Yes."

"And you also testified Samantha Armstrong told you everything about Greg Maston and the rape and she didn't tell anyone else about it, is that also correct?"

"Yes."

"Did Greg Maston ever call Samantha Armstrong or try to get in touch with her after the alleged rape?"

"Not to my knowledge."

"Did she ever see him?"

"I don't know. She didn't say."

"Come now, Mr. Marks; didn't you testify earlier she told you everything?"

Skyler remained silent, smiling smugly. He could tell from her rising color that, despite her composure, he had cut through her. Rebecca continued questioning. She was buying time; she was on a fishing expedition. Skyler was curious what she hoped to find.

"Just before Samantha left for college, she had an eighteenth birthday party. Is that correct?"

"Yes."

"You know that because you were there, isn't that correct?"

"Yes."

"Isn't it also true Greg Maston was among the guests?"

"Yes. I believe he was there."

"Did you talk with him?"

"I believe so."

"Let me read to you a statement from page 46, beginning at paragraph four, of the sworn statement made by Samantha Armstrong prior to this trial, which has already been accepted into evidence in her absence:

> Prosecutor Hiller: *When was the last time you saw Greg Maston?*
>
> Samantha Armstrong: *The last time I saw Greg Maston was at my birthday party. He came up to me with Skyler Marks. They were together.*
>
> Prosecutor Hiller: *Did they arrive together?*
>
> Samantha Armstrong: *I'm not sure whether or not they arrived together. I didn't see either of them until they were there – right there next to me. I don't remember whether or not he, Greg, said anything to me. He may have wished me happy birthday. Shortly after Greg and Skyler came over to me, I had a headache and went upstairs to my room for some medicine and to put a cool*

> *cloth on my face. I think I fell asleep for a few minutes, because the next thing I remember, Emily, my best friend, was knocking at my door telling me to go downstairs; people were looking for me.*

"Now, I ask you again, did you speak with Greg Maston at Samantha Armstrong's birthday party?"

"Yes."

"Did you arrive at the party with Greg Maston?"

"No."

"Did you arrange to meet him at the party?"

"No."

"Did you have any idea he would be attending her party?"

"No."

"Isn't it true the whole firm was invited?"

"I believe that is true, but I have no actual knowledge of that."

"Wasn't Greg Maston considered to be part of the firm, even though he was not a lawyer in the firm, but rather the firm's accountant?"

"Yes, I believe he usually attended firm functions and monthly meetings."

"Then doesn't it stand to reason that Greg would be invited to the birthday party?"

"Yes, but I guess I never really thought one way or the other about Greg or his attendance at firm functions or meetings."

"That is interesting, considering your interest and concern for Samantha. If, in fact, you believed she had been raped by Greg Maston, wouldn't you be concerned about her seeing Greg and being in the same room with him?"

"If I'd thought about it, yes; but I didn't. In retrospect, I would have done things differently," Skyler said solemnly, sorrowfully, as if he truly felt bad for his oversight.

"Did you see Samantha Armstrong talking with Greg Maston on the night of her party?"

"I don't really remember. I think everyone talked to Samantha; after all, it was her birthday party."

"Did you at any time see them alone together?"

"No."

"Did you at any time bring Greg Maston over to Samantha to say hello?"

"I don't remember."

"Shall I reread Samantha's deposition?"

"No. I remember what you said; I just don't recall any time at the party the three of us were standing together, or any time we were near in proximity."

"You practice criminal law, Mr. Marks, don't you?"

"Yes."

"Would you say over the years you have developed a keen sense for detail?"

"Yes," Skyler said proudly.

"Then can you explain to us why you do not remember Samantha and Greg standing with you at her birthday party, especially given what you knew?"

"Objection. Your Honor, he has repeatedly said he doesn't remember. That question, no matter how many times counsel rephrases it, has been asked and answered," Prosecutor Hiller stated.

"Your Honor," Rebecca responded, as she glanced at her wristwatch and the empty chairs of her assistants, "I withdraw the question. Mr. Marks, you stated you have eaten at a restaurant by the name of MacArthur Station. Have you ever taken Samantha Armstrong to MacArthur Station?"

"I believe so. It is close to our office. I go there quite often for meetings."

"Yes or no? Did you take Samantha Armstrong to that particular restaurant?"

"I think so."

"Your Honor, could you please instruct the witness to answer yes or no?"

"Yes," Skyler said, interrupting.

"How many times did you take Samantha to that restaurant?"

"We went there several times over the summer."

"How many times does several times refer to? Approximately?"

"Approximately, a dozen times."

"Have you eaten there with Samantha since the time of the rape?"

"Yes."

"Did you ever see Samantha Armstrong take anything that did not belong to her from any restaurant?"

"No."

"No salt and pepper shakers?"

"No."

"No ashtrays?"

"No."

"Did you ever have to ask for another steak knife because one was missing?"

"That's not something I'd remember."

"Is it possible Samantha removed a steak knife from the table and took it out of the restaurant in a pocket or a purse?"

"Anything is possible, but I don't remember Samantha ever taking anything that wasn't hers."

"Nothing you can recall?"

"No."

"Do you think it would be in character for her to steal anything?"

"No."

Looking up from her notes toward the separating rail, she saw Philip at the swinging gate looking anxious.

"Your Honor, may I have a moment to confer with co-counsel?" Rebecca asked.

"Two minutes, that's all."

As all eyes focused on them, Philip whispered, "Agent Lloyd and I have stumbled on what we think is some startling evidence. We need a recess. Ask for two days. Unless you'd prefer I be the one to make the motion and explain it?"

"No problem," Rebecca said. "How long?"

"Monday should do it."

Judge Bingham recessed the case until Monday, instructing Skyler to appear as the first witness. Rebecca anxiously returned her files to her briefcase and followed Philip out of the courtroom.

Chapter 53

Monday morning the courtroom filled in anxious anticipation. It was clear to courtroom viewers the artist, already beginning the pastel lines, felt the electricity of this day unlike any other. As his hands captured what his eyes saw, swiftly he supplemented color to what had begun in subtle gray hazes.

"Mr. Marks," Judge Bingham said, "let me remind you that you are still under oath. Counsel, you may proceed."

"You stated you were aware Samantha Armstrong drove a red Saab, is that correct?" Philip asked, watching the jury as Skyler responded.

"Yes."

"You also stated you did not see Samantha Armstrong on the evening Greg Maston was murdered. Is that also correct?"

"Yes. I believe that is accurate."

"Have you ever been in the Armstrong Saab?"

"Yes."

"Were you in the Armstrong Saab at any time on the day Greg Maston was murdered?"

"No."

"I have here in my hand a receipt from a rental agency. Could you read it for me?"

"Okay," Skyler said, taking the pink sheet from the attorney's hands.

"Just begin at the top. Could you tell us what agency the receipt is from?"

"The Classic Rent-A-Car Company."

"And what is the name of the person who rented the car?"

"T. S. Mark."

"Could you tell us the type of car that was rented?"

"According to the receipt, it looks like it was a Saab."

"Isn't it true the date of the rental is the day before the murder of Greg Maston?"

"Yes."

"Isn't it also true the return date is the same as the date of the murder?"

"I . . . Yes."

"Objection. I've had enough of this, your Honor," Prosecutor Hiller stated. "Defense counsel has not established the relevancy of this receipt, nor has he laid a proper foundation as to its authenticity."

"Your Honor," Philip replied, "I understand the prosecutor's concerns; but I believe if you would give me a moment, it will quickly become relevant."

"Overruled. But I warn you my patience has a limit."

"Thank you your Honor," Philip replied confidently. "Could you tell the court what the number of your license plate is?"

"F-U-N-4-M-E."

"Is that a specialized license plate?"

"Yes. It was a gift from a client when I purchased my car."

"And you drive a dark green Jaguar. Is that correct?"

"Yes."

"Isn't it true you drove your Jaguar just outside the city limits the day before the murder of Greg Maston?"

"I'm not sure."

"Objection as to relevancy."

"Counsel, I have to agree. Where are you going with this?"

"Your Honor, I believe it will become evident within a few minutes if I am allowed to proceed."

"That is all I will give you. You may proceed."

"Thank you, your Honor."

"Isn't it true you rented the red Saab mentioned in the receipt?"

"I don't know what you are talking about. Why would I rent a car?"

"Well, I have an idea, but let me ask again. Did you rent the Saab in the receipt?"

"My name is not T.S. Mark."

"Yes or no?"

"No."

"You have a brother, don't you?"

"Yes."

"He is younger than you?"

"Yes."

"And his name is Thomas Steven Marks?"

"Yes, but I don't know what he has to do with any of this."

"Does your brother look like you?"

"I have been told we resemble each other."

"So much so, you have been told by many people that you look like twins. Is that a fair statement?"

"Yes."

"Your brother lives in Michigan. Is that correct?"

"Yes."

"Was he here for Thanksgiving?"

"Yes."

"Did he need a rental car?"

"I guess so. I really don't remember."

"Isn't it, in fact, true your brother drove a red Saab when he returned to Arkansas for Thanksgiving?"

"I don't remember."

"Is it possible your brother drove a red Saab when he returned to Arkansas for Thanksgiving?"

"I suppose anything is possible."

"So is it fair to say it was your brother who actually drove the rented red Saab?"

"A lot of people drive rental cars. My brother doesn't have anything to do with this."

"Not directly. You might be correct in that statement. But it was you who rented the car for him using his credit card; isn't that true?"

"Well, I—yes."

"And the salesperson used his initials and then missed the "s" on Marks because that is how you read his name as he typed it into the computer. Isn't that correct?"

"He wasn't a typist. He typed each letter with his forefinger. It took forever. He said his secretary called in sick."

Philip didn't wait for Skyler's editorializing. He pressed on, following his outline of questions as closely as possible.

"Is it fair to say you did, in fact, drive a red Saab during the two days before Greg Maston was murdered?"

"Not—"

"Yes or no?"

"I'm not—"

"In fact, before you answer that question, you may want to consider the fact I have a sworn statement from the cab driver who remembers driving you to the rental agency. Additionally, I have the original log the cab driver kept and turned into his company for the specific day you rented the Saab. The cab driver, a Mr. Nate Williams, is willing to testify as to the authenticity of each document." Philip interrupted, handed to the prosecutor both the sworn statement and the log book. "Your Honor," Philip said, "once counsel is finished reviewing the statement and the log, I would request they be entered into evidence under the business records exception in the interest of time."

"I have no objection to counsel referring to the documents at this time; however, I will not stipulate to the entry of either until I am satisfied by the testimony of Mr. Williams. With that objection, each will be so marked as exhibits; however, the acceptance and entry of each will be held until after further testimony," the judge said.

"Now, Mr. Marks. Did you rent the red Saab indicated in the receipt?"

"It's possible. I've rented many different cars over the years for my brother as a favor. I may have rented it and dropped it off to him so he had a car when he was home, and never gave it another thought. It's been several months. My memory is not clear."

"So you are admitting it is possible you rented the red Saab and drove it."

"It is possible. Like I said, he usually leaves his car in Michigan and flies home."

"Isn't it also true you borrowed the Saab from your brother during the time Greg Maston was murdered?"

"I have my own car I like to drive."

"Then could you explain why you felt the need to drive a rented Saab?

"Like I said, I don't remember driving it. If I did, I'm sure it would have been at my brother's request."

"Are you familiar with a business by the name of The Key Maker?"

"I've heard of it."

"In fact, it is fair to say there is one about two blocks from your home, isn't it?"

"Maybe. It's a few blocks. I've never counted."

"I am handing you a receipt. Do you recognize it?"

"It appears to be from The Key Maker."

"It is in fact your receipt, is it not?"

"I'm not sure."

"Let me help you. You had two keys made. Car keys—a door key and an engine key."

"I occasionally have keys made so I have extra sets in case I lose my keys or lock myself out. "

"Isn't it true the car keys were made for the rented Saab?"

"I don't recall having any keys made recently."

"How is it the receipt came into existence?"

"I'm not sure it is mine."

"You dispute the receipt is yours? The salesman will testify he recalls cutting the keys for you and believes that is your receipt. Now, would you like to answer the question again?"

"I just don't remember. I've made several sets of keys over the past years for cars I own and cars I rent. It is expensive to replace lost keys to rental cars, when the rental car company replaces them. I like to avoid problems I can anticipate. The receipt might be one that is related to keys I had made. I just don't remember."

Philip raised his eyebrow at Skyler and paused, posing for the jury. "Why did you make an extra set of car keys for a rented vehicle?"

"My brother has a habit of locking his keys in the car, just like me. I'm sure if I made an extra set of car keys, whether it was for him or for me, I thought having a spare set would save us a lot of trouble. You know, just in case. I am a very busy man. I don't remember small details like the dates and reasons I had spare keys made."

"Well, I thought of that, so I spoke with your brother. Would you be surprised that, according to your brother, Tom, he has never locked his keys in any car? In fact, he was unaware you had a set of car keys to his rental car."

"I don't tell him everything. I didn't want to make him feel bad; he doesn't like to admit he is forgetful."

"I see," Philip said, with intentional skepticism. "So it is fair to say you had and kept a set of spare keys to the rental car."

"Maybe. I really don't recall."

"Your Honor, I would like to ask my co-counsel to assist me with a demonstration. May we proceed?"

"With caution."

"Thank you, your Honor."

"Attorney Smalley is holding up a license plate. Could you read it for the court?"

"A-U-T-O-4."

"She is now holding up a second license plate. Could you read it for the court as well?"

"Where did you . . .? That is my license plate."

"In fact, it is your license plate. It was removed from your Jaguar by court order this morning after you arrived. Could you read it for the court?"

"F-U-N-4-M-E."

"Thank you. Now Attorney Smalley is holding up another license plate. Please read that one as well."

"A-U-T-O-4."

"Thank you."

"Attorney Smalley is now holding up both license plates that read A-U-T-O-4. But there is one difference between the two, isn't there? Can you tell the court what it is?"

"Objection, your Honor," Prosecutor Hiller said. "While this has been entertaining, I fail to see where counsel is going with this."

"Counsel?" Judge Bingham asked, his tone clearly ordering a response.

"If the witness is allowed to answer the question, I believe the court will understand the relevance of the license plates and the line of questioning."

"Once again, I will only tolerate so much. Proceed."

"Thank you, your Honor," Philip said, before turning toward Skyler, being careful not to interfere with the jury's view of the seemingly twin license plates.

"Do you see a difference between the license plates?"

Skyler stared at the two plates for a moment before answering. "There is more space between the "O" and the "4" in the one she is holding in her right hand, than in the one in her left hand."

"That is correct. If I might ask Agent Lloyd to assist," Philip said. Agent Lloyd approached with a bottle of turpentine and a rag. All eyes were on him as he took the one without the space between the "O" and the "4" and carefully removed paint from around the "4". Prosecutor Hiller did not object as he watched the show. He was curious. The courtroom silence echoed his curiosity.

"I present the new version of the plate. The cleaner, real license plate. Could you read it for the court?"

"This is absurd. It doesn't prove anything!" Skyler responded defiantly.

"Please read it."

"F-U-N-4-M-E."

"Thank you," Philip said, taking a file from Agent Lloyd. "I have in my hand an analysis from the FBI crime laboratory. It details an analysis of paint scrapings that were taken from your license plate."

"I don't know anything about that," Skyler said, smiling casually.

"I also have in my hand a receipt from Hank's Hardware. The receipt lists the mixture that exactly matches the license plate. Also," Philip said, "a search was made this morning of your garage. This can of paint was discovered. A sample has been taken to the F.B. I. Crime Laboratory for comparison with the report from your license plate."

Philip took the can from the uniformed officer who approached him. "I would ask that these items be marked into evidence."

"Without objection, it shall be marked."

"Now, I'd like to ask you again. Did you drive the rented red Saab on the day of Greg Maston's murder?"

"I don't remember."

"Isn't it true that, not only did you drive the rented red Saab, but you put the altered plate on the Saab, making it look exactly like the one owned by the Armstrongs and driven by Samantha Armstrong?"

"No. Why would I do that?"

"Well, that's what we're trying to figure out. Perhaps you would like to explain how the paint got on your license plate?"

"Your Honor, do I really have to put up with this harassment? I haven't been charged with anything. I'm not on trial here!"

"Mr. Marks, please answer the questions—unless you would like to take a brief recess so the prosecutor can consider charging you. Counsel, you may proceed, but let's get on with the relevancy of your line of questioning."

"Thank you your Honor. If the court would bear with

me just a moment. . .Mr. Marks, wouldn't it be fair to state you picked up Samantha in the red Saab after you placed the altered license plate on it? That you then drove her to your office, left her in the running car, in the passenger seat, while you went into the office and murdered Greg Maston?"

"Objection," Prosecutor Hiller called out. "Counsel has no proof; his scenario is purely speculation, and we claim surprise. We would also ask that any such evidence be turned over to our offices immediately."

"Your Honor, all the evidence we have has been turned over to the police department and logged into evidence. We have also presented it—or will present it— here today in this courtroom."

"Counsel, do you have further proofs you wish to offer?"

"Yes, your Honor."

"You may proceed, with the caution that speculation is not to be part of your line of questioning. You are treading a fine line. Mr. Marks has not been charged with anything before us today. Whether or not he, or anyone other than Ms. Armstrong, is charged is purely speculative at this point."

"Yes, your Honor, and now I wish to call my next witness."

"Does the prosecutor wish to reexamine the witness?"

"Not at this time, but I reserve my right to recall the witness," Prosecutor Hiller called out, not looking up, as he fervently scrawled notes on the pad in front of him.

Philip continued. "I wish to call Agent Everett Lloyd of the FBI to the stand and request he be sworn in."

Those in the crowded courtroom listened to procedural formalities as the FBI agent was sworn in. Finally, Philip took a deep breath and began questioning Agent Lloyd regarding the evidence found at the scene of the crime.

"Agent Lloyd, can you tell this court how it is you became involved in the Samantha Armstrong case?"

"I became involved when Samantha asked for assistance in prosecuting the alleged rape of her by Greg Maston."

"Did you find evidence a rape had occurred?"

"There was no actual physical evidence, other than a tape of Samantha Armstrong confiding in Skyler Marks. I understand this is the same tape that has been introduced into evidence."

"Was there anything specifically that interested you in Samantha Armstrong?"

"Yes."

"Can you tell this court what that was?" Philip looked at the jury as he spoke.

Agent Lloyd reached into his inside jacket pocket, pulled out his leather encased notepad and flipped it open. He quickly found the pages needed and let his steel blue eyes survey the room before meeting the eyes of the jury. "For many months the Federal Bureau of Investigations has been watching Skyler Marks."

"Objection," Prosecutor Hiller interjected. "There seems to be no relevance to this line of questioning nor any correlation between the charges against Miss Armstrong and the murder of Greg Maston."

"If counsel will permit me to follow a series of questions, the relevance will become abundantly clear," Philip said.

"Overruled."

"Please continue, Agent Lloyd," Philip prodded.

"It became apparent there was a problem that existed between Samantha Armstrong and Skyler Marks."

"Can you define what you mean by the word 'problem'?"

"Yes. It appeared Samantha Armstrong was being stalked by Mr. Marks. We became involved upon a formal complaint made in Michigan by Miss Armstrong and her attorney and then, later, upon request for investigation and assistance by the Prosecuting Attorney in East Lansing, Michigan."

"Can you explain how you proceeded and what your findings were?"

"We had the phones tapped pursuant to a federal warrant. Conversations were taped which reflected curious behavior on both the part of Samantha Armstrong and Skyler Marks."

"I see you are referring to something you are holding. Could you explain, for the record, what it is you are referring to?"

"Yes. I keep a notepad for each case I work on. The notepad I have in my hand contains the notes I made in reference to my investigation of Mr. Marks and the alleged rape of Miss Armstrong by Greg Maston. I wanted to be as accurate as I can be, so I brought it to refer to."

"Thank you. Now, can you please define what you mean by curious behavior?"

"Yes. Samantha Armstrong was very reluctant to talk with Skyler Marks; yet there were times she enjoyed talking with him."

"While that behavior sounds curious, it isn't illegal. Can you tell us what, if anything else, you discovered?"

"We weren't sure until Samantha Armstrong was hospitalized, but the pieces began to fall together when we spoke with her doctors."

"Objection. No foundation; hearsay."

"If this witness is allowed to testify, it will later be proven by both medical records and testimony from Miss Armstrong's physicians as to what Agent Lloyd is stating. I move this testimony be allowed in the interest of time and judicial economy."

"I'll allow it with the precaution anything not substantiated will be immediately stricken from the record, and you will be personally held and sanctioned."

"Thank you, your Honor," Philip said confidently.

"What pieces began to fall together?"

"Samantha suffers from a multiple personality. When things become too much for her to handle, she has a second personality that takes over."

"A second personality? Can you explain?"

"The tapes obtained under the federal warrants have conversations that don't make sense. Samantha began referring to Skyler Marks as Tom."

"Were you able to figure out who Tom was?"

"Yes. We believe it is Tom Marks."

"Are you certain?"

"Yes."

"What makes you sure?"

"Once we confirmed the conversations had been both heard and transcribed accurately, we began to investigate further. We discovered Skyler Marks has a brother, Tom, whom Samantha Armstrong is fond of. Additionally, we discovered Tom Marks has a girlfriend by the name of Stacey."

"What does Stacey have to do with Samantha?"

"Under hypnosis, Samantha Armstrong, in her second personality, responds to the name of Stacey and, in fact, talks about Tom."

"When you say second personality, what exactly do you mean?"

"Samantha Armstrong is one personality. Stacey is another. Samantha has a multiple personality brought on by trauma."

"Objection! Your honor, while this is interesting, this witness has no personal knowledge. No foundation; no facts in evidence to support his statements. Further, Agent Lloyd is not an expert in mental illness nor is he a medical expert of any kind!"

"Sustained. Counsel, please refrain from asking your witness questions for which he is not qualified to answer, unless you have laid a proper foundation."

"Yes, your Honor," Philip responded, continuing his questioning unaffected by the judge's reprimand.

"Isn't it true you have, in fact, carefully marked the portions of the tapes and the corresponding transcripts with Samantha Armstrong's digressions?"

"Yes. Additionally, tapes have been made of Samantha's hypnosis therapy."

"Your Honor, I would ask the court note the tape recorders that have been placed on the table before the jury be examined and noted they have been previously marked into evidence and the last tape of Miss Armstrong's hypnosis therapy be admitted into evidence. Furthermore, let the record reflect I am handing to the prosecution the chain-of-custody log of the tape since it was made."

Prosecutor Hiller reviewed the log and then returned it. "Your Honor, I have no objection, but I reserve the right to *voir dire*, object and ask the record be stricken once the tapes are played."

"Without objection."

"Your Honor, before we begin, I have two sworn depositions from two voice experts who will be available for testimony, stating the voices on the tapes are Samantha Armstrong and Skyler Marks. I would also like to admit these depositions into evidence."

"Without objection, so moved."

Travis Armstrong was in a haze. He watched. He listened. He closed his eyes and took a deep breath. His baby!

How much she had endured without any support, alone in the world! How could they have let things get so out of hand? Why had they been so blind?

The click permeated the room as the reel, filled with brown shiny ribbon, emptied slowly into the clear reel of the first gray box. The tape hypnotically captured the full attention of the listeners. To the captivated listeners, the machine clicked off too quickly. They wanted more; they wanted their curiosity satisfied. A click from the second tape, then the third. The utterances were similar. Skyler's prompting sexual comments. Samantha turning into Stacey, following Skyler's lead.

Travis wanted the words to stop. He felt every pair of eyes that swept over him and his family. He was glad Anne was at the hospital so she didn't have to endure this.

Philip's voice boomed into the hush that had fallen over the room when the tape recorder clicked off. "Your Honor, at this time I wish to call Dr. Wilhelmina Martins."

Lively whispers buzzed through the courtroom for several seconds before the judge banged his gavel, forcing immediate silence.

"You may proceed."

As the witness was sworn and Rebecca listened to her training, qualifications, and education, she placed a clean page in front of her and began taking notes, meticulously listing additional questions for Philip to ask the court-appointed psychiatrist. She wished Skyler were still present so she could see the last vestiges of his smug look crumble.

"Dr. Martins, can you tell this court how you are involved in the case against Samantha Armstrong?"

"I was requested by the court to be the independent psychiatrist in reviewing the mental state of Samantha Armstrong."

"There were, in fact, two other psychiatrists reviewing Samantha Armstrong's case. Her own psychiatrist, Dr. Levanstein, and one requested by the prosecution, Dr. Ty. Have you had the opportunity to confer with each of them?"

"Yes. Samantha sees her psychiatrist, Dr. Levanstein, three times a week for an hour each session, and then as needed. The length of time has increased or decreased, as needed, during her stay at the hospital."

"And the psychiatrist for the prosecution, Dr. Ty; do you

know how often he spent with her in the hospital?"

"Yes. According to my discussions with him and in reviewing his reports and notations in her chart, he spent a total of forty hours with Miss Armstrong."

"Do you feel forty hours is enough time to make a proper evaluation in this case?"

"Yes, I do."

"How many hours have you spent with Samantha Armstrong?"

"Approximately sixty."

"Do you feel you have had a chance to make a proper evaluation?"

"Yes."

"What is the difference between the sixty hours you spent and the forty hours spent by the prosecutor's psychiatrist?"

"I have approached this case from a variety of psychological angles as well as by piecing together a profile of emotional and mental conditions to ensure nothing was overlooked. Samantha Armstrong has had a number of traumas to deal with. I wanted to explore every medical option."

"And have you been able to explore every medical option?"

"I believe so."

"Could you share that information with us?"

"Samantha Armstrong is suffering and recovering from medical conditions which include prescription drug abuse, hypoglycemia, anorexia, and migraine headaches. Additionally, she suffers from posttraumatic stress syndrome as a result of a rape. All of these conditions have resulted in the development of a multiple personality that enables her to deal with things she could not deal with as Samantha."

"Before we get into the specifics of what you just stated, can you tell this court if you believe Samantha Armstrong is able to stand trial?"

"I do not believe Samantha Armstrong can, at this time, stand trial, due to both her mental and physical conditions."

"Do you believe she is capable of murder?"

"I'm not sure I can answer that. I believe anyone, under the right circumstances can kill."

"Let me rephrase the question," Philip said slowly, in a friendly voice. "Do you believe Samantha Armstrong committed the murder of Greg Maston based on your evaluation of her?"

"I believe she was afraid of him and he hurt her deeply."

"Can you define hurt?" Philip interrupted.

"I believe the posttraumatic stress syndrome she suffers from was brought on by a rape, which she believes to have been committed by Greg Maston."

"Now," Philip pressed on, "do you believe Samantha Armstrong committed the murder of Greg Maston?"

"No. I believe she was too fearful to be near him in any way and could not have emotionally handled being near enough to him to have murdered him."

"But you did say she also suffers from a multiple personality, which this court also heard testimony about. Could her other personality have committed the murder?"

"That is possible, but not probable."

"Possible, but not probable. Could you explain more specifically?"

"The second personality is stronger than Samantha, but it is not a dangerous or culpable personality. It is a sexual, flirtatious personality—a personality type that is not usually thought of as one that has a profile that includes homicidal tendencies."

"Would you then say it is unlikely either personality murdered Greg Maston?

"Yes, that is my assessment."

"Your Honor, I move to dismiss the charges against Miss Samantha Armstrong."

"Counsel, I do not believe there is sufficient grounds for dismissal, but I will listen to your argument. Please proceed."

"Your Honor," Prosecutor Hiller interrupted, "upon Agent Lloyd's request and the FBI, I requested samples of evidence be sent to the FBI labs to confirm the authenticity and physical makeup of the physical evidence found at the crime scene. Based on the findings I was just sent by messenger, I concur with counsel's motion."

"May I be advised of those findings?" Judge Bingham asked, folding his hands patiently on his desk, as an official copy of the report was placed on both his desk and the defense counsel's.

The prosecutor read: "The strands of hair which

matched Samantha's DNA did not match the hair color she had used on her hair for a Halloween party a few weeks before the murder, signifying the strands were from a previous occasion when she had been in the conference room, or perhaps with Mr. Maston, prior to Halloween. The additional strands of hair found on the buttons of the shirt on Greg Maston's body indicate there is a possibly there was a third person in the room." Prosecutor Hiller paused, allowing the silent judge and jury to absorb the information. He looked into the sober faces of the jurors, whose speculations were almost visible. "That theory has been discarded as of this morning. The third set of hair samples has been matched and identified as having come from a Miss Melissa Senger, Samantha's dormitory roommate at Michigan State University. There is no evidence to support Miss Senger has traveled outside Michigan at or during the time of the murder of Greg Maston. Nor is there any evidence to support she had any knowledge or relationship of any kind with the victim. Furthermore, we can find no evidence or information Greg Maston has ever been to Michigan; yet there were strands of hair belonging to Miss Senger present at the crime scene. Miss Senger is available to testify and verify our findings. DNA testing of the hair found and that of one taken from Miss Senger are conclusively a match. I offer this forensic science laboratory report into evidence," Prosecutor Hiller said, pausing as he took the report from his assistant's hand and walked it to Philip's anxious hands.

"Counselor, do you have any objection as to the acceptance of the report into evidence?" The surprised judge asked.

"No, your honor. There is no objection." Philip said, handing the report to the court clerk to be marked as an exhibit.

"You may continue," Judge Bingham said to Prosecutor Hiller.

"The second piece of evidence involves broken fingernails. Curiously, they have only recently been tested; the results have just arrived at our office this morning, as well. The torn fingernails, believed to be Miss Armstrong's, were tested as to their age and were found to have dried to the point of being broken off at least six months before the murder. The age of the nails and the time of the murder do not match. Additionally, there were scrapings of skin found under those nails that have conclusively been found to be from the body of Mr. Maston, and which have been previously offered by the prosecution and accepted into evidence. We now believe these new tests, determining the age of the fingernails, indicate they had been planted after the murder and the scrapings were intentionally placed on them." Prosecutor Hiller paused and took a deep breath as he looked around the courtroom, resting his eyes carefully on the jury and then on Judge Bingham before continuing.

"In other words, it is now our belief, while Miss Armstrong is probably guilty of not using good judgment, that is all she is guilty of. Someone has tried to frame her for a murder she did not commit."

The silence in the courtroom was complete. Not a rustle of clothing could be heard as all eyes focused on Judge Bingham, who sat reading the laboratory reports from the FBI. Finally, he spoke.

"We will take an hour's recess. I will give you my decision at that time." He struck the gavel once, perfunctorily, before disappearing through the door behind his chair.

The artist looked around the room. Sketching rough outlines of the shocked faces in the room, he quickly filled several pages. The excited jury filed out, the stunned faces of the audience whispered, possibly premature congratulations murmured to the Armstrongs; each made interesting composites, each stroke of the pencil captured the fusing of emotions that the day's quick turnaround of events had produced.

Travis sat speechless. He didn't want to breathe. He couldn't move. Could it all really be over? Did they have enough evidence *yet* against Skyler? He looked at his sons who had been by his side for weeks. He was proud of them, more than he had ever expressed. They whispered between themselves, no more bar review books in front of them, just briefcases with files. They had passed the bar despite the chaos. As they waited anxiously, Travis decided he would tell his sons just how terrific they were, once this was over. They deserved that. So did Samantha. He wished he could call Anne and Samantha, but he didn't want to leave the courtroom until he knew for sure. He couldn't get their hopes up if . . . He shuddered; he couldn't think about it. She'd been through so much, and she still had tough times ahead. Where had all the years gone?

Rebecca, Philip, and Agent Lloyd entered the attorneys' lounge with Prosecutor Hiller, who shut the door behind them.

"Thank you for your help," Rebecca said looking at Agent Lloyd and Prosecutor Hiller. "If this doesn't get Samantha off, I'm not sure what will."

"We are not out of the woods yet. We still don't have enough evidence to convict Skyler Marks, or anyone else, of Greg Maston's murder." The prosecutor sighed with frustration.

"That's not entirely true. Skyler Marks may have bigger problems than rape or murder charges. He may have crossed the line with the Castriano family." Agent Lloyd said matter-of-factly, pulling out a second notebook.

# # #

Solemnly, the jury filed in and the audience was silenced by Judge Bingham's gavel.

"Your Honor, at this time, I'd again like to make the motion to dismiss the charges against Samantha Armstrong," Philip stated above the buzz in the crowded courtroom, not waiting for the judge to specifically address anyone or offer his decision.

"I have no objection," Prosecutor Hiller called out over the growing buzz.

Hearing the pounding of the gavel against the wooden plate, the crowd silenced again. Those who had begun to stand up took their seats.

"In the case of the State of Arkansas versus Samantha Armstrong, based on the information recently presented in this courtroom, in addition to the prosecutors' concurrence in the motion by defense counsel, the pending matter before this court in reference to Samantha Armstrong is dismissed. Furthermore, this court wishes her a speedy recovery . . ."

No one heard the rest of Judge Bingham's statement as excited talking filled the room. The gavel released its final bang. Tears filled Travis Armstrong's eyes as he hugged his sons. Cameras flashed. Hands were shaken. Thank you's were echoed. Hugs and kisses were exchanged freely. Philip, Rebecca, and Agent Lloyd smiled at one another as they gathered up their books and files and heard echoes of praise from Prosecutor Hiller and the Armstrongs.

"Good thing you three aren't a permanent team; you might put me out of business," Prosecutor Hiller said, as he smiled at the group.

"Thank you for putting up with such an odd presentation of evidence. We really appreciate it," Rebecca said.

"Don't thank me; thank Agent Lloyd. He presented me with quite a different picture than the evidence from the crime scene showed. I wasn't authorized to release any knowledge of that evidence for fear of tainting the FBI operation."

"What?" Rebecca said, looking from Agent Lloyd to Philip to Prosecutor Hiller.

"Are you two going to fill us in?" Philip asked.

"Well, that all depends on whether you two will stick around to help us prosecute the real murderer," Prosecutor Hiller said.

"You've got our attention," Rebecca said as she watched the courtroom empty into a hall filled with reporters and cameras. "But there's one question I've got to ask. If you knew Samantha didn't murder Greg Maston, why'd you put her at risk of being convicted?"

"She was never in real danger," Agent Lloyd said. "We weren't sure she didn't murder Greg Maston, given her state of mind, until I spent a few weeks following Skyler Marks. He has some interesting friends and some bad habits."

"So why didn't you arrest him?" Philip asked, surprised at what he was hearing.

We had to let him think he had gotten away with framing Samantha for Greg Maston's murder, so he could lead us to the rest of what we wanted."

"Hmm," Rebecca murmured, putting his comments together. "So you wanted him to feel comfortable enough to make mistakes, but scared enough after he'd taken the stand, he'd have to dispose of any links between himself and the murder."

"Very good," Agent Lloyd said.

"What exactly was the rest of what you wanted?" Philip asked curiously.

"For starters, the head of an abortion ring that has left several young women in this county dead or sterile; a series of young women who have been brutally beaten to death; a number of sting operations against the Castriano family that suddenly went sour and then, top that off with an ambitious vindictive attorney who took too many shortcuts, despite his brilliant legal mind, and who bought one too many cops." Agent Lloyd listed Skyler's offenses and illegal connections as if he were ordering hamburgers.

"All of it led to Skyler Marks?" Rebecca whispered in disbelief.

"The same."

"Why Samantha?" Philip asked.

"Lust, greed, control, stolen innocence, the profile on Skyler Marks is endless. Our head guys have had quite an interesting run at putting his profile together. We are looking for Skyler's offshore bank accounts, which we believe must have deposits from payoffs for a variety of crimes." Agent Lloyd motioned the group out of the lounge into the now quiet hallway.

"Have they arrested Skyler?"

"No. We're following him and the Castriano thugs. When we impounded Skyler's car for the license plates, we decided to check for samples. A lot of interesting things were found, including the inner tire tubes. Two were filled with cocaine, two with cash. The boys found a smorgasbord of samples from the trunk that may resolve a number of crimes."

"How did you ever think of looking inside the tires?" Rebecca asked.

"We didn't. One of the police mechanics pulling apart the Jaguar just happened to comment on what a nice car it was and how it was a shame the owner didn't do a better job matching the tires."

"So the guy has different tires. That's not a crime."

"You're right. Except, in this case, why would you drive with two worn tires and two new tires? Skyler Marks had enough money to replace all four tires. The wear on the tires would have given him a poor ride. It just didn't make sense."

"So . . .?"

"I remembered Texas border cases I've read about. A lot of drug trafficking occurs inside tires. So we got the dogs; they went crazy. We opened the tires and there it was. Bull's-eye!"

"Unbelievable. I never would have pieced that together."

"Now we're hoping Skyler and Mr. Castriano find each

other. It will be interesting to see their encounter. We are quite sure the tires belong to Mr. Castriano, who won't be happy Skyler didn't deliver."

"You mean you aren't going to arrest him now, based on all you have?"

"We believe Skyler has hidden the money he hasn't been able to get out of the country. We are looking for keys that might give us a hint as to the hiding places."

"How did you get that idea? The money, if there is any, could be buried in his backyard."

"True, except we found one key already. That's what leads us to believe there are others. The boys are checking airport lockers for a match on the key. We're convinced once we find the locker, we'll find large bills suitably packaged for traveling. You know, a million dollars fits nicely in a flight bag if it's in the right denominations."

"You seem to have it all figured out."

"Not yet, but we're close."

"Aren't you worried he is a flight risk or that the Castriano family will take him out? Should I worry about the safety of Samantha?" Rebecca asked impatiently. "Especially now the trial is over and he's no longer sequestered. If he reads about the trial, he'll wonder if he's now a suspect."

"We'll wait. We'll watch. It'll be like stealing milk from a baby. No one will be harmed; there is no real threat. Castriano will want to know where his drugs and money are before he erases Skyler. We have Skyler Marks so closely monitored we can hear him breathe. We want more than him; we are going for the bad boys as well as the money. We don't want Skyler, or the Castriano clan, locked up only to be released to millions of hidden dollars. Worse yet, millions they can spend on their slimy lawyers. No offense intended," Agent Lloyd said, placing a friendly hand on Rebecca's shoulder.

"None taken. I hope you are right. I'd like nothing more than to see Skyler behind bars," Rebecca stated with conviction.

"We have a lot riding on this operation. We know what we are doing. We have been at least two steps ahead all the way." Agent Lloyd smiled proudly.

"Gee, thanks for sharing," Rebecca declared sarcastically. "I guess we all should be glad you are on our side."

Chapter 54

Samantha looked delicate and beautiful, like a miniature pink rosebud atop a thin stalk, about to bloom. She sat motionless in the new pink and white cotton robe from her mother, with a box of raspberry croissants on her lap. She gazed out onto the small but well groomed lawn of the hospital, grateful her physician had made arrangements for her to use the staff deck every afternoon. Samantha, cocooned in her thoughts she was glad were her own, wondered why her mother was so distracted.

"Why are you so fidgety?" Samantha finally asked her mother, not able to take another series of fingernail taps against the plexiglas patio table, annoyed they had intruded into her stream of inner consciousness.

"No reason," Anne sighed, taking another sip of her coffee. "I just thought we should all take a vacation together, get some sun. You've looked so much better these past few weeks, since you've been allowed to sit outdoors. You always look better with a little color. I'm really happy you are wearing makeup again; your skin has a heathy glow. You've been through so much." Anne kept looking toward the balcony door.

"Things must not have gone as well as we hoped, Mom. I'll be fine, no matter what. Please don't worry."

Anne sighed deeply before sipping her cooling coffee.

"Mom, you did it again! You only sigh when you are upset. What is wrong?" Samantha asked, concerned, suspicious she wouldn't be told the truth, regardless of how many questions she asked her mother. As she waited for a response, she began counting backwards the months she'd spent in the hospital. So many things had happened; so much lost time.

"Nothing. You're being silly. I'm fine! I'm just anxious to get you home," Anne replied, her eyes focusing on her coffee cup.

Samantha knew her mother was avoiding her stare, as

she focused on drinking the remainder of her coffee. Samantha drank her strawberry milk shake and tugged at her croissant. It wasn't difficult for her to eat when they sat outside. The fresh air gave her hope she would get well and be free of her problems. Her daily outdoor time had conditioned her to look forward to her meals. Most of her headaches had stopped and she had survived the withdrawal of the concoction of drugs she had been living on.

The nightmares, the dreams, the voices, all still puzzled her but she was working through them with her psychiatrist. She had decided, several weeks before, she could build a facade she was getting better. She knew everyone, including her psychiatrist, was happier with illusion than reality. As long as she appeared to be getting better and her progress was marked, they left her alone. Samantha still preferred being alone. She did feel stronger, better able to cope. She felt confident she would eventually be able to heal herself. She didn't mind the voices inside her anymore either. She had spent so much time alone, she actually began to feel better knowing they were there. They made her feel less alone. She accepted the voices, the dreams, would go away, just as they came, after her psychiatrist had explained one day she had created them as a defense mechanism, as a way of coping. Surely, when this was all over, they would leave and she would be normal. The voice inside her that used to haunt her had vanished for the most part, once she was able to confide in her doctor and in Rebecca about everything. Yet she knew there were things she might never remember, she might never be able to face. But she was trying. That was the important thing, everyone told her. She wasn't sure what she believed any more. Samantha learned to agree with everyone and do as she was told. It was her only way back home, back to school, back to John. It was Samantha's turn to sigh as each thought provoked another question.

Samantha wasn't sure of her fate and her future; but she was sure, before all was said and done, she would have her questions not just answered, but resolved. And no one would ever hurt her again. She had promised herself that much.

"There's nothing to worry about Samantha. Everything will be fine, really," Anne said, seeing Samantha's strained face as she again looked toward the door. This time she saw the large, dark, handsome figure of her husband.

"How are my two beautiful women?" Travis asked, planting a kiss on each of their foreheads before sitting between them.

"Where are the twins?" Anne asked, searching her husband's face for clues as to what happened in court.

"They'll be along in a few minutes. They had errands to run."

Anne stared at Travis, trying to read his expression. She couldn't. She was afraid to. What if it was bad news? What would she do? How would they handle it? What would they tell their friends? She looked away from Travis. She didn't want to know the answer. Not here, not now. Not in front of Samantha.

"It's a beautiful day, and I don't want to interrupt your outdoor time; but I wondered if we could return to your room for a few minutes? We've all got some things to discuss and, by now, the twins are there waiting for us." Travis said this casually, as if he were asking for another cup of coffee.

Anne followed his lead without responding. She stood, grabbed her purse and sweater, and watched. Samantha, intrigued at the conversation of her parents and the odd facial expressions between them, remained motionless in her chair.

"Come on, sweetheart. We can come back outside this evening if you want," Anne said, noticing Samantha's stillness.

"I'm not moving until I know what's going on. People are always whispering and talking as if I am not there, and I want to know. If something has happened, then you need to tell me now," Samantha stated softly, plainly, moving her eyes from one parent to the other and then back again, still making no motion to leave.

"Samantha, honey, you are right. But we need to go back to your room, and then we'll all talk. Would you like to walk, or can I push you in your wheelchair?" Travis said, lifting Samantha from her chair as if he hadn't heard her protest.

"Fine. Whatever. But I'll walk. I've been pushed around too much," Samantha said, wincing as she watched her parents motion her through the glass patio doors before they would take another step.

The walk back to her room felt long and strained.

Samantha felt uneasy walking in the awkward, silent shadows of her parents. As they neared her room, she sensed the stares of the nurses. Something was wrong. She turned pale, immediately frightened.

"Stop," Samantha said in a low voice, her teeth grinding together. "I want to know right now. What's wrong? I can feel it. Everyone is staring at me."

"Sweetheart, it's not that anything is wrong. It's finally right again," Travis said to his daughter, holding her shoulders firmly, looking into her sharp blue eyes.

Samantha stiffened at the touch of her father. She still didn't like the touch of any man, not even her father. She didn't understand what was going on. She looked to her mother. Her mother's face looked as confused as her own felt.

"I don't understand—"

Travis interrupted, putting his hand on the door leading to Samantha's room. "We'll let Rebecca explain. She's inside waiting with a few of your friends."

Samantha walked into her room, slowly, cautiously, curiously. Within seconds, the curtain was pulled from around her bed and she heard a chorus of voices echoing "Surprise!"

Samantha looked around, not understanding, unconsciously pulling her robe more tightly around her body. Rebecca walked over to her and put out her hand. Samantha shook it, as Rebecca said, "We've done it. You are free! As of this afternoon, all of the charges were dropped."

Samantha looked around the room and then back at Rebecca in disbelief. "It's over?"

"Yes," said the twins in unison.

"And we've brought you a cake with a file in it, just in case they change their minds," Taylor joked, smiling fondly with Tad at their sister as plates were passed around amid the laughter.

"We've saved the best for last," Philip said as the door opened again, revealing Agent Lloyd with John beaming, following behind.

"Samantha, it's so great to see you!" John said, stretching his arms out toward her. "I've missed you."

"John! But how did you know? How did you . . ."

Stretching a curled pinkie finger, John grabbed Samantha's pinkie finger, wrapping it around his.

"I never forget a pinkie swear," John grinned, squeezing his grip more firmly.

"Samantha, I hope you don't mind. I asked John to fly down for the end of the trial. Your parents agreed, and Emily and Agent Lloyd made the arrangements."

"Thank you all so much," Samantha said, not able to control the tears falling through her thick lashes. Hugging Emily in thanks and standing close to John, she noticed how happy everyone was. Still, she felt discontented; she wasn't sure why. She knew Rebecca would fill in the details later, but she couldn't help but wonder if they would take her home or leave her there.

Why wasn't anyone talking about taking her home? As the conversation died down and people began to leave, Samantha waited. It was time for the dinner trays to be jingling down the hallway. What was to be her fate?

"Samantha," Rebecca said, pulling her aside from John and from Emily's stories of college life and classes. "I'll be staying till Saturday. We'll have a chance to go over everything then. I hear you'll be home by the end of the week, and I'll see you there. We've got to run. Besides, I'm sure you want to spend some time with John. Have a good evening!" She gave Samantha a reassuring hug and whispered "and by the way, you'll be safe from Skyler from now on." Samantha nodded slowly, in grateful disbelief, as she watched Rebecca walk out of the room followed by Philip and Agent Lloyd. Samantha's family soon found their way out as well, her mother already taking suitcases home in preparation for Samantha's forthcoming discharge.

"You've got a good friend in Emily," John said, when they were finally alone. "Hey, that tray doesn't look bad for hospital food! We've had worse in the dorm."

"It's not bad. They've got me on a high-calorie plan," Samantha said, feeling as if no time had passed between them since they were last there together. "Emily *is* a good friend; like a sister to me. I'm glad you two get along."

"I'll tell you what, as soon as you're released, I'll take you out to dinner and a movie. Would you like that?"

"I'd love it, but . . ." Samantha hesitated. She was afraid to go on.

"Is there a problem?" John asked, watching Samantha's

full mouth turning to a pout as she bit her bottom lip.

"I . . .." Samantha sighed, breathing deeply, trying to calm herself.

"It's hard for me being with a man . . . being touched, even on the shoulder by my father's hand. My psychiatrist says I will get over it, but I need time—"

John put his fingers gently up to her mouth to stop her from talking. "I understand. We have all the time in the world. Let's make a deal, okay?"

"What kind of deal?" Samantha asked curiously; suspicious of any deal with a man.

"We'll start over in the fall at Michigan State. We'll take one day at a time. I'll even let you knock on my window in the middle of the night, and I'll help you unpack."

Samantha smiled, remembering the day they had met. Finally, she nodded in agreement; and John, being sensitive to the words of caution she had given him, didn't move to touch her. Instead she heard his hearty voice.

"All right?" he said, as he gave her the thumbs up sign and then the "pinky swear" sign.

Samantha smiled more brightly than he'd ever seen her smile. And for the first time in months, she was beginning to feel there was hope, real hope, she'd be normal again.

Chapter 55

Samantha lay on her bed as she watched the doorknob. She was anxious to see it turn and reveal John's handsome figure. It had been great these past few months! It was like starting over. Except John was nearing completion of his master's and she was still at the beginning of her first term of college. Now they were both a year older; but she was many years wiser. She threw her creased copy of *Cosmopolitan* onto the floor, nestling her head against the soft pillows on her bunk bed. Carefully, Samantha moved her hand toward the inlaid wooden box Nana gave her long ago, flipping the meticulously polished lid open. The smooth box mesmerized her. She turned it over and over, inspecting every crevice in it, burning it into her memory. Flipping it over faster and faster, testing her memory of the markings on each side, she accidently dropped it.

Samantha gasped as she watched the music box roll helplessly across the carpet. Scooping it into her hands, she clenched it, afraid to check for breakage. Slowly she released her fingers from around the box. Sighing in relief, Samantha smiled, convinced there was no real damage. Carefully she set it down on her desk. Hearing a clank, her heart sank. The bottom separated from the box. Tears sprang to her eyes as her fingers took the pieces in hand. Desperately, Samantha tried to fit the bottom back into the box. She had to make it whole again, perfect again. She inspected it more closely. Why wasn't it fitting?

Carefully Samantha looked inside the box. She didn't want to disturb the inner workings. Cotton balls. It looked as if cotton balls were stuffed inside the box. What were they doing there? Were they supposed to be there to hold the musical mechanisms inside? Slowly, she pulled at the cotton. If she removed just a little, she hoped, the bottom might fit again. Tugging gently at the cotton, she froze when she heard metal rubbing together. Something metal fell on her lap. She closed her eyes; she couldn't look.

Samantha felt the pieces in her lap before she opened her eyes. They felt odd. She had to see the contents of the music box; surely the delicate music could not be made from such awkward and large pieces as those she was feeling? She opened her eyes and carefully placed the music box beside her, protected by the comforter. She looked down. Pushing aside the cotton, she found three small keys, wrapped in the cotton. Where did they come from? What were they doing inside Nana's music box? How long had they been there? They must have been put there by Nana! Who else had enough access to the box to make it into a hiding spot? Only Nana, Samantha surmised. Nana must have wanted her to find the keys, to find what they went to, to give her a last present, a final memory. She was comforted by that thought. Nana had given her something she could think about in the silence and serenity of her room. She vowed to herself never to tell anyone about the keys. Quietly, reverently, she placed them back inside their hiding place, inside the exquisite music box. Eventually they fit, with the cotton snugly wrapped around them. The keys were protected. The box was protected, the base was returned to seal the box as if it had never been separated. Carefully, she inspected the box. It was as if the secret had never been revealed. Her secret safe. To all others, the box was virginal, old, but still in its original condition. She smiled, knowing she was the only one who knew the truth. She and Nana.

Samantha sighed, her eyes closed and her mind and body relaxed. She listened as the music box finished playing: *London bridge is falling down, falling down, falling down; London bridge is falling down, my fair lady . . .*

Slowly, as she relaxed, she let her body ease. She drifted, tried to picture John. She wanted to dream about him and then wake up to him kissing her into reality. He had promised to take it slow with her, and he had. She found it easy to want him, easy to care about him. She focused on his face. All those months in the hospital, she had memorized every detail of his face from the photos he'd sent. It was easier now seeing him every day. She could recall it in an instant.

But as quickly as John's face came to her, it was replaced with the faces in the shadows of her dreams. The pieces of the faces, had now become whole and recognizable. She saw *him* first; the face of Greg Maston. Lying there. Face down. Instinctively, she knew it was him. Covered in blood. Then Samantha saw herself, smiling. Calmly wiping things, the lamp, the tables, the chairs, the doorknob . . . There was so much blood. Oozing from everywhere. It was so red. . .

Skyler. Where was Skyler? He had caused this. Not her. He should pay; not her. She watched herself moving coldly about the room.

She heard laughter and voices. Music. The music box was playing, but she didn't see it. She tried to piece it together. It shouldn't be there; it should be in her room, in Nana's room . . . but not there in the darkness. Was someone touching it?

The familiar voice, the one that liked to direct her and laugh at her, began. Instantly Samantha recognized it, easily deciphering it from the rest. It called her weak. It had told her she couldn't have any man until she'd gotten rid of the man who hurt her. Samantha knew the voice was right. She had no choice.

Tom. Her handsome Tom. He was there. He appeared out of the darkness. To rescue her. He always did. He saved her from the faces, from the mean voices. His image calmed her. He took care of her. He always did; he said he always would. She turned. A baby was crying in the background. She tried to find it; she wanted to help it. The crying came from so many directions, but never the one she chose. And then it, too, stopped. Blood began to spurt from the walls around her. Then, almost instantly, it stopped. She blinked in horror. The rest of the voices came. The faces too. They began to laugh and chant—until the body rolled over. And she saw his face, calm, peaceful. Dead.

The voice. It was there again. Loudly but calmly. It mesmerized her, again chanting she had been brave and rational and right. Stacey's voice was right and true and strong. Stacey had helped her face up to what she'd needed to do. Now Stacey and Tom would help her begin her life again . . .

Samantha awoke as she heard the quiet knock and saw the dormitory door open. The music box, safely beside her, had silenced. She reached up and placed it carefully on her desk to avoid dropping it again.

Sleepy-eyed Samantha turned her head and blinked approvingly toward her handsome, confident John as he moved across the room toward her. Instinctively, she smiled. She was fine. She was cured. She *was* innocent. She slipped her hand away from the crumpled and badly worn legal words that had remained in her pillow case through all those changes of linen, for over a year. She no longer needed the law. She no longer needed anyone, except John.

Samantha paused as she looked at his handsome face. Perhaps he would help her find the answer to the puzzle of the keys. But then again, maybe not, she reasoned. After all, look what happened last time she confided in a man. Nana's voice rang loudly in her head, *Serenity in Silence.*

Hugging John, Samantha silently retorted to Nana, *Safety in Silence.*

About The Author

Rosemarie E. Aquilina is the eldest daughter of Dr. and Mrs. Joseph and Johanna Aquilina and the mother of three children, David, Jennifer and Johanna. As a resident of Lansing, Michigan, she is the owner of a Lansing based law firm, Aquilina Law Firm, PLC, primarily representing clients in family law related matters. Rosemarie E. Aquilina also serves as a JAG Officer in the Michigan Army National Guard and is also employed as an Adjunct Professor at the Thomas M. Cooley Law School. Rosemarie E. Aquilina is Michigan's radio talk show host of "Ask the Family Lawyer" heard weekly throughout the state on the Michigan Talk Radio Network. With an English Education Degree from Michigan State University and a Juris Doctorate Degree from Thomas M. Cooley Law School, Rosemarie E. Aquilina combines her education and her passion for writing in this suspenseful fictional legal thriller. She enjoys hearing from fans! Please send your letters to:

Rosemarie E. Aquilina
229 N. Pine Street
Lansing, Michigan 48933
e-mail: aquilinalawfirm@aol.com

Quick Order Form

Postal Orders:

Porch Swing Press
2258 Courtney Circle Court
Ann Arbor, Michigan 48103
U.S.A.
Telephone: (734) 213-1370

Please send me _____ books at $15.95 each$ ______

Michigan residents please add 6% sales tax $ ______

Shipping:
U.S. Shipping: $4.00 for first book;
$2.00 each additional
(International Shipping: $9.00 for first
book; $5.00 each additional): $ ______

Check enclosed for this amount: $ ______

Ship to:
Name: ______________________________
Address: ____________________________
Address 2: ___________________________
City: _______________________________
State: __________________ Zip Code:__________

NOTE: Ordering questions, call (734) 516-1370.
Please allow 4-6 weeks for delivery.